The Walls we build

Praise for Jules Hayes

'An absorbing story of injustice and family secrets set against a vividly-drawn wartime backdrop. The finest of story-telling, a real page-turner, an enthralling read. I unreservedly loved it.' *Anne Williams, Being Anne Book Blog and RNA Media Star 2019.*

'Passion, intrigue and family secrets drive this complex wartime relationship drama. A page-turner. I loved it.' *#1 bestselling author, Nicola May.*

'A compelling story of friendship and the secrets we keep for generations. The poignant and moving narrative had me enthralled.' *Critically acclaimed author, Sarah Ward.*

'I was hooked from start to finish, which is a rare feat in historical fiction. Jules Hayes has written an exceptional cross-genre novel that will appeal to all readers. Simply outstanding.' *The Book Magnet.*

'A big bold, multilayered epic about lives and loves shaped by secrets echoing down the generations. Poignant and beautifully written. I whipped through it.' *Author, Laura Wilkinson.*

'Fascinating historical fiction. A story entwined with real-life facts relating to Winston Churchill's household at Chartwell.' *International bestselling author, Glynis Peters.*

'A pacey well-written narrative that keeps the pages turning. It's a thriller, a love story, and it has historical and political context as the events play out in the shadow of the great Winston Churchill. A story about family secrets, the ripples of which reach out across generations. There is something about this book that plants into the reader's mind, and roots it there long after the last page.' *Author, Debz Hobbs-Wyatt.*

The Walls We Build

By

Jules Hayes

In memory of Harold Hayes
12th April 1906 ~ 25th September 1981

Miner, soldier, maker of rissoles, and my grandad

~ Out of intense complexities, intense simplicities emerge

1

Frank

February 2002

Frank lifted his head a fraction and listened to his wife shuffling around in the bedroom above. She was keeping out of his way, just as she'd been doing for more years than he wanted to admit. He slumped further into the armchair that she'd placed strategically so he could look outside, and not bother her. With his chin resting on his chest, he scrutinised his useless body, knowing he'd never achieve the miraculous recovery his old employer had managed fifty years before.

Finally, Frank turned, his line of vision settling on the glass panels of the patio doors, and through those, towards the silver birch that stood as an arboreal chandelier in the harsh morning frost. He clocked the untidiness of the garden; bushes not pruned, last summer's bedding plants long dead, and the grass was a bloody mess. He hated to think what was happening down at his allotment, although Richard would happily sort it, the garden too. Frank would love to see more of his favourite grandson, but instead, here he was, confined to this one room, hearing the familiar creak of footsteps on the stairs as Hilda made her way down. He could gauge every one of her movements around the house, always knowing exactly where she was. Now, she'd be loitering on the other side of the sitting room door. Waiting for him to die.

He should call Richard. Do it now. There were secrets he needed to share with his grandson. Where was his mobile? On the table in the hall? Frank pushed himself into standing, but his knees collapsed as a sharp pain ricocheted throughout the front of his skull. Excruciating. Just like the last time, although this was worse. Much. He couldn't see his wife but sensed she'd crossed the threshold into the room; he tried to call out. No sound came from his lips and in the lull that came before the real tornado he managed to move his head. There she stood, red hair now white and wispy, her face expressionless. He tried again, tried to say the words, *Richard* and *phone*. She turned away.

Frank didn't want this to be the last thing he saw. The back of a woman he'd once loved so much but whom he'd come to despise. Instead, he found what he wanted to see, the full and vibrant image of a life half shared and of a woman so different to his wife, in every conceivable way.

2

Florence

Westerham, Kent
May Day 1928

With her legs splayed out and her back leant against the biggest oak in the village, which was conveniently situated at the rear of the church and away from prying eyes, Florence finished the last puff of her cigarette. She placed it on the parched ground and used the scuffed heel of her boot to extinguish it properly. The *countryside's like a tinderbox*, her dad had told her; the last thing she wanted was to start a fire. *Odd weather for the time of year*, everyone she spoke to lamented. She loved her village but, my God, the people in it could be boring.

Florence undid the top button of her new blouse that she'd changed into earlier, revealing more of her chest than her mum would be happy with. She rested both hands on the top of her thighs, the memory of Frank helping her up from the baked grass of the village green after their picnic with little Anna still vivid. For moments she allowed the warm thrumming between her legs to flow, pushed the pad of her right forefinger, hard, into the area just below her pubic bone, and let out a small moan. It was a sensation she often got when thinking of Frank Cullen. Brusquely, Florence catapulted herself into standing.

Smoothing down her skirt she took a mint from her pocket, popped it in her mouth and trotted towards the main road that would take her back to the village's ongoing May Day festivities. The church's clock said five. The cusp between late afternoon and evening. Her favourite time of day.

Florence stopped by the graveyard's stone wall that fronted the church and heaved herself up onto its uneven mossed ledge, taking out an aged mirror and lipstick from her purse. She dabbed the lipstick on her cheeks and rubbed it in, then put some on her lips. Peering at her reflection, she puckered her mouth and liked the result, although she couldn't help but feel it was all a waste of time. Because there was only one man in Westerham for her. She wiped off the lipstick. Frank wasn't keen on too much make-up. Hilda never wore any.

With too much force she propelled herself off the wall. Frank had said that after walking Anna home he'd be coming back later for the dance. Florence had a feeling that he might have had to carry the little girl some of the way home. Anna had been full-on since ten that morning; she'd be tired, bless her.

Frank had been different today. Did that trouble her? She wasn't sure but she really hoped he wouldn't change his mind about coming to the dance. And with a thudding guilt in her stomach she hoped too that Hilda wouldn't alter her reclusive habits of the last four years and turn up.

The afternoon's events had come to an end and most of the villagers were already heading for the evening's festivities, which were always hosted in the village hall. Hunting for the buffet table, Florence wove her way into the depths of the space. She was starving.

She spotted Frank at the far side of the room. He'd changed his clothes, his trousers were perfectly creased and he wore a newly laundered shirt. His dark brown curls were slicked back revealing the vibrant violet of his eyes. He was talking to Hilda's dad. She flattened down her own unkempt hair, rearranged her blouse, took a deep breath, and made her way over.

'Hello, Mr Wells, nice to see you here,' she said. 'I bet Anna's worn out, isn't she?' She was speaking to Hilda's dad but looking at Frank.

'She is, and thank you, Florence, for looking after Anna.'

'I love looking after her.'

Mr Wells coughed. 'Just been saying to Frank that it's 'bout time him and our Hilda got married.' He wiped his chin self-consciously.

'It is.' She attempted to do up the top button of her blouse as she spoke, but failed. 'Is Hilda or Mrs Wells coming along later?'

'I don't think so, and I'll be leaving myself shortly.'

'Mrs Wells should come and enjoy herself.' She paused, uncertain. 'Hilda too.'

'Too many of the villagers make comments to our Hilda. Not surprised she doesn't want to come to be honest. Mrs Wells has stayed home to keep her company.' A second of silence followed and Florence could tell Mr Wells wasn't sure about the next sentence but he said it anyway, and to her surprise. Mr Wells rarely exposed his thoughts. 'Eighteen's too young to be cooped up inside all the time.'

Too young to have a child too. 'Bloody people,' she said instead.

Both Mr Wells and Frank stared at her, Frank suppressing a smile. She was unsure what Mr Wells' expression was saying.

'I'm sorry, but you know what I mean,' she finished.

'I do, Florence. Unfortunately, I do,' Mr Wells said, gloom drooping over him.

'Give Mrs Wells my best,' Frank interrupted. 'And tell Hilda I'll see her soon.'

Mr Wells' red and weathered face, already skeletally thin, was even more emaciated tonight. 'Why don't you come around tomorrow, lad?' he said to Frank.

'I'm working at Chartwell in the morning.'

'Pop in on your way? I'm sure Hilda'd like to see you.'

'It'll be early. But I will, yes.'

'Good lad.' Mr Wells' eyes moved towards Florence, his gaze lingering.

She really wished she hadn't put on the rouge. 'I'll save some of the May Day cake for Hilda and Anna,' she said. 'I made it at Chartwell with Mrs Cunningham yesterday.'

'You're a good girl, Florence, really. I know that. Like Hilda is…' His hollow cheeks collapsed a little more. 'You've always been there for our Hilda – when she lets you be.' He hitched up his trousers. To Frank he said, 'See you bright and early then?'

Frank inclined his head and Mr Wells strode off through the thickening village crowd.

'Poor Mr Wells.'

'Yes.' Frank turned and looked at her. 'You got changed too.'

'I did.'

'Nice blouse. Green suits your eyes.' Her heart picked up its beat. 'Hardly any gin in the punch this year,' he carried on, gesticulating towards the huge crystal bowl filled with purple liquid sitting in the middle of the long trestle table.

'That's because of what happened last year,' she said with a grin.

'The Harper girl found blotto in the graveyard? It *was* funny.' He pulled out a flask. 'Frank to the rescue.'

'Is that gin?'

'It is.' Florence leant over the table and grabbed one of the postmistress's tongue and pickle sandwiches. 'Hungry?' he said, laughing.

'Always hungry, you know me. Appetite like a horse.'

'Always did have. For everything.'

'Did you ask Hilda to come to the dance, Frank?'

'I didn't. I knew she wouldn't.'

'She's been stupid putting off marrying you.'

He poured a good measure of the gin into two glasses, then filled both up with the punch using the ladle. He handed one to her. 'Let's enjoy ourselves, eh?'

She took a sip, the alcohol slit her throat and she coughed. 'That's strong. So, you're working at Chartwell tomorrow?'

'I am. Mr Churchill requested me and Benjamin to do the bricklaying.' He'd already finished one glass and was pouring himself another, which was unlike Frank; he wasn't a drinker. 'You want the first dance?'

'Why not? No more parties until Christmas. Might as well make the most of it.' She really hoped she hadn't coloured.

They did three very conservative foxtrots as half the village looked on, including Frank's mother and sister, and drank another cup of punch with his added gin. It was Frank's idea to go outside.

'Need some air,' he said undoing the top button of his shirt.

They made their way into the relative coolness of the village hall's back terrace. She peered upwards to a simmering night sky: a huge black sea scattered with silver shrapnel.

'Beautiful, aren't they?' Frank said.

'They really are. I never tire of looking at them.' She missed a step, and looked towards him, his image blurred.

They walked unsteadily towards the graveyard where earlier she'd put on, and taken off, the lipstick.

'Flo, I'm sorry that you and Hilda aren't getting on as well as you should.' He pushed himself up on the wall. 'When was the last time you saw her properly, for a chat?'

'Christmas time. She avoids me.' She caught his eye. 'Avoids everyone but you, and your sister.' She fiddled with her hair. 'It's not your fault.'

'You were so good to her when it happened. You, and your mum.'

'Hilda avoids my mum too. I miss Hilda, if you want the truth.' And she did.

'I think Hilda misses Hilda.'

'And I love Anna. Since she was born I've loved her.' Clumsily, she heaved herself up next to him. He held onto her as she shuffled her bottom backwards.

'Me too.' He lolled sideways with the effort of helping her.

She'd never seen Frank drunk. She placed a hand around him, steadying him, although she didn't feel very steady herself. Her fingers touched the hardness of taut back muscles. He leant towards her, not quite coordinated. 'You look beautiful tonight.'

'Do I?'

'Yes.' A frown fell across his brow. 'All this time, and now…'

'What?'

'I'm not sure…'

'About what?'

'Hilda.'

He leaned closer, and when his lips touched hers something inside sprang to life, but Hilda's image was there, and clear. Frank wasn't hers, no matter what he'd just said. She hesitated, as did Frank. An instant chilled in time. His lips had moved away from hers a fraction, but so near she couldn't see the expression on his face. He touched her cheek. Feather light. And then he nudged closer. Florence tasted the punch on his breath and something deeper. Him. As his tongue gently touched the roof of her mouth, a hot iron ran up her spine and into the nape of her neck, and she tried not to think about Hilda. Through the fug of her gin brain and breaking the stillness of the evening, she heard what sounded like keys dropping to the ground and then light, rapid footsteps. Frank pulled away and turned his head to scan the lane.

He slid off the wall; the spell severed. Florence would never know if it was the noise or something else.

He didn't explain, or apologise.

Not properly, for years.

*   *   *

Florence's head was still thick from last night's gin punch – and embarrassment – although it didn't stop her from surveying the pile of papers teetering on the edge of Mr Churchill's desk. It was understood she was not to touch a thing in the library, or look at any correspondence Mr Churchill, *too cavalierly leaves lying around*, Miss Cunningham, Chartwell's ad hoc cook and her mum's friend, had said. *I know what a nosy parker you are, Florence, known you long enough.*

Mrs Churchill had mentioned this particular rule to Florence once, and once only, because that was the mistress's way. Florence liked Mrs Churchill even if sometimes she could be a bit cold, with the staff and her own children, but as her mother had said, *that's the way of the well-heeled.* Randolph, the Churchills' eldest, was an obnoxious piece of baggage, so Florence sympathised with the mistress's iciness towards at least one of her offspring.

Reluctantly, she turned away. It was true though, Florence thought as she made her way to start on the dining room, she was too nosy. One day it would get her into trouble. The year previously she'd known about the plans for the General Strike long before the newspapers

– and Mr Churchill's response to it. She'd liked him a
little less for a few days but the feeling didn't last long.
He had a lot of responsibility, did Mr Churchill, so much
to think about, and probably why he didn't always make
the right decisions, that's what her dad said. But
Florence liked to think she understood the master a bit,
because there was a big part of her that one day wanted
to do something useful in the world, and she was certain
that was Mr Churchill's aim too. Despite all his mistakes.

Florence began work. Activity was helping to dampen
the threatening headache, as well as thoughts of Frank,
and guilt about Hilda. She patted the floral green
upholstered chairs and tied back the opulent curtains.
No expense spared, that was for sure. It was a good
thing Mr Churchill liked writing articles for the
newspapers.

The master had been in his *building mood* for weeks,
but as was so often the case he'd been called away on
important business as Mr Baldwin's Chancellor of the
Exchequer and was leaving tomorrow. Through the
dining room's arched windows that faced the Wealds she
saw Frank carrying his tools. Mr Churchill would be out
there any minute, giving intricate instructions to the
bricklayers on the ongoing construction work of his
beloved kitchen wall. She'd normally wave to Frank, but
today she caught herself. Growing up really wasn't all it
was made out to be. He hadn't really meant what he'd
said the night before, changing his mind about Hilda.
People often didn't say what they really meant; she knew
that. Drunk or not. Look at her; she hadn't said what she
wanted to say either.

Florence walked back to the library, but not before first stopping by the mirror in the hallway. She pulled one of Mrs Churchill's cashmere scarfs from the coat stand, draped it around herself and twirled a few times, pretending she was in a grand London house and admiring her reflection while she did so. She pushed an unruly strand of dark hair behind her ear, and then unravelled the elegant slate grey fabric and carefully put it back.

In the library she tried to ignore the tempting pile of letters and began dusting around Mr Churchill's many books.

3

Frank

Sticking a hand inside his jacket pocket, Frank felt for the bag of pear drops his sister had pilfered for Anna from the vicar's cabinet. For once he'd managed to make his serrated and solitary sibling giggle with his joke: *the pear-sucking vicar, the sanctimonious old git.*

It was a cool morning but as he walked up the Wells' path he felt the perspiration pooling on his back. He did need to have a proper talk with Hilda although he hadn't planned on it today, and so early. Seven in the morning with a bit of a hangover wasn't the best time for this. He'd told Mr Wells he'd come though. And he needed to get this over with.

Mr Wells answered the door, obviously just about to leave for work. 'Frank, lad. Glad you're here. I had a word with Hilda last night when I got home. She's ready. You ask her today.' Mr Wells was more determined than Frank had ever witnessed before and more hotness spread through him, then hollowness. 'I hope to hear good news later, lad.' And off he went to work; although Mr Wells' main toil of the day was already over.

Frank took a step inside and immediately the waft of clean washing hit his nostrils.

'Frank!' Anna rushed towards him.

He ruffled her head. 'Is Hilda up yet?'

'Hanging out the washing already.' She grabbed his hand. 'I had a nice day with you and Flo yesterday.'

'I'm glad about that. We always like looking after you. You go up to your room, love. I'll go and find Hilda. I can't stay long, have to go to work.'

'To work with Mr Churchill?' Her face lit up.

'Yes, with Mr Churchill,' he said, grinning.

'When can I go with Miss Cunningham to Chartwell and play with Mary again in her little house? I liked that. I like Mary. I like her mum too, and Mr Churchill.' It had been Clementine Churchill herself who'd suggested Anna go to Chartwell and play with their youngest daughter.

'Ah, Anna. I'm sure Miss Cunningham will take you again soon.'

Four-year-old Anna liked this reply and happily trotted upstairs.

He made his way into the garden and studied Hilda as she reached up towards the washing line. Her small waist pulled in further by the cord of her apron, temperamental red hair held in place by a headscarf. Her complexion a milky white. So different to Flo. In so many ways.

She gave him a rare smile. 'Dad said you were coming over this morning.'

'I can't stay long. Have to meet Benjamin. We're at Chartwell today.'

'Mr Churchill off again on his travels?'

'Seems so.'

She pegged up the last piece of bedding. 'Say hello to Flo for me.' Watching his expression carefully, she walked towards him

'You should've come yesterday.' He nodded at the loaded clothesline. 'It's time you stopped taking in washing and went back to the bakery. You loved that job, Hilda. You need to become part of the world again.'

'Perhaps you're right.' She turned away to retrieve the peg basket.

'Come inside. Let's have a quick cup of tea.'

It was Frank who filled the metal kettle and put it on the stove. Hilda had sat down. He put the tea in the strainer and went to sit next to her. Her hand rested on the kitchen table, the skin around her nails red and sore from the laundry work. He placed his own over hers, flinching at its coldness.

'I've something I want to talk to you about.' He heard Anna moving around in the bedroom above.

Hilda looked at him, the sea green flecks in her irises glittering, tiny pinpricks of emeralds in the kitchen's early morning sun. Eyes that missed nothing.

'I never wanted you to feel as if you still had to marry me, Frank.' She pulled her hand from underneath his. 'It's why I've been so hesitant these past years.' Her brow puckered in the way he'd once found so enchanting. 'I was only thinking of you.'

He swallowed, coughed to clear his throat. 'You could have married me when you first knew you were pregnant. No one would've been the wiser.'

She played with a strand of hair and Frank thought he'd never seen anyone as beautiful as the woman sitting opposite him. She held his gaze.

'The thing is, Hilda—'

'I've spoken to my dad... and I'll marry you, Frank.' She hadn't taken her eyes off him. 'If you still want me, that is?' She touched his face.

After waiting four years for those words flatness settled like lead inside of him. He didn't reply.

Hilda sat up tall in the chair. 'You've changed your mind haven't you?' She patted down her apron. 'I've heard what people are saying.'

'*What* are people saying?'

'That you'd be better off marrying Flo.'

'Flo and me are friends. Like you and she used to be. Like the three of us used to be.'

'I know about—' she began.

'Frank, do you want to go in the garden? Hilda, can we?' Anna said, appearing at the kitchen door.

The kettle began whistling and Frank checked the clock that sat on the kitchen dresser. 'I need to be leaving, Anna, I'm sorry.' He took hold of the child's hand, unsure if she was disappointed or not, her features often as inscrutable as her mother's.

Anna needed him.

Hilda rose and with purpose kissed him on his lips. She smelt of the outside and a hint of lemon. 'So, shall we get married?' She smoothed down the frayed collar of his shirt.

He looked at Anna. Looked at Hilda. Swallowed. 'Yes. We'll get married.'

'Good.' She rested her arm on Anna's shoulder. 'Why don't you see Frank out, sweetie?'

Anna's entire face became illuminated at her mother's good mood.

This was the best thing for Anna. Frank saw it already. And he did love Hilda. He'd always loved her. Flo didn't want him; she'd been tipsy at the dance and had been flirting. She meant nothing by it. But that kiss.

There was something about Flo that was so raw, untamed, free. He glanced at Hilda and said no more.

Anna walked to the door with him. 'Next time, can you tell me stories about Mr Churchill, the house, and his children again? I like those stories.'

'I know you do, love.' He bent down and kissed the top of her head.

Frank made his way towards the far end of the village where Benjamin was picking him up, his thoughts still in the kitchen, reminiscing how Hilda used to be, before Anna, how the three of them used to be; *thick as thieves*, everyone said. Hilda used to laugh, maybe not as much as Flo, but when she did it was loud and rich, and because of its infrequency, so infectious, so powerful. As Mr Wells had rightly said, the village gossip *had* strangled Hilda. She'd changed beyond all recognition.

He walked, passing by the track on his left that would take him to the woods where the three of them played as children, and memories swamped him; of when he'd made friends with Flo and probably fallen in love with Hilda. If you could fall in love at seven.

'Boys aren't supposed to cry.'

Frank looked up to see two girls standing by the old oak. It was the redhead who'd spoken. She was so beautiful that he could hardly look her in the eye. She sat down next to him on the hard autumn ground, close, and without being asked.

'What do you know?' Frank snapped, quickly wiping the tears from his face. 'You're just a kid.'

'So are you,' she said quietly, studying him. She touched his arm. He flinched. But only a bit.

'Leave him be, Hilda,' the pretty dark-haired girl said, sitting on the other side of him, vigorously pushing at the autumn leaves with her foot.

The crunching foliage grated through his skull. The throbbing, which had started in his temple, began to spread and his ear was killing him. He'd stomped from his house after yet another beating from his drunken dad, making his way straight to the woods. His tears were mostly due to the thump his dad had deposited on his right ear but also partly because he'd left his little sister to face the continuing wrath of their dad. He'd thought about bringing Jem with him, but he wanted to cry, let it all out and he didn't want his sister to see his tears. It was enough his father was always calling him a crybaby.

The redhead held up her hand and touched his face so very gently. 'There's blood in your ear. Is that why you're crying?'

Frank nodded, deciding that despite himself he liked these girls, and envisaged more ribbing from the boys in his class.

The other girl spoke. She had deep brown hair, sand-coloured skin and was taller than the redhead, bigger. She looked stronger. 'This is Hilda,' she nodded towards her flame-haired friend. 'And I'm Florence. Don't call me Flo, my mum and Dad don't like that.'

He stretched out his legs, pushing away the leaves surrounding them. The hurt in his head was dying down, although he could still hear the distant buzz. 'My name's Frank, Frank Cullen.'

'Did your dad do that to you?' Hilda said. 'Mr Cullen isn't it, your dad?'

'You know my dad?'

'Everyone in the village knows your dad. He drinks too much, that's what my dad says,' Florence chipped in.

Hilda pulled a handkerchief from her coat pocket and wiped away the congealing blood. She had really pretty hair. Like fire.

'Do you want to be our friend?' Florence said.

Frank did want to be their friend but worried how it'd look to the other boys in the village. He nodded hesitantly.

'We start school next year, and then we'll see you there too,' Florence carried on. 'Hilda'll look after you.' She glanced at her friend. 'She looks after me.'

'I don't need looking after.' He studied Florence. He'd have thought it'd be Florence looking after Hilda. 'Especially by… girls.'

'Suit yourself,' Florence said.

Hilda hadn't said a word.

'Let's play tag,' Florence said in a softer tone.

It was Hilda who offered a hand to pull him up. 'One day you'll be grown up and then your dad won't be around,' she said in a whisper.

Frank nodded but in reality couldn't comprehend a life without his dad and didn't really know what Hilda meant. But he really liked her. He liked Florence too.

They played tag and although his ear still hurt he forgot about it as he had fun with his new friends. Later they trundled back to Florence's house where her mum made them dripping sandwiches and hot tea. Her mum checked his ear and he heard her telling Florence's aunt what an awful man his dad was. He wished Florence's mum were *his* mum.

As they'd been growing up Florence was always the breath of fresh air in the threesome, the one who brought the humour. Hilda, more serious, the one who protected him and Flo with the sharpness of her tongue. No one in the playground could outsmart Hilda with words. And Frank: he was never quite sure what he added to their little group and sometimes thought it was enough just being a boy.

Frank crouched down, sitting on his haunches, not wanting to think about the past anymore. Finally he heard Benjamin's horn.

The small truck swung into the indent on the lane. 'Get in, mate, running very late,' Benjamin shouted.

It wasn't until he was halfway to Chartwell, in the back sitting with all the bricklaying paraphernalia, Frank realised he'd forgotten to give Anna the pear drops.

The mortar wasn't the right consistency but it was Benjamin's batch so Frank said nothing.

'Get a move on, Frank. Need to get more down in a day than the old man or I'll never hear the last of it.' Punctuating the sentence, Benjamin spat out a mouthful of phlegm onto the sodden ground.

Frank wiped his brow and stood up tall, stretching out his six-foot frame, nodding towards the little building – Mr Churchill's Wendy house – only a few feet away. 'The master's added a chimney, I see. Brickwork's good.'

'Yes, it's a fine piece of workmanship,' Benjamin said, standing up straight after meticulously pointing the mortar on the last brick he'd laid. He rubbed his chin.

'Although to my eye the bricks aren't in perfect alignment, but it's good… and nice for Mary, but I think the old man just liked building it.' He glanced at Frank. 'You want children?'

'I do. I like them. Have to find myself a wife first, though.'

'The redhead still bucking?'

'Hilda's her name.' Benjamin could sometimes be audacious with his remarks, and usually about women. Even Clementine Churchill wasn't spared, but Benjamin meant nothing by it, not really.

'Florence'd be a better choice. Everyone says so.'

'Everyone should keep their noses out.'

'Maybe,' Benjamin said. 'But you know, lad, maybe they're right. Sometimes we don't see what's in front of us, hanker for what's far away, the most difficult. Easy doesn't always mean wrong, just as difficult doesn't always mean right.'

'Keep the philosophising to yourself, eh?' Frank replied. Benjamin had the habit of often being right. Frank glanced upward looking at the building that was Chartwell. Perhaps he would see Flo inside. He'd ask her opinion later. Have a debate, like she, Hilda and he had always done – before Anna.

Benjamin was about to reply when his attention was taken with the appearance of Chartwell's owner. He nodded at Frank in warning. Both men began working again.

Winston Churchill stopped short at a red rose tree, its buds formed but not yet in bloom. He bent forward and, hampered a bit by his girth, poked the ground around the tree with his stick, then stood up, pulled at his wellingtons, readjusted the black homburg hat, and without a rush finally tottered towards his beloved wall.

He peered at the little children's house, which sat near to the wall-in-progress, then at Frank. 'What do you think of our *Marycot*?' he drawled.

'It's a very fine Wendy house, sir. Anna loved coming to play with Mary. Really good of Mrs Churchill to let Miss Cunningham bring her. I bet your children love playing in it?' Then remembered to add, 'Sir.'

'Mary does. Of course, Sarah is too old. It's good that other children can enjoy Chartwell and not only my own. Miss Cunningham…' He appeared to falter. 'Knew Marigold. Looked after her very well when Marigold's nanny was away.' He placed the palms of his hands flat on his chest, which was covered in his customary all-in-one suit. Plum-coloured today, matching the colour of the bricks Frank thought with a smile. He noted Churchill's thick fingers, and manicure, but two nails on his right hand were jagged, like a real bricklayer's: like his own. A sad expression fell over Mr Churchill's face. Perhaps he was thinking of his daughter, Marigold, who'd died. He didn't know what to say and so said nothing.

The great man looked at him, and hadn't yet addressed Benjamin. 'Are you married, Mr Cullen?'

'No, I'm not sir,' he replied.

'In my experience, every man should get married. I married Clementine, and I'm living happily ever after.' He pulled a cigar from his pocket, enjoying his topic. 'A man needs a good wife as he needs good friends.' Churchill petted the cigar. 'You know about Brendan Bracken? He's my friend, as is Beaverbrook, but two very different men. Different friends for different dilemmas, and sometimes…' Pausing, he twisted off the end of his Romeo and Julieta. 'It's not the friend whom you thought would listen and advise in the correct way. That always surprises me. Advice is paramount. Asking for opinions is paramount. Knowing which opinion to take heed of is paramount.'

Churchill peered at the ground and hunched his shoulders but Frank saw the smile. 'Not that I always take advice. But, I always listen.'

Frank moved forwards, and taking out a box of matches, he deftly lit the cigar. 'Good advice, sir.'

'It is. I only ever give good advice.'

'You do, sir.'

'I am always right. Ask Mrs Churchill.' He picked up a stray trowel and tapped a brick with it. 'The plum bricks work well.'

'They do, sir. Wise choice,' Benjamin said.

That hadn't been Benjamin's opinion earlier.

Churchill's face shone with pleasure; everyone who worked for him knew he loved a bit of flattery.

'I shall be back in a week or so and will carry on,' Churchill said, moving closer to the wall and inspecting the newly laid bricks. 'I think you could do a better job with the pointing, Benjamin?'

'Of course, sir,' Benjamin replied tightly.

'This wall has to be perfect for Clementine.' He sucked deeply on his cigar. 'It has to be perfect.'

'Of course, sir.'

The smoke plumed upwards towards an uncomplicated azure sky. 'It is immensely good to see you both here.' His illuminating gaze appraised both men. 'There is tea or lemonade up at the kitchen, and I hear, apple pie. Ensure you go.' He pushed the homburg hard onto his head. 'It's always wise to remember that the stomach governs the world.'

'I hope you have a good day, sir, and a good trip,' Frank said.

'I will be back to lay two hundred bricks and write two thousand words, every day,' Churchill said, his smile wry.

Frank had read that line in *The Daily Mirror*. Mr Churchill had said it to Stanley Baldwin. Frank knew that Mr Churchill knew that he knew and that Benjamin had no idea what they were talking about.

'And read, sir, as well?' Frank pushed.

Winston Churchill examined his employee's face. 'Oh yes. A man is nothing without reading. Miss Cunningham tells me that you are a keen reader?'

'I am, sir. Anything I can get my hands on.'

'Clemmie and Sarah have been sorting out my books.' He wiped the trowel with a handkerchief he'd retrieved from the pocket of his suit. 'Decluttering me, they say. I have several copies of the same books. I will tell Sarah to give them to you. History books, some biographies. If you are a reading man you should take me up on my offer.'

'I certainly will, sir. Th… thank you.' Frank heard his own stutter. 'So much for your generosity.'

Churchill turned away, jabbed his stick in a nearby rose bush and then, his back towards his workers, held up his arm in goodbye. 'Remember the pie.'

*   *   *

It was late afternoon and the sun's rays were whispery cool.

Frank and Benjamin were sitting outside Chartwell's kitchen door, Frank drinking tea, Benjamin lemonade. There was no apple pie in sight and Miss Cunningham had retired for an hour before preparing dinner for the Churchills. Frank's stomach was grumbling in anticipation.

It was Flo who finally brought out two enormous slabs of pie. She put the plate on the ground. 'Miss Cunningham said I'm allowed to give you more, if you'd like more.' She fixed her eyes on Benjamin as she spoke, avoiding Frank's.

Both men grabbed their portion. Flo went back into the kitchen and returned with the entire pie, which she cut in two. 'Here you go, I don't know where you two put it all!'

'Do we use a fork?' Frank said, attempting joviality, recognising her awkwardness. Because he felt the same.

'I give you permission to use your fingers today.'

He picked up a chunk and took a huge bite, munched and swallowed. 'Is it your night off?'

'I'm about to leave now.'

'Wrap up your pie and take it with you,' Benjamin said. 'And walk Florence home.'

'I'm stopping off at Hilda's on my way,' Frank said to her. 'I've some sweets I forgot to give Anna earlier.'

'Be back here at first light, Frank,' Benjamin said.

As they left Chartwell's grounds the light faded fast. It was Florence who was the first to speak. 'How's the wall coming along?'

'Good. Between you and me, Churchill's a better bricklayer than Benjamin.'

Flo giggled. 'Better than you?'

'Maybe.'

'Did you speak to him?'

'Who?'

'Mr Churchill.'

'I did, yes. He's offered to give me some of his books.'

'He likes you.'

'It rubs Benjamin up the wrong way.'

'Benjamin can be a bit funny sometimes,' she said.

'He's all right though, really. He's good to work for.' His pace slowed. 'I saw Hilda this morning. She's finally agreed to marry me.'

Florence slowed too.

He glanced at her open face that reflected the paling light. 'Last night…'

'We were drunk. We're friends, Frank…' As he'd thought. 'I know you love Hilda. Because you do, don't you?' The lilt in her voice at the end of the last sentence echoed into the lane.

'Hilda needs me. Anna needs me. I don't think her dad would ever forgive me…' He stopped walking and turned to her, tried to smile. 'I can't change my mind. Not now.'

'Do you want to?'

'I can't.'

'No.'

'Go and see Hilda soon, Flo. Have a chat,' he said quietly.

'I will.'

'Everything's all right then? Between us?' he said.

'Of course it is.'

'Hilda's still your friend, you know.'

'She doesn't let me in. She's turned into a recluse. And she's never really told me what happened, just clammed up.' She looked up at him. 'You know, don't you, what happened?'

He nodded. Hilda had told him and with this telling he'd construed an affirmation of her continuing love for him. It had brought him closer to her.

And made it totally impossible for him to leave.

4

Florence

Her heart was burdened, aching, but Florence was determined not to let it show. She was being stupid. Frank hadn't meant what he said. Her dad said alcohol made you say the truth, but her dad was often wrong in affairs of the heart. Frank was only saying he *had* to marry Hilda. He didn't *have to*. He *wanted* to. Of course he did. He'd always wanted to marry Hilda. Since they were children.

They stopped outside the Wells' front gate. 'Maybe I should go and give Anna the sweets. Have a chat with Hilda now? You go home?'

'That's a good idea.' He pulled out the sweets and gave them to her.

She took a peep inside. 'You should've taken them out your coat, they've gone all gooey being in there all day.'

'You're right.' He plunged both hands into his pockets. 'Let me know if Hilda says anything… I'll catch up with you tomorrow at Chartwell?'

She nodded and watched as he loped away. Last night really had been a mistake and lifting her shoulders, she prepared herself for Hilda.

Mr Wells answered the door, his ruddy complexion and sunken cheeks more pronounced than ever. Hilda's mum and dad hadn't handled the whole situation with Hilda and Anna at all well, but they'd done what they thought was best for their daughter, and many parents would have kicked Hilda out. Not Florence's, though. No, not hers, but they wouldn't have pretended her child was her mum's either.

Mr Wells was staring at her. 'Hello, Florence. Nice to see you here lass.'

His trousers were caked in mud and the familiar smell of farm hovered around him; probably just returned from work. He didn't venture from the doorway.

'Can I come in, Mr Wells?'

'Of course, sorry. Hilda's in her room—'

'Flo.' A quiet voice. It was Anna.

The little girl pulled her inside. Mr Wells nodded to his granddaughter, and muttering about getting washed-up, returned to the kitchen. Everyone knew Anna was Hilda's daughter. Florence had no idea why Mr and Mrs Wells were keeping up the pretence. It was doing Anna no favours, and it was doing Hilda no great service either. Since Anna's birth Hilda hardly left the house and had little interest in anything, only the church. Hilda, who'd once been so inquisitive, so full of curiosity for the world, was now just, and only just, existing. She'd withdrawn completely. And what was Florence doing to help her friend?

Coveting her man, that's what.

'Frank came this morning,' Anna said, grabbing at Florence's coat sleeve, indicating for her to bend down so she could whisper in her ear. 'Frank's going to marry Hilda.'

Florence cupped the girl's face. 'I know, lovely.'

'Will I go to live with them?'

She hesitated in her reply. 'With your sister and Frank?' Anna was only four but knew the situation. How could she not?

'With Hilda and Frank, yes,' Anna replied without artifice.

'Of course you will.'

Anna pulled Florence towards her again. 'You do know don't you, that Hilda's my mum?'

Florence bent down lower so she was on the same level as Anna's face. 'I know. It's a special secret.'

'What's a *bastard*?'

Florence swallowed the lump surging in her throat. 'Don't be worrying about words like that.'

Frank marrying Hilda was the way it was always supposed to be. And it would be so good for Anna. The best thing for Anna. Florence loved Anna. Everyone did. Apart from Hilda. She had no idea what Hilda had been thinking these past four years, but then again she never had, not really, despite them being best friends. Hilda should have bitten off Frank's hand before now, but Hilda had always been a law unto herself: strong, single-minded, and purposeful. Different to her. And why Frank loved Hilda, not her.

Florence smoothed the hair away from Anna's face. 'You stay downstairs. I'm going to talk to… Hilda.'

'She doesn't like me in the bedroom with her in the daytime.'

Anna would be better away from this house. With Frank, and Hilda. Florence's heart plummeted, and only a fraction of her brain gave any room to the thought of her and Frank, and Anna, together. She stood up quickly, dizzy with the maverick thought. She swore she'd never drink gin again.

She made her way up the stairs and knocked on Hilda's bedroom door; the latch on the other side rattled.

'Anna, go away, I'm resting,' Hilda's voice carried through the wood.

'It's Florence. I've come for a chat. Please let me in.'

Silence. Florence studied the door's peeling paint. Hilda had never told her who Anna's father was and Florence had never asked; Hilda had never given her the chance to, that's what she told herself. At the time she'd fleetingly thought Frank was Anna's father, but knew from early on that this wasn't the case, although it didn't stop the rumours circulating, because Frank truly wished Anna *were* his child.

Finally, she heard the dull thud of footsteps on the lino floor of Hilda's bedroom. The door clanked open.

'Flo.' Hilda's face was paper white, her red hair tangled and falling around her shoulders, but still beautiful. 'Come in.' A long pause. 'If you must.'

'Aw, Hilda, don't be like that.'

Hilda leant against the doorjamb and rubbed her temple.

'Are you ill?' Florence asked. She did look horribly pale.

Hilda's face took on an amused smile, changing her whole expression. 'No, I'm not ill. Just tired. How are you? It's been a while, I thought you were avoiding me.' She pulled her mass of hair into a ponytail as she retreated back into the room. 'Come sit on the bed.'

Florence sat down. 'I thought you were avoiding *me*.'

'You haven't tried very hard recently.'

'That's not fair.' Florence undid her coat, suddenly feeling too hot. 'Anna looks happy,' she said, changing the subject.

'Anna's fine. Why've you come, today?'

Florence touched Hilda's slim thigh. 'You're my friend.'

Hilda shuffled away from her. 'Look, Flo, you were great when Anna was born, and what you do for her now – you and Frank. I don't know what I'd have done without you both.' She rubbed the palms of her hands down both thighs and then stood, pulled her narrow shoulders back. 'But it's all going to be fine now.'

Florence sank into the soft bed. 'Frank says you've agreed to marry him.'

Hilda fiddled with a strand of hair that had fallen over her cheek. 'He's told you?'

'Yes, I saw him today at Chartwell.' Something told her not to say they'd walked here together.

'And you saw him at the dance last night?' Hilda waited a second. 'Dad told me. Thanks for taking care of Anna.' She studied Florence intently. 'Everyone's right. It's time I stopped being stupid and marry him… before someone else does.'

Another wave of heat consumed Florence. 'You do love him… don't you?' The words jammed inside her throat.

'Of course I do.'

'You should set a date, and perhaps move away with Frank and Anna, make a new start.' Her insides fractured. But she wanted Anna to be happy. She wanted Frank to be happy. She even wanted Hilda to be happy, although looking at her now Hilda didn't seem that joyful. 'Away from here, and the memories.'

Hilda buttoned up her cardigan. 'I know what everyone thinks.'

'About what?'

'That Frank should marry you.'

Hilda was playing with her. Clever Hilda, who'd always protected Florence, since school, and in so doing, controlled her a little too. Florence's discomfort made it so she could hardly breathe in the enclosed space of the room.

'You know what the village is like.'

'The village likes you. Everyone likes you. You're lucky, Flo. Nice mum, nice dad. Nice job. Nice life.'

If truth were told Florence envied Hilda's beauty and cleverness, and had always wanted to be more like her. It had never crossed her mind that Hilda might envy her. 'Maybe you're right. But it's you who Frank loves and wants to marry.'

Hilda leapt from the bed. 'Would you like some tea?'

'I would.' Florence plucked the sweets from her coat pocket. 'Frank forgot to give Anna these. Pear drops. Let's go down and give them to her.'

'Yes. Let's. Look, thanks for coming.'

'So, we're still friends?'

'Of course we are.' Hilda's tone was as flat as Florence felt.

5

Frank

Mr Churchill returned from his four week long London trip and had carried on building his kitchen wall, as well as starting to excavate the pond in Chartwell's extensive grounds. It was Frank's last day working for Benjamin before moving to Nottingham, and he was spending it knee deep in mud, digging out. This wasn't his job but he didn't mind, not for the old man.

It was just after lunch when Frank looked up and saw Mr Churchill approaching the water's edge. He was aware from what Flo had said about the old man's bathing habits that he'd probably just emerged from the first of his two daily dips. Mr Churchill wore a jumper with old mortar clinging to his sleeve, a brown homburg today, and was sucking on his customary cigar. Ready for work.

Frank made his way up the muddy bank, although because of the characteristic bent position of Mr Churchill's head, Frank wasn't able to see his expression.

'Mrs Churchill's secretary tells me this is your last day with us?' Finally he looked up and caught Frank's eye. 'You will be off with that new wife of yours?'

'Mrs Churchill remembers everything, sir. Yes, I am. Hilda, Anna and me'll be leaving for Nottinghamshire tomorrow.' Frank took the last step upward, away from the bank's edge.

Churchill coughed and held out his hand in assistance. 'It is a very good thing you are doing. Highly commendable. And yes, Mrs Churchill does remember everything. She likes to be kind to her staff.'

So the Churchills knew about Anna, or at least Mrs Churchill's secretary did. With hesitance, Frank held onto Mr Churchill's hand as he heaved himself up and then watched his employer discreetly wipe the same hand on the bottom of his jumper.

'Mrs Churchill's very kind, sir. She gave me the books. I really appreciate it.'

'They would only have ended up in the Commons. I hope you enjoy reading them.'

'I've already read *The Memoirs of John, Duke of Marlborough* by William Coxe, sir.'

'Ah, my illustrious relative? Good.' He peered at Frank. 'It is a good thing, to read, and to be interested, and to be inquisitive. To attempt to be more in life, strive for what life hasn't easily given to you.'

'Yes sir, it is.'

Frank didn't know if he should mention the salt and pepper pots delivered by Miss Cunningham to him and Hilda on their wedding day. A wedding day played out in the local registry office with only his mum, Flo, Anna, Jem, and Hilda's parents there. He decided it would be rude not to say anything to Mr Churchill. The blood filled the capillaries in his face. 'Hilda and I very much appreciate the wedding gift, sir.'

Churchill coughed again and lifted his head. 'Mrs Churchill, all her work, of course.' Frank remained silent, unsure if Mr Churchill knew about the gift. It would have been Miss Cunningham who'd quietly had a word with the mistress. Churchill carried on. 'I am truly sorry about your father.'

'Sir?'

Churchill carried on. Unflinching. 'Gallipoli.'

'It was a long time ago, sir.'

And it was. 1915. He'd been only eight. He'd known Hilda and Flo a year by then. Gallipoli and the Dardanelles had been one of Churchill's mistakes during the Great War – a poor judgement – although the outcome was a good one for the Cullen family. Because his father hadn't come home.

'My gravest mistake.'

'As I say, sir, a long time ago.'

'But you miss your father?'

'I can't say I do, sir.'

'I understand.' Churchill rested the palms of his hands on a wide chest in thought. And Frank convinced himself he did understand. Miss Cunningham had told him about Mr Churchill's troubled relationship with his father, Randolph, the third son of the 7th Duke of Marlborough.

Churchill turned away. It was time for Frank to leave.

He made his way back via the kitchen garden and took one last look at Winston Churchill's *Marycot*. He'd build one like it for Anna and the other children he planned to have with Hilda; he hoped with other children that Hilda's relationship with her daughter might improve.

He braced himself to go and see Flo on the way back to his mother's home, where they'd been staying since the wedding. Anna had been sleeping in Jem's room until two days ago, but then Jem had come home from the vicarage for a few days leave. Anna had then moved into his and Hilda's room. It had been the only time he'd seen Hilda relatively happy about having to be in such close proximity with her daughter. It had become blindingly obvious, and very quickly, that his new wife saw sex as a duty rather than something to enjoy. Frank made his way down the narrow gap at the side of Flo's parents' cottage, stopping short when he saw Anna sitting on a small wooden stool.

Hilda had palmed Anna off with Flo again.

Anna hadn't seen him. His line of vision moved to Flo, who was meticulously tending the flowers her mum was famous for growing; she hadn't seen him either, in a world of her own.

Anna's legs hung in mid-air, swinging in rhythm to the song she was singing to herself; she seemed so far away. Frank noticed this a lot with Anna. She was a bright girl and remembered everything, noted everything in her quiet way. You didn't think she was taking notice of the world around her but then suddenly, from nowhere, she'd make a pithy observation about something she'd seen or a person she'd come into contact with. He knew this vexed Hilda, who didn't quite know how to cope with her daughter. Or didn't want to cope with her daughter.

A memory of the time he'd first taken Anna to his mother's for tea came to him. Jem had been on leave from the vicarage and had taken to Anna immediately. His sister was an unsettled girl and had been since those dark days when their father had started coming home drunker and drunker. In the caverns of his mind he understood why his younger sister was the way she was.

Guarded, never truly happy. Spiky. Even Jem's physical appearance was jagged, skinny, and bones that jutted out from all the joints of her body. No roundness to Jem, only sharp angles. But Jem and Anna had formed an immediate bond.

That night as he'd walked Anna back home, she'd said to him, 'Jem's sad.' She took hold of his hand, 'Like me.'

'Why are you sad?' he'd asked.

'Because of Hilda, but I'm not sure why Jem's sad, her mum's nice.'

Frank knew why Jem was sad but of course said nothing to Anna, said nothing to anyone, including Jem.

His thoughts hooked around, returning to the present. Anna was singing and the song carried across the placid spring wind, towards the gate where he still stood.

'I'm forever blowing bubbles…'

It was the melody Miss Cunningham often sang to Anna, and one which – so Miss Cunningham had reported – the Churchills' little Marigold had often sung to herself. Anna really was entranced with the Churchill family, but didn't understand the sadness surrounding the song. It was rumoured Marigold sang it just before she'd passed away, and that both Mr Churchill and his wife now could not bear to hear it.

As Anna finished, she glanced up and finally saw him. 'Flo's looking after me this afternoon, Frank.'

Anna liked being with Flo and a wave of inexplicable sorrow razed through him. Flo looked up, her face shone.

'I can see that. Are you annoying her?' he said gently to Anna, and with a grin.

Anna's expression crumpled into discontent. 'No, I'm not. Hilda says I can stay as long as I want. I think Flo's mum's giving me tea.'

Flo had moved away from the flowerbed and was standing by them. She ruffled the little girl's head. 'You mean your mummy, Hilda?'

Anna screwed up her face. 'I suppose.' She looked up at Frank, the muscles in her face relaxing. 'And you're my dad?'

'I've told you, yes. I'm your dad now and you should start calling me it.'

'Anna,' Flo interrupted. 'Can you go inside and do me a special favour?'

Anna nodded.

'Water from the tap and squeeze that special lemon in it. Do it well, like you always do.'

Anna's face lit up at being asked to do something. 'I will.' And off she went inside.

'She must have picked up that song from Miss Cunningham,' Frank said.

'Probably. Miss Cunningham goes to visit Hilda occasionally. She's very fond of Anna. She's a strange one sometimes, isn't she, Anna?' She carried on, not expecting an answer. 'She sometimes pretends to be the Churchills' Marigold, sometimes she tries to be older and then pretends to be Sarah Churchill. Sometimes, I think Anna just gets really confused. But to be honest, it's hardly surprising.'

'Yes, true. Poor Anna. Poor Hilda,' he said without thinking.

'You don't have to feel sorry for your wife and child, Frank. You're there now to look after them. Put the past behind you all,' she took his hand, 'and that includes your past too.'

Flo couldn't possibly know. His family's secret was buried as deep as the ink blue ocean he'd only ever seen in books. He studied her open face. No one knew, only him, and Jem. And his mother.

'I've come to say thanks for everything,' he said. 'And for coming up with the idea to leave Westerham.' He attempted to read her features. Going to Nottingham had been Flo's idea. She knew he had cousins up there, although a part of him had deflated when he realised Flo was instrumental in Hilda agreeing to move.

She straightened up and wiped her brow. 'I'll miss you, Frank, but it's the best thing for everyone.' Her eyes flicked towards the back door. 'I've been over to see Hilda. She seems happy.' She took a few steps toward him. 'And you're happy now?'

'Course I am. My cousin's got me a job at the colliery in Notts.'

'The pit? But you're not a miner. You're a bricklayer.'

'Not many jobs up there for bricklayers and the money's better at the pit.'

'You'll hate it. You love being outside.'

He shrugged. 'I've arranged an allotment.'

'That's good.'

He pulled out a cigarette and offered her one. She took it. The smoke swirled above them. 'Will you write to us? Maybe come and visit when you can?' he said.

'Of course I'll visit, and write. Take care of Hilda, and Anna.'

'I will.' He threw his unsmoked cigarette to the ground and squashed it with his foot. There was nothing left for him to say. Because he couldn't tell her. It was too late. And anyway, there was Anna.

'Tell Hilda I'll drop Anna back later,' she said.

'Will do.'

He left her standing in the garden puffing daintily on the cigarette her mother would not approve of, her dark hair blowing in the gentle wind.

Frank made his way back to the main road. Back to Hilda, his wife.

6

Florence

2002

Florence studied the date on the newspaper – October 27th 2002 – still bemused she'd made it to the twenty-first century. For the fourth time that morning she flicked through *The Times*, abruptly stopping at page eight and the photo tucked away in the bottom right corner. Holding the paper closer, and noticing with resigned dismay the ropey veins swamping the back of her hand, she touched the image. A handsome man stared back. Frank's grandson looked very like Frank.

Today's feeling of urgency was partly due to seeing Richard Cullen QC's photo, but it was mostly instigated with the news of Hilda's death the day before. Hilda hadn't lasted that much longer than the husband whose life she'd made a misery. Florence wouldn't be going to her funeral. There was no love lost between them, and hadn't been for years.

'Florence, my love, how you feeling today?'

Florence was both glad and relieved that her favourite nurse was back on duty. Celia bustled towards her bed, the familiar smell of cigarette smoke draping the air around her. The other residents often complained, but Florence didn't. She liked her nurse, and she liked the smell. It reminded her of a past that was so long ago and yet not so long ago, of Frank, and

Mr Churchill, although cigars had an altogether different aroma.

'I'm feeling fine, thank you, Celia,' she replied in a raspy voice. Florence inhaled. Yes, the smell was definitely stronger than normal today, and at the grand old age of ninety-three Florence decided she quite fancied a puff. It wasn't as if it'd kill her off any sooner.

'Anything interesting happenin' in the world I should know about?' Celia's eyes took in the opened-out newspaper.

'It's yesterday's.' Florence folded it and placed it on her bedside tray. 'Did you manage to post the letter I gave to you just before you went off on holiday?'

'Holiday? You are joking aren't you?' Celia's pleasant face opened up into her lovely smile. 'Me and Mr Celia decorated the lounge.'

'You two know how to live it up.'

'We have our moments. I did post it. Don't worry. First class too.' She filled Florence's glass with fresh water, most of it ending up pooled on the tray and soaking half the newspaper. 'Sorry.'

Florence wiped away the liquid with her hand towel while Celia eyed up the grapes. 'Have some, they're delicious.'

Celia popped two in between her lips. 'Was it a letter to an old flame?' She gently pulled the pillow from behind Florence's head, pummelled at it, and then, with care, returned it to its rightful place. 'You dark horse, you,' she added.

'No, young lady, it certainly was not.'

Florence rested her head back onto the fattened pillow and let her thoughts wander off. Back to

Chartwell, an afternoon in the spring of 1940, and another letter. Time was running out. She had to tell someone about her and Frank's secrets before the end came.

Secrets and denial: if there'd been fewer of the former and more understanding of the latter, all of their destinies would have taken a different path, especially the woman whose existence had been affected the most.

Florence's own life would have been altered too, but… she'd been happy with the arrangement of the last forty years, more than happy.

It was auspicious that she'd written to Richard Cullen so close to Hilda's death. She hoped he'd reply, or better still, call, and soon. Frank's grandson was the perfect starting point. Frank had been so close to him. She should have spoken to Richard at Frank's funeral; such a wasted opportunity. She had no idea why she hadn't. Guilt probably, she was willing to concede.

Florence looked up at Celia who was perched on the edge of her bed flicking through the damp newspaper. 'I have another favour to ask.'

'Another letter?'

'No.'

'Fire away.'

'Could you take me to the bottom of the garden and give me a fag?'

Celia roared with laughter, helped Florence into the wheelchair, and together they disappeared into the cavernous grounds of Westerham's Waterside Nursing Home.

7

Richard

2002

Richard Cullen QC checked the digital display that hung on the court building's main foyer wall. October 26th 2002 and 4:56 p.m.

'Come on,' his lead researcher said, flicking her head towards the back entrance, a coil of auburn hair escaping her immaculate bun. 'Let's attempt to avoid the press.' Nell tucked the stray strand behind her ear and moved him forward at the same time. 'I booked your favourite restaurant for the celebrations.'

'You were optimistic,' he said, noticing a photographer he recognised from *The Times* lurking on the back steps to the building. Quickly, Richard dipped his head.

'I could always cancel, but knew I wouldn't have to. Another piece of shit behind bars.' She turned towards him. 'Congratulations, Mr Prosecutor Extraordinaire! You going to call Gillian to let her know?'

'Was just about to.'

He tapped on his phone, first Gillian's mobile, no answer, and then the home landline. No response. 'I'll call later. Come on, let's celebrate.'

The sun was dipping in the London skyline as they made their way to the restaurant to meet the rest of the legal team, and as per their routine, they spoke about the case only during the preliminary cocktails, and then it was off limits.

Before food started appearing at their table, Richard disappeared to the restaurant lounge. He tried Gillian again. Still no answer, which was unusual. She would normally have called him, always keen to know the verdict.

Richard put his mobile into the side pocket of his briefcase, catching sight of the two letters that had arrived in the morning's post, which he hadn't had time to open. He pulled both out. The first one was from Nottinghamshire County Council. He opened it and scanned the contents; about Grandad Frank's allotment. Redevelopment. An end of an era, that was for sure. The terrible sadness and grief overcame him again thinking of his grandad Frank and the hours they'd spent in that allotment. He really had to make time to go up to Nottinghamshire to see his gran Hilda very soon. He put the council letter in his inside jacket pocket.

The second envelope was from a Florence Miller, the return address a nursing home in Westerham, Kent: the birthplace of both his grandparents. Richard had never heard of her. He was intrigued but his mind was on other things, and the unopened letter was put into the back compartment of his briefcase – non-urgent correspondence.

He was about to put his mobile away too when it pinged an incoming text. Must be Gillian.

Gran Hilda in hospital. Stable but poorly. Will keep you up to date with any news. No need to rush up though, son, I know you're full-on. But I think she'll be joining your grandad Frank

sooner rather than later.
Hope the case is going well. Verdict yet?
Dad.

Glancing up at the glass partition, which separated the restaurant from the lounge, he saw waiters and waitresses filling the table with food. He'd reply after the dinner. He looked at his dad's words again.

Yep, they really were nearing the end of an era.

Richard put his mobile inside his jacket pocket too.

Before leaving the restaurant Richard had replied to his dad's text, asking which ward his gran Hilda was on. He'd call the hospital in the morning. If Gran couldn't speak on the phone, he'd leave a message with the nurses, to tell her that he, Gillian and Beccy would be up to visit next weekend.

As he made his way to the tube station his head had the feel of an impending hangover, but he still managed to pick up some way too expensive handmade cupcakes from the Deli. Over the years it was a thing he did, and now a ritual on the successful outcome of a case. It was past nine and the dense throbbing at his temple persuaded him to splurge and take a cab instead of his usual journey along the Central Line back to leafy Ealing.

To him, not a true Londoner, it still seemed ostentatious getting a taxi; Gillian always insisted on using them. His wife, solidly middle class, solidly sensible, and solidly keen to ensure she lived the life she believed her family had the right to lead. Unfortunately, as was the way, all her hard work had bypassed their daughter, backfired spectacularly. Richard grinned in the darkness of the hot London taxi. Beccy. His pride and joy. Like him, not Gillian. His thoughts, though, were unfair because Gillian did have a social conscience and he admired that about her. She was a special needs teacher and her students adored her, but with her own child Gillian was too hovering. Too in Beccy's face. He knew it, his parents knew it. Beccy lived it.

He clambered out the taxi and paid, the successful outcome of the case encouraging him to give an unusually large tip.

Approaching their Victorian property, which sat on the corner of a quiet road, he saw a silhouette at the front door and knew instinctively it was his daughter.

As he fumbled with his keys, Beccy beat him to it. Her dark blonde hair was pulled back into a ponytail, wide brown eyes outlined with pink, she'd been crying. She wore no make-up, which was unusual, as she'd taken to wearing a terrifyingly large amount since acquiring her first boyfriend. Gillian disliked Carl. Richard though, was extremely fond of him.

Beccy's normally silky skin was blotchy and red. Her slim legs were encased in black leggings and she wore an old black jumper. He had a premonition the tears were connected with twenty-three-year-old Carl, who had no job and lived at home with his hard-working single father. Carl wanted to be a musician and he was indeed a superb saxophonist, but he earned no money, only what he made from busking. Richard could see why Beccy had fallen for him. Of course, Gillian couldn't, and had been blaming him for the last six months that if they'd sent Beccy to a private school this would never have happened. Beccy meeting a bloke. Richard couldn't understand her logic; Beccy had met Carl last summer at the local nightclub in Ealing.

He handed his daughter the box of cupcakes.

'You won,' she stated, trying to smile.

'We did.' He glanced over her shoulder into the voluminous hallway, catching a whiff of lilies. Jesus, how many times had he told Gillian not to buy those bloody flowers. Death in a sniff. 'What's wrong?'

'My mother is wrong.'

'Is this about Carl?'

She looked at him with those puppy eyes. 'No. It's not about Carl. It's about me.'

'What's happened?' He heard footsteps on the landing. 'Your mum?'

'She's been on the phone for the last three hours looking for clinics.'

'Clinics? Are you ill?' He really wished he hadn't drunk so many Margaritas.

Gillian appeared and Beccy slunk back into the kitchen, slamming the door behind her.

'What's going on?' he asked his wife.

She eyed the box of cupcakes. 'You won?'

'We did. I didn't think we'd pull this one off.'

'You can pull anything off.'

'I got a text from my dad. Grandma Hilda's been taken to hospital.'

'Oh, Richard. Do we need to go up?'

'He says not, not yet.' He leant against the hall wall. 'She's old, though. Hasn't been the same since Grandad Frank died.'

'They say don't they, that the one remaining doesn't last long.'

'They do. What's going on with Beccy?'

She slumped onto the bottom step of the stairs. 'Beccy's pregnant.'

'Ah.' No wonder the phone remained unanswered earlier. The vein in his forehead pulsed.

'Is that your only reaction?'

'I don't know what to say. But I don't think ringing up clinics is the best way forward today. We need to talk about this as a family.' He touched her face. 'Together.'

'She can't have a baby. She's only seventeen.' She peered at him. 'I'm sorry to land you with this tonight, of all nights.'

He sat beside her on the step. 'I take it Beccy doesn't want an abortion?' He guessed that would be his daughter's reaction to this news. Christ, this was going to be a tough one.

'No, she's adamant.'

'We have to be careful how we handle this. Hold off on your search for clinics. Please?'

She nodded. The movement imperceptible.

'The baby's definitely Carl's?' he carried on.

'I can't believe you asked that.'

'Just checking,' he said, nudging her arm in an attempt at playfulness. He often found with his wife that in times of stress levity could be a good thing. Tonight, unsurprisingly, it wasn't working. Fatigue washed over him. 'I like Carl,' he said.

Her shoulders sagged further. 'Carl's dumped her.'

'Oh.'

'A baby will ruin her life.'

'How many weeks?'

'Can't be more than eight.'

'Are you sure she *is* pregnant?'

'Three pregnancy kits, plus the two I bought earlier.' She glanced at him. 'She has a brilliant life ahead of her. She's worked so hard.'

'I know, I know. But Beccy's Beccy. She's strong minded… like her mum.'

Finally, she managed a smile.

He stood and took off his coat. 'Have you really been looking for clinics?'

'We need to know the options.'

'There are two options. Beccy keeps the baby, or she has an abortion. She'll be able to go to the NHS for a termination.'

'You're not pulling the state thing on me with this one. Beccy goes private. Don't go on,' she said. 'Please. I'm going to bed, and I'm sleeping in the spare room.' She looked at him. 'I'm not being difficult. But I know I won't sleep. And I don't want to disturb you. And you've been drinking, and you'll snore.'

'Do I always snore when I'm pissed?'

She smiled properly. 'You do.'

'We'll talk in the morning.'

She kissed him on the cheek and he smelt her spicy perfume. 'Congratulations on the case, Richard. I'm so pleased for you, and proud.' She made her way upstairs.

He took off his shoes and walked through to the kitchen where Beccy was sitting at the table, the cupcakes in front of her, untouched. He opened the lid. He wouldn't mention Hilda at the moment.

'They're awesome cakes, Dad. Are you going to tell me to get rid of my baby?'

'No, I was going to ask you if Carl really had dumped you.'

'No… I dumped him.'

'Thought so. Why did you tell your mum he'd finished it?'

'Dunno really. She might try and make him marry me or something ridiculous.'

'I don't think that's on the agenda.' He laughed, and then fell silent. Waited. 'Do you love Carl?' he asked finally.

She took a bite of the mint and chocolate cake, the iridescent icing falling onto her jumper. 'I do, but better if we split, I think. I'm sorry, Dad.'

'You can finish your A Levels. Go to uni when the baby's older.' From the moment Gillian had told him the news he'd been carefully considering his reaction towards his daughter. There was no point antagonising her tonight. They were all tired. It would go nowhere; as obviously it hadn't.

'Get you!' But the smile dropped away. 'Dad, can we not talk about it now?'

'Okay.' He flicked on the kettle to make coffee. 'Do you want one?'

She rubbed her stomach. 'Nah, caffeine's not good for foetuses.'

'They broke the mould when they made you, love.'

'You always go back to being a Notts boy when you're stressed.' She smiled up at him. 'I'll be okay.'

'I know you will.'

He pulled a cupcake from the box and managed to get the whole thing in his mouth. Munching he studied his daughter, her face not blotchy anymore, the evidence of tears gone. 'I think it's time for you to hit the sack.'

'You mean it's time for *you* to hit the sack?'

He smiled. 'It is. We'll talk tomorrow, okay?'

'Okay.' She began packing away her stuff.

*   *   *

The next morning and very early, he hadn't been able to sleep thinking about Beccy's pregnancy and Gran Hilda, Richard got up and made his way to his ground floor study. He put his mug of coffee on the desk, sat down, and dragged his briefcase towards him. Despite the upheavals at home he needed to start preparing for the next case. He flipped back the leather and the letter from Westerham, and Florence Miller, stared back at him, poking out of the 'non-urgent' pouch. Richard opened it, reading the words quickly.

Florence Miller, a woman he'd never met was requesting a visit. She had information she was keen to share about his family, she explained. Richard picked up the coffee and gulped it back. He would have to go and see her, although God knew when.

His mobile interrupted his thoughts. He'd leave it to go onto voicemail, but checked the caller. His dad. He looked at the digital clock on the wall, 6:10 a.m. He took the call.

'Hello, son, I'm sorry to call so early.'

'It's okay… everything all right?' He knew it wasn't.

'It's your gran. She died in hospital last night. Unexpected in a way.'

'Oh Dad, I'm so sorry.'

'They thought she was stabilising, but she had a massive heart attack.' He paused on the other end of the line. 'It was thankfully quick, she wouldn't have suffered.'

'That's good. Let me talk to Gillian and we can organise.'

'Okay.'

'Dad?'

'Yes, Richard.'

'You ever heard of a Florence Miller?'

'Not that I recall, why?'

'I'll tell you when I see you, it's not important.'

'Give my love to Gillian and Beccy.'

'I will. Take it easy, Dad.'

8

A week later

Richard and his family were heading northwards out of London.

For the first thirty miles Gillian hadn't said a word. Beccy sat in the back and was unusually quiet too. His cotton polo clung to his chest; he turned up the air con. This was going to be one hell of a few days. Grandma Hilda's funeral was tomorrow.

His dad had suggested all of them staying at Hilda's house, *seeing as it's empty*, he'd said with some black humour, hiding his grief. His dad had adored his mother, as had his younger brother, Richard's uncle – Nick – and both more than they'd adored their dad. It had been Richard who'd filled that void for Frank. He'd had a special relationship with his grandad, and had always felt less for his gran Hilda he admitted to himself. He glanced in his rear-view at Beccy. She'd loved Hilda, closer to her as a kid than she'd been to Frank. It was one thing that mother and daughter had in common, both preferring Hilda to Frank. The family did seem to be polarised regarding his grandma and grandad. He moved his eyes back to the road. The news of Hilda's death had stopped abruptly talk about the pregnancy. Their daughter's bombshell, for this week anyway, had been put on the back burner.

Richard missed his grandad still. Gillian never relished their visits up north but he loved them. He dreamt of retiring to the north one day, but knew this dream was unlikely to become a reality with Gillian. He put his hand on her knee, and she placed hers over his, gave him a tight smile. She was thinking about Beccy.

As a family they'd get through this.

At Watford Gap finally one of the women in his life spoke.

'Great-grandma Hilda lived a long life, I suppose,' Beccy said. 'We were lucky to have her so long. And that she was still living independently. It's pretty amazing really.'

Gillian turned her head to answer. 'Yes, Hilda was a bit of a force. Always more to her than met the eye. An underlying tragedy in her life somewhere.'

Richard glanced at her. 'I never thought that.'

'Trust me. There is… was.'

'Yeah, I think so too,' Beccy echoed.

'My dad's asked me to hang around for a while and sort out the house. I can't say no. But can you imagine all the stuff?'

'Wish I could stay and help,' Beccy said.

'You're off on half term next week, so you could if you wanted. Keep me company,' Richard replied.

Gillian interrupted. 'I don't think that's a good idea. Beccy and I have things to sort out.'

The car descended into silence again. He and Beccy both knew what that meant. Richard kept quiet. He'd only be gone a week. Nothing could happen in a week.

*   *   *

His mum, together with his aunt, had prepared the traditional funeral tea, which was being held in Frank

and Hilda's home, a home his grandparents had
inhabited for fifty years, although the second house
they'd owned in Nottinghamshire. His grandad though,
had kept his allotment in the village where they'd once
lived, probably only because of his attachment to the
Wendy house and wall he'd built within its parameters.

Richard's memories were still so vivid of his grandad
and most of those recollections centred around their
companionable visits to the allotment: Frank, a man
with so many more interests than casual acquaintances
could ever be aware of, although Richard had always
recognised his grandad's disenchantment with life,
covering him like a second skin. Richard identified with
it, because despite his success in the field of law, he felt
much the same. He was more like his grandad than his
dad, and it was why they'd been so close. Both wanting
something different to what they had.

Richard had wanted to be a pianist. His grandad had
wanted to be a scholar, like the man whom Frank had
admired most in the world; although Winston Churchill
had not found the academic path easy, not as easy as the
global myth of him indicated.

Richard was not a pianist because he didn't have the
talent. His grandad had not been a scholar because he
was born into the wrong family, the wrong class, and
somewhere along the way on his life's journey his
grandad had given up. Frank had been so proud of his
grandson's achievements and Richard had never told
him that really he'd wanted to be a pianist. Often
recently, he'd wished he had.

Richard viewed the overflowing buffet table. Hilda
had been a woman who kept herself to herself;

nevertheless, living to your early nineties it was never going to be a small gathering. The modest house heaved and there were several people there he didn't recognise.

He noticed an old lady sitting in the corner, quite alone. He turned to his dad and whispered, 'Who's the oldie over there? Maybe get Beccy to go and sit with her? She looks isolated.'

'Bit of a surprise. That's Frank's sister,' his dad replied, rubbing the scar on his left cheek in agitation.

Richard tried to retrieve a long-lost name from his memory banks. 'Jemima?'

'Yes, Jem.'

'She didn't bother turning up for grandad's funeral. I've never met her,' Richard said.

'She lives in the middle of nowhere, near Dublin. She moved there years ago,' his dad explained.

'She's come all the way over from Ireland?'

'She has, son.'

'Grandad never talked about her.'

'Probably some family disagreement that's festered for years. Dad never had anything to do with her, or her child, but Mum always kept in touch,' he explained. 'Jem came to stay a lot when I was a kid, when Dad went off on his jaunts to London. Her visits tailed off in the latter years, though. But as I say, she and your grandma kept in touch.'

'I'll ask Beccy and Gillian to sit with her.'

'Good idea, son.'

Gillian and Beccy both looked a little put out that they'd been given the duty.

He introduced himself. 'Hello, Jemima, we've never met. I'm Richard, Jim's son, and this is my wife, Gillian, and Beccy, my daughter. You've come a long way, I hear?'

'I couldn't miss Hilda's goodbye.' She looked directly at him; her eyes rheumy but still possessing the sharpness of a woman who'd maintained all of her faculties. 'I am sorry I couldn't come to Frank's.' She paused. 'I really was unable to.'

'It's fine,' Richard said. 'I'm sorry that we've met under such sad circumstances. Were you close to my gran?'

'Yes, I got on with Hilda. Always did.'

The inference was that she hadn't got on with his grandad, her brother. Frank.

'Excuse me, Jemima, but I have to mingle,' Richard said.

Her face creased like parchment paper. 'It's nice to meet you.'

He left her in the capable, but reluctant, hands of his wife and daughter.

Richard was standing in the kitchen tipping back a large sherry (and surprising himself at how much he was enjoying it) when he felt a gentle touch on his arm. It was a robust-looking lady. Mid-forties he guessed. A strong smell of cigarettes hovered around her.

'Are you Hilda's grandson?' she asked.

'I am. Richard Cullen.'

'I'm sorry to intrude, I feel a bit uncomfortable being here, to be honest.'

'It's fine, really. I'm sorry if I don't recognise you.'

'No, you won't recognise me. You don't know me.' Her eyes took in the room and she pulled her black cardigan around her ample body. She had lovely eyes. Sparkling and roguish. 'I'm a nurse. Celia.'

He raised an eyebrow in question.

'At The Waterside Nursing Home… in Kent.'

'Ah. I'm a little confused?'

'One of my patients, my favourite to be honest, sent you a letter. She gave a telephone number for you to call her. You haven't replied, or called. I know you've been tied up, and I'm sorry…' Her eyes glittered. 'Again.'

'Ah, yes, of course. I did plan to reply.'

'I'm really fond of Florence, the lady who sent you the letter. She seems to have taken a turn for the worse and she's agitated about this. She asked me to come. Today, here, to the funeral. She wasn't able to be here. Her health you know, she's in her early nineties.'

'That's very kind of you to help her, Celia. The letter didn't say much.' He gave her his most encouraging smile. 'Please make yourself at home. Eat and drink, there's mountains of food.'

'Thank you.' She took a breath. 'I think Florence would like to see you, Mr Cullen.'

'Do you know what it's about?' His eyes swept over the kitchen, the house. 'I've got a lot on at the moment.'

'I understand and I'm so sorry.'

Celia's brittle confidence slid away and Richard's natural empathy clicked in. He could see she felt awkward and out of place. She must have felt strongly to turn up, and obviously liked her patient very much. He was always drawn to people who went further than their job demanded. Put in the extra mile. They were the people you could trust, the people who remained true to their beliefs, the people who didn't bullshit you. Celia was such a person.

'Come through, let's go upstairs where it's quieter,' he said.

She followed him up the stairs and into a bedroom. He moved the pile of mourners' coats to the side of the bed. She sat down while he rummaged around his briefcase to find Florence Miller's letter.

He read it again. 'She knew Hilda and Frank when they lived in Kent, when they both worked at Chartwell. Do you know anything more than what's in the letter, which isn't much?'

'I do know, but Florence wants to talk with you directly about it.'

'I can't make it to see her until I go back down south, which will be a while.'

'Florence thinks there'll be documents, things in Hilda's house that might help?'

'I haven't started properly on it all yet.'

'You're a solicitor, aren't you?' she asked.

'Barrister.'

'Well, Florence thought you might be the right person to know.'

'Know what, Celia?'

She stood up, pushed her hand through bleached blonde hair. 'Every family has secrets, and I think Florence needs to get this cleared up before she dies.' She smiled. 'She thinks she's going to pop her clogs, I told her it's not going to happen yet.' Her smile dropped. 'But you never know with these oldies.'

'Are you going to tell me? That's why you're here, isn't it?' Richard said.

'Frank and Hilda had another child, a girl, apart from your dad and uncle.'

He did begin to wonder then if a mad woman from an attic somewhere had inadvertently popped into his grandma's funeral. 'I think you, or… Florence Miller might be mistaken. I think my dad, and his brother, would know if they'd had a sister.'

'Perhaps, but I really don't think so. Florence might be old but she hasn't lost her marbles yet. The girl was in fact your grandfather's stepdaughter. Frank married Hilda when the girl was four, and that was when they moved away from Westerham and to,' she took in the house, 'not here. They moved here at the start of the war, Florence told me. When the trouble started.'

'Go on.'

By the end of his conversation with Celia, Richard's world had imploded a little more.

The funeral guests had finally left. Richard encouraged Gillian and Beccy to go back with his mum and dad. 'I need to stay and start sorting things out,' he explained.

His dad offered to help.

'It's fine, Dad, you go back with Mum, Gillian and Beccy. I'll sleep here tonight. I'm restless, and I'll get started on sorting out Gran Hilda's stuff.' Maybe his dad wanted to help. It was his mum. 'I thought you wanted me to do it, Dad?'

'I do, son. I can't face it. I'll look at everything after you've sorted through.'

Richard rubbed his dad's back. He was determined not to bother him with Celia's revelations, just yet. He'd wait until after he'd seen Florence Miller in person.

Gillian interrupted. 'Do you want me to stay with you? As long as I can leave with Beccy first thing.'

'No, it's fine but thanks for offering. I'll give you a call before you leave in the morning.'

'I could stay up here with you, Dad,' Beccy said.

'That sounds like a good idea—'

Gillian interrupted, 'I don't think so, things to do, stuff to sort out. Time's an issue.' She paused purposefully. 'And we've already discussed this.' Another beat of time. 'Richard?'

'I could stay here for a few days,' Beccy said. 'It won't make any difference to… things.'

'You could, but I'll be longer,' Richard said. 'You'll be bored after a day.' He wanted her to stay.

'I won't. I'm like you, I like it up here.'

'Best if you go home with Mum, Beccy.' Gillian was looking too cross.

Beccy huffed but had the good grace to say nothing more. Richard wondered if the hormones were already kicking in and mellowing his daughter. He looked at her. Looked at Gillian, and remembered Beccy being small. One day he'd like a grandchild. He didn't know why he was thinking that but he was. Better not say anything to Gillian.

His mum rescued the situation and clasped hold of Beccy. 'Come on, I've made shepherd's pie for supper.'

They hadn't mentioned Beccy's pregnancy to her grandparents.

'Oh! My favourite,' Beccy exclaimed, grabbing hold of her grandma's hand.

Still a child.

But his mind was already moving back to thoughts of Celia. He'd put on his barrister's hat and would keep it on for the next few weeks while he investigated what Celia had told him about Frank, Hilda, and a woman of whom up until today he'd never heard a thing.

He needed to meet with Florence Miller and find out about his grandad Frank, and Gran Hilda.

9

Due to a stream of visits from relatives and general socialising with his family, whom he didn't ever see enough of, Richard hadn't got started on his mission of sorting through Grandma Hilda's stuff as soon as he'd liked. He'd be in Notts for longer than expected.

That morning, with some files he'd retrieved from the box nearest the loft's mouth stuffed in his rucksack, he'd decided to visit Frank's allotment. He got off the bus and was standing at the top of the alleyway that led to the patches of allotment land. The narrow path was cold the year round and yet as a boy holding his grandad's hand he'd never noticed the damp stagnant air, only impatient to get to their destination and start work.

His grandad was steadfast in his memory, as were Frank's tales about the war, the Churchills, and Churchill's bricklaying. Frank had been working class, a staunch labour supporter, a big union man his entire life, and despite having once worked for Churchill it had baffled Richard that his grandad held the wartime leader in such high esteem. But then his grandad – the miner, bricklayer and ex-soldier – had often baffled him. Frank had been a complicated man, a man of many layers. He'd loved Frank to distraction but knew that for others his grandad Frank hadn't always been the easiest man to get along with. And those others, Richard knew, included his wife, Gran Hilda.

Not long before his grandad had died, Richard had asked him how he could be so wedded to the trade union and yet still idolise Churchill. Frank had shaken his head and a rare grin had appeared on his face.

There has to be order, there has to be a leader, there has to be discipline. People judge Churchill now in the context of the modern day. His victories, his genius was of his time, the era we were living in then, and should be assessed as such. As should his mistakes, of which he made many. Who doesn't? You can't vilify the man and ignore what he achieved, just as you can't exalt him without acknowledging his mistakes. Churchill made mistakes. People now just see one thing or the other, they don't look at the whole picture. I'm a union man through and through, but it doesn't stop me from knowing when other union men take things too far, when they break the rules of democracy, which some do, and endanger the cause. Doing what the bloody other side do all the time. It's what gave Churchill – and the Tories – the ammunition to come down hard, like he did in Wales at Tonypandy.'

Thinking of his grandad's speech, Richard began making his way down the alley, which was starved of light due to the enormous shadows cast by the houses, rows of terraces that stretched downwards towards the apex of the pit tip that personified the area. The pit, which gave most of the villagers their livelihoods before the mine stuttered to a final stop, and closed eight years previously.

Even now Richard wasn't sure what his grandad had been trying to say. Maybe that we all make mistakes and it's the common ethical goal which is important to keep in mind. Frank had been ruthless in his dealings with union disrupters, the hard core. His grandad, maybe like Churchill, never thought he might be wrong, and was often completely undiplomatic and unwavering when sorting out these hiccups. Churchill, although a unique leader, an imposing man – Richard believed, and independent of his grandad's rhetoric – was flawed. Churchill had been, there was no doubt, brilliant and often insightful but he was also tactless, single-minded, and ambitious, with a frequent disastrous lack of judgement. Richard had always thought Churchill's proclamation that he *followed his destiny* was code for, *follow any given opportunity*. Churchill was a chancer: Richard had once dared to say to this to his grandad.

'You might be right, my lad. But at least he lived with the consequences of the chances he took.'

Richard was beginning to see a strong and disturbing parallel between Churchill and Frank.

He stopped walking and pulled out the file of letters and leaning against the end terrace stared at the headed notepaper from Chartwell. It told Richard clearly that his grandad had brushed across the life of the great wartime leader, and not only because he'd once worked for Churchill.

The batch of letters looked as if they hadn't been touched for years.

He sat on his haunches and took a closer inspection of the correspondence addressed to Frank and Hilda, from a hospital further north. The letters were in date order and started in January 1939, just before the outbreak of war. That was when Anna Cullen was first admitted to High Royal Mental Hospital, as it was known then. At the bottom of the pile was a sheet of paper containing Anna's admission information.

Number of Admission: 3286
Admitted: January 11th 1939
Age: 15
Previous place of abode: Nottinghamshire
Age on first attack: 15
Religious Persuasion: Church of England
Name of nearest known relative: Mother, Hilda Cullen.
Stepfather: Frank Cullen. Biological father: Unknown.
Relieving Officer: TM Parker
Facts observed by NA Proctor: Acute decline into insanity.
Cause not known. Depressed. Suffering with malnutrition
and has received medical treatment for stomach pains.
Diagnosis: Insane
Other facts communicated: Can read. Born with normal
intelligence but now shows signs of diminishing intellect.
Obsession with Winston Churchill and particularly the
Churchill's deceased child, Marigold Churchill. Obsessive.
A morbid interest in death and babies.
Rejects all knowledge of both parents.

Breath caught in his lungs and for seconds he found it difficult to breathe at all. Celia had told him about the psychiatric institution, and that Anna Cullen was indeed still alive, and still residing within it. When he'd spoken to Celia at his gran's funeral, he'd thought Florence Miller was perhaps suffering from early dementia symptoms, making it up about Anna Cullen and High Royal. This documentation proved she wasn't. He leant forward. He knew his dad and Uncle Nick had no idea; they could never have kept this from him.

Frank and Hilda had managed to keep it from everyone.

He struggled to stand as he rallied between anger and sadness. Surely they would have a reason to have kept it all a secret? He would find out and in a heartbeat of a moment knew the other letters would throw light on this discovery.

The thought of a fifteen-year-old girl being shipped off to a mental asylum, because that is what it would have been back in the thirties, dragged a pensive and haunted feeling through him. During his legal career he'd heard nightmare stories about such institutions and he struggled to understand why his grandparents had sent their daughter to such a place. He reread the admission letter. Anna Cullen had been perfectly sane right up until the months before she was admitted for assessment. Assessment. What a joke. Once taken to a place like High Royal a poor sod would never leave. And Anna hadn't. According to Celia she was still there. A seventy-six-year-old woman.

What the hell had Frank and Hilda done?

He cast his mind back over the last few days, the funeral, things people had said. Things people hadn't said. In his mind's eye he saw Frank's sister sitting awkwardly talking to Beccy and Gillian. He would bet his life Jem knew something and Florence Miller knew more than what Celia had told him.

He contemplated calling his dad. No, he'd deal with this himself. He put the letters back in his rucksack and squinted into the greyness of the horizon and his overcrowded mind moved to Beccy. He'd been surprised at her news, but not shocked. This stuff happened. He knew of at least two other colleagues whose daughters had found themselves pregnant at the wrong time of their lives. But… from memory, they'd been university age. Beccy was only seventeen. Gillian was right of course, Beccy was too young to have a baby. But it wouldn't be the end of the world if she did. The end of the world for him would be Beccy, or Gillian, dying. That was catastrophic, not an unplanned pregnancy. He and Gillian had been married eighteen years, known each other for much longer, and ironically pushed into tying the knot because of Gillian's surprise (not a surprise really, oh how they'd shagged in those early years) pregnancy. It was more than ironic that with a marriage certificate they were unable to produce more babies. His dad had told him only recently that Hilda had found it difficult to conceive too, and that Hilda had always viewed Jim's birth as a gift from God.

Richard looked again at the date of Anna Cullen's admission details – very soon after his dad had been born. And, of course, Hilda had had a child before giving birth to his dad and Uncle Nick. Anna. How could Hilda have kept that secret? Because that child, Anna, had obviously been illegitimate and Hilda didn't want anyone to know. But that theory didn't work because clearly Frank had married Hilda and given Anna his name.

Richard walked and thought. The Wendy house in Frank's allotment. Anna's existence explained why Frank had built it. Even as a child Richard's logical mind had questioned why his grandad had constructed a toy for a girl when he had only boys. Now he knew why. Frank hadn't built it for a potential daughter that Hilda had never conceived with her husband; his grandad had built it for a daughter that had been conceived with someone else. Who was Anna's father? Was it Frank maybe? Had Frank loved Anna? Resented her? Is that why he sent her off to an asylum?

Richard could not believe this scenario. He couldn't. Perhaps it was Hilda who was behind her daughter's incarceration. Or perhaps they did it as a joint decision.

He began to jog.

10

Frank

July 1928

When Frank got home from Florence's, the house was unusually quiet, the kitchen's smell was bland, and there was nothing cooking on the stove. Frank opened the oven door; nothing in there either. Turning, his stomach grumbled and he noticed Jem's scarf tied on the back of the kitchen chair.

It was strange having his sister home. Time off from the vicarage only happened occasionally: God's appointed didn't believe in holidays, or kindness. Frank couldn't believe Jem had stuck it out this long, but guessed she'd rather be there than here, with him, although Jem and Hilda got on well, more so since Anna's birth it seemed. Jem didn't like Flo though, at all. The roots of her animosity went back years. He would have been eight when he was around at Flo's house, without Hilda, who had the measles and was confined to home. His little sister had turned up at Flo's door upset; Jem didn't say why, but he knew it was to do with their dad. Flo wouldn't let Jem stay and play with them, and he'd taken Flo's lead and sent Jem back home. Later though, Flo had felt guilty and told him to go home too, to comfort his sister. He didn't – not until much later – when *he'd* wanted to leave. Jem had never forgiven Flo, and from that day on, Jem carried her dislike for the effervescent vivacious Flo like a baton.

And Jem always held her resentments fast.

He opened the oven door again, as if by doing so a meal would miraculously appear. Three women in the house and it looked as if there'd be no food tonight. Thinking about Chartwell's magnificent fare, with force, he pulled a chair from underneath the table and sat down, his father's irrational rages pushing into his mind. Frank inhaled and tried to take stock. He *wouldn't* be like his father. He hated him, even now, even when he knew his body was rotting somewhere far beneath the sea near Russia.

He stood and walked to the window where he saw his mother in the small patch of garden, the last rays of the late evening July sun reflecting off the silver streaks in her hair. She'd been growing fruit and vegetables and was busily picking the rhubarb. He glanced at the clock. There was no way she'd be making a pie tonight, not if she hadn't even started on the tea.

She looked up, saw him, and made her way inside, holding an old basket stuffed with rhubarb and bringing a draught of fresh air in with her. 'You're home early.' She plopped the basket on the table and the ripe vegetables cascaded onto the chipped wood.

'We need to get ready for the journey up north.' His eyes moved to the oven, the table that was bare of cutlery, the bloody rhubarb. 'No tea tonight?'

She wiped her brow, which was covered in tiny beads of sweat. 'Hilda and Jem said they were sorting it out, with help from Anna.' She smiled. 'I think they're on strike.' She returned the stray rhubarb to the basket.

'I'm starving,' he said.

'Don't worry, Hilda's mum said she's made enough soup to feed us all.'

'So you knew they wouldn't bother?' He forced a grin. Jem got away with murder with their mum, but he knew why. His mum trying to make it up to her daughter. He and Jem didn't talk about what ate at both of them, but understood each other in the way that a brother and sister could and yet still be distant.

His mother interrupted his thoughts. 'I know they've been having a nice time together, and that's what's important.' She peered at him. 'Stop it, Frank. Please.'

He shrugged. 'Flo's looking after Anna.' Glancing at her, he continued, 'You look tired.'

'I'll miss you.'

'I know.' He took her in his arms but it was a clumsy embrace. His mother wouldn't miss him. She would find life easier not having a man around who reminded her of her dead husband. Frank looked too like his father and he despised that fact.

Deftly, she untangled herself from his awkward clasp. 'I'll go round and pick up the soup. There's homemade bread from yesterday. I'll make a rhubarb pie later and you can take it up to Nottingham with you tomorrow.'

'I'll go find Hilda.'

'She'll be in Jem's room.'

Frank made his way up the narrow stairs and heard the faint sound of giggling that he recognised as Hilda's. A foreign sound these days. He knocked. As a rule he never set foot in Jem's space. An unsaid rule.

'Wait a minute,' Jem shouted.

Frank hesitated a moment but then opened the door. Jem's jaw lowered at the sight of her brother looming in the doorway. She was sitting at the dressing table, Hilda perched on the bed.

'There's no tea.' He tried to say it light-heartedly. 'And Hilda, why've you palmed Anna off with Flo again?'

'Anna's fine. She wanted to go to Flo's,' Hilda replied. With her vibrant red hair free from pins and such, she looked like a Celtic queen. 'Come over, Frank, sit next to me.'

He took a few steps inside.

'No. Do not come in,' Jem said under her breath.

'Don't be silly. It's only Frank,' Hilda said to Jem.

'*Don't* come in.'

'Jem—' Hilda carried on, confusion peppering her voice.

'Jem, c'mon,' he said.

'*Do not* come into my bedroom,' Jem hissed.

Frank turned on his heel. 'I'm going out, to fetch Anna.' He glanced at Hilda. 'There's no tea. You two should be ashamed of yourselves.'

As he walked out the door he heard Jem mumble under her breath. '*You* should be ashamed of yourself, Frank.'

He almost fell down the stairs and nearly knocked over his mother as he made his way through the cramped hallway and towards the outside.

The warm air hit him and after a few hundred feet of swift walking he calmed. What was wrong with him? Tomorrow they'd be taking the train up to Nottinghamshire to start a new life. But as his heels hit the ground with a startling force, the guilt he felt about his sister coursed through him.

He'd be glad to be gone. Start anew. Away from this house, his sister, and the always beating sense his mother and sister blamed him: because he was a man. Flo was right. They needed to get away.

* * *

Florence, Jem and his mother were at the train station to see off the newly formed Cullen family.

Frank moved the suitcases to the edge of the platform and looked at his watch. The train was delayed and wouldn't be leaving for another ten minutes.

'Don't leave them too near the edge, Frank, they might slip down onto the tracks,' his mum said, her face creased into an expression he couldn't decipher and a similar countenance he'd seen on her face at her husband's memorial service. A mixture of grief and relief.

'We might as well get on.' He began humping the suitcases through the open door of the train.

Hilda moved towards his mother, touching her arm as if in apology for his flash of anger. 'Thank you for having us, and come to visit when we've settled in. You must.' Hilda then turned to Jem. Put the palm of her hand on her sister-in-law's cheek. 'Stay in touch.'

Frank saw tears in his sister's eyes. He hadn't seen her cry for years. Not since that long ago day when Flo wouldn't let her come into the house and play with them. He knew she hid the other tears. He held out his arm to embrace Jem. She stepped sideways and wrapped her arms securely around herself.

It was Hilda who gently pulled him away from Jem's vicinity and then slowly, but still with her eyes on Jem, Hilda turned to Flo, saying, 'Thanks for all your help.' She moved nearer and whispered close to Flo's ear, although Frank still heard, his heart dropping to the ground. 'You really should stay off the gin, Flo.'

Many years later Frank would wonder if he'd left his heart splattered on the train platform alongside Flo. It had been Jem near the graveyard that May Day evening. Who did Jem loathe the most, him or Flo? He decided his sister disliked most people. Only Hilda seemed to get through.

Stunned, Flo didn't reply. Frank searched her face, trying to tell her with his expression that he was sorry. She shook her head, bent down and hugged Anna. 'Be a good girl for your mummy and daddy.'

Hilda pulled Anna towards her, a gesture of ownership rather than warmth. 'She'll be good, won't you, sweetie?'

Anna shrugged her tapered shoulders and Frank tried to ignore the tears he saw forming in her eyes as Hilda shuffled her daughter into the carriage.

He got on the train and as it moved away he watched Jem staring at him from the platform. Her arms still folded firmly across her chest. The same expression on her face as when their father's empty coffin was lowered into the cold earth.

Disgust mixed with anguish.

Frank made a promise to himself that day that he'd make a better job with his family, his children – and his grandchildren – than his parents had made with theirs.

11

September 28th 1928

The Nottinghamshire Post

Winston Churchill, Chancellor of the Exchequer, And

His Little House At Westerham, Kent

During his summer holiday Winston Churchill has become a trade unionist. He helped to build a house on his estate at Westerham, laying the bricks himself.
Mr Churchill has been invited to join the Amalgamated Union of Building Trades Workers. Mr Churchill appreciated the humour of the idea and consented to become a member of the union.

Frank, Hilda and Anna had been living in their new village in Nottinghamshire for just over a year and neither he, nor Hilda, was particularly ecstatic about the place, or the house. It was too small and suffered with rising damp. They both missed the Kent vistas, although away from the colliery and the pit tip this part of the world offered its own pretty countryside, which up until now they hadn't had time to appreciate. Or the inclination. That was more the problem. Frank spent most of his days in a dark hole, the remainder at the allotment.

And Hilda. She didn't appear that interested in exploring her new space, only absorbed in the local church and its activities. Her faith had worsened not improved. He did indulge when occasionally she became more like the Hilda he'd loved; the one he saw in rare moments inside the bedroom, although he was left wondering if her enthusiasm was an artifice, and an artifice which was as strong as her real and suffocating love of God. Sometimes he went to church with her to show solidarity, to show his love, not for God though, but for Hilda. He'd hoped she'd change in a new place where no one knew about her past. She hadn't, and he was left pondering why they'd bothered to uproot themselves from Westerham. Away from Flo.

However, in the autumn of 1928 things weren't that bad, not really. Soon Hilda would be pregnant and the house would be full of children. Anna would love that. And so would he.

Frank hated the pit but the money was good and mostly he liked his workmates, although him not going to the pub and his reading habits did place him a step away from them. In his darker moments as he shuffled along on his belly at the pit face, he told himself that he could always go back to bricklaying. The article he'd read in *The Nottinghamshire Post* had made him feel odd. Disjointed. He wasn't living the life he wanted to live and saw that life slipping away, day-by-day. He was reading less, no time for it. Hilda had once been a lover of books and it had been one of the things they'd always had in common, but since getting so involved in the local church she never picked one up, only the bible. It was as if he were on a slope, unable to stop moving downwards, edging himself along nicely, allowing the unhappiness at work, allowing himself not to read books, and hoping it was a direct trade for his sacrifice of Flo, and happiness with Hilda.

Today Frank had all day free. He'd forgotten it was the Sabbath, something he was apt to do. Gradually over the past year he'd cleared his new allotment. It'd been overgrown and in a right old state; its previous tenant had died five years before and so it had been lying unused since then. He'd weeded, ploughed up the soil, getting it ready for the first seedlings. He'd been disappointed with the amount of sun the plot got, or more to the point, didn't get, but he'd make do. Frank was getting good at that.

He'd also laid the foundations for his own little *Marycot*. A Wendy house for Anna, and for her future brothers and sisters. It wasn't on Mr Churchill's scale but it would be more than adequate. It had a door that he planned to fix with a lock, and one small window. He also wanted to build a tiny pretend fireplace inside, like Mr Churchill had done. He contemplated whether he should build a pretend chimney too.

He found himself grinning. Things really weren't that bad.

'Dad, are we going to start the bricks today?' Anna had appeared, as if from nowhere. He hadn't heard her footfall on the stairs.

'I think today's the day.'

Hilda had followed her daughter downstairs, she was wearing her best dress and a little hat perched on the side of her head, her hair set free, cascading onto her shoulders, like the red shimmers of a setting sun.

'Frank, it's Sunday. I'm taking Anna to church,' Hilda said in the controlled tone that never boded well.

'Hil… Mum, Dad says I can go to the allotment with him.' She looked pleadingly at Frank. 'We're going to start building my Wendy house. Please?'

'No, Anna. Church first. Then you can go and join your dad,' Hilda said.

'C'mon, Hilda. Anna doesn't need to go to church… and atone for her sins.' He shouldn't have said it, knowing it as soon as the words dropped from his mouth.

To anyone else Hilda's expression would appear unchanged.

Rapidly he tried to back pedal. 'I mean—'

'I know what you mean, Frank.' She looked at Anna. 'It's probably better I go without you anyway. The Sunday school teacher says you're so disruptive.'

'Go and get changed and go with your mother to church,' he said to Anna. 'Make your way down to the allotment when you get back. You can help me then.'

Hilda buttoned up her coat. 'No, Anna sweetie, go with your dad.' In a split second her face had softened. Frank noticed this a lot with Hilda concerning Anna. It was as if she tried to be nice to her daughter, but in the end it was just too much effort; something else overtook her. 'It's all right,' she finished, glancing at Anna with a slice of affection. 'The Sunday school teacher says you ask too many questions.' She slid a look towards Frank. 'Not a bad thing.'

'It's certainly not,' he said, hearing relief in his own voice.

'I'll be late. There's cold meat in the larder for you both,' she said, her voice placating.

'You not home for dinner?' Frank asked.

'The vicar asked me to join him to eat at the vicarage.'

'You were taking Anna to the vicarage, for her dinner?'

'Frank, leave it, please.' She collected her bag, checked herself in the mirror. 'You two have a good time.' She left the house.

'Dad, she wouldn't take me to the vicarage.'

'Course she would. C'mon, missy. Let's go and build a house.'

Anna grinned. 'I love you.'

Frank was already opening the door. 'I love you too.'

12

It was after three when Frank and Anna returned from the allotment. As he fried up potatoes to go with the cold meat from the larder, and helped by Anna, he heard a knock at the door. He opened it. Rod Lambert stood there peering at him, while his son, a twelve-year-old Hugh, lurked behind.

Frank didn't like the young Lambert lad, didn't like his father much either, but he worked alongside Rod, who'd been at the pit forever, so he tried to make the most of them knowing each other; tried to hide his antagonism for the older man. And Maisie, Rod's wife, often helped Hilda out if she needed someone to keep an eye on Anna. He liked Maisie, and Anna had made friends with their daughter, Rosy. Anna needed a friend. Besides Rosy, she hadn't made a connection with any other children in the village. Anna remained quiet and introverted, sensitive to the world around her, and was emotionally – Frank tried to think of the word – frangible.

He forced a smile, the wooden spatula he was stirring the bubble and squeak with still held in his hand.

'You cooking, man? Where's that wife of yours?' Rod said.

Frank heard Hugh snigger and at the same time Anna disappeared into the front room. He ignored Rod's question. 'What can I do for you, Rod? About work is it?'

'Coupla things. Work, the mineshaft pulley is being looked at and so our shift's cancelled in the morning.

You have a day or two off.' He peered over Frank's shoulder, into the kitchen. 'Thought you'd like to know.'

He still hadn't invited Rod or his son inside. 'Well, that's good of you to come round, and inform me.'

'Inform you? Bloody hell, man. I've come t'tell you.' Hugh sniggered. 'I thought we could go to the pub later, for a pint.' Rod's expression levelled into a smile. 'That's when you've made your dinner.'

'Thanks for the offer, but I have things to do here at home.'

'Suit yourself.' He seemed to think for a moment. 'While I'm here, I notice you've started building sommat on your allotment. I don't think that's allowed, you know.'

'I think there's nothing saying I can't build on my own allotment.' Frank took a step back. 'I don't think I'm contravening any rules.'

'Think you're clever, dun't ya, with your big words? Well, seeing as you're my mate, I'll not make a fuss.' He made a point of looking at the spatula again. 'You're a funny 'en, Frank. Max Betts says you're a supporter of that bastard Churchill, that you used to work for him, laying bricks?' Rod spat into his palm and slicked back his cowlick. 'Think you're different, don't you?' He didn't wait for Frank to reply, which Frank had no intention of doing anyway. 'You're not, you're just bloody odd.'

Rod stepped into the kitchen, his eyes immediately resting on the pile of books sitting on the tiny kitchen counter unit. Frank had recently been given them by, of all people, the vicar. He'd been a bit surprised at the man-of-the-cloth's cast-offs. Flaubert's *Madame Bovary* and *Sons and Lovers* by DH Lawrence. The thought did cross his mind the widowed vicar was taking an interest in Hilda for reasons other than her devotion to God. A week before he'd asked her outright and she didn't speak to him for the rest of the day, finally saying later that evening: *You'd never have said that if it wasn't for the reason I have Anna. Don't deny it.* As he peered at the books, which he hadn't even looked at yet, he wondered if she'd been right.

Rod steamrollered on: 'Reading and building kids' houses isn't right. No wonder Hilda always looks so bloody miserable. My Maisie says your Anna's an odd 'en too.'

Hugh giggled, and Frank noticed the young boy was chewing tobacco. He really had to put his foot down about Anna going over to theirs, try to persuade Rosy to come here more often, although he knew that wasn't something Hilda encouraged. Maisie and Rosy Lambert were all right, but something shouted at him about both Rod and his son. He had to talk to Hilda.

He walked forward, nudging Rod and Hugh back out the door, then moved outside to stand with them. Looking down at Rod – he was a small man – and trying to keep his temper Frank said, 'Thanks for letting me know about tomorrow. Give Maisie my best. And Rod, I don't think letting your son pick up your habits is doing him any favours.'

Frank licked the spatula before Rod could reply, and went back inside, closing the door, although not before hearing Hugh say, 'You going to punch him, Dad?'

'Not this time, son.'

There was nothing more in the world that Frank wanted to do at that moment than punch Rod. The palm of his hand where his nails dug into his skin pulsed.

Anna had returned to the kitchen.

'You all right, love?' he asked her.

She nodded. 'What did they want?'

'Just came over to tell me I don't have to be at the pit tomorrow. I've a few days off. Might be nice if we go somewhere. You, your mum and me. Take a bus into Derbyshire?'

'I'd like that.'

'Good, c'mon the bubble and squeak'll be ready in a minute. Go and pull the leaf up on the table in the front room, there's a good girl, or we'll be eating dinner at suppertime.'

'I wonder what Mum had for dinner?'

'At the vicar's house?' He piled two plates high with the green-looking potato mess. 'Nothing as good as this.'

'I hope she's not still mad when she gets home.'

'She won't be, especially when I tell her we're going away.' He bent down so he was on eye level. 'Anyway love, she wasn't mad. Not really. You know what your mum's like.'

Anna nodded too stoically for a girl so young.

*   *   *

Anna was clearing the table in the front room when Hilda stepped into the kitchen.

'You have a nice time?' Frank asked, leaning against the wall.

She took off her coat, hanging it on the back of the larder door. 'It was lovely.' She poked her head into the front room. 'Where's Anna?'

'She was clearing the table…' He heard movement in the room above. The lightness of the day had evaporated. Anna had disappeared to her bedroom as soon as she'd heard her mother return, as she'd vanished too when Rod and his godawful son had come to the door. She'd seemed so happy with him down at the allotment, helping him lay the bricks for her little house. 'We've only just had our dinner but I can make some tea for you if you're hungry.'

He'd got better at doing some of the meals since moving to Notts. He'd had to learn. Some days Hilda just seemed to forget to cook. He knew she was down that she was still having her monthlies. But it'd take time. He'd saved up some money and could afford two separate rooms for a night or two in a Derbyshire guesthouse. It might be easier if they were away somewhere.

'No, I won't be hungry tonight,' she said. 'The vicar's lunch was huge, but thanks.'

Lunch. It was dinner. Even Miss Cunningham had called it dinner out of earshot of the Churchills.

'Rod Lambert's been around to let me know I'm not working tomorrow, probably the next day too. I've told Anna we can take the bus into Derbyshire, stay a night or two. It's time we had a bit of a holiday.' Her face remained expressionless. 'Hilda?'

'Why don't just the two of us go?'

'Because we can't leave Anna, she's only six… c'mon, Hilda, stop it.'

'I'm sure Maisie Lambert will look after her. And Anna likes Rosy.'

'She doesn't like Hugh, though, or Rod. I'd rather we didn't farm her out. Some fresh air'll do her good.'

'I don't think I want to go.'

'For Christ's sake, she's your daughter.'

'And I'm your wife and I'd like to go away with you alone.' She moved towards him. 'I'm sorry about this morning, and I'm glad Anna went with you to build your house.'

Her sweet breath touched his cheek. She rubbed up to him and he felt himself harden. Too often Hilda was parsimonious with her affections but today she allowed him to kiss her, his tongue hesitantly finding hers. As he felt her hand moving to his groin his anxieties about Anna, Rod, everything, dissolved.

She rubbed his erection. 'We'd have such a nice time, just the two of us. Anna'll be bored tramping the hills. We can stay in bed and then go walking, Frank, like we used to do back in Westerham. Remember those long treks through the wood? And Flo wouldn't come with us because she said she hated walking?'

'I do remember.' His hardness waned with the mention of Flo. They hadn't seen her since they'd left Westerham, but true to her word she wrote regularly, and always addressed to both him and Hilda. Flo wasn't one to hold a grudge. It was one of the things he loved about her.

He'd mentioned the May Day dance to Hilda only once since the train station incident. She'd shrugged it off, as if it didn't matter. And perhaps it didn't. Flo was getting on with her life. The kiss had been a mistake for her; he saw that now. Bloody Jem, loitering in the shadows of the village, sticking her nose in, wanting to make everyone else's life as miserable as she was making her own. But then guilt washed over him about his sister. What he'd allowed to happen.

'So just the two of us go into Derbyshire tomorrow?' Hilda broke into his thoughts.

'And Anna?'

'She can stay at Maisie's. She'll enjoy it. Please, Frank? There's nothing wrong with the family.'

'I don't want Anna staying in the same house as Hugh.'

'I need a proper break—'

He heard the kitchen door open and Anna appeared. Had she been listening?

'Love, how do you feel about staying at Rosy's for a night or two?' he said.

Anna glanced at her mother. 'I thought we were going on holiday?'

Frank put his arm around her shoulder. 'Your mum and dad need a bit of time alone, love. You can come with us next time.' He took a sideways look at Hilda. 'Can't she?'

'Of course you can, Anna. You like Rosy, she's your friend, and Maisie, you like Maisie?' She bent down to Anna's level. 'Mummies and daddies need time alone sometimes, sweetie.'

Anna touched her mother's cheek.

Frank hoped it was only him who noticed Hilda's miniscule flinch.

* * *

The next morning as Hilda packed a small suitcase, and just as he was about to take Anna to the Lamberts', the postman opened the gate, leaning his bicycle up against the wall.

'Letter from home, I think, Mr Cullen. For Mrs Cullen.'

'Thanks, Tom. How's your morning been?' he asked absent-mindedly, recognising the sprawling handwriting. He'd hardly had any correspondence from his mother or sister since coming here; only Flo had written.

'Not bad.' The postman pushed his black cap onto his head. 'Not as busy as usual,' he said, pulling his bike into an upright position and climbing back on it. 'Maisie Lambert says you're off for a few days? I'll save any post for you, if there's more, for when you get back.'

Frank waved him off. 'Thanks.'

'Who's it from, Dad?' Anna asked, her overnight bag slung over her bony shoulder.

'It's from Jem, I think.'

'Oh! Tell me what she says in it. Open it, Dad. I miss Jem, and Flo too.'

'I know you do.' He put the letter in his pocket. 'It's addressed to your mum. I'll read it to you when we get home from Derbyshire.' He scanned her face. 'You all right, love?'

'Rosy and me are going to play houses.' She said it with no smile.

'You'll have a fine time. You'd be bored with me and your mum.'

They started walking.

Frank handed the letter to Hilda, who was ready to

leave. She had on her best suit, a rustic brown. He loved that suit. She wore a hat tilted to one side, her hair pinned loosely at the back, her skin as unclouded as the blue sky outside. She looked happy and he tried not to think that the reason for this was that they were leaving Anna behind.

'It's from Jem,' she said, looking at the handwriting. 'Did Anna get to the Lamberts all right?'

'Yes, Maisie's there. Rod's at the allotment. Hugh's at a mate's house, thank God.'

She glanced up. 'What do you mean?'

'I don't like the boy and I don't like Anna being around him. He has all the hallmarks of his father.'

'I think you're getting the Lambert men mixed up with your dad.' She waited for his reply; he remained silent, she carried on: 'There's nothing wrong with Rod, or Hugh. Honestly, Anna'll be fine.'

'Am I allowed to know what Jem's said in her letter?' he said.

She checked the carriage clock on the mantelpiece. 'We need to be going or we'll miss the bus. We can read it together on the way to Matlock.'

Jem had written to tell Hilda, and by default, him, that she was getting married to her employer's son, William Barnes. Jem had told him she couldn't stand William, and Flo didn't rate him at all. *A gossip as well as being dull*, Flo had said.

Why the hell was Jem marrying him? A question that, as the bus trundled out of Nottinghamshire, he asked Hilda.

'I'm worried about Jem,' she replied. 'She doesn't love him, you're right. I don't know why she's decided to marry him. I really don't.'

He shrugged. 'Maybe you should write back and tell my sister this isn't a good idea? She'll listen to you.'

'I don't think that's my place. Jem's a grown woman. It's her decision. I just hope she doesn't live to regret it.'

'You don't regret marrying me, do you?'

She wavered only a second. 'Of course I don't. And you Frank, do you regret marrying me?'

'I don't, Hilda.'

'Sometimes I think you do.' She glanced at him. 'I love you, and why I thought it better we went away alone.' She said it in a voice suggesting of the night to come.

He placed his hand on her knee.

She carried on, her voice dropping in volume. Two old ladies sat in the seat in front. 'There's something we should talk about, Frank. Jem, and your dad.'

He continued looking ahead, his stomach tightening.

'I know why you and Jem were so glad when your dad didn't come back from the war. Jem's told me, Frank.'

'What did Jem tell you, exactly?'

'Your dad—'

'She told you recently or have you always known?'

'She told me the day you came into the bedroom. You couldn't do anything, Frank. Jem knows that, really.'

'That's not how it seems.'

'I thought it was you who she was scared of… that's when she told me the truth.'

'Bloody hell. Me? Who do you think I am?'

'Shush, Frank.'

'She blames me for not doing anything,' he said in a whisper.

'You were a child, not much older than Jem. The whole village knew about your dad, his drinking.'

'Jem hates me.'

'She does not. But I think it's coloured you, as it's coloured poor Jem. Made her make bad decisions. And Frank—'

He huffed, still not looking at her. The old lady in front moved her head at the guttural sound. 'Sorry,' he said, and turned towards Hilda. 'What, love?'

'Bad things happen.' Her words caught quietly in her breath. 'A bad thing happened to me, and you saved me. You couldn't save Jem. But it doesn't make all men bad. Rod. A child – Hugh.'

He sank down into the bus seat. 'You think I'm overprotective of Anna, don't you?'

'Yes, I think you are.'

'I love her.'

'And she'll be fine at the Lamberts,' Hilda said. 'And don't worry about Jem. Maybe she'll be better off married than working in a job she hates. At least she'll have her own house. William's not bad off.'

'Did you talk to Jem a lot about—'

'No. Not a lot. Hardly anything. It wasn't your fault.'

'My mum knew,' he said finally.

'Leave it, Frank. Please.' She delved in the envelope. 'There's a wedding invitation.' She peered at it. 'Next month.' Tears immediately formed in her eyes.

'What's the matter?'

'She's obviously pregnant.'

He put his arm around her, his movement nudging the seat in front.

One of the old ladies turned around. 'Love's young dream, eh? Off for a little holiday? Nice to get away together. Make the most of it, before the little 'ens come along.'

The lady didn't seem to notice Hilda's tears.

They spent two idyllic days and nights in Derbyshire. And despite Hilda assuming that Jem was pregnant (which she was as it turned out) Frank had never seen Hilda so relaxed and this feeling was transported to the bedroom.

They would make their own baby.

* * *

It was Frank who went to pick up Anna on their return and although she was pensive he convinced himself it was just her way. Maisie assured him she'd had a lovely time and in his post-euphoric Derbyshire glaze he chose to believe her.

Four weeks later and after a visit to see Dr Faversham, Hilda announced she was pregnant. The next ten weeks were ten of the best in Frank's life. Like a dog in the sun of a long awaited summer he basked in his wife's happiness. At every available opportunity he went down to the allotment to finish building the Wendy house for Anna, and when she could, Anna came with him. Her grumpiness at being left behind with the Lamberts had finally evaporated. She even seemed happy, looking forward to having a sister to play with. *It might be a boy*, Frank had said. *It might, Dad, but I'd really like a baby sister*, she'd replied.

Frank didn't care what flavour came out of Hilda's belly, he really didn't. The joy he felt inside had even encouraged him to look for a job with a local building firm. He was still a member of the union. Hilda's pregnancy and having read the article about Mr Churchill becoming a member had galvanised him. However, when Hilda's miscarriage happened at fourteen weeks, he attempted to reconcile himself to the fact he would never have children or grandchildren with Hilda and so abandoned the idea of a return to bricklaying, punishing himself by staying at the pit.

The happiness he'd witnessed in his wife, in Derbyshire, Frank never saw again.

13

Richard

2002

Richard had reached the outskirts of his grandad's old allotment. He slowed and began walking in between the individual plots, the autumnal mud sticking to his expensive trainers. Finally he arrived at Frank's. It looked sad and overgrown, made worse when compared to the neat well-kept plots surrounding it. The allotment sat on the edge, secluded from the others, and the wall that Frank had built back in the late 1930s helped it be more delineated, protected. Frank had always liked his privacy. Keeping people out. Perhaps keeping himself in.

Richard sat on his grandad's wall and peered at the Wendy house – the *Marycot* – as Frank sometimes called it. Richard had always been intrigued with Frank's stories about Churchill: his bricklaying, his painting, his writing, reading, his general polymathy. Richard stared sadly at the newly landscaped pit tip. Since he received the letter from the council, he'd thought it would be a sorrowful day – the day his grandad's constructions were knocked down. Even after Frank's unexpected first stroke, when his ability to move and talk was minimal, the old man had made it clear he wanted to keep the allotment in the family. And Richard *had* kept the allotment, although it had lain unused since Frank's first stroke. Why had Frank been so adamant to keep it? Nostalgia, probably.

'Richard Cullen?'

A deep growly voice brought him away from his thoughts. Richard looked up. 'Yes.'

'Don't you remember me, lad?'

'Mr Lambert? Jeff? Of course I do. Great to see you again. How long's it been?'

Richard slipped off the wall. He remembered Jeff from his and Frank's visits to the allotment all those years ago. Frank had tried to stay away from people in the village and had made a point of avoiding them. Richard though, did remember Jeff Lambert. He and his grandad would sometimes bump into him. Jeff hadn't changed that much, still lean, visibly older, but recognisable.

'Long time ago,' Jeff replied. 'When you used to come here with Frank. I was at your grandad's funeral, the church and the cemetery afterwards, but we didn't talk, lad.'

'Sorry about that. It was a busy day. You weren't at my grandma's funeral, were you? I didn't see you. Sorry, if you thought I'd ignored you.'

'You didn't, lad. I wasn't there. I wasn't in touch with your gran.'

Richard plucked a memory of a vague story about Jeff's dad, Hugh Lambert, and his grandfather, Rod. Frank hadn't got on with either of the men. Hugh Lambert had died in the war from what he remembered, and when Jeff was just a baby. Rod had died before the war. Richard didn't really know the full story as to why Frank didn't like the Lambert family, although now he possessed the greatest desire to know.

'How are you?' Richard asked politely.

'I'm all right. A few more years left in me yet.'

Jeff surveyed the allotment, the wall and Wendy house. 'Your grandad liked to build. Loved his bricklaying. My grandma told me that a group of allotment owners wanted him to get rid of,' he gesticulated around, 'but he were having none of it. Frank built them back in the days when you didn't need planning permission. No one liked messin' with Frank, my gran told me.'

Richard now did retrieve something. The mind of a barrister. A fight between Frank and Hugh. Before the war. 'Go on, Jeff.'

'Your gran's gone now… there was talk about a girl, a daughter back before the war.'

Christ, why was this info popping up now? Probably because Hilda was dead. No one had mentioned anything and now information was pounding at him from every direction. He didn't immediately address the subject of his grandparents' mysterious daughter. 'Frank and Hugh had a fight, didn't they? Before the war?' Around the time Anna was taken to High Royal, Richard calculated quickly.

'Jesus, I can't be that precise,' Jeff said. 'But yes, acrimony between my dad and Grandad Rod, and your grandad I reckon, according to my gran.'

How in God's name had Anna remained a secret? Was that why Frank and Hilda had moved house and village? He looked directly at Jeff. 'Did my dad ever say anything to you… about the girl?'

'No, never. I remember my own mum saying something. And my auntie. I can't say it was mentioned much, but my auntie, my dad's sister, spoke about a girl.

She was friends with her when they were kids, before your gran and grandad moved from the village.'

'Does your auntie live locally?'

'Rosy? No, she moved down to Bodmin in Cornwall back in the early sixties. Disconnected from the family. I haven't seen her for years.'

Richard could almost feel the synapses snapping into newly formed pathways of reasoning inside his brain. He'd ask his researcher, Nell, to look Rosy up, find a number for her. Rosy knew Anna as a child; she would know something.

Jeff nodded towards the Wendy house and carried on, 'It'd explain that? Maybe the girl died and your grandad and gran wanted to forget about it all?'

'I think you've got the facts a bit mixed up, to be honest,' Richard lied. 'Anyway, if that was the case surely Frank would have got rid of the Wendy house?' He pried for information.

'Get off! Your dad – Jim – and his brother loved playing in it!'

Richard pasted a smile on his face. 'It's great to see you again, Jeff. Take care of yourself.'

'They hope to be getting rid of all this.' His gaze took in the land that surrounded them. 'Before the end of the year. For redevelopment. More housing.'

'Yes.'

'We've set up a petition, though.'

'Good for you.'

'Might be effective, you never know.'

'You don't. I'd be happy to sign it, and my dad too.'

'I'll get something to you both.' He moved to leave. 'Do you have any kids?'

'Yes, one. Rebecca, Beccy. Seventeen now.'

'Still a baby really, though.'

Richard smiled wryly. 'Not really. They grow up fast these days.'

'In all days they've grown up fast, don't be kidding yourself there.' Jeff turned. 'I'll be seeing you. Don't forget about the petition.'

Richard's head throbbed. He pulled himself back up onto the wall and took in his grandad's abandoned allotment. Pieces of bamboo strewn over what was once the area where Frank had grown sweet peas – they'd been his gran Hilda's favourite flower and the only flower Frank had ever grown in his patch. *This land is for growing food not flowers*, his grandad would say, always remembering the war and the frugality it had instilled within everyone who'd lived through it. *But for your grandma I always make an exception. She loves these flowers.* Richard would pick the flowers, then he and his grandad would make their way back up to the top of The Avenues, catch the bus to the next village and give them to Hilda, who, as Richard recalled, was never that keen to receive them. Frank was always trying to make Hilda happy. Richard suspected it had been a thankless task for his grandad. Gran Hilda never seemed content and now he wondered if it had anything to do with Anna.

He stared past the detritus of the allotment and focussed on the Wendy house, then at the wall. Frank had told him he'd built them because he wanted to lay bricks, that bricklaying was a therapy for him, as it had been for Winston Churchill. But Richard recognised now that the wall was like a comfort blanket for Frank, keeping people out. There had been only one time he remembered his grandad getting mad with him; the day he'd started (for no reason he could recollect now) digging around the wall. He'd have been around six and the only time on the receiving end of Frank's wrath. After the incident Frank had made it up by giving him a fireman's lift all the way back to the bus stop. Richard had loved that.

Putting the rucksack on his back and deciding not to catch the bus, he jogged the five miles to his grandparents' home thinking about what Florence Miller knew.

14

Florence

Chartwell
15th November 1932

Westerham Evening Standard

Hindenburg Defeats Hitler In The German Presidential

Elections

Mr Hindenburg beat Mr Hitler in a troubled Germany's Presidential election.
However, it would seem Adolf Hitler and his party, the NSDAP, is on the rise.
There is war-mongering talk within parts of Westminster, and notably from Mr Winston Churchill, that Adolf Hitler, utilising the discontent within Germany, is a potential menace for Great Britain and her allies.

Mr Churchill had been in a foul mood for weeks so Mrs Churchill was going up to London a fair bit alone and always leaving Mary in the care of her governess who, Florence often thought, was the girl's second mother. Why did people have children and then ignore them?

Florence put Mr Churchill's dark canine mood down to him being at home too much since the crash in America and the financial depression that had then

ricocheted into Britain and the rest of Europe –
including Germany – she'd gleaned from page four of
today's newspaper, which Mr Churchill's valet had left
on the kitchen table. It was Frank who'd encouraged her
to read the inside of the paper as well as the front
headline.

She and the rest of the staff had heard Mr Churchill
blasting off about Adolf Hitler. The master always
seemed to reach his crescendo on this topic soon after
dinner, when it wasn't unheard of for Mr Churchill to
throw a plate, or a glass brimming with cognac, or both,
in anger and exasperation at the supposed rise of Mr
Hitler. On many occasions she'd been the one clearing
up the aftermath. Florence didn't really understand:
from what her parents had said there was no way a
strange little Austrian would ever rise to power in
Germany. *Absolutely bloody preposterous*, her dad had said.

The staff, and his own family, avoided Mr Churchill
as much as possible when he was like this, which was
more often than not these days since he'd been hounded
from the front benches, (she knew all this from the
valet's conversations with Miss Cunningham.) Mr
Churchill though, continued to work at Chartwell *like a
man possessed*, that's what Miss Cunningham said. Writing
and painting, and so much reading, and then there was
the bricklaying too. Florence had no idea how he could
take – or fit – it all in. He was a whirling dervish of
activity: even when doing nothing he was doing
something. Thinking. You always knew when this was
happening as he had the habit of placing idle hands, his
palms, on the front of his chest. She'd noticed he did
this too when something was perplexing him, although

after much observation she'd come to the conclusion he did it generally when he was ruminating and not doing.

She folded the paper; she really shouldn't be reading it. The last thing she needed was to be caught reading when she should be working. Two weeks before, some correspondence had gone AWOL from Mr Churchill's study. He'd blamed her (through Mrs Churchill), but she'd never laid eyes on it, and definitely hadn't moved it. After being on the receiving end of Mr Churchill's temper she'd thought she'd lose her job. A week later the papers turned up. On Mrs Churchill's instruction her secretary had taken the papers, then gone away on leave for a week with them still in her bag.

She rose from the kitchen chair and made her way to the door that led outside to the herb pots, which sat near the entrance, so cook could retrieve them easily. As she bent forwards to pull a handful of fennel, she smelt the aroma of cigar and stood up straight, automatically touching the hair that always strayed from underneath her work cap.

Mr Churchill stood just outside the door.

'Good morning, sir,' she said.

'And a fine morning it is, Florence.'

Mr Churchill studied her but said nothing more.

'Is there something you would like, sir?' she said finally as a mild fear surfaced. What'd she done wrong now?

'I would like to apologise about those bloody missing papers. I thought you had mislaid them,' he said, looking directly at her, a smile beginning to slide onto his round face. 'Not Mrs Churchill's fault, she has so much to do.'

'No, sir, it wasn't Mrs Churchill's mistake at all.' She didn't say it was the secretary's. Mrs Churchill's secretary didn't like Florence and she didn't want to make things worse for herself. She held the fennel tight in her hand. 'I'm just glad they turned up, sir.' And she was. Because even though she was certain it wasn't her who'd moved them, she'd felt guilty because she did often have a gander at his papers.

'My apologies, Florence,' he said with a theatrical flourish, and then peered at the fennel. 'What is on the menu for tonight?'

'I've no idea, sir. Miss Cunningham is here for a few days, taking over Cook's duties. Cook's gone to spend some time with her son in Bournemouth.' She took a breath and felt brave. 'Miss Cunningham doesn't as a rule plan very much in advance. I'll give her the fennel and she'll decide.'

'Ah, yes, Miss Cunningham, a little on the culinary spontaneous side, eh?'

'I think so, sir.' She tried to dampen her emerging grin. The master did so make her laugh.

'We have known Miss Cunningham for a long time. Before Chartwell, before…'

Florence didn't know what he was about to say but guessed he was close to mentioning his fourth child. Miss Cunningham had known Marigold, said she was a lovely little girl. It was so sad she'd died.

'I hope you enjoy whatever Miss Cunningham decides to make for tonight, sir.'

'I'm certain I will.' He took a puff of his cigar and threw it onto the ground. 'Have a good day, Florence.'

'And you too, sir.'

He walked past her and shuffled off in the direction of his studio. He'd be gone most of the day, she knew this because he was wearing his painter's clothes. She waited until he was out of sight and picked up the smouldering cigar, took a puff, felt dizzy and then pulled a handful of mint leaves from the pot, stuffed some in her mouth and chewed. Miss Cunningham would kill her if she knew she was smoking the master's discarded Romeo and Julietas.

She couldn't believe he'd apologised to her, but then again that was the master all over. She'd been working for the Churchills since she was fifteen and the awe she felt towards him had only grown stronger over the years, and more so these days. She could see why Frank admired him so much. Frank wanted to be like Churchill; although no one could or would ever be like the master. *Broke the mould* was the expression her mother used. The valet had told her once that to all intents and purposes Mr Churchill was a self-taught man. She thought about Frank, in many ways he was too. He'd always had a book on the go. It had been Frank who'd told her that although Winston Spencer Churchill was from aristocratic stock, born at Blenheim, a direct ancestor of the Duke of Marlborough, he hadn't gone to Oxford or Cambridge and had only just scraped into Sandhurst; places she didn't know about but places that she saw as being important, for men anyway.

Frank liked to teach himself things. He wanted to know things. *Has a thirst for knowledge that lad*, her mum had said. Before Anna, Hilda had been the same. Frank and Hilda were always top of the class. Best at maths, best at spelling. Both best at everything. She could never have compared to Hilda, and anyway, the kiss on May Day was a long time ago now. She'd got over it, sort of, and she was sure Hilda had by now too, although Jem still avoided her. She knew it was Jem who'd told Hilda about her and Frank kissing on the wall.

She put the fennel on the sink, turned and noticed the freshly cooked ham sitting on the range stove. Picking up a carving knife and turning around to make sure the kitchen door was closed she sliced off a thick piece from its end. It melted in her mouth. Miss Cunningham's hams were the best; she hacked off another hunk and munching, sat back down. She opened up the newspaper again, and as she flicked through looking for the page that talked about London society gossip – her favourite bit – she thought about the letter she'd received from Frank a few weeks before. She and Frank kept in touch via letters, although she always addressed hers to both Hilda and Frank. Only Frank replied though, generally. It was Jem and Miss Cunningham who wrote the most to Hilda.

Florence was getting on with her life. She liked working at Chartwell and was happy with her lot. One day she'd look for adventure, but not quite yet. Two of the local lads from the village had courted her, as had Jem's employer's son, William Barnes. She'd given him a chance, not her best decision, but pickings were sparse in Westerham. When she'd finally turned William's offer of marriage down, he'd moved his attention to Jem; Jem who Florence thought would *never* get married. But Jem had married William, and their wedding was the last time Florence had seen Hilda, Frank and Anna.

The wedding tea had been a bit awkward, on many fronts.

She pulled out her little bag she kept under Chartwell's kitchen sink when on duty, and took out Frank's letter. All was not well with Hilda and Frank, as all was not well with Jem's marriage either. Maybe she was the clever one – not getting married, turning down William. She pushed the old and jaded thought of marrying Frank to the back of her mind. Not having a man controlling her suited just fine. Well, perhaps maybe Mr Churchill did a little by the fact he was her master but it wasn't the same, at all.

She read Frank's letter. Pouring his heart out (as much as Frank could), he spoke about Hilda's battle to get pregnant, and miscarriages, about the black thoughts that overwhelmed him whilst working in the darkness of the mine. He asked if she would visit them sometime soon. That it would help Hilda, and that Anna would love to see her. Not once did he mention he'd like to see her, but she did so want to see Anna. She did wonder though if her turning up would help Hilda. But the past was behind them. Hilda had been her best friend since they were toddlers. All would be well.

That evening she asked Miss Cunningham if she could take a long weekend to go see Frank, Hilda and Anna Cullen.

15

Florence's feelings about visiting the Cullens teetered around the equivocal; it had been Frank who'd taught her that word. She liked it and said it quietly to herself a few times sitting in the railway carriage that was taking her up to Nottinghamshire.

It was good getting away from the village, and Chartwell, because despite their amicable meeting near the herb pots, Mr Churchill really was unbearable at the moment, and his mood was rubbing off on the mistress who was becoming just as intolerable.

Florence was reticent about seeing Hilda and as much as she looked forward to seeing Anna, she foresaw this visit was going to be difficult – on many levels. Hilda was depressed about the miscarriages (she'd had two), whilst Frank disliked the pit and was desperate for other children. Poor Anna; two unhappy parents. She sensed Frank had plunged into a dark mood – perhaps like what she was seeing on a daily basis at Chartwell. Frustration and the inability to affect events led both Mr Churchill, and Frank, towards deep places. *The dark hole*, her mum called it.

As the train sped through Northamptonshire countryside she worried the relationship between Hilda and Anna still hadn't overcome its beginning and that Frank marrying Hilda, taking on Anna, had made no difference at all. Sadness enveloped her thinking this, but time *had* moved on, and as Florence had healed she'd remembered with fondness the old Hilda – as she'd been in the years before Anna. She really had hoped Frank and Hilda would be happy, and Anna would benefit.

The man sitting next to her had fallen asleep, his head dropping onto her shoulder. She tried to shuffle sideways but he woke up and apologised. She nodded politely, still thinking of her friends.

'Off somewhere nice?' he said.

'Yes, I am.' She pulled a newspaper from her bag and felt him watching her read.

'Like reading the news do you?'

She turned to look at him. 'Women generally do like to know what's happening in the world, and,' she moved a stray hair away from her eye, 'generally speaking, most of us can read these days.'

His expression dropped into confusion, or disbelief, or both. He didn't answer and thankfully nodded off again, but this time his head hanging in the opposite direction.

Florence stared at her lap, thinking about the general direness of a woman's lot in life, the tethered relationships they often had, and needed it seemed, with men; the lack of independence, of education, the way women had little choice on how to live their lives. They were expected to marry, have children, keep house – and women from the lower classes, especially so. And if a woman was unable to produce the much-wanted baby, then… well… then, what was she there for? It was a question and conundrum that Florence had thought about often of late.

She wished Hilda could carry a baby full-term because she felt this would make everything right for the

Cullen family. Hilda had done so with Anna, why couldn't she again?

Hilda and Anna met her at the train station and Florence was relieved to see Hilda's face shine at the sight of her.

'It's good to see you, Flo. Thanks for coming.' Hilda hugged her enthusiastically and Florence relaxed.

Anna had grown and was now close to Hilda's height, but so very thin, like a sapling tree. Florence moved nearer to her. 'How's my girl?'

A grin broke on Anna's face. 'I'm glad you've come, Flo.' She took hold of Florence's hand and stroked it.

'Where's Frank?' Florence peered around as if he'd suddenly appear.

'He's at work. Doing a lot of overtime,' Hilda said.

'Is money very tight?' Florence asked, wishing she hadn't. It was none of her business.

'It is. But no, he doesn't need to be making himself more miserable than he already is.'

'Oh, Hilda.' Then she stood back and studied her old childhood friend, who looked very different to when Florence had last seen her. Although only still twenty-three, fine strands of grey had appeared in her voluminous red hair, and yet in a strange way she looked even more beautiful. Matured. As Florence scooped Anna up into her arms she felt years younger than Hilda and a shiver swept through her.

'Are *you* all right?' Hilda asked, noticing the tremble.

'I'm fine.' She smiled. 'Someone just walked over my grave.'

Anna grimaced. 'That's not a nice thing to say.'

'It's just a saying, Anna, honestly,' Florence replied.

'I don't want you to die, Flo.'

'I'm not going to die, silly!'

Anna's grimace turned to a scowl. 'There are worse things than dying though, aren't there?'

'Like what?' Flo asked softly. She noticed Hilda looking straight ahead and not listening. Where were Anna's thoughts coming from? She'd always been sensitive and fragile. Had those traits worsened since their move, rather than improving, she couldn't help but ask herself.

'Like being locked up,' Anna stated.

Florence rubbed Anna's head and didn't reply.

Hilda had stopped walking and said to Florence. 'Have you seen much of Jem?'

'I don't see much of her. I was never her favourite person, as you know. We don't get on, not like her and you do.'

She half expected Hilda to deny this about Jem but didn't and Florence's already dipping spirits fell a bit more.

Anna was quiet on the bus journey home. Florence and Hilda talked trivia. It felt as if so many things were off the conversational agenda. They talked about the Wendy house that Frank had built for Anna, but Florence *felt* the unsaid conversation: about Hilda and Frank's other children that were never meant to be. The miscarriages. They talked about the weather a lot, Florence remembered years later.

'I bet you love your Wendy house, don't you?' she asked Anna.

Anna's face remained resolutely grumpy and troubled. She only moved her head in reply. Florence's worries about seeing Hilda were swamped by her concern for Anna.

All was not well with the little girl.

By the time they stepped off the bus the early winter sun was spent, the November evening approaching briskly. In the grim half-light the village appeared flat, consumed, without joy. On first impression everything about the place was depressing, from the rows of houses that loomed ominously in front, to the huge pit tip overtaking the horizon in the distance.

The bus dropped them at the top of a long wide street, with houses – in terraces – laid out each side. Hilda told her they were known as The Avenues. Housing built specifically to home the colliery workers. There were ten houses on each side of the street, Hilda informed her, spreading out sideways and each house backing onto a separate smaller avenue. The house opposite starting the next avenue down, and so on. Thirteen avenues spread downwards. Florence totted it up in her head: two hundred and sixty houses, two hundred and sixty families. She wondered where the rest of the luckier colliery workers lived.

Florence took in the street that seemed to go on forever and at an incline downwards. Her eyes were drawn to the green land at the end of the long road – the allotments Hilda told her – and beyond that the monster of a pit tip, which signified the end to The Avenues. From where she stood Florence could see that at a certain part of the year, or even part of the day, much of the allotment land would be in shadow. She imagined Frank, reading books on what fruit and veg bloomed with little sun, and then held Anna's hand while Hilda hurriedly crossed the road ahead of them.

Frank and Hilda lived on the fourth avenue on the left side. They had a tiny front yard, with an outside toilet, and a garden even smaller than the one at home. They entered the kitchen via the front yard and Florence was shocked at how miniscule the space was. But the place was pristine clean.

The kitchen, and later she was to find, the whole house was adorned with other people's clothes and bedding. Hilda was still taking in washing to make money, still didn't want to be on display to the world. Florence wondered if anything had changed at all inside Hilda's head. She conjectured the state of Frank and Hilda's marriage and the feeling of gloom that had been crowding in on her since arriving at the bus stop suddenly became a physical sensation, choking.

She viewed what would be her surroundings for the next few days, thinking back to their village school and the cleverness of her two friends. They deserved more than this. The problem Florence saw with her friends was not related to Mr Churchill, personally, at all, but it wasn't the first occasion that Florence had seriously doubted the political motivations of her employer. Women had been able to vote since 1928 (the vote of the fairer sex was not something Mr Churchill was in favour of and never had been, she certainly knew that) and although she was loyal to her employer in the domestic sense, she did not plan to vote for the Conservative party. She admired Mr Churchill. He was a man who on a personal level she'd trust emphatically, because working for him she couldn't fail to understand his honourable side. Mr Churchill was a hard taskmaster; a perfectionist, a gambler by nature, an egotist, quick to flare into a temper, but he would always respect and try to understand an adversary's point-of-view – for a short period of time anyway.

As magnanimous in defeat as he is jubilant in victory, the valet often said. Florence wasn't sure she entirely agreed with him. As she'd become more politically aware, the more she'd questioned Mr Churchill's policies. Of course, she had to keep her opinion quiet in the house about this; but then again being a woman she'd had to keep quiet about any political opinion. Only Clementine Churchill was allowed to have a political stance at Chartwell – and if truth were known – only if it generally agreed with the master's.

Years later it was implied that Clementine Churchill had a mind of her own and *did* disagree with her husband. Florence had never been witness to this – only perhaps in domestic matters – where Churchill acquiesced because he scored points with his wife, which he could then redeem at a later date.

How had Frank voted? Labour all the way down the line. Like her, Frank was able to separate his 'love' and admiration for Churchill from his politics.

'Make yourself at home, Flo,' Hilda said interrupting her thoughts. Florence went into the front sitting room. Anna was already curled up on the settee reading a book. 'Anna, why don't you go over to Rosy's house and play, so's me and Flo can talk?'

'I'd rather stay here, with Flo, Mum.'

Thank goodness she was now calling Hilda Mum. Florence sat next to her, rubbing her twig-like arm.

Maybe Hilda and Frank didn't have enough money to buy food and this brought her mind to the ham and huge piece of Dundee cake Miss Cunningham had pilfered from Chartwell's pantry. She returned to the kitchen where her suitcase still sat, and opened it. She pulled out the luxury food and took it into the front room, giving it to Hilda.

'Oh Flo. This's so kind of you.'

It was the first time that day Florence saw Hilda smile properly. 'Thank Miss Cunningham,' she said convivially. 'She sends her best wishes too.' She turned to Anna. 'Go to your friend's, lovely, and I'll come and collect you later. It'll be more fun than staying here with us.' Florence held up the cake, courtesy of Fortnum and Mason's. Miss Cunningham had taken a big risk with Mr Churchill's Dundee. 'This'll be our pudding after tea.'

Anna grinned but it soon fell away, as Anna's grins were apt to do. Something was always stopping the girl's moments of joy.

'Rosy's brother's at home today,' Anna said quietly and to no one in particular.

'Well, of course Hugh's at home, sweetie,' Hilda said. 'He lives there, silly.'

Anna got up from the settee without saying a word.

'I'll see you later, Flo?' Anna shouted from the kitchen.

'Yes, I'll get directions from your mum.' Florence got up and walked to stand by the sitting room's window and watched Anna open the back yard's wooden gate, wondering why she was so reluctant to go and see her friend.

'How is Anna?' she asked Hilda, but her eyes remained glued to the window analysing Anna.

'She's fine.'

Even now it was difficult for Hilda to talk about her daughter, finding it almost impossible to talk of how Anna had come about. It had been Frank who'd given Florence, in snippets, some of the story.

'I'm so sorry about the babies, Hilda. But it *will* happen, I know it will.'

'*The* babies. You mean *my* babies?'

'Yes, that's what I mean.'

'I just get so tired with it all.' Hilda walked into the kitchen; Florence followed and watched her put the ham in the pantry. Hilda leant against the wall. 'How is it I fell so easily with Anna? And the pregnancy and birth was so… undemanding? In the middle of a Welsh nowhere she was born, the place my mum took me to quietly and in shame to have the baby I didn't want. There was no midwife, only my mum and a farmer's wife who'd delivered more than a hundred calves in her lifetime, but never a human baby. It was so easy, Flo.'

'You never talk about it.' Florence thought about her next words carefully. 'What happened, can you tell me?'

'I'm sure Frank's told you.'

'Not much. You tell me. Please… if you want to. Only if you want to. Frank's only ever mentioned bits, and only to protect you, from me thinking badly of you.'

'Do you think badly of me?'

'You know what I mean.'

'You mean how I am with Anna, don't you?'

Florence nodded reluctantly.

'I try to love Anna properly. I really do.' She held her arms across her chest. 'And Frank adores her, which is good. But I just want us to have our own children, together. It's not much to ask, is it?'

'It's not. Frank's a good man.'

'He is. I should have left him for you, shouldn't I?'

'No, Hilda. It was never like that. I'm sorry—'

'About the dance? Don't be.'

'Look, I don't know what Jem saw, or what she told you. But nothing happened. We were drunk.' She looked up at Hilda. 'Frank was always yours.'

It had occurred to Florence more than once that Hilda's sudden change of mind about Frank had been entirely due to Jem's information and that Hilda had thought she'd lost her hold.

'It doesn't matter now, does it? I'm here,' Hilda gesticulated at her surroundings, 'and you're not.' She peered through the kitchen window. 'You were the lucky, one, Flo. Always were.' Hilda returned to the sitting room and Florence followed. 'Do you want to know, what happened? How I fell with Anna?' Hilda said, perching on the end of the settee.

Florence smiled encouragingly. Why hadn't she asked Hilda before? She and her mum had helped the Wells family when they finally realised Hilda was pregnant. Florence hadn't been able to go to Wales with Hilda and Mrs Wells, as she'd started her job at Chartwell by then, but she'd been there for Hilda on her return, looked after the new baby, and had loved Anna immediately, as had Frank. But then Hilda began to retreat, only allowing Frank in but refusing to marry him. Florence had let it go because she hadn't wanted to intrude, didn't want to delve where she wasn't wanted. But she now realised she'd been completely wrong. Hilda had wanted to talk and she hadn't been there for her. Had she herself felt too uncomfortable? Perhaps she had, and too young too to understand the subtle complexities – just as Hilda was too young to have a baby.

'Tell me,' Florence said finally, and went to sit next to Hilda.

'Can you remember when I used to go to the cattle market with my dad?' Hilda began. 'The farmer he works for would send him. My dad always had an eye for cattle and sheep. I loved going with him—'

'I do remember. Your dad said I couldn't go to the market with you both. I don't think I ever forgave your dad that.'

'Well, I wish you had come that day with me, and then it wouldn't have happened. The market was full of men, of course. I wandered around, I liked the freedom and my dad was busy buying and selling. Behind the market there were the latrines for the farmers, covered to keep out the rain and weather. That day, a farmer from another county was there. New, no one had seen him before. Old. Quiet. I was near the latrines – behind them – I was dying for a pee. My dad'd told me to hold it in until we could get to the tearooms. I couldn't hold it and I didn't want to bother my dad. I didn't think anyone could see me, but he, the out-of-towner, must have been looking. There and then, he grabbed hold of me. I tried to scream but he stuffed his filthy handkerchief in my mouth. Before I knew… '

'Go on,' Florence said gently.

'Only moments. I knew what was happening, but didn't, if you know what I mean?'

Flo shook her head in denial, the image far too strong.

'Then he got up, muttered something about me smelling of piss and left. I never saw him again.'

'Did you tell your dad?'

'No. I told him nothing.'

'Your mum?'

'No. And by the time I knew I was carrying a baby, it was too late. My mum and dad never guessed, and I didn't really. I didn't get that much fatter. No morning sickness.' She laughed sadly. 'It was such an easy pregnancy, and so easy to get pregnant. And then soon after we came back from Wales, with Anna, I saw an article in the newspaper. A man from the next county had been trampled to death by his own horse. It was him Flo. The bastard.'

'Did you say anything then?'

'There was no point. He was dead.'

'Why didn't you ever tell me?'

'I don't know.'

'Your mum and dad stayed behind you. They sent you to Wales to have the baby to make it easier for you. You got through it. Frank loves you. He's never held it against you. It made him love you more.'

'He fell in love with Anna. Which was a good thing. Because I never did. How could I?'

Florence shook her head. 'He fell for you years ago, long before Anna.' She touched Hilda's arm. 'I tried to help when I knew you were pregnant. I tried to be there for you.'

'I know you did, and you were, and I appreciated it. You and Frank were the best.'

Florence smiled. 'I've another little present in my suitcase.'

'What?'

'Cooking sherry. Shall we have a glass?'

Hilda half-smiled. 'Yes, let's.'

The two women drank one glass each and then Florence helped Hilda gather up the washing that was strewn throughout the house.

After asking Hilda where Rosy lived, Florence left her getting the tea ready. As she walked in the direction of Rosy's house she mulled over what Hilda had finally told her. God, poor Hilda. But she had Frank now. Hilda should let it all go. Get on with it, as her mother would say. Her mother though – like her dad about truth and alcohol – wasn't always right, and thoughts of Hilda troubled her as she made her way to pick up Anna.

Rosy lived at the bottom of the long road and on the thirteenth avenue. Prone to superstition Florence was surprised they'd built a number thirteen. The Avenues should have stopped at twelve or gone on to fourteen, missing out thirteen. Rosy Lambert's house was on the left side of the street. She walked around to the back door, knocked, and a boy answered. Untidy dark hair, wide-set eyes, full cheeks, narrow lips, his body on the plump side. Mushy, her mum would call him. Unkempt looking, as her father would say. Although in a way, he was strangely pretty. About fourteen, fifteen, but Florence had never been good with ages. Rosy's older brother, Hugh, she assumed.

'Who are you?' he asked, his voice deep. She now pegged him for a definite fifteen, perhaps even sixteen.

She stepped nearer to the door and smelt tobacco. The boy was chewing some.

'I'm Anna's…' She didn't know how to introduce herself. 'Auntie, I've come to collect her. Are your mum and dad in?'

'No. Not here.' He stepped to one side. 'The girls are upstairs, in Rosy's bedroom.'

'Aren't you a bit young for tobacco?' she said lightly.

'It's none of your business.'

'Can you go and get Anna, please? Tell her Florence is here.'

She waited on the doorstep but managed to peer into the back sitting room. It was exactly the same layout as Hilda and Frank's home. But this place reeked of tobacco. She was absolutely certain she saw a cockroach in the darkest corner of the room. She swallowed holding in the sick.

Anna appeared, a larger framed girl following her, a mass of unruly blonde curls and a meek expression.

Rosy said, 'Does Anna have to go?'

'She does,' Florence replied. 'Where's your mum and dad?'

The boy interrupted. 'At work, Mrs nosey parker.' He grabbed at Anna. 'Anna likes coming around when there's no one here, don't you, Anna?'

Rosy seemed incapable of speech and only shrugged. Every hair on Florence's body lifted.

Anna stood next to Florence, glued to her hip. 'See you soon, Rosy.'

The boy put his arm around his sister and grinned. 'See you soon, Anna.'

'Stop it, Hugh,' Rosy said quietly. She said to Anna, 'Sorry.' But then Rosy yelped. Hugh was gripping his sister's arm tight.

As they walked back home Florence asked herself what Hilda and Frank were doing living here.

She must talk to Frank.

Sadly, Florence saw very little of Frank on her visit. He was always at work and she wondered if he was avoiding her. It was something Frank was apt to do if there was something he didn't want to talk about.

During her stay, Anna didn't go around to Rosy's again, but Anna did take her to Frank's allotment to show her the Wendy house. Anna was proud of the key she owned and the two of them sat inside for a good hour eating the remnants of the Dundee cake and drinking squash, but whistling outside interrupted their convivial impromptu picnic. Anna suddenly stiffened.

'What's wrong?' Florence asked.

'Nothing.'

'Who is it?'

'Hugh.'

'You don't like him do you?'

'No.'

'Why don't you like him, Anna?'

Anna shrugged and Florence noticed a crumb of Dundee on her lips. She brushed it off gently. 'Why, Anna?'

'He… locked me in here… took my key and locked me in.'

'Is that all he did?'

She shrugged again.

'Did you tell your mum?'

'Yes, that he locked me in.'

'And what did Hilda say?'

'That I make too much of things, that Hugh was just playing,' Anna croaked.

'How long were you in here?'

'A couple of hours.'

'Did you tell your dad?'

'No, Hilda… Mum told me not to bother him.'

Florence was gradually drawing a picture of the Cullens' life in Nottinghamshire. 'Perhaps you should tell your dad?'

'Maybe.'

That one word marked out how much older Anna was inside her head than what showed in her scant and child-like body.

Florence told Frank when finally on her last day there she was able to spend an hour alone with him. The hour was both warm and excruciating. She'd tried to forget how Frank made her feel but it all came flooding back, and in the house he shared with Hilda this gave her an overwhelming sense of shame. And so she attempted to keep to the problem of Anna, which was easy to do, as she was so worried about the girl.

Florence had no idea if he'd acted on what she'd told him and on her return to Westerham wished she'd made more of a fuss.

It wasn't until after the war that Florence found out about Frank's brush with the police in the autumn of

1938, and it was much later still when she discovered why a twenty-one-year-old Hugh Lambert had dropped any accusations against Frank.

16

Frank

Nottinghamshire
July 30th 1936

The Daily Herald

Civil War In Spain

Prime Minister, Stanley Baldwin, has made it clear in his speech today that Great Britain in no way supports the Spanish Left wing Popular Front party. He is keen Great Britain will not be seen to be taking any side in Spain's current civil conflict.

Mr Churchill said from his home in Kent, "The threat of Soviet Bolshevism, at this time, is of more crucial importance than the threat of German militarism."
Mr Churchill went on to say that he regards the civil strife in Spain a result of "dangerous communist infiltration…"

Frank lay on the settee with a cushion propping up his head, reading the paper. The unrest in Spain had been causing massive debate and sometimes violent arguments at the colliery. He knew at least three blokes who were determined to go and fight for the

Republicans, and against the fascist bastard, Franco. He'd thought about it himself.

He sat upright and looked at the clock on the mantelpiece. Anna was due home soon. There was no way he'd leave Anna, no matter how much he agreed with the Spanish Popular Front and despised what General Franco was getting away with. He didn't agree with Churchill on this. On this, Mr Churchill had it very wrong. Couldn't the old man see that what was happening in Spain was the beginning of something else? He was just a working class man with no proper education, but he saw. Saw where it could all go. Why couldn't Churchill?

Hilda was doing some paperwork and accounts for the vicar and said she'd be home late. He'd made rissoles for tea with the leftover stuff from the larder. He'd make sure Anna ate, and then make his way to the pit for the long night shift ahead. He tried not to feel angry that Hilda should be looking after Anna. The relationship between mother and daughter had got worse, not better. It was Anna's birthday next month, her fourteenth. He knew Hilda hadn't even thought about it, but he had. He'd got her a new dress, together with a matching pair of shoes, buying them with the bonus he'd made mining the biggest amount of coal in a month. The bonus he hadn't told Hilda about. He glanced at the clock again and heard the latch on the gate outside. Good, Anna was home a bit early. They had plenty of time. He went into the kitchen and put the frying pan on the hob. As he dropped in a knob of lard, Anna opened the door.

'Hello, Dad.'

She appeared more sad than usual. Her dark curls flat and lifeless, her face was a pasty white, narrow shoulders hunched up.

'Everything all right at school, love?'

'Oh, you know.'

'No, I don't. You have to tell me.'

'I just get ignored at school. No one likes me. And Rosy was off today, so I had to sit on my own all dinnertime.'

'Aw, love. I used to hate it when I had to sit on my own at school at dinnertime.' Gently, he pulled her inside and helped her take her coat off. 'Is Rosy all right?'

'Hugh pushed her down the stairs. She's hurt her ankle, so had to stay home.'

'What do you mean he pushed her down the stairs?'

'He said it was an accident. He was in a rush to get to work. Was doing a double shift at the pit or something.'

'Bloody Hugh. I hope she's all right.'

'It's not broken but swollen.'

'I'll be seeing him at work later. I'll have a word.'

She leant up against the tiny kitchen table and tucked a thick strand of hair behind her ear. She was the image of her mother, everything, from the exquisite alabaster-white skin, to the arresting green of her eyes. He knew Hilda hated that she looked like her. Poor Anna. She could never win. If she'd resembled her father Hilda would have punished her for that. After every miscarriage Hilda's emotional treatment of her daughter worsened a little bit more.

Jem had been to stay a few months before and although his sister had managed to spectacularly avoid him for the whole week she was there, he did manage to have one decent conversation with her. He'd asked her to have a word with Hilda about Anna, because Hilda listened to Jem. He wanted Jem to try and persuade Hilda to be just… nicer to her daughter.

Frank didn't know if Jem had said anything, and if she had, it obviously had no effect. If Anna had a different mother she wouldn't be as fragile and brittle as she was. She'd always been sensitive, but her own mother's treatment of her had made Anna's natural leaning to the melancholic a given.

He studied Anna. Physically she had really blossomed in the past six months. Still thin but with curves forming in all the right places. He tried not to notice, but sometimes couldn't help it. In profile she was even more striking than her mother, or would be in a year or two. He noticed when he was out in the town with her, the stares and admiring glances from the youths, and even from men as old as himself. He wanted to punch those people. He wanted to keep Anna safe.

'You're miles away,' she said, bringing him back to the present. 'I think they're burning.' She poked the rissoles with a fork. 'My favourite. I love you, Dad.'

'Go and lay the table, as I have to leave in an hour.' He flipped over the four rissoles sizzling in the pan.

They ate quickly and he was glad to see Anna mopped up everything on the plate.

'Best ones you've made for a while,' she said, beginning to clear the table.

'Leave it, love. Come and sit on the settee with me and tell me about school. Which subjects you're enjoying?'

She plonked herself next to him, laying her head on his chest. 'If it weren't for the others I'd love school.'

He smiled. 'You'd rather have a governess?'

'I remember Mary Churchill, you know. The *Marycot* at Chartwell. I loved going there to play with Mary. I wish the others in my class were like Mary.'

'I think Mary got the good end of it all, being the fifth child. Her parents had got into the swing of parenthood by then.' He looked at her. 'Being the first can be hard. I was the first.'

She stuck her head deeper into his chest. 'Was it hard for you?'

'A bit.'

'Grandma Cullen never comes to stay.'

'No, but it's a fair way for her.'

He felt the vibrations of her head on his chest as she nodded. 'I like Jem though.'

The inference was that she didn't like his mother so much. 'When you're a bit older you can get the train to Westerham by yourself and visit Grandma, maybe stay with Jem? See Miss Cunningham too.'

'That would be nice.'

'So what's your favourite subject at school?'

'Science. Mrs Beadle says it's my best too.'

'That's good.'

'I want to be a nurse. But Mum says we can't afford it.'

'We can, don't worry.' He checked the time. 'I have to go to work soon.'

'I know, can we just stay like this for a bit longer?' she asked, lifting her head.

'Course we can.'

The pair of them must have nodded off and it was the shrill voice of Hilda, who'd returned from her unpaid work at the vicarage, which woke them from a snatched slumber.

'Frank,' she shouted, 'you should be gone by now. It's past five.'

He woke, disorientated, felt the small weight of Anna jump away from him.

'And you, young lady.' His eyes were open now. 'You should be clearing up the tea things, doing something useful,' Hilda said in that clipped tone. Another miscarriage had edged her further towards the depths, and further away from her daughter.

Anna hadn't said a word. She disappeared upstairs to her bedroom.

'Why do you do this?'

Hilda sat down. 'I don't know.'

Shaking his head, he got up, collected his work stuff and left the house without saying a word. During the half hour walk to the colliery he thought about why Hilda did it. Nothing was changing. It never would.

* * *

By the time Frank was inside the shaft cage, and as he heard the familiar sound of the chains taking him and the others on his shift down into the bowels of the earth, his anger towards Hilda finally subsided.

The previous shift was waiting to be taken back up to daylight. The cage thudded to a stop. The fifteen men trundled out. Frank, along with Max Betts and two others, were earmarked to make their way to the pit face.

Hugh should have been there, waiting with the others to be taken back up, but was nowhere to be seen.

The finished shift loitered near the shaft. Usually there was a crush to get in the cage, men dying to get back up to ground level and the pub. There wasn't today.

Frank turned to the foreman. 'What's going on?'

'Trouble on the face. There's been a collapse at the east end. No one's been able to get though. It's really tight.'

'I take it that someone's stuck in there or we wouldn't be down here?'

'You're the best, Frank. The only one from this shift who has a chance of getting through—'

Max interrupted. 'Are you mad, gaffer?' His question directed to the foreman. 'You can't send anyone in, not until we know it's safe.'

'A man is missing, probably stuck, we have to do something.'

'Who is it?' Frank asked. He already knew.

'Hugh Lambert.'

Many things passed through Frank's mind. He didn't like Lambert. He never would, but he was more than aware, as the foreman was, that he was the best man to get Lambert out. For all of Hugh's bravado and keen confidence, Hugh was petrified of the dark and enclosed spaces. Hugh, never as a rule, took the face jobs, and earned less because of it. Frank hated working at the pit but had been surprised at the ease he'd taken to being down a black hole. He wasn't claustrophobic, something which had come as a bit of a revelation.

And today was a day when Frank was willing to risk his life, not for Hugh, by God not for Hugh, but simply because it was a life, his life, that seemed so meaningless. Hugh had had his mishap on just the right shift. Even the thought of Anna couldn't take the feeling away from Frank that his life these days wasn't worth living.

'What the hell's Lambert doing on the face?' Frank said finally.

'We keep him away as much as we can but today we needed him there. It's a job, Frank,' the foreman said.

'The collapse, is it structural or could there be another reason, like Hugh being careless?' Frank asked.

'I was there on my last shift,' Max said. 'In that section, and everything looked good. It might be Hugh. He may well have just got clumsy with one of the timber poles.' He glanced at Frank. 'You know how bloody useless he can be.'

'Will you do it?' the foreman asked Frank.

'I'll come in with you, mate,' Max said. Max was friendly with Hugh. They were a similar age. Not everyone disliked Hugh as much as Frank did; he did know that. Hugh's loose mouth and propensity to all sorts of unsavoury behaviour seemed to be lost to many in the pit, and the village; most took him with a pinch of salt and many liked him because of his devil-may-care attitude. Frank was self-aware enough to know that it was generally only to him, and Anna, to whom Hugh was such a pariah. Maybe Rosy too. Hilda didn't have a problem with Hugh either. In a microcosmic moment in the depths of the earth a jab of understanding hit him; that as Hilda was so wrong about so many things, that *he* might be wrong about Hugh. And anyway, he liked

Maisie. She'd be devastated if anything happened to her son, and so soon after losing her husband, Rod.

'No need, Max. No point both of us going in. I'll do it,' Frank said.

He and the foreman walked the half mile to where another shaft would take them lower, onto the pit face.

'See what you think when you get down,' the foreman said. 'If it's too dangerous and you need help, come back and we'll have a rethink. I just want to assess the situation. You know what you're doing, Frank.'

And down Frank went, alone, only carrying with him the tools of his trade. He emerged from the small shaft, dipping low under the ebony black ceiling, and saw immediately where the problem was. Ahead of him there had been a small collapse, but it wasn't a major disaster. He'd seen it before. A localised problem with a timber beam that had been made unstable. He shone his lamp into the blackness and on his stomach made his way to a mound of rubble blocking the passage. Hugh would be behind there somewhere. He shouted Hugh's name and his own voice echoed back. Hugh wouldn't hear him; the worst-case scenario was that he was unconscious. Frank spent an hour, if not more – time on the face often became meaningless – fixing up another pole adjacent to the small collapse, and then when he was happy with that, he began to dig hard into the rubble. Sweat leaked from every pore and as he worked, the anger towards Hilda dissipated, even the inbuilt rancour he felt towards Hugh melted away in the dank darkness.

At the point he sensed he was nearly through, he shouted Hugh's name again, his voice croaky from the viscous dust. He was certain he heard something, a human groan.

'Hugh, you little runt, you there?'

As he spoke he felt rather than heard a deep rumble of movement and turning over from his belly onto his back saw a shudder of the rock above him, felt crumbles of loosened debris fall like hundreds of tiny spiders onto his face.

'Hugh! Make your way through the hole, man, now. Wake up!' Frank quickly began pushing into the in-way he'd been working on and finally saw a dim light. Hopefully, it was Hugh's torch.

'Is that you, Frank? I've broken my arm. I can't move it.'

'Like your sister nearly broke her ankle, Hugh?' He couldn't resist it. 'Get yourself out.'

'I hit the pole by accident. I hate the face…'

Then Frank felt a more insistent rumble, not crumbles of earth now, rocks. He peered to where Hugh lay. 'Now, man. Get out, forget your arm. It's not your leg, you can move. Forget the pain, just get out. The thing's going to collapse.' Frank knew Hugh would find it hard to move. You needed your arms when flat on your belly at the face as much as your legs. But they needed to get out. It crossed his mind only for a moment to get moving himself. Hugh had a way out now. It was up to him. Frank didn't want to die down there. He didn't want to leave Anna.

He pushed his arms through the gap. 'Grab my hands and pull.'

At last Hugh did as he was told and as Frank grabbed at Hugh's left arm, the earth began to come down in a deluge. Together, and with Frank nudging Hugh along with his knees, they made their way the few hundred feet to where the space between ground and the coal ceiling became larger. As they both sat up they heard and felt, rather than saw, the disintegration of the black ceiling. As dust and debris blew with force towards them, he pushed Hugh, and with both of their heads bowed and leaning forward, they carried on, Frank making sure Hugh, who was in obvious agony, wasn't far behind. Finally they approached the secondary shaft that would take them upwards to the next level, where the foreman waited. Frank shoved Hugh into the small cage, followed him in, then pulled on the chain and almost immediately it began to ascend.

Hugh was taken straight to the infirmary and after a debrief with the foreman, Frank – persuaded by Max – went to the pub, where he was lauded as a true hero, simply because it was common knowledge he didn't like Hugh but had put his life on the line to save him anyway. After that day Frank became somewhat of a legend at the colliery, and even more so when he went on record defending the foreman who had sent him into a dangerous situation. Because of Frank, the foreman wasn't sacked, even keeping his hallowed position at the pit.

When Frank returned home drunk, the first time since the village dance, he found he couldn't get into the bedroom. Hilda had locked him out. As his head hit the cushion and lying on the settee, he tried, again, to understand his wife. He really did try.

His last two thoughts before he fell into a disturbed sleep were that he didn't like Hugh but was glad the runt was alive. The other thought; he had to sort things out with Hilda. They had to try for another baby.

He continued to believe that a baby would make everything all right. For all three of them

17

Richard

2002

When Richard returned from his grandad's allotment, still thinking about Jeff Lambert's words, his dad was sitting on Gran Hilda's back door step waiting for him.

'Hi, Dad. What you doing here? Why are you outside?' he managed to pant. There were more hills on the jog back than he remembered.

'Forgot the key. I wasn't planning on coming down, but thought I would.'

Jim Cullen was not spontaneous. Richard noticed his dad shivering. He unlocked the front door. 'C'mon. It's freezing out here.'

'Where've you been?'

'The allotment. Down memory lane.'

'You loved your grandad.' His dad followed him inside.

'I did.' Richard flicked the kettle on. 'How's Gillian and Beccy?'

'They're fine. Got off early this morning.'

'Good. You don't have to be here, you know. I said I'd sort it.'

His dad sat down on a kitchen chair. 'Jemima came to see us after we got home.'

'Lots of secrets—'

'That's why I've come, son.'

'About Anna?'

'You know?' Jim fidgeted, took off his coat. '*How* do you know?'

'Why've you never told me?'

'I didn't know, not until Jemima's visit last night.'

'What did she say?' Richard asked.

'That Nick and I have a sister.'

'A half-sister, and she's still alive.'

'We didn't know. Nick and me didn't know.' His dad's voice was muted.

'I can't understand how this could've gone under the radar for so long.'

'Anna was never mentioned. Never.' His dad rubbed his cheek, petting the scar. 'I remember Frank going away a lot in the fifties, through to the eighties. Maybe four or five times a year. Mum said he went to meet up with his army buddies. She was always on edge when he went.' His dad was standing now. 'And I remember… one of my mates, this would be in the mid-sixties, saying he'd bumped into my dad on the train going down to Kent. My mate was off for some sort of training course near Westerham.'

'And?' Richard said. 'That's where grandad Frank came from, him and Gran. Maybe he was visiting family, friends?'

'He told my mate he was on a meet up with his army pals in London. A few days later, my mate saw Dad in the town he was doing the course. In the local greengrocers buying fruit and veg.'

'Did your mate speak to him?'

'No, he left it. Said he just felt Frank didn't want to be questioned, and he, my mate, knew Frank had lied to him about his destination. He let it drop. He thought my dad was having an affair or something. I never said anything to my dad about it.' He looked at Richard. 'I didn't have the same relationship with him as you. I never questioned him.'

'What do you think he was doing down in Kent, if not on a reunion?' Richard asked.

'I've no idea. Maybe something to do with Anna?' He paused as if saying her name was painful. 'But Anna's in a hospital up in Yorkshire, from what Jemima said. So I don't know why he visited Kent so regularly.'

'It might have had nothing to do with Anna?'

'You think he *was* having an affair? The thing is, son, my mum and dad's relationship always seemed… difficult, but as a kid you just accepted it. But now looking back there was something odd about his "jaunts." But for me and Nick it was normal.'

Something clicked inside Richard's mind. Florence Miller, Celia told him, had lived in Kent all of her life, with her American husband and children. Just outside Westerham, where Florence, and his grandma and grandad, had been born. Richard sensed a connection. Florence had been widowed in the early sixties, but remained in the house that she and her husband had shared since marriage, just after the war. 'Why has Jemima decided to tell you now, Dad?'

'I really don't know. She wouldn't tell me much, just the address of the hospital, psychiatric hospital, and she gave me a few photos of Anna of when she was young and more recent ones. I still can't believe it.'

'Why now, though?' Richard was asking himself rather than his dad.

'She's getting older, but I think she suspects Hilda would have kept a lot of correspondence. Have you started on the stuff up in the loft? I suppose you have, that's why you know.'

Richard shook his head and told his dad about Florence Miller's letter. 'You heard of her?'

'You asked me that before. No. Mum never mentioned her, at all.'

'Can you remember a woman at Grandma Hilda's funeral? Thirties, bleached blonde hair?'

'Yes, I wondered who she was.'

'Florence Miller's nurse, at the nursing home. Florence's known all along. Florence was Frank and Hilda's friend donkey's years ago. Apparently she wanted to tell me about Anna at Grandad's funeral, but didn't. I didn't even know she was there. Did you?'

His dad shook his head. 'She must have just come to the church. So many people there.'

Richard lifted the kettle. 'Tea?'

'I will. There's whisky in the top cupboard. Add a drop for me. I came on the bus.'

'Maybe on Grandad's jaunts he was visiting Florence?' Richard said.

'Perhaps. My mum never knew if he was. As far as we were concerned he was off on his reunions. Maybe my dad *was* having an affair – with Florence.' He stared at the floor. 'I wouldn't put it past him.' His dad rubbed his chin. 'Jem used to come a lot to stay when Dad was off, before she moved to Ireland. After that she came less. In the latter years Mum went over there.'

'Did she?'

'She did.' His dad flopped down on a kitchen stool that was far too small to accommodate his substantial frame. 'Do *you* think your grandad was having an affair with Florence?'

'I don't think so. I really don't.' Spontaneously, Richard gave him a bear hug. 'I could do without this.'

'What's up, son?'

'Oh, another conversation, another time.' He'd retrieved the whisky and put a fair measure in both mugs. 'I'll get to the bottom of this.'

'I know you will.' Jim took a gulp of the whisky-tea. 'I've brought the photos to show you.' He pulled them out from his overcoat pocket and laid the four of them on the work unit.

A little girl. Around five or six. Skinny, serious looking. Dark hair that tumbled onto her shoulders. China white skin. She wore a pretty pinafore dress of the time with a blouse. Richard saw immediately the resemblance to Hilda despite the difference in hair colouring. Information on the back: *Anna 1932.*

The second photo was of the same girl, a little older, and Frank standing next to the Wendy house in the allotment, behind them a sea of sweet peas. Anna looked about ten in that one. *Anna in the allotment: 1934*

The third photo was of two women standing by an old sycamore tree. One older woman and a younger woman. He thought the younger woman was Anna; she wore a smart dress that he dated to the 1950s. The older woman wore a plain white pinafore, her eyes and expression totally vacant, the folds in the skin of her face heavy. Her hair well greyed.

Richard flipped over the photo: *Jemima and Anna, High Royal Hospital, 1951.*

The old woman was Anna. She'd only have been around twenty-eight. She looked ancient and nothing like the young girl she'd been. His heart heaved for a woman he did not know. Then his mind flitted to Beccy. He wanted to tell his dad about the pregnancy but now wasn't the time. Too many other things to think about.

Finally he looked at the fourth photo. Again the older lady, looking even more advanced in years. With another woman. Not Jemima, as in the first photo. Someone else. He flipped straight over to the back.

Anna and Florence. 1953. He took a closer look. It was taken in a different location to the one by the sycamore trees. More urban, like someone's back garden. Pretty flowerbeds, well-tended. He homed in on Florence. How old would she be? Early nineties now. She'd perhaps be in her mid-forties. A very handsome woman, Richard noted. He studied the photo. Had Jemima taken it? Probably, as she'd given them to Jim. In the right corner of the image he saw a fragment of something. He got up and went to retrieve a magnifying glass from his briefcase, which he sometimes used in court when observing photographic evidence. Sitting back down on the floor cross-legged he scrutinised the image. A trousered leg and a shoe on its foot. Richard peered at the shoes, Frank had worn the same make of shoes for decades his gran Hilda had once told him; the reason for her impartation of knowledge he couldn't remember now.

Richard was certain the leg and shoe belonged to his grandad Frank.

His dad spoke. 'I'm going to see her.'

'Anna?'

'Yes. She's my sister.'

'Hold fire, Dad. Let me work out what's happening first. Please. I've already found some documents. I'll find out more and I'll keep you in the loop. And we'll go and see Anna together.'

'That my parents could do this—'

'There'll be a reason. There's always a reason for everything and it's been my job for the last twenty odd years to find those reasons.'

His dad touched his shoulder and poured more whisky into the mug, which was devoid of tea. 'I'm going to Nick's later to tell him.'

'Okay. I'll call you when I know anything. Is Jemima still around?'

'She's at the Savoy in Nottingham still. Plans to stay for another three days.'

'Good.'

Swilling out his cup and putting it on the wooden draining board, his dad left.

Richard picked up his phone and called his home number. No answer. Of course there would be no answer, Gillian was at work. He called her mobile. Straight onto voicemail. He tried Beccy's mobile. No answer. He laid the phone on the table, not understanding the feeling of apprehension in the lining of his gut. He picked up the phone again and punched in the school's number where Gillian worked, which took him straight through to her office.

Finally. 'Gillian Cullen.'

'It's me, darling.'

'Richard, I'm glad you caught me. I'm leaving early. I've persuaded Beccy to go up to the Peaks for a few days, a chill and a chat. Then thought we could pick you up on the way back.'

'I'd have liked to have come with you both. Fancy a few days climbing.'

'We're not climbing. Just walking and talking.'

'Beccy loves climbing.'

'She's worried about the baby.'

'She wants to keep it doesn't she?'

'Yep. Look, I think a few days of mother daughter chats will be productive.' She paused. 'One way or the other.'

'Sounds good. I can't get Beccy on her mobile.'

'I think she's switched it off. Carl, you know?'

'When are you leaving?'

'As soon as I get home.'

'Okay.'

'How's it going?'

'Interesting. I'll tell you when I see you,' he replied.

'Intriguing!'

'Love you.'

'Love you too. See you soon. Gotta go, Richard.'

She hung up.

He'd forgotten to ask where they were staying but guessed the same B&B they'd used before when the three of them had gone up there for climbing weekends. Jack Sivers' place.

He made his way upstairs to the room he was sleeping in and got changed from his sweaty clothes, then, walked onto the landing and opened the loft door, pulled down the ancient ladder and lumbered up into the damp and rambling space.

18

Richard grabbed at the box where he'd found the admission form for Anna. There was still so much more stuff to go through. Two more boxes sat beside it, similar ageing process on the cardboard so he figured they'd been put in at the same time. He manoeuvred all three boxes to the loft's mouth and then scrambled back down the first few rungs of the ladder. He'd eaten nothing and felt the whisky's effects, nearly missing a rung.

Finally, he managed to get them down and took them into the room he'd slept in the night before. Quickly, he realised the correspondence had been put in date order. He started at the bottom of the first box.

He studied the correspondence, which dated back to 1928. Some letters with the Chartwell heading. He picked those first and sat on the edge of the bed, somehow expecting correspondence from Churchill himself, but Richard knew really that this wouldn't be the case. The first one he read was signed by a Betty Cunningham. He remembered his grandad mentioning a Miss Cunningham. She'd been a part-time, on and off cook at Chartwell and for a member of staff had been close to the Churchills.

As he rummaged through he saw that each lot of letters were in a 'pile' pertaining to each writer: a chronology of correspondence from each sender.

This first lot from Miss Betty Cunningham.

October 1928 – a letter asking if the Pyrex dish was holding up well.

Benjamin says he's missing Frank and he hopes Frank's enjoying his new job.

November 1928 – I am so sorry to hear about the miscarriage, Hilda. My best to you and Frank. Be patient, God will deliver.

Letters dated Easters and Christmases, 1929 through to 1931. A few more in this period reassuring Hilda about her miscarriages. Richard counted two short pregnancies up to now. Poor Hilda. Some mentions in these letters asking how Anna is faring. A few mentions of Jemima and her son, Nathan.

November 1932 – Hope you enjoyed the ham and Dundee cake Florence brought with her. It sounds as if all is well up in Nottinghamshire.

Correspondence then thinned out until the mid-thirties.

July 1936 – I've heard your sad news. (Another miscarriage) Stay strong. News coming from Spain isn't looking good. Give my love to Anna. Jem says that she is so very thin, and remains an anxious girl.

March 20th 1938 – Lovely to see Anna at Westerham. I'm so glad you allowed her to come, Hilda. She's growing into quite a lovely young woman, even Clementine Churchill remarked on her beauty to me – very unlike Mrs Churchill! From what I gather Anna had a lovely afternoon at Chartwell. It was so good of Mrs Churchill to invite her with some other young people from the village, although unfortunately Master Randolph and his rowdy London friends were here, which I think, rather spoilt it all for the youngsters. Anna helped me a little in the kitchen, but she spent a good few hours in the grounds with the others her age, having fun I believe, and doing what young people do! And so I was surprised when Anna asked Jemima to organise an early train home for her. Florence and I, and Jemima and Anna's grandma, had hoped she'd stay for the full week.

His grandad had once told him that occasionally the Churchills would invite local villagers to come to Chartwell – an organised event. Richard had imagined these events to be a little like the garden parties at Buckingham Palace, only obviously, a much less grand affair.

He picked up the next letter.

November 1938 – Congratulations. I have sent Jim a little something. I hope to see you when you next visit Westerham and I can meet him properly. Isn't it terrible news about Chamberlain? I worry about being overrun with Germans. How is Anna?

December 1938 – Christmas wishes.

October 1940 – I had not realised you had moved, Hilda. I hope this letter finds you well. Stay in touch.

Summer 1943 – I hope Frank is safe and well in his posting in Africa. Hilda, I am a little concerned, Mrs Churchill has received a letter from Mr Churchill. Hilda, could you contact me? Mrs Churchill has given it to me for safekeeping. I hope to give it back to Frank at the earliest opportunity. Best that way, Mrs Churchill's secretary says, as it's so busy here at Chartwell.

With this last letter Richard sat up straight. Would Miss Cunningham still be alive? He doubted it, and might not have kept the letter anyway, and if she had maybe the letter she spoke of had found its way back to his grandad and he'd got rid of it himself. If Miss

Cunningham had been in her mid-thirties at Chartwell before World War Two, she could be well over a hundred.

He texted Nell to do the legwork for him on Miss Cunningham, and also to look up Rosy Lambert, Jeff Lambert's aunt. The efficient Nell asked no questions, saying she'd get back as soon as she had information.

The next pile consisted of official letters, which had been sent to his grandparents from High Royal Mental Hospital. A massive pile, charting Anna's time there.

He sorted through them, comments about Anna's physical health but in reality mapping her disintegration. Entries about her condition, an obsession with birth, babies, with Churchill and his family, particularly, Marigold Churchill, with whom it seemed she had a strong connection; so much so that Anna believed she was the dead Churchill's child.

In between 1948 and 1953, Richard speed-read trying to get the general gist. Anna was more stable, and never violent.

In the years in between 1953 and 1982 there were no more letters from High Royal Hospital to Hilda and Frank. And no letters from Florence to Hilda, or to Frank. But they could just be lost.

He sifted through the correspondence again, looking for clues. He placed the photos his dad left with him on the floor and looked at the one of Florence and Anna, with the trouser leg, and knew instinctively that photo was definitely not taken at the institution. He looked at the date again. *1953*.

Richard moved onto the next pile. This lot from Florence Miller, most of the letters addressed to Frank.

He flipped through looking for anything interesting. He wondered if Hilda had known about these letters before Frank's death, or if she had found them after he died. He suspected the latter.

The one that lay at the top was dated the summer of 1940, postmarked Devon, and sent to Frank in a convalescent home in a village near Westerham. Richard knew so little about his grandad's past, which was quite normal he felt, for the third generation. For his dad and Uncle Nick to know so little though, he found not only disquieting, but also disturbing.

What was the secret that had halted his grandparents from acknowledging that Anna existed? Surely it couldn't have been only the fact that Anna had serious mental health issues? His extended family seemed on the whole open-minded and liberal.

In the letter Florence asks if they (she and Frank) might meet up in London.

I've spoken with Jem and I know Anna has been institutionalised.

Why didn't you tell me, Frank? I don't speak with Hilda anymore so please say yes to us meeting. I need to know more about Anna.

Florence Miller had known about Anna from the very beginning. Why had it taken her so long to come forward? Richard sensed Florence's closeness to the girl.

More letters from Florence, and these to Hilda. The early ones dated to the late twenties and early thirties, affable enough between the two friends, but then the correspondence peters out, until October 1940. But one from Florence to Hilda, acknowledging Anna has been sent to High Royal. The tone of Florence's letter was terse. There were no response letters from Hilda available for him to look at to gain a sense of his grandma's mindset at that time.

At the bottom of this clutch he pulled out one more, and then saw a large parcel wrapped in tissue paper. He slid it out, putting it to one side, reading the letter first.

From Florence, addressed to Frank, postmarked London, which had been sent to a British command base address in Cairo. November 1942.

Dear Frank,

I hope all is well in Africa – as well as it can be. I did receive your letter about Harold, and thank you for your kind words about Edward. Edward has asked me to marry him and of course I have said yes, but perhaps we won't tie the knot until after the war, which I hope with your efforts in Africa will be nearing its end soon. But how wonderful that you have met up with Harold in that far-off country. It sounds as if you got on well. And your comment that he has been very helpful to you. What did he do? Teach you to ride a motorcycle?! Your news about Hugh Lambert as you can imagine, didn't sadden me at all, as I'm sure it didn't you either. If what you suspected was true, and I believe it very well could be, the world is well rid of him. So perhaps, Frank, we have one thing to thank Mr Hitler for.

On a more serious note, and I don't want to burden you, but we do have to talk about Anna on your return, because I know you will return.

I hope you will be able to speak properly to me then.
Your loving friend,
Florence.

PS Edward and I had tea at the hotel in Marble Arch last week. It was nice to be back there, and I only ever think of you with fond and grateful memories.

When you are home, you must concentrate on Hilda and your children.

Richard spent some time reading that letter. From what he could see, his grandad and Florence had been close. Hilda and Florence hadn't been. Something about the last part of the letter referring to the hotel in Marble Arch jumped out to him. He looked at the photo of Florence again. She'd been a good-looking woman. But then again, so had his grandma Hilda, who had been a true beauty. Beccy had made the comment on more than one occasion that she'd wished she'd inherited her great-grandmother's looks. His mind did a curveball, diving into Beccy's pregnancy. If the baby were a girl, perhaps Hilda's redhead genes would come out in Beccy's offspring. Beccy would love that. He brought his thoughts away from his daughter and a potential granddaughter, and back to Florence and his grandad. Had there been a relationship between the two? Had Frank been unfaithful? Was that the reason his grandparent's marriage had always seemed to him – not that he thought about it too much as a kid, if in truth at all – a little cold. He stared at the photo, the trouser leg and foot that could well belong to Frank. Of course this proved nothing, and Florence had been married. But only until the early sixties, when she'd been widowed, and according to Celia, she'd never remarried.

He sat back and stretched out his own legs, allowing his mind to go into free fall, let that lateral thinking flow.

He'd assumed Anna had been in the institution all of her life, yet here in this photo she was somewhere else, with Florence.

He needed to let it all drift over him.

He pulled out the second envelope. This one from Frank to Hilda.

February 1943 Tripoli, Africa.

Inside he found a newspaper clipping folded into six. Dated January 1946, announcing that Churchill was to receive *The Order of Merit* medal. The clipping must have been placed inside the envelope later than when the letter had been written. There was something else too. Nestled in the corner of the envelope, its ribbon neatly wrapped around the silver medal. Richard took it out and gently unwrapped the dark blue, white and red striped ribbon, holding the medal in the palm of his hand. The tears built. His grandad had never told him, or his own sons. An image of George VI peered at him; he turned the piece of silver over and read the inscription.

For bravery in the field.

He'd always known his grandad to be courageous and despite the mystery of Anna, this only confirmed his assumption. He read the clipping. His grandad had won a medal. Richard knew that despite Frank keeping his medal secret he would have been elated to have received recognition for his part in the war, and that he had received that recognition – as had the man Frank had most admired in the world. Winston Churchill.

Frank had saved clippings all of his life. An avid reader of newspapers, a voracious imbiber of books. Frank. A miner, a bricklayer. A hero. A working-class man who'd never reached for his dreams. Frank had been so proud of him when he'd made it to the Bar. His grandparents had never been well-off enough to help him financially, but they attended his graduation ceremony, and Frank had even come to London (a city he despised) to sit and listen in on his first big case. Richard remembered that evening as if it were yesterday. After court his grandad had taken him to Marble Arch for dinner, said he had good memories of it, probably the only good memories from London. Richard had asked him what had happened at the hotel, realising now that Frank had only mentioned it because his gran wasn't there.

The penny fell. Florence.

He read Frank's letter to Hilda.

March 1943.

Hilda,

I miss your letters, love. Please don't stay cross with me. I might not return and then I really feel you might regret, a bit, not writing to me more often.

I like to hear about Jim and Nick. I miss them, and you.

As you've probably read from the newspapers we have victory over here in this god forsaken desert. Although the men in my unit, including me, respect the Nazi General, Rommel, as much as our own Montgomery. War is a very strange thing, as is life, but we have to make the most of it.

If I could change things, I would, I really would.

I want to tell you something. Winston Churchill came to speak with the troops, and he recognised me, remembered me, from Chartwell. He asked about you, and Florence. I can't believe he remembered, but he did. I think it might be because his daughter,

Mary Churchill, seems to have taken Flo under her wing a bit during this bloody war. It would be nice if you and Florence could stay in touch. As I said in my other letters, Flo knows about Anna, and has been to see her. Flo is your friend, Hilda.

I don't want to rattle you, but have you made time to go see Anna? I know you find it difficult, but for me, could you?

Anyway, I was going to tell you something. I was put forward to receive the Military Medal. It's a long story, but I told my commanding officer that I couldn't take it. I had to explain to Mr Churchill himself too. I need to talk to you about why I wanted to refuse. They say I have been brave, a hero, but I'm not, Hilda. Mr Churchill said I had to take the medal, that to refuse would be an act of disrespect. So I have a medal.

But Hugh Lambert is dead and I should not have a medal.

I have to go now. We have a few days to recover, but then the 7th Armoured Brigade will be on the move. To Italy. Time to sort out that bastard, Mussolini now.

I love you Hilda, and the boys. And Anna.
Your husband,
Frank

Richard rubbed his eyes and swigged from a bottle of water, finishing off a litre, and as he did so his mobile pinged in the sound of a text. He scanned the screen, really expecting it to be Gillian. It was from Nell. All the information he needed on Miss Cunningham. She'd died in 1986. A spinster and had lived with her great-niece for the last five years of her life in Chesterfield. The great-niece still lived there and was alive. A Mrs Fiona Trott. Born 1951. Nell had sent a contact number and address. She also sent an address and contact for a Rosy Magson, née Lambert. Lives in Bodmin, Cornwall with her husband. Both still alive.

Nell had once worked as a civilian for the Metropolitan police. She was a Godsend.

His eye was drawn back to the package wrapped in the brittle tissue paper. Gently, as if he were opening an ancient manuscript he unwrapped it. Three thick books. He took out the top one and laid it on the floor, opened the cover. A dry volume on one of Churchill's relatives. He opened the cover, feeling as if he should have gloves on.

To Frank Cullen,

Enjoy reading, enjoy bricklaying. Remember, the walls we build are not to keep people out but to keep our mind within. The greatest mistakes we make are the mistakes that eventually give meaning to others. It is only for us that the mistake is a true tragedy. Often we are our own wall.

Winston S Churchill

May 1928

He checked the other two books and found no more personal messages, but each one signed by Winston S Churchill. He wrapped them back up and placed them in the box. He knew about Frank's fascination and admiration for Churchill, he knew because occasionally Frank talked about the politician, when he was in the right mood, which had happened more regularly as Richard moved towards adulthood. His dad had told him that over the years and as Frank became more involved in the unions, Frank talked less about a man who was seen by most miners as the devil himself. An anachronistic aristocratic Tory. After the winter of discontent his grandad ceased mentioning Churchill at all. His trade union friends up until then had indulged him, his dad had said, but this goodwill ran out in the bleakness of the 1970s. Richard gazed at the box. The incongruity of his grandad's life tucked through him.

He made his way downstairs and flicked the kettle on for tea, deciding to forgo the whisky. Would Fiona Trott have kept the correspondence that Miss Cunningham might have been in possession of? Suddenly he thought that maybe it *had* been sent onto Frank, and was still undiscovered in the other boxes. He trekked back upstairs, had another look, but found no such letter.

What he did find was a letter addressed to Frank, from Chartwell. 1953, written by Clementine Churchill's secretary.

She thanked Frank for spending some quality time with Sir Winston, and would like to thank him in advance for his discretion "concerning our Prime Minister."

Richard did a double take at this and checked the date again. 1953. During Churchill's second term of office as Prime Minister. He scrabbled around his memory. That would be the summer of Churchill's *secret*. The information about this had only become public in the mid-eighties, but it seemed his grandad Frank had known about Churchill's stroke long before that. Of course he had. Richard grinned, remembering witnessing the trade union get-togethers at Frank and Hilda's house in the late seventies. By then Frank's connection to Churchill had been well hidden.

158

He returned to the kitchen and called his parents' home.

'Dad, can I use your car?'

'Course you can, son. Where you off to?'

'I'm starting with Jemima.'

'Better call the hotel first, make sure she's not out and about. A sprightly thing, is Jem,' his dad said down the phone but Richard could see him frowning, rubbing his scar. 'Do you want me to come with you?'

'No, better alone I think.'

'Let me know what happens.'

'Will do,' Richard said.

'I'll bring the car over, son.'

'Okay.'

He called Jemima's hotel. The receptionist put him through to her room.

'Richard Cullen?' she asked. Her voice's tone didn't hint at any surprise at his call.

'Could I come over for a chat?'

'Of course. If you want to hear what I have to say. By all means. Please come.'

'I'll be there in an hour.'

His dad brought the car. Richard dropped him off back at home. 'Let's keep this to ourselves, Dad?'

'Yes. For now.'

19

Frank

October 2nd 1938

The Nottinghamshire Post

Winston Churchill's Speech In The House of Commons:

Summary Of The Munich Agreement

"…We are in the presence of a disaster of the first magnitude which has befallen Great Britain and France. Do not let us blind ourselves to that.

… And do not suppose that this is the end. This is only the beginning of the reckoning. This is only the first sip, the first foretaste of a bitter cup which will be proffered to us year by year unless by a supreme recovery of moral health and martial vigour, we arise again and take our stand for freedom as in the olden time…"

Frank stared at the wall of the Wendy house. *How had it come to this?* It had been a disastrous year for Europe, although a good one for him and Hilda, he'd thought. It had been whilst Anna was on her visit to Westerham in March when Hilda had told him she was expecting again. He hadn't hoped for the best with another pregnancy, but Hilda had managed to carry the baby through the danger period and now was only a month away from her due date. He admitted to himself that the bliss he and Hilda were experiencing had blinded him to Anna's low mood, a mood that had worsened since her early return from Westerham.

His gaze dropped to the newspaper. Ten years since they'd moved to Nottinghamshire. In many ways so little had happened in that time, although today, everything had happened. Frank's eyes swept over the small space. Without the little table and chairs it seemed so empty.

When Anna had appeared at the gate of the allotment he'd known something was wrong. At first he thought it was to do with Hilda and her pregnancy, but soon found out that it was nothing to do with his wife; and yet everything to do with her. He wanted to comfort Anna, make her feel better. He told her to go and sit inside the Wendy house, and then he'd gone back and put a damp cloth over the concrete he'd mixed for the foundation of his new wall. Returning, he took out the table and two small chairs, and made his way inside, to be with her. He held her close. When the pain came he tried to tell her it was normal. He'd done everything he could to ease her discomfort.

Frank stared at the little door, and as if he were drunk, it elongated and stretched. Blurred. He rubbed his eyes. He hadn't touched a drop of alcohol since the Hugh pit incident. He didn't want to end up like his father.

Although today he knew he'd turned out worse.

Leaning back he tried to calm himself. He attempted to stretch out a leg but despite having taken out the furniture, the Wendy house he'd built was much smaller than Winston Churchill's. He could barely move. God knows how he and Anna had managed earlier.

As Winston Churchill's children had grown out of their father's indulgence, so Anna had grown out of her father's. At fifteen she only came down to pick up the fruit and veg to take back to Hilda. These days she hardly ever went inside. He threw the newspaper onto the floor and rubbed his hands together violently.

Cramped, he picked up the bottle of water Anna had forgotten to take home with her to refill; of course she'd forgotten. She'd remembered to take the beetroot though, so that was good. He'd told her things needed to look as normal as possible. The hot sweat he'd worked up clearing things, the mess, the blood, had become cold and sticky. He swigged the dregs of water, and again allowed his eyes to take in the small space. Cleaner than it had been for years. He'd made sure he'd done a good job.

Frank's thoughts were interrupted by the high-pitched tone of whistling that he recognised immediately. It was Hugh, who had an allotment two patches away from his – it was his dad's allotment, although Rod had died four years ago of an unexpected heart attack. Frank still didn't like Hugh. After the accident at the pit they'd fallen into a few months of laboured friendship but it hadn't lasted long. Only last week Max Betts had told him that Hugh, after too many pints, had been bad-mouthing Hilda in the pub, telling everyone who'd listen that Hilda didn't look after Anna properly. Frank hadn't said anything to the little bastard yet; he'd been biding his time.

But now this. He didn't want to get into the Hilda thing now. Not now. He needed to get rid of Hugh and get on. Thank God Hugh hadn't turned up earlier.

Hugh poked his head inside. 'What the hell you doing in there, Frank?'

'Having a rest, what does it look like?'

'Looks like you've been doing some spring cleaning.'

'You got nothing better to do?'

'I saw Anna on her way back home. Upset, she looked.'

'Anna's fine. Keep your nose out.'

'You and Hilda should keep an eye on Anna.'

Frank peered at him and didn't answer. He shouldn't involve himself in conversation. Get rid of Hugh as soon as possible.

Hugh carried on, 'She's on her own too much in the village, that's what Rosy says. Like I said, you and Hilda should keep an eye on her. I'm trying to do you a favour, Frank. You should know what's going on.'

Hating himself for replying Frank asked, 'What d'ya mean?'

'What I say. The quiet ones, and all that.' He spat out the tobacco he was chewing. 'Get my meaning?' Frank did get his meaning. Hugh peered around the little building. 'You taken the table and chairs out?'

He must have had a nose around at some point, Frank didn't know how because as Winston Churchill had done with his *Marycot*, Frank had installed a proper lock too. He'd wanted it to be as much like the great man's building as he could make it. Anna had loved having her own key. But she was a child no longer.

'None of your bloody business,' Frank finally grunted in reply.

'You're a grumpy bastard.' Hugh moved his face away.

Frank suspected Hugh was looking at the wall he was halfway through building on the west side of his patch. The pulse in his neck quickened and despite the temperature hot sweat trickled in between the crevices of his curved spine. He had the greatest desire to punch Hugh for turning up now and getting in the way. It took all his willpower to not strike out at him and hold onto his temper.

Hugh's face appeared again. Red and bloated for someone so young. He was a heavy drinker like Frank's dad.

'You shouldn't be building walls on here,' Hugh said. 'What you doing, trying to keep everyone out? Bloody walls and kids' buildings.'

Frank heaved himself out from the small house and stood up tall, the newspaper crunching within the tightening fist of his hand. Hugh shrank away from him. Hugh Lambert wouldn't be signing up for a would-be war with Hitler, not that Hugh Lambert would know anything about what had happened at Munich. The miner didn't read newspapers.

'I think you should just go and start your work.' Frank's tone was measured, controlled, and not how he felt.

Hugh huffed but turned quickly making his way towards his own allotment.

Frank stooped down and returned to the small space. He smoothed out the newspaper and his eyes dropped to the words again.

Winston Churchill was predicting war in Europe.

He uncurled himself and leaving the Wendy house made his way to the unfinished wall he was building. He uncovered the concrete, gave it a stir and placed the cloth back on top of the metal bucket. Partly filling in the hole with earth, he trod it firm and then poured the concrete on top to form the wall's extended foundation.

Later, another day when it had set, he'd begin to lay the bricks.

20

The next day
3rd October 1938

The Daily Mirror

Churchill Applauds Cooper's Resignation.

Chamberlain Wrong To Appease Hitler

Mr Duff Cooper has made a speech to the House of Commons explaining his reason for resigning as First Lord of the Admiralty.
Cooper has always opposed Neville Chamberlain's appeasement policy.
Privately, Cooper has voiced the opinion that the Munich Agreement is "meaningless, cowardly, and unworkable."
Mr Churchill applauded his decision.

Trying to distract himself with the world's news and away from the confusion of the day before, and still reading the paper, Frank stepped through the door into the kitchen. How could anyone think the Munich Agreement was a good idea? There were reports coming out of Germany that Hitler was now confiscating Jewish land and property. *Redistributing.* Most blokes at work refused to believe a war was imminent. He was at a loss with both their and Chamberlain's narrow-mindedness, as he was at a loss as to what had happened the previous day in the allotment.

His first thought after it had happened was to call the police, that was what he'd been going to do – tell someone – but Anna had become hysterical, saying she wanted no one to know, especially Hilda. He'd thought of Hilda and her extended eight-month stomach and convinced himself telling her would cause a problem with this much-wanted pregnancy. And that would destroy Hilda, and him. And Anna was adamant for them to say nothing. So he hadn't.

He was later home than he'd anticipated, the gaffer at the pit had asked him to do overtime, an extra night shift, and there was no question they could do with the money, more so than usual as Hilda had stopped taking in the washing. He peered at the clock. Just after 7 a.m., and then at the dish Miss Cunningham had given them when they'd got married. It had a huge chip on the side and was why the sky-blue bowl had found its way from Chartwell's kitchen to the Cullens'. The beetroot it held was what Anna had brought home yesterday from the allotment. Wetness covered the skin on his back and he wiped away the moisture forming at his hairline. The offer of an extra shift couldn't have come at a better time. He needed to be away from home to try and gather himself, but on the other hand guilt devoured him because he hadn't been around for Anna.

This should have been a special time in the household, but after yesterday his delicate contentment had evaporated and as he'd worked all night in the pit's bowels he'd tried to work out how best to deal with it.

Hilda came into the kitchen just as he was taking his coat off. 'You're a bit late. You must be starving.'

He glanced at her huge stomach and the look of fulfilment nestling precariously on her face. 'I'm not that hungry, to be honest.' He kissed her on the cheek. 'How you feeling?'

'Really good.' Her face shone with an understated happiness and his gut puckered a bit more.

'Anna at school?' he asked as lightly as he was able.

'No, she's upstairs.'

'She all right?'

'No, she's not.'

The pain in his belly became sharper. 'What's wrong?'

'Nothing serious, Frank. Stop worrying. She's come down with something, that's all, so I told her to take the day off.' She scrutinised his face as if gauging his reaction. For once Hilda's disinterest regarding Anna was a blessing. 'Everything'll work out,' she said.

He touched her stomach and tried to smile. It was as if she knew. She couldn't know, not unless Anna had said something, but Anna couldn't have said anything to her mother. Hilda wouldn't be this calm if she had.

'The baby's been moving today,' she said. 'With the grace of God, and no upsets, this pregnancy will be fruitful.'

They were having another child and everything was going to be fine, but the mention of God and His grace brought another wave of pain inside Frank's stomach. 'It's got nothing to do with God—'

'Don't speak about the Lord in that way. You know I don't like it.' She pushed inferno-red curls behind her ears, but Frank saw the hint of a smile and finally allowed himself to relax a little.

She went to the stove to check on what he could make out as stew. She placed the bowl of beetroot on the table and then added some vinegar. Just the way he liked it.

'Perhaps Anna's got flu. It's going around,' he said.

'Perhaps.'

'I'll go up and see if she's all right.'

'Your breakfast's ready. Leave her be.' She rubbed her stomach. 'Everything's going to be fine now.'

'Yes.' Thoughts of Anna and his wall preoccupied him. He grappled around inside his head trying to find a subject not connected with domestic things. 'It's not looking good in Germany, with Hitler.'

'Women in the village say that if war comes the miners won't have to go.'

'You know that if war comes I have to go.'

'You don't have to.'

They both looked up at the rattle of the door that opened up to the stairs.

Anna seemed to float into the tiny front room. He was sitting at the table and as always in the middle of the week only one leaf was put up. He took in his food, the sick feeling rising into his gullet.

Anna moved towards him and his heart missed its rhythm. She was as pale as winter, and even whiter than she'd been the day before on leaving the allotment. She didn't seem to see him, or her mother.

Hilda felt at her daughter's forehead. 'You don't have a temperature. I've no idea what's come over you.' She said it matter-of-factly, even for Hilda.

Frank pushed his plate away, untouched. 'She needs to rest.' He looked at Anna, who stared past him. He got up and putting his arm around her led her back to the stairs. 'Come on, love. Back to bed.' She shook off his grip.

Hilda sighed and took over, taking hold of Anna's arm. 'Come on, young lady. Less of this. I've enough on my plate.'

Anna's face was blank, unseeing, but then she grabbed her mother's arm with a force that took Frank by surprise. He managed to summon up some normality of speech, gently pulling Anna away. 'Anna, calm down. Your mother's pregnant. Be careful, love—' He shouldn't have said that.

Anna thrust him away with violence which shocked him, and then looked at her mother, not uttering a word.

Hilda recovered quickly. 'You need to rest, Anna. Go back to bed and I'll bring you breakfast up in a minute.' She guided Anna towards the stairs.

In a moment, which both Frank and Hilda missed, and with a potent and unexpected force, Anna pushed Hilda hard. Frank was never sure afterwards if it was by mistake or on purpose. Hilda tripped on the edge of the hearth, seemed to teeter and then fell, landing hard on her back, crashing into the fireplace.

Frank took hold of his daughter, moving her away from Hilda, although already she was docile again. 'Anna, my God, stop it, what the hell are you doing?' He knelt down beside his wife, blood on her temple where her head had struck the mantelpiece. 'Are you all right?' he asked in a whisper. 'Here take my arm.'

'I can't move. Pain in my stomach… the baby…'

He glanced up at Anna who hadn't moved.

For a long moment Anna focussed on him and appeared to come back from a place no one would willingly go. She shook her head, still peering at him but her face vacant.

Hilda had begun to cry and with her red hair torn free she said in a whisper. 'Frank, get her away from me.'

Anna stood as a statue watching her mother. Frank still kneeling beside Hilda. His daughter stared through him and slowly walked to the table. She sat down, placed her elbows on its surface, then took Frank's knife and fork, dragging the plate of stew, as well as the bowl of beetroot, towards her.

Anna began to eat as her mother began to haemorrhage.

21

'The beetroot's very good this year, isn't it, Dad?' Anna's voice was level, flat.

Frank held Hilda's hand and looked up at his daughter. Something had happened to her mind, and Christ, he wasn't surprised. He wanted to tell Anna that everything was going to be all right. But then he looked at Hilda, her eyes glazed over, barely conscious. He had to get the doctor. Anna would be no good to go and get help and he couldn't leave her here alone with Hilda. God knows what would happen. He made his decision quickly.

Without saying a word, carefully he pushed a cushion underneath Hilda's head. 'I won't be long, love. I'm going to get the midwife.'

She opened her eyes, and pulled at the arm of his sleeve. 'Don't leave me with her, Frank, not with Anna.'

How had it come to this? 'I'm going to put Anna upstairs in her bedroom. Don't worry.'

'Lock her in. The devil's inside her,' she whispered.

He had no intention of locking Anna in her bedroom. 'It was an accident. Anna didn't mean to hurt you. You'll be fine. I won't be long.'

'My baby, she's killed my baby…' Tears trickled slowly down his wife's cheeks.

'Shush, the baby's fine.' He was getting good at lying. And as if he were floating above, with horror he examined the scene below. Him, Hilda, Anna. An unborn baby. And the other baby, on the periphery.

He was certain his and Hilda's baby was not fine. If this had occurred in any other way he'd have let the grief and disappointment engulf him, but Anna's actions had shocked him and he knew they were directly related to the day before, and what he'd done, and what Anna had asked him to do. Keep the secret.

Her mother bleeding and all Anna did was to carry on eating. The sweat on his back and underneath his armpits cooled, becoming glutinous. The irony of the situation was eating into him like the causticity of the substance he used to get rid of cement from his clothes. He wished there was a chemical to rub this thing away, and off his soul.

All night on the coalface he'd worked through this feeling and for once had been glad to be a hundred feet under the ground, coal dust clogging up his throat. During his backbreaking shift he'd managed to forget for a few moments, hacking so hard at the seam of black gold that by the end of his stint he'd mined more coal in one session than ever before.

He moved towards the table and Anna didn't even glance up. She squashed a piece of beetroot with her fork and pushed it to the edge of the plate, sliding it off the side and onto the lace tablecloth.

Finally she said to Frank. 'Anna's dead.'

He bent forwards and put his lips near to her ear. 'Anna, perhaps we should tell your mum?' He tried to find her eyes, but she'd turned away. 'I'm so sorry love—'

'No. Don't tell. Promise me, swear,' she whispered back. 'She'll hate me even more.'

'Is that why you hurt your mum?' Frank had his own thoughts about why Anna had hurt her.

'I'm Marigold now.'

In a hushed tone so as Hilda couldn't hear: 'Anna's not dead, love. It's Marigold who is… and your—'

'I'm forever blowing…'

'Anna, stop. Come on, let me take you to your bedroom, have a lie down.' He thought she'd protest, but docile, like an animal, she rose, not looking once at her mother. 'Quickly,' he said, hearing the desperation in his own voice.

Once upstairs he opened the bedroom door and ensured she was sitting on her bed before leaving. Her coat was pegged up on the back of her door. For quickness he pulled it off so as he could wrap it around Hilda before he left the house. It was the coat Anna had worn yesterday on her visit to the allotment. Flecks of blood covered its hem and he remembered her pain. He turned, closed the door as quietly as he could, and despising himself, turned the key.

Walking downstairs he made to place the key in the pocket of Anna's coat, and as he emerged at the bottom of the stairway, but before he opened the door into the front room, he felt in the pocket and pulled out what he'd touched inside. As he yanked out the handkerchief, the smell of tobacco hit him. A unique smell, stronger than the brand many of the lads at the pit used.

Apart from one lad. Frank pushed the tobacco in his own pocket.

He went to check that Hilda was still conscious. She was. He placed Anna's coat over her, telling her that

Anna's bedroom key was in the coat pocket. Hilda lay on her back, eyes closed. 'See you in a bit, love,' he said.

She made no response.

The midwife didn't live on The Avenues. It was a fifteen-minute walk. He sprinted and was there within five. She had her coat on within seconds. Frank bolted back home, and the midwife arrived twenty minutes later. She'd called in at the doctor's house on the way.

When Frank returned he could hear Anna banging on her bedroom door. Hilda hadn't moved. The midwife came in and took over.

'Is that Anna upstairs?' she asked.

He nodded. 'She wasn't herself. I had to lock her in her bedroom when I came to get you.'

The midwife nodded but said no more about Anna. 'Hilda's not good. The doctor'll be here soon. We'll have to take her to the infirmary.'

'Will the baby be all right… will Hilda be all right?'

'What happened, did anything cause this?' She glanced to the ceiling.

Frank only hesitated a second. 'Anna pushed Hilda and Hilda fell into the fireplace. It was an accident.' And it was an accident. His whole life was shattering in fast and defined moments. He wished Flo were here. He needed someone to talk to. He hadn't seen Flo for an age.

The doctor knocked on the open kitchen door and entered without invite.

'What has occurred, and how long ago?' he asked. He was a short man, bald head. A man of few words was Dr James Faversham, not from these parts, from nearer to where Frank and Hilda, and Flo, had been born. This fact endeared the Cullens to the doctor to a level not enjoyed by many in the village.

'About half an hour ago. Hilda lost her footing and fell into the fireplace,' Frank replied. 'Are she and the baby going to be all right, doctor?'

'My car's outside. We need to get Mrs Cullen to the infirmary.' He looked at his watch and ignored Frank's question. 'My wife is holding one of her luncheons today. She would like me to get back for it.'

Panic was a rising storm tide inside him. Why was the doctor talking about luncheons? 'Hilda's not going to lose the baby, is she, doctor?' he asked.

'I hope not.' The doctor spoke directly to the midwife. 'You may go home and get ready for your shift at the infirmary, I hear it's a busy time. I'll handle this, Mrs Lucas. I plan to stay at the hospital with Mrs Cullen. Could you please let my wife know and give her my apologies?' He then addressed Frank. 'Please, I need to examine Hilda, you may want to leave the room.' He paused. 'What is the noise upstairs? Is that Anna? Isn't she at school?'

'She's poorly, having the day off.'

The doctor made no more enquiries, too preoccupied to question the quiet wails echoing through the ceiling.

The midwife took herself to the door that led to the staircase. 'I'll go and see what's troubling your daughter, Mr Cullen.'

He pulled away the coat he'd placed over Hilda earlier and found the key from its pocket. 'I locked her bedroom door.' He handed it to Mrs Lucas. 'Please could you stay with Anna for a bit?'

'I'm afraid I have to be at the infirmary,' she said. 'Anna'll be all right at home. She's fifteen, soon be starting work, for goodness' sakes.'

'She's not well—'

'I'll give her some aspirin, Mr Cullen.'

'I can't leave her, and I have to go with Hilda,' he replied.

The doctor interrupted, his face too grim. 'Frank should accompany us.'

Mrs Lucas nodded whilst looking at Hilda. Her expression, together with the doctor's, told him what he didn't want to know. It was all his fault. Everything.

'I'll go and get one of the Lamberts to sit with Anna. That's all I can do,' she said softly.

'No!' he shouted. He took hold of the midwife's arm and said more quietly 'I'll be back as soon as I can. Please stay with Anna.'

'Mrs Lucas, stay and see to Anna,' Dr Faversham said, his tone pragmatic. 'I'll explain to Matron that you'll arrive at the infirmary later than expected. Please, we have more important matters to deal with.' He glanced at Frank, 'Go and make tea or something while I examine Mrs Cullen.'

In confusion Frank did as he was told and five minutes later Dr Faversham came into the kitchen holding Hilda upright. Frank abandoned the tea.

'Come on, Frank, time to go,' the doctor said, his face ashen and drawn. Hilda's even more so.

Frank took his wife's other arm. 'C'mon, love.'

As they stepped outside into sheets of rain, Mrs Lucas came to the kitchen door. 'I'll stay with Anna.

She's not good. I think she needs to see a doctor too. But don't worry about her, I'll look after her.'

Feeling the cold dashes of rain, like razor slices on his face, he glanced first at James Faversham then at Mrs Lucas. 'I'll get back as soon as I can.' He tried not to think about the next few hours.

Mrs Lucas nodded but Frank and the doctor were already opening the gate and making their way through, with Hilda propped up between them, heading to the doctor's car.

Frank saw the neighbours' curtains fluttering and was relieved it was only Mrs Lucas who'd witnessed his daughter's madness.

Despite the drama of James Cullen's entry into the world, Frank's son slipped from his mother's womb without any of what Frank's mother would call 'theatre'. He slithered onto the back seat of Dr Faversham's car with ease and confidence, which would mark Frank's firstborn's character, and many years later, his first and only grandson's character too.

Through the heartache of that morning the thing that stuck the most in Frank's mind was the doctor saying the F-word under his breath as he stopped the car only at the top of The Avenues as Hilda shouted that her baby was coming. The *fuck* was directed at the fact it was Frank who'd accompanied them and not the midwife, although Dr James Faversham did a wonderful job cutting the cord in the back of the car and even managed not to get too worked up about the blood saturating his brown leather seats.

These were the things on which Frank focussed, instead of thinking the unthinkable of losing his baby, or his wife. Or both.

Frank held his red and wrinkled new born, and as his child took its first breath in a world that he was coming to believe he didn't understand, a clear image of Anna as a baby stabbed at his mind. He thought about the secret she'd instructed him to hold tight and his mind was overtaken with a thick fog. He thought too about his old employer, about another time when he'd witnessed the interactions between Winston Churchill and his children. Often Mr Churchill wasn't the best father but he'd always been a loving one. Frank had seen that, heard about it from Miss Cunningham. Randolph was the biggest disappointment to his father, but Frank recognised the solid love Churchill held for his son. He'd seen the devotion and care the old man had put into the building of his *Marycot* for his children.

The same as Frank had put in for Anna and her Wendy house.

But deep within the fabric of who he was Frank saw the love, which had been growing within him as he'd watched Hilda's belly expand these past eight months, reaching its crescendo as he helped deliver his son. It was of a different calibre than his love for Anna. And because of the unravelling of events in the past thirty-six hours, and despite the adoration and amazement that oozed from every pore of his body for both his wife and son, he disliked himself. He saw more of his father in him than he wanted to see and less of the man who he'd revered for the past ten years at Chartwell.

He peered at the walnut face of his child, at the thatch of black hair, and told himself that everything would be all right. And he tried not to think about the other baby.

The atheist-minded Frank made a deal with Hilda's God: if Hilda and the baby survived he would tell his wife everything. *Dear God, it's my promise to you.*

Dr Faversham wrapped the baby up in the blanket he kept in the back of the car and checked Hilda's pulse. 'It's as steady as can be expected but we need to go. She's dropped away from it all a little. Make sure Hilda's head is supported, and keep the baby warm.'

Again, Frank did exactly as he was told. He held the baby tight and named him there and then: James, after the doctor, although Frank was only ever to call James Jim.

He loved Jim immediately. If someone had asked him to gouge his eyes out to save his son, he would have done so with no hesitation. As the doctor drove to the infirmary, more like a racing car driver than any staid pillar of the community, and as Frank held Jim tight, he allowed himself to think of Anna. Did he love Anna this much? He did, but the sum of his love for Hilda and Jim was greater than the individual: that's what he told himself.

And how he explained it to Mr Churchill five years later in an African desert.

Hilda nearly lost her life that wet and slate grey day in 1938. Frank truly believed she did not, purely because of the love flowing from her for her new son; love like an age-old stream running through ancient rocks. He thought then of writing to Flo, asking for her advice, even asking her to come and visit, so as he could tell her everything, confide in her, as he'd always done. But something stopped him and he knew what it was: on Flo's first visit, all the way back in late 1932, was when she had met a young Hugh. What age would Hugh have been then? Fifteen, sixteen perhaps. Flo had been concerned about Hugh, about him being in such close contact with Anna. But Frank had shrugged off her concerns, or pretended to, because he'd mostly agreed with her. But Hilda had chosen to see no problem with either Hugh or his family and at that time Frank hadn't wanted to aggravate Hilda. He'd known Flo had wanted to talk to him about Anna, and with shame, he admitted to himself, he'd avoided the conversation as much as he could. He'd ignored her concerns (even though they echoed his own – always so difficult when you know someone is right), so now he felt as if he couldn't go to her. That was why he could not contact Flo and confide in her.

A long time ago Mr Churchill had said that everyone needed a friend they could trust. Churchill had trusted Brendan Bracken, and perhaps not so much, Beaverbrook. Frank trusted Flo but couldn't spill his guts to her, not now. He could only confide in someone on the periphery of his life about what had happened, and like Churchill, he had to be selective in the friends he spoke to. Sometimes, like Churchill with Beaverbrook, it was better to seek counsel with the one you are not close to, or don't even properly know. Someone you've admired from afar, someone who holds your respect, even if sometimes that person has done things they are not proud of; a flawed person. As the seeker of solace knows himself to be too. To reveal yourself to another who shows similar character blemishes is an appetising route to travel in the quest for redemption and forgiveness.

As Frank sat with Hilda in the infirmary, a part of him wanted to leave and go comfort Anna, the other part not wanting to abandon his new son and wife. Frank deluded himself with the fantasy that by the time he returned home Anna would be back to her old self. But he knew this wouldn't be so and wondered how he was going to handle it. To come clean. Tell the truth. That was his deal but already he'd floundered on his promise.

It was what he should have done but he did not.

He did not tell Hilda because he'd sworn to Anna he would not.

And not delivering on his part of the bargain with God for the rest of his life Frank bore the price of his duplicity.

22

Frank stayed with Hilda all night at the hospital, although the matron would rather he hadn't. Dr Faversham's favouritism of him though, made it so it wasn't a problem. The bigger problem was Anna. Mrs Lucas had ended up staying the whole day with her, telling Frank afterwards she couldn't leave, and leave she didn't, making her bed on the Cullens' settee. He had no idea how he'd ever repay her.

When he arrived back to a home that seemed empty without his wife and the eternal smell of drying laundry, Mrs Lucas was in the kitchen preparing herself some dinner. He wondered how she'd managed to find anything in the spartan larder.

'Frank, you're back. Dr Faversham came earlier and told me the baby and Hilda will pull through. How are you, love?' Mrs Lucas wasn't the midwife now but a concerned villager.

'Hilda's very ill. But the surgeon says her womb isn't ruptured, the blood was coming from the placenta. Miraculously the baby's well, a whopping six pounds and two ounces. Big for a premature baby, the midwife on duty said. It's a boy.'

Mrs Lucas turned away from the carrot she was chopping. 'That is big. I'm so pleased. Little boy, lovely. What've you named him?'

'James… after the doctor. I owe Dr Faversham everything. But I'm already calling him Jim. Hilda agreed to the name. But it was my idea,' he finished, as if it being his idea was important.

'The doctor'll like that.' She took in the small kitchen. 'I had to make myself a bit at home—'

'I don't know how to thank you.' He tilted his head to the ceiling. 'How's Anna?'

'She's calm now, but won't speak. Not eating.'

'Is she in her bedroom?'

'Curled up on the settee. I got up and she came downstairs and took my place.' She tried to smile.

'I'll go in and see her.'

She found his eyes. 'What's happened, Frank? Was there a reason Anna pushed her mum?'

'She didn't mean to hurt Hilda, or the baby.'

'No, but Anna's unusually upset. I've tried to tell her that it's not her fault. It does seem an extreme reaction.'

'Anna'll be all right. She's in shock.'

'Perhaps, but she's always been such a sensible girl.' She lapsed into quietness and then carried on, saying gently, 'I've asked Dr Faversham to come around later to examine Anna. Maybe suggest some medication he might be able to give.' She paused. 'He might decide that Anna should be admitted… if she doesn't change, just on a temporary basis.'

'What do you mean, "admitted"?'

'Hilda'll be coming home with the baby in a few weeks, if all goes well, and I know it will. If Anna stays like this, how on earth are you and Hilda going to cope? I'm sorry to bring this to light, but I'm thinking ahead.'

'Everything's just got too much for Anna. She finishes school soon and has been worried about what she's going to do. Her and Hilda have been arguing. Hilda wants her to help with the laundry. Anna has other ideas.'

'What does Anna want to do?'

'She wants to be a nurse, a midwife, but Hilda's dead against it.'

'Why?'

'Says we can't afford it.'

Mrs Lucas remained quiet for seconds, but then said, 'I could have helped you. I could have helped Anna.'

'Get her into nursing you mean?'

'Yes. Anna's a sensible girl. Perfect for the vocation of nursing.' She edged her eyes to the front room and then studied the worn lino of the kitchen floor.

Not now, though, was what she was thinking. He wanted to tell Mrs Lucas everything. He'd promised himself and Hilda's God he'd tell the truth. He hoped to an elusive God he'd be a better father to Jim than he'd been to Anna.

He shared none of this with Mrs Lucas but said instead, 'I'll go and see Anna. Does she know Hilda's well and… about the baby?'

'I haven't said anything. Best not to, I think, at this stage.'

'Shall I say anything?'

'I'd say not. Give her a cuddle. Tell her another day.'

He walked through to the front room where Anna lay on the settee, on her back, with her eyes open, looking upward, towards the grey ceiling that needed a layer of paint. The coat he'd retrieved from her bedroom to place over Hilda lay over her, as a blanket. It was bloody cold in there, especially after being in the hospital where the heat at times through the night felt as if it were suffocating him. The coat reminded him about the tobacco he'd found inside the pocket.

'Anna, love. How are you? Mrs Lucas says you're feeling a bit better?'

She made no sound; her only reaction was to close her eyes.

He perched on the side of the settee next to her. 'Talk to me, love.'

She pulled up her knees, making herself into a ball. Frank swore she'd lost weight overnight.

'Tell me.'

Silence.

'Tell me about Hugh, Anna.'

She stared through him.

'Love, how do you feel? They'll be missing you at school.' He thought about what he'd just told Mrs Lucas about the nursing. 'You need to finish school properly so that you can go and do the training to be a nurse. That's what you always wanted to do, isn't it, love?'

She opened her eyes. '*I'm forever blowing…*'

'Anna, stop it.'

'Their little girl was ignored and she died. Marigold, that was her name, wasn't it, Frank?'

'The Churchills' daughter? She died because she had a throat infection. That's why Marigold died.' He ignored that she had called him Frank. She hadn't called him by his first name since Westerham. 'I'm your dad, Anna, and I love you.'

She closed her eyes.

'Anna. We have to tell your mother. Let me tell her.'

'No. Never. Marigold says no. Please. Swear?'

'Marigold's dead, love… as is—'

'Marigold's back. She says not to tell what happened. Swear again you won't. Hilda will be mad. She's always mad about everything. She knows.'

'Knows what, love?'

'Knows Marigold's come back.' She stared at Frank. A captured animal. 'Swear you won't tell her.'

'I swear, love, I won't say a thing. Just you get better.'

He stood and looked at his watch, calculating what shift Hugh Lambert was on. Nights, he worked out. It was just after lunch and Hugh would be at his allotment. 'I love you very much, Anna.' He swallowed. 'I'll make everything all right.'

She didn't answer.

When he returned to the kitchen Dr Faversham had appeared.

'How's Hilda and the baby?' Frank asked.

'Both doing well.' He glanced at Mrs Lucas. 'I'm here to examine Anna. Mrs Lucas here says she isn't well at all. I've arranged for another nurse to come and take over from Mrs Lucas, who really needs to get some proper rest and resume her work at the infirmary. Come outside a moment, Frank.'

They stepped into the yard.

The doctor carried on, 'I need to assess Anna.' He took a breath, coughed. 'But if I see fit, I believe it might be prudent to admit Anna for a short time to High Royal.'

'High Royal? The asylum?'

'A mental hospital.'

'Anna's not mad. You know her and Hilda's history. It's been hard for Anna.'

'And it looks as if it may become harder for her. Come, it's freezing, let's go back inside.' As they entered the kitchen he addressed Mrs Lucas. 'Can you give us a moment?'

'Of course.' Mrs Lucas herself made her way outside and disappeared into the toilet situated in the Cullens' front yard.

'Frank, is there anything I should know? Anything that's happened recently that could have caused this change in Anna? I know she'll feel guilty about causing an early labour in her mother, but this reaction is extreme.'

This was Frank's opening, his chance. 'No, there's nothing more to know.'

'Give me an hour with Anna.'

As Frank shrugged he heard a quiet knock on the door and then it opened.

'Ah, Nurse Dawkins, good timing,' Dr Faversham said to the woman standing in the doorway. 'Mrs Lucas is just—'

'Yes, I know. I've seen her,' Nurse Dawkins said.

'Frank, this is Alma Dawkins and she'll be staying with Anna for a while. Put your mind at rest.'

Alma Dawkins held out a gloved hand to Frank. 'Hello Mr Cullen. Congratulations are in order, I believe?'

'Yes, they are. Thank you for coming.' Glancing at the doctor, he said, 'I'm off for a bit then.'

'Yes, you go and do something to take your mind off things. Anna's in capable hands,' the doctor said kindly.

Frank made his way to the gate. Any hands were better than his.

He walked quickly down the fourth avenue, towards the alleyway that led directly to the allotments. He slowed his pace, allowing the dankness to wash over him. Despite having saved Hugh Lambert's life, he didn't trust him. But he'd always liked Maisie; she'd been the main and driving reason he didn't want Hugh to die on the pit face. And in truth it had come second nature to save the skin of a workmate. The thought had only crossed his mind for a moment not to help, but as everyone had told him afterwards if he hadn't Hugh Lambert might well have died. As he walked past his own allotment Frank wished dearly he hadn't bothered.

Hugh was turning the soil with his fork when Frank arrived and hadn't noticed he had a visitor. Frank watched him lay the fork up against the wire fencing and pull out his tobacco. He was tall, some said he was a good-looking bloke, but he'd always seen Hugh as too pretty and too rounded for a man. Although twenty-four, he still had some filling out and hardening up to do. Although his gob had been fully formed for years.

Frank walked towards him, slowly, and was outwardly relaxed, although the familiar knotting inside his stomach engulfed him.

Hugh tipped his head. 'Frank—'

Frank leapt forwards, and so adeptly that Hugh had no time to clock what was happening. He punched Hugh in the face and heard the crunching of his nose. Blood flowed and in shock Hugh made no move apart from holding a shaking hand to his face.

And then as if time had slowed and realising what had happened Hugh said: 'What the fuck… '

Frank stepped away, giving himself room. He then lifted his leg high and kicked Hugh hard in the stomach. Hugh fell onto his knees. He tried to speak, Frank saw that, but no words came from his mouth. Frank hadn't said a thing and didn't intend to. He moved in again, punching Hugh again, but harder this time, finding his target to the side of his nose. More blood as the skin above his eye split wide open. Frank pulled back, got ready and punched again, and again. And again. Hugh was on the hard ground, he'd collapsed onto the fork that had fallen away from the fence, a prong poked into his cheek, and more blood. Hugh was motionless but moaning, lying flat on his back, his left arm held to his face.

Frank lifted his right leg, waited a moment, waited for Hugh to say something. Silence apart from Hugh's low-grade murmur of pain. With all the strength he could gather, and thinking of Anna, of Hilda, his new son, he stamped down hard on Hugh's shoulder. He knew from the angle of Hugh's arm, and the force and velocity of his own foot, that he'd break the bastard's limb. The same arm broken during the accident at the pit. He could almost envisage the line of Hugh's healed bone snapping for a second time and as he heard Hugh's unearthly wail he knew this was so. Feeling as if a force had taken him over, Frank picked up the garden fork by its prongs and belted Hugh twice more with the wooden handle.

Hugh didn't look very pretty now.

Frank was making to turn away when Hugh finally spoke, his voice cracked, a whisper. 'Is this about what I've said about Hilda? Just pub talk,' he managed to gasp. Hugh touched his own face and then looked at his hand covered in his own blood. 'You're mad, Frank, bloody mad. I think you've broken my fucking arm.'

'Your dirty mouth. Not just Hilda is it? I've heard what you've been saying about me too.' Frank considered for a moment his next words. 'This isn't for that though. By God, no it isn't. You know what this's for.'

'I don't know what you're talking about,' he rasped. 'I tried to tell Anna—'

'Shut up. For once shut your gob. It won't go down well with your mates at the pit. Max, the others, what you did to my daughter, if they find out.'

'C'mon man. I didn't mean anything by it. We're neighbours, workmates, you saved my life.'

'Biggest mistake I ever made. Shut up, Hugh, just shut the fuck up.'

Hugh tried to stand but fell backwards, letting out a feral yelp. 'But I'm telling you, you need to take more care, you and Hilda, with your girl.' He gulped. 'No wonder Anna—'

'Keep your nose *out*.'

'Look, I won't say anything, I *haven't* said anything. It's your business. I'm sorry what I said about you, and Hilda.' Tears flooded Hugh's fleshy cheeks.

Frank turned and walked calmly away.

He made his way to his own allotment and went to sit inside the Wendy house. What was Hugh talking about? About Anna? Trying to wriggle out of what he'd done. Well he knew what Hugh had done. Was it any worse than what he'd done? Him and Hugh, as bad as each other.

It wasn't until an hour had passed that he heard the commotion. He found out later it was Rosy who'd found her brother, coming to get him for a late dinner.

After Rosy had gone to the police, they'd wanted to question him that afternoon.

The police did come and question Frank the next day, but by then Hugh Lambert had made it clear he wasn't pursuing Rosy's complaint of Frank beating him to a pulp. The whole village knew it was Frank and most conjectured it was to do with Hugh's malicious talk about Hilda.

Although in a few days there would be more gossip to keep them going.

23

'He's just beautiful, Hilda.' Frank held Jim tight to his chest.

'He is, isn't he, and feeding well, too. I didn't feed Anna. She never wanted my milk. She never wanted me.' Hilda gazed at her son with adoration, leaned over and touched his head. 'What's happened to you?' She peered at Frank's hand.

Frank looked at his bandage. 'Nothing, I had a bit of an accident at the allotment.'

Hugh was telling everyone it was all a big misunderstanding. It was already being whispered that Frank wasn't the sort of man to go this far. Frank was more than aware opinion would be that Hugh probably had it coming, and people would question very little what had started the disagreement, assuming it would be blokes' pit stuff, or related to Hugh's gossip about him and Hilda neglecting their daughter. And more specifically, about him. Max had mentioned that Hugh's gossip was becoming more vicious and vile, but it had taken a bit of persuasion on Frank's part to get the information out of Max. Hugh was spreading rumours about him and Anna. Frank swallowed. Hugh seemed to be everywhere in the village, like a noxious gas. But he'd saved Hugh's life, hadn't he? No miner ever forgot that. Frank had become iconic after the Hugh accident and was in high demand to work with on the pit face, like a lucky mascot. Frank was a big union man too, clever with words; the men respected him. No doubt Hugh deserved what Frank had given him, most miners decided.

'How's Anna?' Hilda asked finally, accepting his explanation.

'She's not good. Not talking, not eating. She didn't mean what she did, Hilda.'

'We can put all this behind us now. Whatever's happened.'

Frank studied his wife's face. Did she know more than she'd let on? She was Anna's mother. Wetness gathered on his forehead. No, she couldn't know.

He tried to smile. 'We can, Hilda.'

She leant forward to take Jim from him; the baby had started to whimper. 'He wants feeding.' She rubbed Jim's tiny back. 'I can't change history. I can't help the way it's all gone with Anna. If I could go back and change things, I would.' A rare tear formed in her eye. 'I really would, Frank. I'm going to be a better mother to Jim, and the other babies we're going to have.' She paused for a second. 'And you'll be a better father too.' She held Jim close. 'Having a son'll be different.'

'I like having a daughter. I love Anna.'

'I know you do,' she said quietly. 'And I do too, believe it or not.'

'It doesn't seem that way.'

'You can have no idea how difficult it's been for me. You really can't. Anna's not easy for me.'

He didn't want to get into this. Not now, and changed the subject. 'Dr Faversham's worried about other pregnancies. Don't get your hopes up about another baby.'

'The obstetrician says I'll heal well, and he can see no reason why I can't have another,' she said stubbornly.

'We'll cross that bridge when we come to it. Get better first.' He perched on the side of the bed knowing it was against Matron's regulations. 'Anna's not well, Hilda.'

He couldn't leave the subject of Anna. He should share the truth with Hilda, but Anna had made him swear, and telling Hilda might tip them further towards the abyss.

'She said she had a bad headache, that's why she didn't go into school.' Hilda broke into his thoughts.

'Inside her head she's not well, I mean.' He fidgeted and finally stood. Jim began to grizzle and with difficulty because of the bandaged hand, he took the baby from Hilda, fending off the sharp pain in his left temple.

Carrying on he said, 'Dr Faversham's spoken to Anna. Assessed her. He feels if there's no change in the next week or two, she should be taken to a hospital… a mental hospital in Yorkshire. To be looked at properly.' His head throbbed. Perhaps with further questioning from professionals Anna would admit the truth, and then he could admit it too.

'I can't think about this now.' Hilda rubbed her forehead.

Tell Hilda. He'd sworn to Anna he wouldn't.

And so Frank said nothing, and from that day the rest of his and Hilda's life together was fated not only because of the hidden truths within the family, but the awful wider truths to come that could never be ignored.

He'd listened enough to Winston Churchill, through his radio speeches and reading the newspapers, to acknowledge there would soon be war in Europe. Frank was a minority in the ordinary working-class communities of the country, believing before many that conflict was imminent.

Frank hoped the minority was right because as much as he would despise leaving his new son, getting away from the village, the curtains that flicked too often, from Hugh, and from his guilt, going to war was something Frank already craved.

Jem had once told him he always ran away, either in his head or with his body. Perhaps his sister was right.

24

Frank left Hilda and the baby just after lunchtime and headed straight to the colliery office, which was situated to the rear of the headstocks. He planned to ask for a few days off.

The gaffer was sitting behind his overflowing desk, his face, as always, a mask of neutral expression. The gaffer didn't often let his feelings show.

'I hear congratulations are in order?' he said in a flat voice.

'They are, thanks,' Frank replied.

'Funny way to celebrate, beating up Hugh Lambert. I'm not going to ask why. But I'm two men down now if you don't come in.' He looked at Frank's hand. 'Men have worked with worse than that – Saturday night injury.'

'It's not my hand, gaffer. Family affairs. I need two days off.'

'You're a good worker, normally. No trouble, normally.' He picked up a piece of paper from his desk, gave it a cursory glance. 'All right.'

Frank nodded and undid the top button of his shirt. It was too hot in the windowless and airless room. The gaffer started to read the top sheet of a pile of papers. The interview was over. Frank got up from the uncomfortable chair. He liked the gaffer, never stuck his nose where he knew it wasn't appreciated.

'Thanks.' Frank was glad to escape the heat.

Nurse Alma Dawkins was staying at the house with Anna. Frank made his way home, avoiding the stares he drew as he walked. The reason he'd floored Hugh was because of what he, Frank, knew. It never crossed his mind that Hugh would come clean as to why he'd beaten the little sod up: Frank understood a man like Hugh. The reason would stay locked between them, and this suited Frank.

He stepped through the door and into his kitchen, which smelt like someone else's house. Alma Dawkins cooked different things to Hilda. He hadn't eaten anything for days, and Anna was eating nothing either, but the nurse had to feed herself. Nurse Dawkins wasn't in the kitchen or the front room. He climbed the stairs and knocked on Anna's door.

It was Nurse Dawkins who said, 'Come in.'

She was sitting next to Anna's bed. The room smelt of cooked vegetables and a dish still full of soup sat on the bedside table. Frank swallowed the acrid sick that gurgled to the back of his throat.

'How is she?'

'The same, I'd say,' Nurse Dawkins said.

'Has she spoken?'

'Nothing, only keeps singing the rhyme about blowing bubbles.'

Frank perched himself on the edge of the bed.

The nurse carried on. 'You need to change the bandage. Lucky it isn't broken.'

Frank nodded. Anna was fast asleep. He stroked her forehead.

'Have you spoken to Dr Faversham?' she asked.

'He wants to take Anna to High Royal,' Frank said wearily.

'Might be the best place for her, Mr Cullen. How's Mrs Cullen going to cope with a new baby, and,' she nodded towards Anna, 'and this? And you'll be at work.'

'Can I have a few moments, Nurse Dawkins?'

'Of course.' She rose from her chair, clutching a book she'd been reading. 'Dr Faversham'll be here in a few hours.' She left the room.

Frank waited until he heard the latch of the door at the bottom of the stairs before he pulled the cover away from Anna's face.

'Love, Anna. Wake up. Talk to me.' He'd make everything better. Anna would be fine, later she'd be fine, but she didn't open her eyes. 'Love, it's me, your dad.' He didn't know what to say. 'Anna, please… be normal.'

She didn't answer.

'Shall I tell your mum? We'll tell her together. Make you right?'

Her eyes flipped open. 'No!' She sat up, her movement so fast it took him unawares. 'No. Marigold died, but she'll come back.' Anna looked at him, her eyes rimmed in vermillion red, and then she grabbed at his face with her open palm. Automatically, he held up his own left bandaged hand; she grabbed for that too. The pain shot through his arm, up to his neck and exploded into his brain. He stopped himself from shouting out, aware of Alma Dawkins in the kitchen below.

He took hold of his daughter and felt her dissolve into limpness within his arms. He carried on nursing her and that was how Alma Dawkins found them fifteen minutes later when she returned with Anna's medication. Frank had asked the doctor what he was giving her. *Nembutal, a barbiturate that will calm Anna*, Dr Faversham had replied.

He stepped away from Anna and Nurse Dawkins gave her the tablet, putting it in Anna's mouth and holding her jaw closed. Anna finally swallowed. The way she held Anna, arms locked to her chest, belied the nurse's secret strength. He could see why Dr Faversham had chosen this particular nurse for this particular job. He moved forwards, wanting to protect his daughter from such heavy-handedness.

'Leave me to it, Mr Cullen, please. Give her a minute and it'll start to take effect.'

Impotence streamed through him. He was useless and he felt less than human. He watched as she pushed Anna down on the bed, laying her out flat. The nurse used her whole body to keep Anna in the exposed position and after no more than five minutes Anna became completely flaccid.

He opened the bedroom door and returned downstairs. There was no way he was letting them take Anna to the nut house. No way at all.

Frank had told Dr Faversham he wasn't allowing Anna to go to High Royal; that they'd make a decision when Hilda was up for making one. Despite his wife's troubled relationship with her daughter Hilda had agreed with him, and her agreeing made him feel better about things. Little Jim had reunited them. They were a family and as a family they'd pull through this. It had nothing to do with anyone else. They would cope.

But Frank admitted he couldn't cope with Anna alone. She needed fulltime care while he was at work. Hilda and Jim wouldn't be coming home for another two weeks. They had some savings but not much. He thought about asking the gaffer for a sub on his wages, but although he trusted the gaffer not to say anything, and that in fact it would be common knowledge by now Anna was not herself – gossip amongst the teachers would see to that – he didn't want it to be common knowledge that they were as skint as they were. He had a phobia about people knowing his business.

Jem's marriage was unhappy but her husband didn't keep her short of money. Frank wrote to his sister, explaining as briefly as he could the problem they were having with Anna, and that they needed some cash to tide them over. Clever Jem would fill in the pieces, and she wouldn't question. He and Jem; good with secrets. But more than anything, Jem loved both Hilda and Anna. He'd thought about asking Flo but decided against it. He wasn't sure why. Perhaps because he didn't want Flo to know, because she *would* definitely question. He remembered her salutary warning regarding Hugh a decade before. No, he wouldn't ask Flo, and when he did write to her a day or two after writing to Jem, he said nothing about Anna, only giving the news of James Cullen's arrival into the world.

Jem sent him a telegram, saying that the money would be coming through in a few days and Frank felt a lot easier.

Before Hilda and Jim came home all went well. Anna still wasn't speaking, but she'd started to eat again and had also begun getting up from her bed, even if only to look through the bedroom window. Frank had told the school she was suffering with a bad cold she couldn't get rid of. Dr Faversham verified the story, surprising Frank by agreeing to put off an assessment at High Royal for the time being. He and the doctor had always got on well. Dr Faversham was a Churchill supporter too. Many years later Frank was to learn Dr Faversham had been on the same continent as him during the war but had not been as lucky as Frank in coming home.

An ermine rug of snow covered the ground when Hilda returned to the house with Jim – now a big baby of ten pounds. The nurse said that if little James had gone full-term he'd have been an enormous newborn. *Whatever made him come out early has done you a favour, Mrs Cullen*, she'd said.

Flo had written, and was keen to come and see them all. He didn't even mention Flo's letter to Hilda. He didn't want Flo to come. Jem had mentioned she would visit and bring their mother but Frank knew that wouldn't happen. He was as far away from his family now as he'd foreseen ten years before.

As they walked down the fourth avenue together Frank's muscles constricted in anticipation of Anna's greeting. How would she take to her new brother? He tried not to show his doubt. He'd led Hilda to believe Anna was better than she really was, hoping if Hilda expected normal, normal she would get. He'd even told Nurse Alma Dawkins she wouldn't be needed today.

When they walked into the kitchen the smell of liquorice – Alma Dawkins' stew – hit them. Frank should have seen the ominous sign then. Stew and beetroot would always remind him of that terrible afternoon, the day after the allotment.

'Smells good in here. Alma obviously likes a bit of fennel,' Hilda said with a smile.

'Is that what that bloody awful smell is?'

'I like it.' She handed Jim to him. 'Is the cot ready?'

'In our room, like you asked.'

'I want him near me.'

'I know.'

'Will Anna be upstairs?' she asked.

'I'd imagine so. Why don't you go up? Leave Jim with me.' He had to give Hilda some credit, she didn't flinch.

'I'll make things better between us, me and Anna,' she said softly and Frank wondered if new motherhood had already smoothed away the thorns.

Frank listened as she made her way up the stairs, feeling easier than he'd done in days. He went to sit on the settee with Jim, half waiting to hear Anna screaming and relieved that after ten minutes he heard nothing. After half an hour and anxious, holding Jim, he plodded upstairs to see what was going on. He knocked on Anna's door. No answer. He went in. She was in bed and fast asleep. He made his way into his and Hilda's room and squeezed by the side of the cot. Hilda lay on their bed, still with her coat on and fast asleep too. She must have said hello to Anna and then gone to lie down. He smiled into the fading light of their room; all day the November sun had been shielded by the heavy blanket of snowy air. He put Jim in his new cot and sat next to Hilda on the bed, waiting to make sure the baby was properly asleep before going back downstairs.

Hilda was exhausted, and so was he. But for the first time in weeks he felt some peace settle. He allowed himself to nod off, just for a bit, then he'd serve up the stew Alma had kindly made. He'd learn to like fennel. Maybe Anna might even eat with them.

He had no idea how long he'd been asleep when he woke up to Hilda's piercing howl.

And the even higher tones of his son's screams.

25

Florence

Westerham, Kent
Two years later
April 1940

Florence plonked a cup of tea in front of her cousin. 'No sugar, sorry. Mum couldn't get hold of any.'

'Tea's not the same without sugar,' Harold said, taking a massive slurp.

'I know.' She rummaged in the back larder looking for food, but all she could find was a slab of hardening fruit loaf. She took it out and sliced it up, stuffing the crumbs into her mouth as she did so. 'I'm starving.'

'You're always starving, but it's the motorcycle riding today, I reckon. Works up an appetite.' Harold raked his hand through army-cut white-blonde hair. 'You've got it now though. In the swing. You love it, don't you, biking? I knew you would.'

'I do. Seems to come naturally to me.'

'It does. We'll finish this.' He shoved the whole piece of loaf she'd given him into his mouth. 'And I'll go through the bike maintenance stuff again.'

'When do you have to leave?'

'Tomorrow night I'm getting the cargo ship to north Africa with my division.'

Harold hadn't had to be conscripted into the army, he was already a soldier when war had broken out. He was her mum's brother's son, they lived in Southend-on-

Sea; she'd spent a week with them every summer as a child. Harold was six years older than her but they'd always been close.

'It's been great learning to ride a motorcycle,' she said. 'I love it, just sorry that when you go I won't have one to practice on.' She cleared away the teacups.

'Have you thought about joining the ATS? It'd suit you. They're looking for female riders.'

'Crossed my mind, yes. Mary Churchill's mentioned it.'

'C'mon, let's have one last spin,' he said.

'I have to be at Chartwell by three, I promised Miss Cunningham. Just for an hour to help out. Mr and Mrs Churchill are down unexpectedly from London later. All hush hush though.'

His brown eyes glittered. 'Dare you to turn up at Chartwell on my motorcycle?'

He knew she'd bite. Her mum'd kill her. But there was something in the air, something about the war that was making everyone do things they shouldn't. Anyway, the Churchills weren't due at Chartwell until later in the evening.

'All right, c'mon.' The feeling of the anticipated exhilaration of riding the motorcycle fast and turning up at Chartwell on it was already pleating through her.

Florence sat pillion as Harold drove them to the deserted track. He stopped by an old gnarled gooseberry bush and climbed off the motorcycle, as she did too.

'Off you go! The road is yours!' he said, holding the motorcycle upright.

She climbed back on the Ariel Red Hunter and stroked the vibrant red petrol tank and still clumsily, kick-started the engine. And off she went.

The freedom, the wind curling through her hair, the noise and smell of petrol, wearing Harold's old trousers held up on her tiny waist with her father's cut-down old leather belt made her feel, oh so alive. She did two up and downs of the track, managing fifty miles an hour, and then finally pulled up beside Harold.

'Nice,' he said. 'You go to Chartwell. I'll wait here.'

'I might be more than an hour.'

He lay down on the damp ground and pulled a coat from his knapsack, then pushed the bag underneath his head. 'No problem waiting. He peered up at her. 'You might want to brush your hair. See you back here,' he looked at his watch. 'Five?'

'You sure?'

'Are *you* sure?'

'I take you up on the challenge, Harold Wilkins,' she said, swinging a leg over the bike, and expertly this time kick-started the engine.

'You've got the hang of the starting. That's the real bugger of riding.'

'I can get the hang of anything given the right teaching.'

'I know,' he said grinning. 'I hope Herr Hitler knows what's coming when you join up, Flo.'

She touched her forehead in mock salute and sped towards Chartwell.

At the gates she stopped the engine and slipped off, walking into the grounds on foot and pulling the bike alongside her, feeling as if she were cheating on the dare.

It was Miss Cunningham who spotted her. Unfortunately she'd been out at the front of the house doing something to the step, polishing it, it looked like. Since war had been declared no one had a well-defined job any more, including the faithful Miss Cunningham. The ad hoc cook took one look at Flo and appeared to go into some sort of shock.

'Florence! What on earth are you up to now?' she asked, her jaw lowering.

Florence waved at her.

'You'd better get out of those trousers, sharpish,' Miss Cunningham carried on in a clear tone of disgruntlement, making no mention of the motorcycle, as if it didn't exist. Florence couldn't wait to tell Harold.

Mr Churchill's valet appeared next to Miss C, and then Florence noticed the black Humber parked in the driveway. The Churchills had got to Chartwell earlier than expected.

The valet walked nearer to Florence, said nothing, only admired the shining and clean motorcycle, (all her work.) He then turned to Florence, and she was sure, admired her in the same way as he purred over the inanimate object.

'Very nice,' he said, an amused smile on his face. 'I do love some aspects of our country's terrible conflict. Good for you, Miss Judson.' The valet always called her by her surname. He was an odd mixture of conservativeness and the New Attitude pervading the country.

'Get that… thing down the side of the house, the east wing entrance, Florence,' Miss Cunningham said loudly. The side wing of Chartwell that wasn't used much, due to its lack of sunlight. 'And change into your work dress immediately. Before Mr and Mrs Churchill see you.'

As Florence pulled the bike to where Miss Cunningham had earmarked, Florence smelt the familiar aroma of the Romeo and Julieta and turned to see Mr Churchill himself peering at her from underneath his painting hat, standing in the shadow of the house, wearing a green-coloured all-in-one paint-splattered suit. What was he doing? He was supposed to be saving the world. She smiled inwardly at the thought that he'd left London, and the war, to finish the picture he'd been agonising over for months.

'Interesting, Florence,' he said, looking at Miss Cunningham. 'You can go inside, Miss C.'

Churchill gave Florence a guilty smile. Miss Cunningham huffed delicately and disappeared through the front door. Mr Churchill carried on: 'Ensure Mrs Churchill doesn't see the motorcycle, or the trousers, Florence.' His smile had turned into an unmeasured grin. 'I don't think she is quite ready. Although I suspect Mary will approve.'

'I'm sorry, sir.'

'Where on earth did you learn to ride a motorcycle?' Mr Churchill asked.

'My cousin, sir. He taught me to ride, and look after it. Properly, check the tyres, everything.'

'Very commendable. But perhaps find another mode of transport to get yourself to work?' He fell silent for a moment. 'Time to find yourself a husband, Florence. Then you won't need such frivolous things to keep you occupied.' He walked closer to her. 'Have you heard from the bricklayer? Frank was his name. Yes, Frank Cullen.'

'We don't keep in touch as much as we should, sir.' Surprised Mr Churchill remembered but then again he forgot absolutely nothing.

'Talented bricklayer, and a man who reads. We should nurture our friendships.'

'Frank and his wife were my best friends.' She heard the despondency in her own voice. 'Frank built a Wendy house for Anna, just like yours. And a wall, like your kitchen wall,' she remembered to add, 'sir.'

'Anna? The little girl who came to play here?'

'Yes, sir. You have an amazing memory,' she blurted out. He nodded. 'I mean sir, you remember so much.'

'It is my job to remember everything.' He looked into the distance, as if in thought. 'Anna, yes, indeed. I remember Mrs Churchill telling me that Anna Cullen had been invited to one of the yearly lunches she organizes for the village youngsters. A few years ago?'

Flo remembered Anna's visit well. She hadn't quite fathomed at the time why Anna had cut short her visit. It had been the last time she'd seen Anna. 'That's right, sir, Anna was invited. And yes, it is your job to remember these things.' Perhaps she was overstepping the mark with her last comment.

'Excellent reply.' He fiddled with a button at the top of the suit, undoing it and looking relieved when his neck was set free, and carried on. 'Mary enjoyed playing with Anna all those years ago.' He moved his hands to rest on his chest and addressing the original part of her sentence – he would often do that – he carried on, 'Frank built a *Marycot*?'

'He did, sir.'

He'd tipped his head in acknowledgement. 'Wonderful to hear. I must get on. And do as Miss Cunningham asked and change your clothing.' He turned, already thinking of something else and Florence inclined her head to a disappearing figure.

Harold was still asleep when she got back to the track two hours later. She told him what had happened, and what Mr Churchill had said.

'Bloody hell, Flo. You should be coming with me to Africa, the Germans wouldn't stand a chance.'

26

One month later
10th May 1940

The Westerham Evening Standard

Churchill Takes The Prime Ministerial Helm As

Germans Advance

It has been announced that Winston Churchill will lead a coalition government after Prime Minister Neville Chamberlain said he was stepping aside.

Sitting at Chartwell's kitchen table with her chin nestled in the palms of her hands, Florence was absorbed in the edited down words from the master's speech.

"…I would say to the House as I said to those who have joined this government: I have nothing to offer but blood, toil, tears and sweat. We have before us an ordeal of the most grievous kind. We have before us many, many long months of struggle and of suffering…"

The ramifications of his leadership had led to the decision that Chartwell wouldn't for the foreseeable future be used as the Churchill family home. Many thought when war had been declared, as they had thought too regarding the Great War – and including Florence – that it would be a quick conflict. But as the New Year began and the 'Phoney War' raged it became clear to everyone this would not be the case.

Florence smiled at the memory of the previous September when Miss Cunningham had fainted as news of war came to them over the radio (she was only out for a few seconds, thank goodness), and Mr Churchill's valet had poured her a large sherry at 11.15 a.m. in the morning.

Florence's small world was changing and she was changing too.

The Churchills were now to be based permanently in London, and it had been rumoured Clementine Churchill hoped the house would be used for evacuees. Miss Cunningham had taken much glee in recounting to Florence's mum (Florence found out years later) that the evacuees and their mothers found the place as boring and uncongenial as Clementine Churchill did herself, and by the end of 1942 the evacuees had found refuge in a place a little more exciting than the Wealds of Kent.

Florence discovered a priceless humour under Miss Cunningham's starched exterior; they had definitely become closer since war had broken out. War seemed to do that Florence decided at the end of it.

It had been a few days before and a rare appearance at Chartwell, surrounded by Clementine, Randolph and Mary (Sarah and Diana hadn't been there) when Churchill gathered together the staff to inform them of their impending job losses. They'd all guessed why – because Mr Churchill was about to bag the job he'd always wanted. Florence was to be kept on as part of a skeletal staff to maintain the house on a basic level, but Orchard Cottage in the grounds was to be kept in full swing through the duration of the war.

She was glad she'd been kept on, but spurred by Mary Churchill's activities in the war effort and the general *Churchillian* feeling that pervaded the house, and even more now that the master wasn't in it, Florence had known what she wanted to do. She wanted to be a part of the war and not just a bystander watching it all happen.

She'd received a letter from Frank two months before, telling her he'd rejected the excuse his reserved occupation of miner gave him to sit out the conflict in the blackness of a mine. Frank had signed up at the local recruits' office in January 1940. *Anything is better than being underground all day*, he'd said.

He'd left Nottinghamshire for training further north in February 1940. It all seemed to happen so quickly; but then again so had the war. Only for Winston Churchill had conflict with Hitler always been a certainty. All through the 1930s as Florence had busily cleaned and dusted his library she'd seen first-hand evidence of his fears and (what the Cabinet called) his obsession with Adolf Hitler, the rise of the Brown Shirts, and the sinister and surreptitious sidelining of the Jews throughout Europe.

Still, Florence had been a bit surprised about Frank joining up, because although she understood he'd want to fight for his country – indeed she suspected fight directly for Winston Churchill – she was incredulous he was so keen to leave his sons. Frank and Hilda finally had their first baby in the autumn of 1938, the second coming along just eleven months later. After a decade of miscarriages Hilda's body was rearing for motherhood.

Florence hadn't been able to get up to see them and their new baby, but had got the distinct impression she wasn't that welcome. That was the undertone of the correspondence from Hilda, and it had thrown her. She'd thought they'd made up on that long ago visit in 1934, but as the years passed and Hilda didn't invite her again, Florence accepted that Hilda had all but severed all ties with her. She did though, still receive a twice-yearly letter from Hilda; she was sure it was Frank who encouraged this.

The letters were full-on about the new baby, a bit about Frank, but Hilda said nothing about Anna. Frank hadn't mentioned Anna in his letters either.

Florence was twenty-eight and considered over-the-hill for marriage and children. But in many ways she was ahead of her time, and although the small-minded collective consciousness of her village labelled her a childless spinster (she had actually heard someone say it), she'd always known this was not to be her destiny, and felt the timing of the war had been designed just for her.

Florence hadn't heard Miss Cunningham enter the kitchen.

'Thank the Lord for this, eh? Make all of our lives easier.' Miss Cunningham looked over Florence's shoulder at the newspaper headline.

Despite her and Miss Cunningham's continuing conviviality with each other, Florence still expected a flick around the ear and ducked sideways through habit. She was always getting told off for reading the newspapers. But the balance of things was indeed adjusting.

'You mean with the master not being in a bad mood all the time? Yes, he's got what he wanted – to be Prime Minister. Mrs Churchill will be pleased too,' Florence replied.

Miss Cunningham nodded. 'We won't be seeing very much of them. Running the country, and a war, being the Prime Minister, and Mrs Churchill will make sure she's with him, every step of the way.' She sat down next to Florence. 'Your mum tells me you have plans?'

'I do. I'll be here until we've sorted everything out, but I plan to join the ATS, the Auxiliary Territorial Service.'

Miss Cunningham smiled. 'I know what the ATS is, Florence. But yes, I think that's a good idea. A young woman like you … well, the country needs you.'

Miss Cunningham stood and walked to the window, which overlooked the expanse of land that led towards Clementine Churchill's rose garden and Mr Churchill's kitchen wall, and of course, the *Marycot*. 'This is a time of great change.' Florence was used to Miss Cunningham's matter-of-factness, she wasn't a woman prone to fancy or profound statements. Florence was intrigued.

'This is your time, Florence. With the help of the Lord,' (Florence had never taken Mrs C as being religious either, not like Hilda had become), 'Mr Churchill will lead us to victory and we will come out the other end of this war a different country.' She glanced at Florence and took away the newspaper from the table, folded it and put in a nearby drawer. 'A country that will see its women differently.'

Still a country where women shouldn't read newspapers though.

As if Miss Cunningham had guessed her thought, she carried on. 'This is the Churchills' time. No reading at work, Florence.'

'Sorry. I hope you're right, Miss C.' She loved the village she'd been born and brought up in, but it was time to move on, war or no war. The too loud remarks she'd heard about her own marriage-less state, as well as about Jem and her all-too-known-about loveless marriage to the son of the vicar, William, was only amplifying her desire to escape.

'But for now, there's work to do,' Miss Cunningham said. 'I want you to clean Mrs Churchill's bedroom so it's ready to dust-sheet up. Then, when you've finished that, come over to Orchard Cottage – there's a lot to be done there. Mary'll be over tomorrow.' She began wiping the table. 'She's taking a break from her work with the Red Cross.' Folding her arms she continued, 'Wouldn't it be rather funny if in the future your paths crossed somewhere else other than Chartwell?'

'I think that's rather unlikely, Miss C.' Florence grinned at her.

'I remember the Great War, trust me, stranger things happen. Anyway she'll be here for a few days taking over Mrs Churchill's role in ensuring we do everything properly. Mary was always the sensible stable child.'

Florence rose. 'I'll get on then.'

'And Florence. Any correspondence you find, just put it in a pile. Mrs Churchill left in rather a hurry last time she was here, so please. Discretion?'

'Always, Miss C.' Florence evaded eye contact. Clementine Churchill's bedroom was tidy, only needing a light clean. She put the huge pile of dustsheets on the floor – they weighed a ton – and began work. She'd sneezed at least five times; carpets really were dust-collectors and she was glad they didn't have them at home. There were some bonuses to being poor.

She sat on the stripped bed and surveyed what she had left to do.

The writing bureau. She'd left that job until last, knowing she'd end up having a read, and wanted time. She smiled into the grey half-light of the room and as if to stop anyone from finding her, made the space even darker by pulling the heavy curtains nearly closed.

She rose and her eyes travelled immediately to Mrs Churchill's personal in-tray. Her hands softly flicked through the envelopes – all opened – and she picked one up. Postmarked Sicily. *My special Clementine, beguiling lady, wonderful woman…*

Florence read to the end. There was nothing too, how would her mum put it… sexual, but it was obvious to Florence that the long trip Clementine Churchill had taken a few years before had been a little bit more interesting than the household had thought. She remembered Mr Churchill's *Black Dog* the months she'd been gone, which had been much worse than any the household had seen before. Frank admired Churchill for his brain and personality; Florence respected him because of the real love he held for his wife.

She placed the letter back safely in the tray and her eyes roamed. A small pile of letters sat on the left edge of the bureau; in the tray Florence knew to be the correspondence Mrs Churchill took from her husband – he couldn't possibly reply to every letter personally, and neither could his secretary. This pile was usually compiled of letters from constituents and people from the surrounding area in Kent. Together with her own secretary, it was Mrs Churchill who dealt with this correspondence. These had obviously been forgotten in the build up to Winston Churchill making his way to becoming Prime Minister.

Florence checked her watch. She really needed to get to Orchard Cottage.

She picked up the unopened letters, pulling one randomly from the middle of the pile. There was something familiar about the writing.

Mr Winston Churchill

She turned the envelope over to see if by any chance there was a sender's name and address. There was. Florence stood up, the letter clutched in her hand.

Frank Cullen had sent Winston Churchill a letter. It had been delivered by ship from France, where Frank was stationed with his regiment, trying to stop the Nazis occupying France. Why was Frank writing letters to Churchill? Was he going mad? She went through all the other unopened envelopes; there were no more from Frank.

She put it in her apron pocket and opened the curtains, leaving the mistress's bedroom with her heart beating fast and sweat dampening her cotton dress.

Picking up her coat from the peg in the kitchen she felt inside the pocket for the cigarette she'd saved, and on her way to Orchard Cottage she stopped near the *Marycot*, lit it and stood for a few moments smoking and reading Frank's letter.

She folded it up and placed it back in the envelope, trying to reseal it. She returned to the house and put it back in the tray, and then with fire in her step made tracks to Orchard Cottage.

27

Six weeks later
26th June 1940

The Daily Mirror

Paris Falls To The Nazis

Hitler's conquest of France has reached its conclusion. Today General Charles de Gaulle made a broadcast to France from England, urging his countrymen to continue the fight against Germany. The armistice, signed by the French on June 22, went into effect on June 25, and more than half of France was occupied by the Germans.

Florence read the newspaper, but from the corner of her eye noticed the frequent glances from the man sitting to the side of her on the bus. Was he admiring her new hat or that she was reading a newspaper? She guessed it was the hat.

Events in France had shocked her; no one could believe it had happened, no one in her village anyway, and certainly no one at a quiet and under-inhabited Chartwell where the subject wasn't spoken about. Winston Churchill, the British Prime Minister was in London, but it was as if the few employees left around Chartwell knew the old man wouldn't want it mentioned, and so, well trained, they didn't, not very much anyway. Mr Churchill was a Francophile and distraught at the events unfolding in France. Miss Cunningham had said she'd heard rumours Mr Churchill would soon be entertaining De Gaulle in London. *Wished I could be a fly on the wall*, she'd said mischievously. *No love lost between them*, she'd finished. Florence really liked Miss C.

It had been weeks since Florence had opened and read Frank's letter to Winston Churchill. She'd put pen to paper lots of times, but each letter to Frank found its way into the rubbish bin. She didn't know what to say or how to say it. In the end she'd decided to confide in Miss Cunningham. She didn't have to tell her how she'd found out what was in Frank's letter to Churchill, but had to make it clear she hadn't found it out from either Hilda or Frank, or a letter she shouldn't have been reading. And so she was on her way to visit Jem in the neighbouring village. Florence could then say with good conscience to Miss Cunningham that she knew what she knew from Jem. If anyone knew anything it would be Jem. Jem and Frank had always had a strange relationship, cool on the one hand, but deep under the skin the brother and sister knew each other's secrets.

It was a ten-minute walk from where the bus dropped her. She covered the ground slowly giving herself time to think. She'd received her letter from the ATS a week before. In the letter was her railway warrant. She was to report to Honiton, Devon Railway Station at 11.00 hours in a week's time. She was more than excited and her exhilaration had only grown when Mary Churchill had made a point of finding her in the garden as she picked herbs, to congratulate her too.

When Florence finally knocked on the Barnes' front door her dress was saturated. The sky clear and vast. Noon and the temperatures already punishing.

Jem answered. 'This is a surprise, Florence.' Her face cracked open a little as if she'd remembered to smile. 'Come in, it's cool inside. Such a hot day.'

Jem took Florence into the neat and tidy front room of her home, where everything was in place and everything had a place. She found Frank's spiritually angular sister difficult to be around, particularly since the horrible scene at the train station years before.

'Would you like water or squash, or tea?' Jem asked.

'Water'd be nice, thank you. Is Nathan at home? I'd like to say hello.'

'He's at school, of course.'

'Yes, of course he is.'

Jem disappeared. Florence scanned the room, noticing only photos of William's family and several of Jem and William's son, Nathan, as he'd been growing up.

Jem returned with a jug of water and two glasses on a tray. 'What brings you here, Flo?'

'I'll get straight to the nub, if that's all right with you?'

'Please do.'

Jem remained standing, her arms hanging lifeless. Florence tried to ignore the tight current of suspicion lingering in the clammy air of the sitting room. It certainly didn't feel cooler inside the house. Florence pulled at the collar of her dress and took off her hat. 'Have you heard from Hilda or Frank recently?'

Jem perched herself on the armchair. 'I have. Frank wrote to me from the convalescent home he's presently in. I've been to see him.' She took a sideways glance at Florence. 'Hilda's coming down soon to take the children to visit him. They'll be staying here. I believe his next posting is Africa.'

Why hadn't anyone told her Frank was so near to Westerham, and that he was unwell? She knew he'd been one of the thousands rescued at Dunkirk but had thought he'd come through unscathed. 'Has Frank, or Hilda, mentioned Anna?'

Jem's eyes wandered towards the mantelpiece, fixing on the wallpaper above it.

'Is Anna all right?' Florence probed.

'Hasn't Hilda told you?'

'Hilda's told me nothing. It feels as if they've been avoiding me.'

'Anna's been admitted to the High Royal Mental Hospital in Yorkshire.'

So it was true – what Frank had said in the letter to Churchill.

She remembered the last paragraph, where Frank hinted that he had more to tell. That he was not the man Churchill thought he was. Florence had wondered about Frank's own state of mind, if she were honest, and felt a bit of embarrassment at his confession to a man who, she felt, would never read such a letter, and a man who literally had the world's fate on his shoulders.

Florence finally answered. 'Why's this been kept such a secret?'

'It's not something you'd want to shout about from the rooftops, is it? Anna's in the best place.'

'What caused this?' she asked. 'Anna's always been… fragile. What happened? Something must have.'

'I think Hilda's pregnancy did it. Anna just couldn't cope.' She took a gulp of water. 'They tried, Flo. Hilda tried to keep Anna at home, but then something happened that made it impossible.'

'What happened?'

'It's better Hilda or Frank tells you. It's not my place to.'

'I can't believe this's been kept such a secret.'

'Hilda and Frank just wanted to keep it all quiet.'

'But, Anna. I love Anna,' Florence said.

Jem's face softened. 'I love Anna too. I don't know what caused this. Hilda doesn't either, and as usual my brother has buried his head in the sand.'

'Frank's stopped writing to me.'

'That's what he does, isn't it? Look, Flo, they brought Anna home briefly last summer, before war was declared, but it didn't work out. Hilda couldn't cope and Anna was sent back to High Royal. You can't blame Hilda. She did everything she could.'

'Have you seen Anna?'

'I went up to Yorkshire a few months ago to see her in the hospital.'

'You should have told me.'

'I hear you're to join the ATS?'

'Yes.' Florence suddenly had an idea. 'I want to see Anna. Do they allow visitors? Do I need to ask Hilda and Frank's permission?'

'Visit before you leave for Devon, you mean?'

'Yes.'

'I don't think that's possible, for the next few months anyway. Anna's under a special treatment regime. I was told I couldn't visit for a while. Only Anna's parents are allowed access to see her at the moment.'

'God, poor Anna. Can I write to her, do you think?'

'You can, but she doesn't read anything.'

'She loved reading.'

'She's not the girl you last saw.'

'Something must have happened that caused Anna to—'

'Lose her marbles?' Jem finished for her.

'Stop it.' Florence's eyes travelled again around the room that although tidy was devoid of care and love. Jem was empty of love too. She tried to find some empathy for Frank's sister because of the revolting man she'd married, because of Jem's tendency to the melancholic.

'I think it's my brother who knows more than Hilda about it all,' Jem said, quietly but with conviction.

'What makes you say that?'

Jem shrugged. 'Just a feeling. But you can't blame Hilda for sending Anna to the hospital. She has her children to think of.'

'Anna is her child too in case you'd forgotten.'

'You know what I mean. And Frank joined up when he didn't have to, leaving Hilda with the mess of it all. As usual. And the war has complicated things for everyone.'

Florence couldn't stop herself, swept her eyes around the room. 'I can't see it's affecting you that much.'

'William's been sent his papers.'

'I'm sure that may well have been good news to you.'

'You know, Flo, I can really see why Hilda and Frank lost touch with you. You were never their friend.' Jem paused deliberately. 'And it's cupboard love for Anna.'

'I really don't know what you mean.'

'Because you knew Frank was close to Anna.'

'That's really not true.' The heat in the room stifled her. 'Why don't you like me, Jem?'

'You're superficial. You see nothing. It's all about you. So self-absorbed. Always were.'

There was something wrong with Jem and Florence was desperate to leave.

'You wanted Frank, and he didn't want you,' Jem carried on, furrowing deeper into the underbelly. 'And now you pretend to worry about Anna. Let Hilda sort out her own family.' Her words draped in the air.

Florence put on her hat. 'Thank you for the water.' She walked towards the door. 'I hope William remains safe and well, wherever he ends up being posted.'

Jem only nodded.

When finally she got back to Chartwell, Florence immediately wrote a letter to Frank suggesting they meet up in London after her training, and then she asked Miss Cunningham if she could use the phone. She'd never asked such a thing before, and had to explain her concerns about Anna to give a good reason.

Miss Cunningham asked no questions and gave her blessing.

Florence managed to speak to the administrator at High Royal Hospital and was told Anna Cullen would certainly still be there and in a position to receive visitors when Florence planned to visit in the autumn.

28

Frank

Parkwood Convalescent Home, Swanley, Kent
July 1ˢᵗ 1940

Frank glanced at the utilitarian clock that hung on the wall of the ward he shared with two other servicemen. One was out in the garden, while Taff was in his rehabilitation session – torture session he called it – and so thankfully Frank was alone. Hilda would be here soon; he hadn't seen her since he'd left for France, although he knew that with the addition of Nick to their family, Hilda was at last mildly content.

What Anna had done to her mother and her baby brother had thrown a darkness over them. It would leave a mark forever, but Frank truly believed that one day Anna would come back to them for good, and that they would be a proper family. That's what he told himself. Always.

Hilda had asked him – not begged, which wasn't her way – to put off joining up, but he'd been determined. Nick had only been a few months old when Frank signed his papers at the recruitment office in the main town. He'd finished his training at the end of February 1940 and was sent straight over to France as part of the British Expeditionary Force. The days had been long and hard in a country that was desperately trying to fend off the Nazi threat. He'd seen, heard and witnessed things that had opened his mind to the tyranny of the world, and the horror of what men (and often women) could inflict on their fellow human beings. Being in Vichy France had almost helped him forget the allotment and his own problems. Almost.

He'd been in France for three months when, foolishly trying to assuage his guilt, he'd written to Mr Churchill. Of course, he didn't think Mr Churchill would ever read his letter, which is probably why he sent it. The letter to Churchill brought his mind back to his family. He'd been ecstatic when Hilda had told him she was pregnant again, but Anna – who hadn't improved – tainted his joy and was, the doctor said, withdrawing more into a world she had created for herself. Since being hospitalised for the second time, Anna rejected completely that he and Hilda were her parents, and her fixation with Marigold, the Churchills' dead child, had become stronger. He'd seen that coming, knowing that somehow Anna was confusing herself with Marigold. So many times he'd decided to tell the truth about the day in the allotment, but then, he'd see Anna's face pleading with him to swear his silence. His guilt moved in and over him as the Germans had moved over Paris: efficiently, relentlessly. A cloak of culpability enclosed him like a straitjacket.

Like the one they'd used on Anna.

After Anna had been readmitted, Hilda only visited her daughter sporadically. Frank's heart was so dense with sorrow and knowing then his plan to sign up, he hadn't known how to ask Hilda to go see Anna more regularly.

She'd seen his angst though, explaining: *I can't go visit Anna all the time, I have to think about Jim, and the new baby*, she'd said patting her stomach. She never mentioned the evening with Jim in their bedroom, or the time when Anna had come home from the hospital for a few weeks. Hilda *had* tried. She'd had Anna home, but it had all gone so terribly wrong.

Every part of his rational brain told him that if he revealed the truth, it would help Anna, but he could not, because Anna had pleaded with him to say nothing. Like the thick timber poles that held up the ceiling of the dark pit face, his whole world was propped up with guilt too. Anna, Jem, and even Hilda, who he'd married, knowing that it was a mistake.

With the loud chimes of the clock his mind came back to the present. If the bus was running on time from Jem's village they should be here soon.

He heard the crying before he saw Hilda and Jim. She walked into the light and airy ward, a wailing Nick clutched to her chest. Jim who'd been walking since ten months, and talking since he wasn't much older, toddled beside her; he looked towards his dad, his expression unsure. Of course it would be unsure, the boy hadn't seen him for months. To Frank it felt like a lifetime and to little Jim it probably felt longer.

He got up unsteadily from his chair; the matron had had him out of bed for a week. *Good to be up, if only in a chair*, she'd said. She'd also encouraged him to spend some time in the garden. It was a lovely garden at the convalescent hospital, surrounded by a high yellow brick wall on its west side. Beautifully pointed, perfect proportions and although the colour of the bricks was different it reminded him of Churchill's kitchen wall, as well as the small wall in his allotment. With this comparison, for a moment, he found it difficult to breathe.

He stood up. 'Jim, my lad, you've grown.' He knew better than to hug the boy, who did seem confused and unsure. 'You remember me, your dad?'

Jim nodded then a smile swallowed up his little face, causing the scar on his cheek to crinkle. Frank's heart fissured.

'Hello,' he said. 'Daddy?'

'That's me!' Frank picked him up. Jim was rigid in his arms. He looked over Jim's shoulder at Hilda; her features were brimming with happiness. His insides unwound. Hilda was coming back. All she'd needed was a family. Then for a moment his gut retracted as an image of Anna, as he'd last seen her – restrained on a bed at High Royal Hospital – materialised.

'It's so good to see you,' he said.

Hilda hugged him awkwardly, because of Nick sitting on her hip. He hoped. 'It's so good to see you. It's been all over the newspapers. Seems your man did us all proud, and brought you back safely.'

In that moment Frank questioned if he should take his leave. He'd intended to go straight back to fighting as soon as the doctor signed him off, but he should spend time with his family, and go to visit Anna.

'Old Winston, eh?' he replied. 'He's a genius. Takes chances. Some call it arrogance, and that might be, but he's the one who'll win us the war.' He embraced her and his groin tightened. 'It's bloody good to see you. And the boys.' He took Nick from her. 'He's grown so much.'

'They do grow.'

'He looks bonny,' he said.

'Nick's a good boy.' She took hold of Jim's hand, like a lioness. 'Jim is too, aren't you, lovely boy?' Almost absentmindedly, and only for a second, she stroked Jim's cheek and looked too sad. Anna was never far away.

Frank pulled up a chair. 'Sit down, love.' Jim climbed onto her knee. 'How are you?' he asked.

'I'm fine. All's well at home. Everyone sends their best wishes, including your gaffer.'

'That's nice of him.'

'He's a nice man.' She fell silent for a moment. 'Maisie Lambert came to see me last week, with Rosy. It's so difficult, Frank.'

'I know it is.' His voice hardened. 'How's Hugh?'

'He got married, quick like. His new wife's pregnant. He's signed up too. It's why Maisie came to see me. I think she was trying to be nice. But Rosy asked where Anna had gone. I didn't know what to say.'

'Have you heard from High Royal?' He swallowed and took a sharp breath. 'Have you been to see Anna?'

Her smooth brow creased. 'The doctor sends me a letter every month. I think that's nice of him. Anna's doing as well as can be expected.' She sat up tall. 'I *have* been to see Anna. But she doesn't know who I am. It's as if I'm a nurse there.' She glanced at him. 'She doesn't love me. She never has.'

'That's not fair, Hilda.'

'You know how difficult it's all been.' Her eyes pleaded with him. 'You *do*, Frank?'

'I know. Just try and go when you can.'

She pulled out a handkerchief and wiped Nick's nose. A silence settled between them and a schism opened wider in his heart.

'So Hugh's signed up?' he said, moving away from the subject of Anna. 'That's a bit of a surprise. As is him getting married, and being a dad. That's why he signed up I'd guess, the little bastard.'

'Frank, your language.' She looked at him. 'To get away from his responsibilities?' She didn't let him answer. 'Yes, it is a surprise. Maisie's devastated.'

He studied her face, deciding to ignore her comment about responsibilities. 'Some discipline'll do him good.' He lay Nick gently on the bed and stood. 'Have you heard from Flo?' he asked finally. Both of them had evaded contact with their old friend, putting off telling her about Anna.

'Not recently,' she said, her voice buckling.

'I'll write to her.'

'If you must. It'll be good when you come home for a bit, Frank.' Almost as an afterthought, 'I miss you.'

He didn't answer. She didn't miss him. Just like his mother had never missed his father.

Hilda and the boys were allowed to stay and eat lunch with him and for a few hours there were no more crossed words or awkward conversations. Children were excellent at diffusion.

Before returning home, they visited the next day and Anna wasn't mentioned once. His gaze fell on Jim, who had no idea his sister existed; he'd been too young when Anna had come home in that fateful summer, before Nick's birth.

'You be a good boy for your mum, Jim,' Frank said.

Jim dipped his chin to his chest, not really understanding but pretending to, wanting to please his dad.

Hilda pulled a small bag of sweets from her pocket and gave them to Jim. 'Only have a couple, mind,' she said. 'And don't give Nick any. He's too young.'

Jim nodded. 'Jem's nice. Gave sweets.'

Hilda checked the ward's clock. 'We have to go, Frank, or we'll miss the train.' She rose.

Frank gathered up his boys and hugged them hard. He kissed Hilda on the cheek, as her lips were a territory that didn't belong to him anymore, if ever they had.

From his window he watched them leave the front entrance, and then he went back to sit on his bed thinking about Jem and her recent visit. After a few moments and in agitation he pushed away the blanket covering his legs. He'd been surprised she'd bothered to come and see him, the meeting between them had been awkward. They'd ended up talking more about Anna than anything else. He felt he couldn't ask about William, as he knew their marriage had been dead before it started. He didn't really know what to say, and could offer no advice, although he knew she wouldn't want any anyway.

It hadn't been until the end of Jem's visit when she asked about what had happened in France, and then they talked normally for a while about the French people and how he'd picked up a bit of French. Jem seemed interested in that, and they'd chatted, almost convivially, but then, from nowhere, she'd asked him what had happened to Anna to make her the way she was. The question was accusatory. As if she knew. Jem had a way of seeing into things and knowing. It was why people found her off-putting, uneasy at her crystal take. *I don't know*, he'd said. Jem had probed no more, got up, and put on her coat. *Look after yourself, Frank*. Shards of flint in her tone. He'd never taken to William Barnes but that day he'd felt a wave of sympathy for him.

The nurse had wheeled Taff back to their ward; his rehab sessions seemed to be relentless.

'You look miserable, mate,' Taff said.

Frank watched the nurse help him onto the bed. 'I'm all right. What about you?'

'Top of the world. Frances and the kids are coming to see me tomorrow. Hope I look a bit happier after their visit than you do after your family's,' Taff said with a tired grunt.

Frank had been sent immediately to a hospital in east London on his return from France, where he'd stayed for ten days before being moved to Parkwood. The severity of the pneumonia he'd come down with in France only hitting him properly when he found out about *Operation Dynamo*, the Dunkirk rescue operation. It had been as if he'd then allowed himself to be ill. The doctor told him he'd been lucky to come through it. Frank was never sure if he meant through the landings and rescue, or the virus that had ravaged the British army.

He studied Taff, who hadn't come out of Dunkirk unscathed. Taff had lost both his legs.

Although the Welshman was still more content than he'd ever be.

* * *

235

Two weeks later and days before he was to be discharged, the porter brought him the post. A letter from Flo. She'd beaten him to it; he'd procrastinated too long. She told him that after her ATS training she was moving to London, and she'd been invited to *something quite posh at the Savoy Hotel, can you believe it? Mary Churchill has asked me. If you are better by then, Frank, and well enough, perhaps we could meet up in London?*

It would be so good to see Flo again. He tucked the letter in his pocket.

He would meet with her and then rejoin his regiment. He wrote a letter to Flo, agreeing to her idea. Then he wrote one to Hilda saying he'd been ordered to join his regiment at Liverpool where they would be getting a ship that would take them to North Africa. He was so sorry he couldn't come up to Nottinghamshire but hoped to get leave before Christmas.

Two days later Hilda sent a telegram telling him she was moving from their house in The Avenues to a village five miles away. Jem was going up to help with the move. That was all she said.

Frank sank deeper but did not change his plan.

29

Richard

2002

Richard was at the Nottingham hotel where Jemima was staying by 4 p.m. He parked in the multi-storey and made his way through torrential rain. As he gave his name to the receptionist he felt a light tap on the sodden sleeve of his coat.

'Hello, Richard,' Jemima said. 'You got caught?'

'Seems I have been, yes.' He studied her face. His great-aunt who he hadn't met until a few days ago. At his grandma's funeral he hadn't noticed how alike in stature Jemima was to his grandad. She'd probably shrunk with age but still stood at a good five foot seven. Frank had been a giant to Richard when he'd been a kid. The gentle giant, his mum had called him. His mum had liked Frank; she hadn't been on the side of Hilda. It seemed his family were polarised, either towards Frank or Hilda. It was obvious that Jem was on Hilda's side.

'There's a nice café around the corner, shall we go there? Not far either. The rain doesn't look as if it's going to stop,' she said with firm conviction and already moving to the door.

'Sounds fine to me.'

Jemima walked slowly and he had to remind himself of her age.

They made their way to the back of the café.

Jemima shuffled onto the bench that leant against a lime-coloured artex wall and Richard took off his coat.

A waitress appeared. Scraped back hair, a nose piercing, heavy eyeliner that suited her pale and oval face. Her youth putting into perspective Jemima's years. The girl was a similar age to Beccy.

'What would you guys like?' she asked, her tone perky.

'Cappuccino, please.' Richard smiled at the waitress.

'And you?' she asked Jemima.

'Hot water with lemon. I don't want the water boiling.'

'On its way.' Her words stumbled out and Richard looked away from her unease.

He put himself in "work" mode, deciding to wade straight in, as he could see there would be no point messing around with Jemima.

'My dad came around this morning, with the information you'd decided to give him.'

'I apologise. It all must have come as a shock.'

'It did to my dad, yes. But not to me. I've already been given the details.'

'Recently?'

'It doesn't matter. Why have you decided to tell the family now, Jemima?'

'It's time. I might not live for much longer. As Florence might either. I'm guessing Florence has been in touch with you? I told Hilda years ago to get rid of her boxes in the loft, but she wouldn't. Poor Hilda.' The waitress came over and gave them their drinks, smiling at him, but avoided looking at Jemima.

'What happened, all those years ago? I've seen the photos. You were in one. Have you kept in touch with Anna?' he asked.

'Yes, I've always gone to see Anna. Hilda found it difficult, and she had the boys to look after.'

'Did my grandad go to see Anna? Or did they just leave her to languish there for the last sixty years?'

'Frank saw her regularly. As I say, Hilda had to think about the boys. But she did go to see Anna, occasionally, but less so in the latter years when—'

'Why was Anna kept a secret, Jemima?'

'That's what happened back then.'

'Anna's still there.'

'Hilda wanted to safeguard her family, her children.'

'But those children grew up into my dad and uncle?'

'It was just easier in the end, and the way things turned out.'

'I've read the admission forms. Anna was normal, then one day, she wasn't.'

'One can only conjecture why Anna lost her mind.' She picked out the lemon from her water. 'In the autumn of 1939 when Hilda and Frank brought Jim home from hospital, something happened which made it impossible *not* to have Anna admitted to a psychiatric institution. On the day Hilda returned from hospital with Jim, as he lay sleeping in his cot next to Hilda's bed, Anna came in and cut Jim's face.'

His dad's scar. He'd told him it had happened in a minor pit accident. 'What made Anna to do that?' he asked.

'I don't know. No one knows.' She played with the piece of wilted lemon. 'I suspect Frank knew why, but that's only my intuition.' She glanced up at him, her expression troubled. 'And because I know Frank so well. But you can't blame Hilda for allowing Anna to be admitted. Hilda couldn't keep Anna.'

He tried to remain rational and calm. 'And that was it? Anna went there and stayed there forever?'

'No. The next summer when Hilda was pregnant with Nick the doctor at the hospital felt it was the right time for Anna to come home. She was on medication, and supposedly much more docile.' She looked at Richard. 'Hilda allowed Anna to come back home. She gave Anna a second chance. Hilda left Anna for only moments with Jim. They disappeared. Anna took Jim. Hilda was out of her mind with worry; she didn't know where Anna had taken her brother. Hilda didn't want to tell anyone, she was too ashamed. She spent an hour on her own looking for them. Then Anna came home, but without Jim. The key to the Wendy house clutched in her hand, which she wouldn't give to Hilda. Hilda found the spare key and went to the allotment and found her baby – your dad Richard – locked in the Wendy house.'

'And then Anna was sent back to High Royal?'

'Yes. What else could Hilda do?'

'And Frank?'

She tilted the glass mug of lemon water, finishing it. 'As usual, Frank did nothing.' She followed the rim of her cup with an arthritic finger. 'As he did nothing for me with our father.'

'My great-grandfather? He was killed in the First World War? Gallipoli?'

'He was.'

'What *didn't* Frank do?'

'I'll leave you to work it out. I loved Anna, and so did Hilda, in her way, as much as she could.'

'Jemima,' he said. 'Did my grandma, Hilda, love Frank?'

She fumbled with the collar of her blouse. 'As much as any woman can love a man after what Hilda went through. And what Frank put her through, in the end.'

'What? More secrets?'

'It's a long time ago now, and it doesn't matter.' Jemima placed her mug in the middle of the table and seeing her resolute expression, Richard knew she wouldn't expand on her comment, although her next sentence told him volumes. 'And if, when, you meet Florence, remember, she was always biased towards Frank. Always.'

Awkwardly, she slid sideways from her seat. 'I'm planning on going to an exhibition. The taxi's picking me up at the hotel in fifteen minutes. It's been good to talk to you, Richard.' She touched his shoulder. 'Hilda wasn't the bad witch, and your grandad wasn't who you thought he was. And Florence… well, Florence has had another agenda her whole life. I'm sorry to shatter your memory of Frank.' She walked to the café's door.

Richard didn't move. He had his theory about his great-grandfather and Jemima and he didn't want to think about it at that moment. He stared at the chair she'd vacated and sadness overwhelmed him. Too many secrets within his family. The waitress came over.

'Would you like another drink? Something to eat?' she asked kindly.

He smiled up at her although he knew it wasn't getting anywhere near his lips. He shook his head.

241

'Not surprised you have no appetite, to be honest. I don't think I would after having coffee with her.' She wiped the table. 'Sorry, I shouldn't have said that.'

'It's fine,' he replied. 'It's what sometimes happens when you get older. Become a bit grumpy'

'I hope I don't ever get old, or grumpy.'

He gave her a five-pound note. 'Well, the alternative for the former isn't a good one,' he said with a grin. 'Keep the change, and thanks.'

'Thank *you*, mister.' She made her way back to the kitchen.

He took out his mobile from his pocket and pressed the contact number he had for the Waterside Nursing Home.

A receptionist answered.

'I'd like to speak with Celia please.'

'Who's calling?'

'Richard Cullen, regarding Florence Miller.'

'Celia's not on today, can someone else help you?'

'I'd like to visit Mrs Miller.'

'Are you family?'

'Friend. Celia will understand.'

'I'll get another nurse.'

The line went quiet. He was on hold.

'Can I help? This is the Sister speaking.'

'I'd like to visit Florence Miller,' he looked at his watch. 'I'd be there early evening?'

'I'm afraid that's not possible, Mr—'

'Richard Cullen. Mrs Miller was a friend of my late grandfather and she has expressed a wish to see me. Celia has been in contact with me.'

'Mrs Miller isn't well at the moment. She's suffering badly with bronchitis so I'm afraid a visit today is out of the question.'

'Can I check in tomorrow to see when she might be able to see me?'

'I'll get Celia to call you. Is this your mobile number?'

'Yes, please, if you could do that I'd appreciate it.'

'Good day, Mr Cullen.'

If he couldn't see Florence, he would make contact with Miss Betty Cunningham's niece, Fiona Trott.

Then his mobile rang out. His dad.

'Just thought I'd let you know I've been contacted by the council about Frank's allotment. It's all definitely approved. The diggers will be there next week. Frank's *Marycot* and wall will be gone forever. End of an era eh, son?'

Richard had known this was going to happen, and it wasn't the end of the world, of course it wasn't, but something niggled at him and he couldn't quite put his finger on it. The scene long ago when he was only a child, as he dug near to his grandad's wall, and Frank being so angry.

'We knew it was going to happen,' Richard said aloud.

'I've been to see Nick, and told him about Anna.'

'Is he okay?'

'As gutted as me, to be honest, son.'

'You told Mum?'

'No, not yet. You spoken to Gillian and Beccy?'

'They're going up to the Peaks for a few days.'

'Gillian made no mention to us of going away,' his dad replied.

'Some family stuff going on, Dad. Anyway, they can pick me up on the way home.'

'True. What's going on? It's not like you to keep family things to yourself. We're not that sort of family.' Richard moved the mobile to his other ear. 'Or maybe we are. You and Gillian are all right aren't you?'

'We're fine.'

'Is it Beccy?'

Richard didn't answer immediately.

'Son?'

'Beccy's pregnant.'

'Ah.'

'You don't sound surprised?'

'Your mum guessed.'

'Jesus, nothing gets past her does it?' Richard said, suppressing a smile

'When's Beccy due?'

'We're not sure she's keeping the baby, Dad.'

'Beccy'll be keeping the baby. Does Gillian want her to have an abortion?'

'I don't want to talk about it now, if that's okay.'

'Of course, son. What's your plan, with the other stuff?'

'I'm planning to go and see Florence Miller. But can't see her until tomorrow, or maybe even another day. I have contact details for someone else who lives in Derbyshire who might be able to help. I'm going back to Gran Hilda's to get my stuff then driving there.'

'You and Gillian, and Beccy need to talk.'

'I'll sort it out. I'll sort everything out.'

Richard disconnected. Shards of unease were settling within and he couldn't pinpoint why. The last time he'd had this feeling was the day before he'd got news of his grandad's death in February. It seemed like such a long time ago already. But the sense of foreboding was just as strong today as it had been then.

The night before Grandad Frank had passed away he'd dreamt of open skies and empty landscapes, of places where no people existed; only time and the gentle lassitude of energy depleting soaked through the image in his dream. No living being, just a pervading feeling of the many who had once lived. When he had woken he'd known it would be the first day without someone close to him in the living world – and that he had glanced something of the next.

When Gillian had called him in his Chambers to say Frank had had a massive second stroke and that he was in intensive care, Richard knew he would never make it to Nottinghamshire in time. And as he'd looked out of his office window that faced a busy London street, glancing up into a particularly clear city sky which, for a moment, mirrored the sight in his dream, and saw a lone kestrel hover high above the building opposite looking into his window, and at him – like a silent angel – its wings so wide and open, he knew. He knew Frank had died. As he'd turned back to his desk the phone that sat next to a photo of Gillian, him and Beccy, taken on a hiking holiday in the Peaks, rang out. It was Gillian again. Frank had died hooked up to tubes and lines, and machines.

Today he was having that same feeling and he couldn't shake it off.

He thought about calling Gillian again, tell her his irrational thoughts but decided against it. It was stupid and he attempted to claw back his objectivity, erase the dream that held his fears.

'You still here?' the waitress asked.

She sounded like Beccy and for an instant he thought it was. 'Sorry…'

'It's no problem, mister. You want another drink? You look upset.' She glanced at his phone. 'Bad news?'

'No. Not really. Not yet.'

She smiled consolingly.

'Thanks, I really do have to go,' he said getting up.

'Have a nice day.'

'You too.'

Richard didn't go immediately. He had to call Rosy Magson née Lambert. He settled back down in the chair and punched in the number.

A male voice answered. 'Hello.' His tone indicating he wasn't a man who liked picking up the phone.

'Hello, is that Mr Magson?'

'Who's this?' he barked back.

Richard raised his voice. 'I'm hoping to speak with Rosy Magson.'

Scuffling with the phone, Mr Magson called out his wife's name and then came back on the line. 'She'll be a bit, takes her a while to get down the stairs. Told the mare we should've had an extension in the bedroom,' he shouted into Richard's ear.

'It's okay, I don't mind waiting.'

Five minutes went by and finally Rosy picked up the phone, breathless. 'Mrs Magson speaking. Who is this?' Her voice quieter than her husband's, more measured.

'I'm sorry to bother you, Mrs Magson. My name's Richard Cullen. I'll try and be brief. Recently my grandmother died, Hilda Cullen. I'll be direct, Mrs Magson. I'm trying to find out about Anna Cullen.'

Silence.

'I hope you don't mind me asking, but my dad and uncle have only just found out that they have a sister.' He paused for effect. 'A sister who's still alive.'

'Anna was my friend, back before the war, before her mum and dad moved. I never quite knew what happened to Anna. My mum and dad never mentioned it. There was talk she'd been carted off. I never saw her again.'

'Yes, she was institutionalised. May I ask you about your brother, Hugh?'

'Bloody Hugh, was probably part of the problem with Anna. He wouldn't leave her alone. Frank knew, and that's why he beat Hugh up. Hugh deserved it. I hated my brother, was glad he died in the war. The world was a cleaner place without him.'

Momentarily, Richard didn't know how to respond to that one and so said nothing. 'Hugh was a fair bit older than Anna, I believe?'

'Yes, Anna was the same age as me. Hugh was seven years older than both of us.'

'Do you believe that Hugh… did something to Anna?'

'I really don't know, but I wouldn't have put it past him.' She went quiet, seemed to be thinking. 'Anna didn't like him, and I didn't blame her, and—'

'Yes?'

Silence.

'Are you still there, Mrs Magson?'

'I am. Anna told me that Hugh was always spying on her, following her. She asked me to say something to Hugh, but I couldn't. I was too scared of my brother. Families, eh?'

'Indeed,' Richard said.

'Even though Hugh died in the war, and was out of my hair, I still wanted to get away from that god forsaken village. I left in the early fifties. I never went back, only for my mum's funeral.'

'Thank you for all this information, Mrs Magson.'

'I'm sorry about Anna. I should have done something.'

'You were no more than a child.' He gulped back what was a threatening lump in his throat. 'It's my grandparents who were at fault.'

'Maybe. Hilda was a cold 'un with Anna, but your grandad adored her.'

'Well, again, thanks for your time.'

'One more thing. Do you know a Florence Miller? She might be able to help you. She was a friend of the family, she loved Anna, she might know something. Amazing woman as I remember. Not like the other women at the time, a bit of a maverick. Mind you, she's probably dead, must be at least ninety.'

'No she's not, and thanks for telling me that.'

'I liked Florence, and so did Anna.' He heard a clatter in the background. 'Got to go, my husband's just dropped something and probably doesn't even realise it, he's so deaf.'

'Thanks for your time.'

She'd already put the phone down.

He really needed to speak to Florence Miller.

30

Florence

London

The Few Speech during the London Blitz

– Churchill's Address to The House of Commons

August 20, 1940

"Never in the field of human conflict was so much owed by so many to so few. All hearts go out to the fighter pilots, whose brilliant actions we see with our own eyes day after day...

... America's President Roosevelt has recently made it clear that he would like to discuss with us, the development of American naval and air facilities in Newfoundland and in the West Indies... The English-speaking democracies will be somewhat mixed up together in some of their affairs...

... Like the Mississippi, it just keeps rolling along. Let it roll. Let it roll on full flood. I could not stop it if I wished; no one can stop it. Like the Mississippi, it just keeps rolling along. Let it roll. Let it roll on full flood, inexorable, irresistible, benignant, to broader lands and better days."

As thousands of others were doing throughout the British Empire, Florence made time to tune in to the

Prime Minister's radio speech. The landlady of the house where she was staying in Soho had allowed all the paying guests to sit in her front parlour whilst they listened avidly to Winston Churchill's words. Florence noted with a smile how at eleven in the morning and straight after the speech her landlady pulled a bottle of cooking sherry from her cupboard.

'One glass only. If you want more I'll add it to your room bill,' she said.

Cramped and sitting at the corner of the rickety table, Florence took a sip; not as good as the bottle Miss Cunningham kept in Chartwell's larder. 'I think I might like another one.'

The landlady's usually neutral expression lightened and she very nearly smiled. 'That's not a problem, Miss Judson.'

'Call me Florence, please do.'

'And please call me Elizabeth.'

'Nice sherry,' Florence said.

'No it's not, but it'll do. Good speech, the old rascal gave.'

'It was. It's his strong point, oration.' Florence was echoing her dad's observation.

'Oration?'

'You know what I mean.' Heat rose on Florence's neck.

Elizabeth grinned. 'I do.'

It was the last line of Winston Churchill's speech that was staying with Florence. All the importance of his words, but it was the image of the Mississippi River on a continent she'd never visited and probably never would – *rolling, rolling, rolling* – that imprinted on her mind. This led her thoughts directly to her last few days at the training camp in Devon. She'd heard rumours from the other girls, although she had no idea where they got their information from, that Randolph Churchill's wife, Pamela – with the *blessing* of Clementine Churchill and the Prime Minister – was sleeping with an American envoy who had been sent to scout out the war waters at Downing Street. The envoy reported immediately back to Roosevelt. The envoy, according to the gossip, had a lot of sway with the American President. Clementine Churchill's approval of Pamela's activities had surprised but not shocked Florence, because she knew Mrs Churchill would do absolutely anything to support her husband, and almost anything to support the war effort.

And Florence would too, if it came to it.

Mary Churchill had been present at the Devon camp on the day Florence had received her motorcycle license, and it was the daughter of the Prime Minister who'd presented her with it, and then gone on to talk about *sweetening up the Americans*, which was the whole reason for the planned buffet supper at the Savoy in October, which Mary Churchill had invited Florence to attend.

Florence had bought a new dress for the evening. Emerald green, she'd even managed to get hold of some stockings. The assistant in the tiny shop just off Wardour Street had sold her a red hat with matching gloves too, telling Florence that with her dark chestnut thick wavy hair, her wide-set "to-die-for" brown eyes, she looked like Anne Sheridan in them. That had done it. Florence had blown her entire week's wages on one outfit. She hoped it would be worth it, even if she were only to manage converting one American she might meet at the buffet to the British cause. Whilst at the shop she'd also picked up a beautiful black and red ribbon that she planned to give to Anna.

Over the last few months Florence had been catapulted into another world. She'd already carried out her first batch of jobs in London, choosing her lodging because there was a tiny back yard with easy access for her motorcycle. She owed her cousin Harold a lot, and had told him so in her last letter.

Florence wondered if the Prime Minister would now eat his words regarding her not being married. It was rumoured it wouldn't be Winston Churchill who would win the war, but the female population of the country. Florence was alive with excitement. Ready. For everything. Especially supper at the Savoy.

'I will put two on the guest list, Florence,' Mary had said. *'So feel free to bring a friend. It will be fun, and safe, the hotel is positively hidden by sandbags, and I swear miles of blackout material for the windows. It's a buffet for the Officers' Sunday Club, but in recognition of the drive to recruit women into the war effort and encouraged by my mother, and my father of course, they have opened it up to us mere females. I hope you can come, Florence.'* Mary Churchill had then laughed mischievously, *'There will be some Americans there too. Part of our "duty" as women will be to encourage the Americans to join the war in the fight against Hitler.'*

Mary had carried on, *'Britain needs to show the Americans it is their war too. The United States cannot remain isolationist. We must do whatever we can to make Roosevelt change his mind.'*

Mary had sounded just like her father.

Florence finished her glass of sherry and stayed another hour in the warm parlour talking to her landlady. It was that day when she and Elizabeth Banwell bonded, and was to be a real turning point in her life, recognising she would never return to Chartwell as an employee. Her life had moved on and there would be no going back.

Elizabeth began to prepare the evening's supper, and Florence made her way out into the small back yard. Methodically, she began cleaning and carrying out the maintenance on her motorcycle; an Ariel WNG, her pride and joy, and just as Harold had taught her.

The oil was low, so she topped it up; she polished the wheels, and the mudguards, she rubbed hard at its leather seat. She also found a fault with the brakes, which after half an hour of reading her manual, she managed to fix. By the time she'd finished it was suppertime.

As she entered the parlour Elizabeth poured Florence a glass of sherry and handed her a cigarette. 'Here you are. For a working girl.'

Florence: a butterfly emerging from its safe but limited cocoon.

31

September 5th 1940

Florence arrived at the café just off Oxford Street at midday. She ordered herself a cup of tea, a scone and waited at a table by the window.

She saw Frank before he saw her. He crossed the street, looking utterly out of place amongst the city bustle and even from where she was sitting she saw his look of concern directed at the sandbags; she also saw how he'd grown prematurely old. The grey at his temples striking, lines like furrows on his once smooth forehead, his six-foot frame hunched in the light military coat he wore, which was wrapped tightly around his body, as if he were crumpling up against the elements.

The sun was high in a crystal-clear London sky. It was touching eighty degrees in the shade.

Frank's face glowed as he caught sight of Florence through the window and a heat of expectancy rose in her too. Nostalgia and a sense of homesickness for Westerham plunged through her, as did the memory of the fledgling love for a man who didn't belong to her. But then, an image of Anna in an asylum dug into her mind. Perhaps Frank had changed as much inside as he had on the outside. Perhaps she didn't know him anymore.

Frank swung open the café's heavy wooden door allowing a burst of heat and noise into the small space. The bombs had abated for the last eighteen hours leaving the population of London not quietened at all, if anything enlivened. War had brought chaos and madness and grief to the capital city but also a consistent stoicism, leaving behind forever the capriciousness of the previous decade. In London Florence felt more encased within the humanity of her fellow human beings than she'd ever experienced within her own village. She met London in its darkest moments, became infatuated with the city as she imagined she could be with a mysterious, dangerous, or even forbidden, lover.

'Flo, you look wonderful,' Frank said, standing next to her chair in full army uniform. His face cracked into a hint of a smile. Good to see him. So good. She made to stand. He placed a hand on her shoulder. 'No, don't get up.' He stared into her face. 'You really do look great. War suits you, Flo.'

'I wouldn't say that. But getting away from Westerham does.'

'I thought you loved it at Chartwell?'

'I did.'

'This war'll last longer than the Great War, you know. You'll be away from home longer than you think.'

The unforgiving sun pouring through the window did him no favours and guilt passed through her at her own enjoyment of Europe's conflict. Frank was part of the war proper.

'Sit down, Frank.' She pointed to the chair. So good to see him.

She asked the waitress to bring two more cups of tea and two more scones. Frank looked as if he needed fattening up.

The waitress placed the scones on the table, scrutinising Frank and his uniform. He seemed oblivious. Florence watched him too, seeing what the waitress saw. A good-looking bloke returned from fighting.

'This is on the house, for our soldier here,' the waitress said, bending forward a little, getting closer to Frank, checking his ring finger. He'd never worn a wedding ring. 'My brother's been drafted. He's in East Africa.' Her face opened up just talking about her brother. 'I didn't even know where Africa was until I looked it up in a book. He'll be all right though, won't he? I mean you are, cos you're here.'

Frank hadn't looked at the waitress once, not directly. She was a very pretty girl and Florence guessed she'd have a lot of admirers. Frank didn't appear to notice.

He answered but was looking at Florence. 'What regiment's he with?'

'First Battalion Essex, Artillery.'

Finally he caught the waitress's eye. 'Your brother'll be fine. Probably safer there than it is in London at the moment.'

'You think so?'

He smiled. 'I really do.'

'If you want more tea and the last few scones, let me know. On the house.' The extra wiggle she displayed as she walked away wasn't for Florence's benefit.

Frank had long since stopped looking at the girl.

Despite the melancholic expression Frank carried there was no question about his attractiveness. But he was married, and married to Hilda, although Florence conceded it wasn't as if she was reluctant to get involved with men before marriage; oh no, absolutely not. In her late twenties Florence was not a virgin and when she allowed herself to remember who she'd had that very first unsatisfactory fumble with, the heat of mild shame bit through her; shame only because the whole experience had been so cold. Her dalliance with William Barnes had been before Jem had walked down the aisle with him, so she didn't feel any guilt about sleeping with a married man. It had though, been a mistake.

Frank had fallen quiet. Florence's stomach tightened as she took in the leanness of his body, the thickness of his hair, the way his violet eyes slanted when he smiled. 'I'm so relieved you got home alive,' she said. 'I would've been distraught… you know, if it'd turned out differently. It doesn't bear thinking about.' From the corner of her eye she spotted the waitress studying them from the counter.

'To be honest,' he said, 'I thought I'd die with the pneumonia and not from a Vichy bullet.'

She found his hand that lay on the table. 'So, you'll be heading back up to Nottingham soon? Spend your leave with Hilda, Jim, and Nick?'

He had the good grace to redden. 'Flo, I'm sorry we've lost touch. Me and Hilda miss you.'

'Maybe you do, but not Hilda.' He was holding her hand, the pressure of his fingers intense.

This was the time to say what she had to say. She thought of Anna and took in the humid air of the café in gulping breaths.

'Life hasn't turned out as I thought it would,' he said quietly.

'No, it often doesn't.' She moved her hand away, missing the warmth of it immediately. She shuffled in her chair. 'Is there something you want to tell me, Frank?'

He looked through her as if not hearing. 'Tell me about the posh bash you've been invited to.'

Liking the subject and still not ready to confront him head on, she allowed the sidetrack. She told him about Harold and learning to ride a motorcycle, that Harold was now in Africa, about Devon and her training, about Mary Churchill. And how she'd spent all of her money at the dress shop. She knew her face shone with enthusiasm as she recognised too, the fizzing in her stomach as she recounted it all.

He smiled at her monologue. The first really proper smile since he'd walked into the café. 'You really are in your element.' He hesitated. 'And you really do look wonderful. Has anyone told you look a bit like Anne Sheridan?'

Florence laughed. 'They have. It's why I ended up spending a whole week's wages on a new outfit.'

'You never change, always full of it, life, no holding you back. It's brilliant about the dispatch riding. I'm proud of you.' The grin dropped from his face. 'You're not quite who we all thought you were.'

'You mean you and Hilda?'

'I suppose. You're special, Flo. Find out which regiment Harold's in, write and tell me.' He pulled a piece of paper from his pocket, turned it over so she had a clear space to write Harold's details down.

She took it and scanned the front page as she did so. Orders from his regiment. 'This says you're going the day after tomorrow? I thought you were on leave, that you'd be going up to see your family?'

258

'Change of plan. Write to me, Flo.'

'Frank, you need to talk to me about Anna. And—'
She bit into a scone, delaying her words, chewing slowly.
Finally she swallowed. 'About what you said to Churchill
in the letter you sent to him from France.'

At this he sank deeper into his chair as if trying to
make himself invisible. 'How do you know about that?'

'It's a long story, and… I'm sorry. Your letter was
filed in Mrs Churchill's "to do pile." I saw it when I was
closing up her room in May. I recognised your writing,
and your name was on the back of the envelope.'

'And you opened it?'

'It's a good thing I did or I wouldn't have known
about Anna. Why on earth did you write to Mr
Churchill?'

If possible he slumped further into the chair and the
unbroken August sunlight pummelled at his features.
Vulnerable, yet too handsome. She couldn't be angry
with him. And, he had every reason to be angry with her.
It was never a pleasant sensation: to be caught out, to be
seen to be doing the irrational. Because writing to
Winston Churchill was definitely a bit ridiculous.

'I needed to tell someone Anna'd been taken to the
mental hospital,' he said softly. 'It was a stupid thing to
do, and I never thought Mr Churchill would read it.'

'You could have told me.'

'I should have done.'

'In the letter, it reads as if you wanted to say more?'

'I was in France. At my wits end. I wasn't thinking
properly.' He peered past her, through the window.
'There's no more I wanted to say.'

'You and Hilda should have told me you'd sent Anna away. What's happened? Why have you and Hilda allowed her to even be taken to a place like that?' He remained silent. 'I've been to see Jem, Frank.'

'It's the best place for Anna. Honestly, it really is. He watched her. 'What did Jem tell you?'

'Not much, that Anna's in the asylum. Why don't you have Anna back home? Surely Anna will get better, at home, with her mum and dad?'

'It's more complicated than that.'

'Tell me.'

'The doctor who's looking after Anna thinks she was jealous of Hilda being pregnant with Jim, and that's what started all this off.'

'And do you believe that to be true?'

'I don't know, it seems plausible.'

It sounded totally implausible to her.

He went on to tell her about what Anna had done to Jim, cutting a three-week-old baby's face. After he'd gone upstairs and put Jim in the cot next to his sleeping mother. She couldn't place the Anna she knew with the Anna Frank was telling her about and in that moment her heart really did reach out to Hilda, as well as for Anna.

He carried on. 'We did have Anna back the summer before Nick was born. Everything was going fine, we thought, I mean Anna wasn't *normal* but we thought she was *safe*, the doctor had said the medication she was on had made her safe.' He rubbed his hands together. 'We believed him' He stopped talking abruptly. 'So we brought Anna home. Hilda wanted to.'

He ploughed on ignoring the new customers who'd sat at the next table.

'Hilda left Jim with Anna in the house. She'd only gone over to the next avenue. When she got back half an hour later, Anna and Jim had gone. Hilda couldn't find them anywhere, and I was at work.'

'But she *did* find them?'

'Yes, after an hour, Hilda went to the allotment, she doesn't know why she did, why she'd thought they would be there, but Jim was.'

'On his own, a baby?'

'Anna had locked him up in the Wendy house. Luckily I'd made a spare key and Hilda could get in to get him. He was all right.'

'Where was Anna?'

'She'd gone back home, locked herself in the outside toilet. I'd got home from the pit by then and could get Anna out, persuaded her. But after that we had to send Anna back to High Royal. We had no choice, Flo.'

'Did Anna say why she did what she did, taking Jim?'

He raked his hands through army-cut hair, squeezed his eyes shut. 'She hardly spoke but said he'd be safe with Winston and Clementine in the Wendy house, that they would look after him. That they would treat him as their child... like Marigold.'

'My God. Anna took everything in you ever told her about Marigold. Anna was always singing that song.'

He leant back in the chair. 'Anna completely refuses to believe Hilda and I are her mum and dad.'

'I'm so sorry.' She pushed her finger into the puddle of spilt tea on the lacquered table. 'What caused Anna to be like this? There has to be a reason? It's not because of jealousy, surely? That's not who Anna is. She was desperate for a brother or sister.'

'The allotment, the Wendy house, Hugh Lambert.'

'Rosy's brother? What about him?'

Frank pulled at the sleeve of his shirt then undid his collar.

'What? You think he interfered with her? Does Hilda know? Is the hospital aware?'

'No, neither know.'

'Have you confronted Hugh?'

'Sort of.'

'Sort of?'

Frank stared out the window. 'I beat him to a pulp.'

'Did he admit to it?'

'He's never admitted to it.'

She watched him closely. 'What makes you so certain he did… what he did? And if it was Hugh, and not someone else?'

'I just know.'

'*How* do you know, Frank?'

'A man knows. She's blossomed. Beautiful, like her mother.'

'You have to sort this out. It's like history repeating itself. And Jem too.'

His eyes left the street vista and darted quickly back to Florence.

She carried on, 'Hilda was interfered with, and now Anna. And… Jem. Your father.'

'Did Hilda tell you about Jem?'

'No, she didn't, I guessed. Only recently that it's all fallen into place. Why does Jem blame you?'

'Because I didn't help. Do anything.'

'You were under seven, how could you do anything?'

'There's something else,' he said.

'About Jem?'

'No. There's something at the allotment.'

'What?'

He dragged his eyes back to Florence. 'Nothing. I'm rambling, I'm tired, still don't feel myself. Nothing, Flo.'

There was more, but the moment had passed. 'You have to tell Anna's doctors about Hugh Lambert. I can't believe you haven't.'

There was something else that wasn't just bothering him, it was eating him alive. She saw it. He wouldn't be telling her today though; he was too on the edge. Her intuition told her that Hugh was a key figure in the mystery and that she'd find out more on her visit to see Anna.

'Is Hugh still in Nottinghamshire?'

'He's joined up, Hilda told me. Not conscripted, voluntarily. With a bit of luck he won't last long. With his attitude and natural ability to annoy people, he might well see the end with a British bullet.' He took a breath. 'He's married too, a baby on the way.'

'Poor woman is all I can say. I did try to tell you years ago, about Hugh.'

'Leave it, Flo, Please.'

She reached across the table and took both his hands. 'Does Hilda know you're not going up to Notts?'

He nodded. 'She sent me a telegram. She's moving house. To a village five miles away. She doesn't want people asking her about Anna.'

'No, she wouldn't.'

'This isn't Hilda's fault.'

'I'm going to go, to visit Anna.'

He rummaged in his pocket taking out a brown paper bag. 'Six ounces of pear drops. Lucky to get them.' He pulled out another. 'Two oranges too.' He handed them to her. 'Give the sweets to Anna when you see her. She still loves them. Don't let them get gooey. The oranges are for you.'

She smiled at him. He remembered.

'So are you seeing anyone, Flo? Do you have a boyfriend, it's none of my business, but you know, you're a good-looking woman.'

'And getting on a bit?' she said with amusement.

'I didn't mean that.'

She caught his eye. 'I think you were the best catch in Westerham. Hilda's a lucky woman,' she said, her tone measured. 'Despite everything.'

'I don't think she'd agree with you.'

'I wish you could talk to me about it, and about Anna.'

'One day.' He pulled a packet of cigarettes from his pocket and offered her one. She took it. Frank leant forwards and lit it. 'You seem sort of happy, Flo.'

'Sort of, yes.'

'You were always the wild one, given a chance. The war's given you a chance, hasn't it?'

She nodded.

'You looking forward to your posh supper at the Savoy?' he said.

'Bit nervous.'

'Don't be, you'll knock 'em dead.'

'You think so?'

'I know so.'

She tried to ignore his admiring glance and was embarrassed at the heat she knew was obvious on her face. She told him about Pamela Churchill and the American envoy, about Mary saying, *we all have to do our bit.*

'Clementine Churchill's no shame, and the old man's just as bad.' He took hold of her hand. 'I'm staying near Marble Arch. Do you want to walk with me? Get something to eat at my hotel? I mean if you have nothing else on today?'

'I'm free today.' The scones hadn't been that good and she was hungry, and Frank looked as if he could do with the company. That's what she told herself.

He stood up. Taller now, his stoop less apparent. The sun catching the violet in his eyes. Frank walked towards the café counter to pay.

'Thanks, mister,' the waitress said. 'Have a good day with your girlfriend.' She put Frank's tip straight in her pocket.

It had been an easy mistake to make. A wartime London population not knowing if they would survive the night was infested with lovers, clandestine relationships, and abandonment. You could almost smell it. Florence could.

After leaving the café Frank held out his arm for her and together they walked through the beating heat of London, and mostly in silence. As they paced, everything and everyone seemed so far away, as if they were not real any more. The only real thing was her work, the war, and walking next to Frank in a city so different from where they'd been born. As they entered Marble Arch he'd relaxed, the deep crevices on his forehead melted away. She saw what other people might see. A couple taking a stroll on a hot summer's day.

Frank placed his arm over her shoulder. 'Here we are.'

They crossed the road. The hotel was bright, catching the late afternoon sun as it pulsated onto the palatial but tired-looking entrance. The hotel's glory decades in the past.

'I've some whisky in my room,' he said to her. 'Shall we go up and have a glass before we eat? Build up an appetite?'

'Good idea.'

'I don't mean anything by it, Flo. We can go straight into the dining room if you'd rather?'

'No, I'd like to go to your room.'

Gently, he took hold of her arm. 'It's the third floor, we'll take the stairs.'

Lives had changed, the world was different in the vacuum of war. Everything was different.

She and Frank were different.

He unlocked the door and pushed it open with his foot. 'Make yourself at home.'

The room was bigger than she'd thought it would be, with a double bed underneath a huge bay window that looked over the massive green of Hyde Park. 'This must be costing you a fortune,' she said trying not to look at the bed.

'I got a good deal.' He pulled a battered suitcase from the sidewall and opened it. Florence recognised it from the day he, Hilda and Anna had taken the train to Nottinghamshire, the day they left Westerham for their new life, and hesitance knocked at her. He took out a bottle of whisky. 'I keep it in here in case the maid gets ideas.' He smiled.

She saw glass tumblers sitting on the table next to the bed. She moved over and picked them up. 'You drink now?

'Not really.'

'A small one for me.'

He held her hand that held the glass and poured the whisky. 'You sure?' She nodded. 'I'm sorry what happened all those years ago after the dance,' he said. 'I've never apologised. I knew that night. And then… the next day Hilda finally saying yes. After four years. I had to, Flo. I had to marry her.'

'I was devastated.'

'Me too.' He took away her glass, placing it on the table, and pulled her to him. She rested her head on his shoulder and the silence and the glitter of sun inside the room fell over them. He took her face and found her lips. She thought she'd taste whisky, but it was the gin of thirteen years before that she experienced. The same ripple of hotness that she's felt all of those years ago drummed up into her groin and settled inside her stomach. Readiness and need consumed her.

Frank pulled away, but with a different hesitation from the church wall. Then he'd stopped for Hilda. Today he hesitated for her.

'I'm sure, Frank.'

'Flo…'

She heard and felt his passion, and knew this thing happening between them was equal. But that day, after so long, it wasn't love she felt for Frank. Not the love it had been all those years before. It, and she, had changed.

She responded to his caresses, his tongue, she led his hand to where she wanted it to go. They fell onto the bed, in silence, and he found the place that ached. Florence gasped; she could not wait any longer and pulled him to her.

It was everything she knew it could be, and more. She allowed herself the freedom to feel the pleasure she'd been searching for and which was now overflowing and consuming her entire body.

The two friends lay spent on the bed; Florence tucked up sideways, her head nestled on his chest, his dark hairs tickling her nose. The August sun dipping in the sky but its feather rays still tumbling through the half-drawn curtains.

It was Florence who spoke. 'This shouldn't have happened, should it?'

He turned. 'Of course it should.'

'This won't happen again. I don't love you, Frank, not like Hilda loves you, and not like how you once loved Hilda.' *Oh, how she loved Frank.*

He traced a finger across her cheek. 'I understand.' He touched her hair, moving a strand away from her face. 'Someone somewhere is going to be very lucky getting you, Florence.'

He never called her Florence, not since they were children. She peered at him and a splinter of guilt siphoned through. Now it was over, Hilda, Anna, Frank's boys were too real inside her mind.

She kissed him tenderly on the cheek and got up, began dressing.

'You don't have to go,' he said, 'at least have a drink before you leave.'

'I don't like whisky.'

'I know.' He smiled. 'Hilda'll never know about this.' He pulled the sheet from his body and got up.

She looked away, not from embarrassment but because it was time for her to leave. 'Never,' she replied. 'It's our secret.'

She and Frank were to share many secrets in the coming years and them sleeping together that one sweltering and bright summer's day in London was the easiest to keep. The only person to know about Frank would be Florence's future husband. If Hilda and Frank's marriage had taught her nothing else, it had taught her to be open with the man with whom she would spend the rest of her life. Her afternoon with Frank showed her what she had been looking for, what she had wanted to physically feel, was attainable. If she had known that day who she would meet at Mary Churchill's buffet, would she have waited? She didn't think she would. Making love with Frank was good, it was real, and instead of hampering their friendship after the war, she suspected it only strengthened it. There was no misconstruction of intent. None at all. Hilda and his family were so far away, not only in location, but in spirit too. Like Frank, Florence was a part of the war and it was that which bound them.

He picked up her hat and gave it to her. 'You will write to me?'

'Of course I will, I always do, don't I?' She watched him, watched his torment. He wouldn't leave Hilda and his boys, and this knowledge calmed her. The time was long past for the two of them.

'Don't forget the pear drops and oranges, and give Anna a big hug from me. I love her, Flo.'

She felt he was going to say more and she hovered at the door, contemplating pressing him again about Anna, but she did not. Now was not the time and maybe Frank was right. This was all to do with Hugh.

'I know you do,' she replied finally.

She opened the door.

'Enjoy Mary Churchill's buffet,' he said smiling.

'I will.' She hesitated. 'I don't regret it, Frank.'

'Neither do I.' It was Frank's turn to hesitate. 'Flo, I plan to come back. And when I do we have to talk… about Anna. About Hilda. If… if I don't come back, there will be a letter for you.'

She left it at that.

As Florence walked through Hyde Park an unsettled feeling followed her. Like a sentient shadow. She should have stayed, found out the truth about Anna but knew Frank wasn't ready to share that truth.

She needed to find out the reason for Frank's disquiet, Hilda's silence.

And Anna's madness.

32

October 2nd 1940

Florence was late getting home from Kings Cross where she'd bought her ticket to go up to Yorkshire to visit Anna; tomorrow's train, 3 o'clock. First though, was the Savoy bash. Tonight. It was time to wear her dress, and try to be someone she wasn't. Her mum had told her not to worry, *born in the wrong household you were, my girl. You'll fit into the Savoy as easily and snug as ol' Cinder's foot slipped into that slipper.* She missed her mum.

Florence surveyed her tiny bedroom but the mirror on the wall was huge and she could see herself in full, nearly. Her feet were missing in her reflection. She didn't mind this though, because she hadn't been able to afford new shoes. But as she looked down at her suede turquoise slip-ons that she'd buffed up with an implement Elizabeth had lent her, she was pleased at the match with the emerald green dress.

She'd straightened her hair with irons and put on the reddest lipstick she'd ever worn. She fiddled with her hat. She loved it but was unused to such frivolity in her headwear. It sat precariously on the front of her head, just as the shop assistant had shown her. The ruffles of red fabric seemed to her to be asymmetrical. She pushed and pulled them but finally, after hearing the church clock outside strike six, gave in. She scrutinised her reflection. Not bad. Not bad at all. Momentarily she thought about Frank, guessing the shine in the eyes staring back at her was due to the afternoon in his hotel.

She picked up the red gloves, checked her hat one more time, and left her room.

Florence was ready.

'You could have come with me, you know, Elizabeth.' Florence went to sit at the kitchen table, but not before shoving a paper handkerchief under one of the legs of the uneven surface.

'Not my thing, Florence. I want ol' Churchill to win the war for us. He is the right man for the job. I mean, he likes a good war doesn't he? But I hate all that upper-class stuff.'

Elizabeth was at heart a staunch labour supporter, *not a commie though*, she was always keen to emphasise. Left in her politics, although it didn't stop her from sleeping with a wealthy man who lived in Knightsbridge. Elizabeth's socialism was a bit like Churchill's domestic communism. When it suited. Wednesdays were Elizabeth's nights with her lover. Florence's room was the one below where Elizabeth slept. Every Wednesday Florence had to sleep with cotton wool stuffed in her ears, and every Thursday morning there was always a late breakfast. The gentleman politely doffed his cap to her on leaving, a huge smile in place. He reminded her a bit of Mr Churchill, the way he was able to appear quite ordinary and at home with the lower class, in a way peculiar to the confident and rich.

'It'll probably be deathly boring,' Florence said.

Elizabeth grinned. 'Probably. Lots of lovely food, though, I'm guessing.'

'I hope so.'

Elizabeth laughed. 'Never known a girl with an appetite like you.'

Florence turned to her landlady, her smile slipping. 'There'll be the sirens tonight again.'

'No doubt. I might ignore them and take my chances.' She smiled at Florence. 'It won't be the local station where you'll be sheltering this evening?'

'I thought the bash might be cancelled, but it hasn't been.'

Cancelling was not the way of their leaders, and as it was becoming increasingly obvious, not the way of the British people either.

Elizabeth surveyed her lodger and her new dress. 'You look lovely, Florence.'

'You must go when the sirens start, promise me you will?'

'We'll see.'

Mr Churchill had forecast *The Battle of Britain* in his summer speech, but no one foresaw the ferocity of the attacks. They had begun in the daylight hours, but now it was only during the blackness of night when the Germans dropped their lethal bombs. She, Elizabeth and the other lodgers had spent nearly every night since the Blitz began in either a nearby spare and unused Anderson shelter, or later, within the ample depths of the London Underground. The smooth sound of the siren caused the city's population to move and mobilise to safety without even thinking. It didn't take long to become accustomed to a new way of living. Many though, after only weeks, decided to forgo their own welfare and stay in their homes. Many paid with their lives. Florence didn't want Elizabeth to be one of the Luftwaffe's casualties.

She understood what Elizabeth meant though, conditions in the air raid shelters were abysmal, but the spirit of the Londoners was astounding. Men and women woke up in the morning, made their way to the earth's surface to find out if their homes were still standing. For many, they weren't and they would spend the day rummaging through their life's belongings, attempting to recover anything useable.

After the first few days of the Luftwaffe's onslaught these people were just glad to be alive. By the end of September 1940, the estimate of civilian casualties was seven thousand. That number would only increase.

Elizabeth reminded Florence it really was time to go if she wanted to get to the Savoy on time. She handed Florence a shilling to get a taxi.

'I don't want you to be late, not after, Lord above, all that faffin' around upstairs. Anyway that hat might drop off if you actually walk anywhere.' She smiled kindly. 'If possible, forget the war for a bit.'

Florence took the money gratefully, and kissed Elizabeth on the cheek. It was Wednesday and Elizabeth was in a good mood, and another reason her landlady was even contemplating forgoing a shelter that night.

Germany had invaded Libya in early September and as she got in the taxi she thought of Frank in the desert, and caught her breath at the great swathe of life that was gulping down all of them. Would anyone go back to being who they'd once been? She thought not. Only perhaps those who had no knowledge of what was happening in the world. People who chose not to follow the news, listen to the radio, because she knew there were many who preferred not to know. And other people, like Anna, where the world they lived within was possibly worse than the world on the outside. She shook her head, trying to get rid of her thoughts. The taxi driver glanced at her in his mirror.

'You all right, love?'

'I am, thank you.'

The driver was a rare breed, as most of the London cabbies were being conscripted, and Florence knew from the difficulties she was having herself with getting petrol that the remaining cabmen were driving vehicles that had to be maintained on rationed petrol in the blacked-out, bombed-out, sandbagged streets of London. She did wonder though if the cab would actually make it to the hotel as it spluttered its way down the street. She held on to her hat as the car sped up, and just as they approached the acute corner, which always took her unawares on her motorcycle.

'Sorry, love. Took me by surprise, the acceleration.' The cabbie laughed turning his head and hitting the pavement hard with the rear right wheel.

'Yes, always good to check acceleration,' she said, holding back a giggle. He gave her a bewildered look. 'You can slow down, there's no hurry.' She really wished he'd concentrate on the road. The thought of being killed by a lax cabbie and not a German bomb brought a wry smile. The irony.

'You're looking pretty, love. The Savoy Hotel you said? Hobnobbing tonight are ya?'

'Sort of.'

'You'll knock 'em dead.' He glanced at her again. 'That green there suits you. Anyone told you that you look like Anne Sheridan?'

Florence grinned at him. 'Yes, they have.' She retrieved her compact and pretended to fuss with her lipstick and the rest of the journey passed in silence.

33

Standing in the outside foyer of the Savoy Hotel Florence fretted at the length of her new dress, the colour, and the hat. She moved to the hotel's perimeter wall, trying to merge with its bricks, but the emerald was a beacon – as the shop assistant had said it would be. Within minutes she was surrounded and couldn't remember ever having been such a draw and wondered if it was the leftover radiance from the hotel room in Marble Arch.

An elderly man who was not in uniform spoke to her; she found out later from Mary Churchill he was a member of parliament, part of the labour coalition, a Churchill dissenter in politics but his friend around the dinner table, as many were.

'Good evening, my dear.' He appraised her and any paltry confidence melted away. She'd spotted a group of women getting out of what looked to her like a very expensive car. Dressed immaculately, wealth wafting.

'Good evening,' she replied.

The man took in the arriving ladies. 'They do this thing all the time, don't worry. Be yourself. Are you one of Mary's?' He didn't let her answer, 'I'm Daniel Dalton. It's a pleasure to meet you.'

'Florence Judson, sir.' She touched her hat and stopped herself from curtseying.

'Your hat looks fine, Miss Judson. And no need for all that.' He pointed to her knees. She'd dipped a little, couldn't stop herself.

She liked him. 'One of "Mary's?"'

'An ATS girl. I know Mary's invited a few.'

'Oh, yes, that's me.'

'And what's your… speciality?'

'I'm a motorcycle dispatch rider.'

His serious and remarkably unlined face spread into a smile. 'Interesting. And are you enjoying your newly found freedom?'

Florence's muscles coiled a little. The men of the country were aware of the limitedness of women's lives, why did they pretend they didn't know? That it had taken a war for women to be given 'freedom' brought stubbornness to her reply.

'It's been given to me because there wasn't much choice?' She couldn't believe she'd said that.

'Ah! You are right, Miss Judson. Forgive me. I see with women such as yourself there'll be no way Herr Hitler will be treading our shores.'

That was funny, and it made her think of Harold.

He grinned and as he did so another man joined them. 'Ah, Edward,' Dalton said. 'A pleasure you could make it. Hopefully the Nazis won't start with their bombs until we've drunk all the best port.' He turned to Florence, 'And bored all the best looking ladies.'

She hoped the MP was being truthful. She didn't feel like one of the best looking ladies. She really wasn't sure about the emerald. She stared at the man who'd joined them. The vision of excellence (that had been the ATS girls' description of a man who was worth using a new pair of stockings for) was only an inch or so taller than her, but stocky. A head of wavy blond hair that wasn't cut in the usual short style she was used to seeing. Brown eyes, not unlike her own, but deeper, less chestnut more chocolate. A wide, open, symmetrical face. Perfect skin, dark, as if he'd spent time in the sun, toffee coloured. He looked like no one she'd ever come across before; like a Greek god from the books Frank used to bring to the woods for all three of them to gawp at.

'May I ask to be introduced to this gorgeous lady, Daniel?' the man said, his accent telling her he was an American.

Florence stepped forward. 'My name's Florence Judson.'

He took her hand and kissed it. 'Very good to meet you, Miss Judson.'

'Please call me Florence.'

'Florence.' He pronounced her name in the most beautiful way, a caress curving around her. The inside of her stomach fluttered and flowed. 'That is a wonderful hat you are wearing. We'd better keep you inside or the Luftwaffe may well spot us.'

Daniel Dalton laughed, but tightly. Florence suspected that Mr Dalton did not like the American.

'Thank you,' she said. 'You're American aren't you?'

He held out his hand. 'I am. Edward Miller,' he said softly. 'It's lovely to meet you. I'm sorry, I should have introduced myself immediately. I'm a doctor in the Medical Corps. Not in uniform, as you see.'

'Edward, I'll leave you with Florence, but be sure to bring her inside soon for the punch,' Daniel Dalton said. 'Mary Churchill is already here, I'm sure she will be keen to speak with you, Florence?' He ambled away.

What would she say now? She couldn't believe she was here. This wasn't her world and yet the man standing beside her made her feel as if it were, by the way he looked at her, spoke to her rather than *at* her. Stood next to her with respect rather than contempt. Edward Miller was way ahead of his time and she never quite knew if this was because he was American or because… he was Edward.

He waited for her to speak and didn't rush her. Edward would never rush her.

Finally she said; 'I must go and find Mary Churchill, please excuse me.'

'I'll come in with you, Florence, if that's okay?'

They moved inside. Florence's jaw lowered as she entered the hotel. The blacked-out curtains that spread across the windows had been covered in splatterings of silver sparkle. Inside were more women dressed in their finest, dripping both jewellery and confidence and Florence silently thanked the shop assistant who, it turned out, had been right; she saw it in Edward Miller's reaction to her.

Edward led her gently through enormous double doors that led into the ballroom, where round tables spread for what looked like an eternity until she realised the room was covered in mirrors along one wall. A group of men stood on the stage playing Glenn Miller tunes.

'Mary's over there, by the band stand.' Adeptly, he led her, nodding to people as he walked. Everyone seemed to recognise him. He was an American doctor; why did everyone know him?

'Do you know Mary Churchill?' she asked.

'I do. Her father asked me to come over to England. I'm here as part of an envoy for the Medical Corps. I'm reporting directly to the Surgeon General, who in turn, is advising the Secretary of War.'

'You're that important?'

He laughed heartily and the crinkles that formed around his eyes told her he was probably older than his golden locks implied. 'No, I'm not, but my big boss is, and I'm here with him learning the ropes, is that how you Brits say it?'

She smiled, easily now. 'Yes, I think it is.' She thought for a moment. 'But America isn't in the war.'

'America will be joining Europe soon. Don't you think?'

'I really don't know.' She loved the way he had asked her opinion. 'But I think that's why you've been invited here, so we can persuade you.'

'Ah, you really are one of Mary's girls.' His face became serious. 'Most Americans are staunchly isolationist. They don't want to get involved in what they see as Europe's problems. Too narrow-minded to see they are our problems too. Roosevelt knows this, knows the mood of his country. He's biding his time until the election. He wants a third term in office, and bringing America into the war will cause him a defeat.' He studied her face. 'But I believe Roosevelt has something else up his sleeve to help Britain, and Mr Churchill.'

'I don't suppose you can tell me?'

'No, I can't, but it will help the Allies, a lot.' He moved closer to her, he smelt of grapefruit cologne, a glorious smell, and said in a conspiratorial tone, 'More than extra soldiers, Mr Churchill, and Britain, needs money.'

'Ah, I see.' And she did see. Her dad had said the war would bankrupt the country, and that they'd be paying for it for decades to come.

Florence glanced towards where Mary Churchill stood, talking to another old man in uniform. He tottered around, he'd obviously already drunk too much of the punch.

Mary Churchill turned and saw her. 'Florence, you're here! Wonderful to see you.' She tapped Edward Miller's arm. 'I see you're already being looked after?'

Edward had turned away for a moment as another person touched his arm, wanting his attention. Mary Churchill winked at Florence; she'd never forget that wink as long as she lived, she really wouldn't. Edward had swivelled around again, kissing Mary Churchill on the cheek. 'It's a great event, Mary, you've gone for broke, I see.'

'We do what we can, Edward, don't we?'

'Attitudes are changing in Washington,' he said to her, his face now serious.

'That is good.' She turned to Florence. 'Florence will be good company tonight, for you, I'm sure.'

'I'm sure she will.' He paused as if thinking. 'So you two know each other from the ATS initiative?'

Florence looked at Mary, and Mary looked at Edward. 'Not exactly,' Mary said. 'Florence was our housemaid at Chartwell, since she was very young. But now, she's doing her bit for our country, as is every single citizen.' She touched his arm. 'We do really need all the help we can get. Ensure Mr Roosevelt knows that, Edward.'

His expression remained serious. 'He does know. And I know, Mary, for certain the Surgeon General is preparing for after the election.'

Mary smiled widely. 'Enjoy the evening, Edward.' Looking at Florence, she said, 'And you too. I'm so glad you came.' She took Florence's hand, whispered in her ear. 'I know it's daunting. Your outfit looks amazing. Well done.'

Florence grinned at Mary, and Mr Churchill's daughter floated off.

'There's another room across the foyer where it's less noisy, would you like to go and have a glass of punch there?' Edward asked.

'That'd be nice.'

She followed him through the ballroom, catching sight of them both in the walled mirrors. Her mum and aunt would die when she told them.

In the hotel's entrance there seemed to be some disruption; people standing by the doors and loitering outside. She heard shouting and looked up at Edward. 'Something's happening. Maybe we didn't hear the air raid sirens, I think we're due a visit.'

'It's not that,' he said, walking towards the door.

Florence was about to follow him. The doorman gently took her arm.

'I wouldn't go out there, Miss.'

She looked at his hand and with purpose unpeeled it from her wrist. 'I'm going outside.'

He shrugged. 'As you please.' By his tone she knew he thought she wasn't supposed to be there, that she didn't belong. Your own always recognise you.

283

Florence saw a group of people outside and heard someone say they were communists from the East End. She walked through the enormous hotel doors, down the steps and found Edward.

'*The Parasites, Ration the Rich!*' they shouted. Jostling, holding up their arms, fists clenched.

The police together with several ARP wardens held them back from the small barriers that had been placed in front of the hotel. She shivered despite it being the mildest of autumn nights. These people were disgruntled and angry. And she could see why; the difference between inside the hotel and inside these people's homes would be obscene.

The policemen were doing their job well, and gradually the gang began breaking up and the surge of relief rippling through the throng of high maintenance partygoers was palpable, although it didn't last for long as the familiar sound of sirens echoed through London. She tilted her head upward, towards the black canopy and the trailing and focussed brightness of searchlights crisscrossing the sky.

'The Germans are here,' she said. 'Have you been through this before?'

'Yes, the last two nights. I'm not a Blitz virgin.'

'Ah,' she said, knowing her face was on fire, feeling so close to this man she'd only just met. 'Hold onto your hat then.'

'I will, but more importantly, hold on to yours, Florence.'

A man had appeared and was talking to the policemen who were holding the demonstrators in check.

'That's the hotel's manager,' Edward said.

After a few minutes the police allowed the demonstrators up the steps of the hotel and inside.

'Come on,' Edward said. 'Let's move to the basement. I've heard there are cucumber sandwiches.'

She smiled. 'Are they allowing the communists into the Savoy?'

'They sure as hell are.' He took her hand as if it were the most natural thing to do in the world. 'I love the British.'

Florence spent all night in the basement of the Savoy Hotel, the horrendous noise from outside muffled but still audible. The Nazi firebombs screeched through the night and to her ear it seemed worse than the preceding weeks. She hoped Elizabeth and her gentleman friend had gone to a shelter.

Later when she and Edward separated and went to their respective sleeping quarters she ended up in a little room adorned with a pink bedspread and a single bed, pink towels and a tiny white Victorian dressing table. Despite the bombings Florence had the best sleep she'd remembered in a while, and when she made her way into the hotel's foyer the next morning she was relieved and a bit excited that Edward found her easily.

He took hold of her arm and led her outside and into the street, both of them silent as they surveyed the thick smoke and smouldering fires in the distance. 'Can I take you home?' he asked softly.

'I'd like to walk.'

'I'd like to walk too.'

'All right, let's.'

As she and Edward Miller walked to Elizabeth's, Florence had the biggest premonition the Germans had found her lodging house, so she moved quickly, as you do when foreseeing a terrible thing that you need to know hasn't happened.

'Slow down, Florence, I can't keep up,' Edward said

He was attempting to be buoyant and unflustered because as they trekked through London the culmination of the Germans' night work became heartbreakingly obvious, and although not a new sight for Florence she saw Edward was finding it difficult to comprehend. He told her months later it was included in a report to which he'd contributed, that was presented to America's President.

They made their way through the carnage, the smell of burning timber permeating the thin early morning gauze of an October sun. They stopped regularly to try and help: reuniting a child with its parents (thank God the parents were alive), helping a man excavate his budgerigar and cage from a pile of rubble. Florence couldn't believe the bird was still alive. The man was ecstatic, holding the cage protectively and ignoring the destruction strewn around him. No home but he still had his pet.

Then, as they approached the street that led directly to Elizabeth's road, Florence heard the most horrific wails. At first she thought it was a woman, the tone high-pitched, guttural. A terrible sound. Edward stopped and scanned the street, people scurried around, many without coats in the coolness of the autumn day. Edward left her side and walked towards the wails. It was a man, elderly, perhaps in his late sixties, maybe even older, the skin on his face covered in soot, emphasising the deep lines carved into his features. Florence followed Edward, who was now standing next to the man, who was kneeling next to his house, digging in the rubble with his bare grazed hands, blood mixing with the dust of the bricks; bricks that had once been put together in such a way as to be his home. Sporadically the man looked up, his expression a question mark, he was desperate for help. The house was only half a house. The bomb had taken away the front completely exposing the inside. Florence looked closer, blue wallpaper on the lower level, what had once been the parlour she guessed; the upstairs floor completely taken out and so the difference in levels could only be seen with the defining mauve of the wallpaper of what was the bedroom above.

The man's wails became louder. 'My wife, my wife…'

Edward gently pulled him away. 'Where is your wife, sir?'

The man pointed to the rubble, a table leg jutting out, a glint of silver, and a knife, which Florence thought had probably been sitting on the table to which the leg belonged. 'We didn't go to the shelter last night. Sat under the table.' He pointed to the heap of destruction.

Florence's gaze darted around, searching for an ARP warden, looking for anyone to help, then, her eyes settled on Edward. He took off his coat and began to move the rubble with his bare hands. Florence began doing the same.

'You might be needing this.'

Florence turned to see, finally, a warden holding two shovels. 'Rare to find them alive after a night like this one,' he said wearily.

'This man's wife may well be alive,' Edward almost barked, already taking hold of the shovel. The warden and Edward began digging while Florence held the man tight.

An hour later it was Edward who discovered the body. Wearing her apron and with a photo frame of her grown-up children still clutched in cold and stiff fingers.

The man put his head on Florence's shoulder and the growling sound of his cries would stay with her forever.

The warden disappeared to find more help.

'I can't leave him,' Florence said.

'I know,' Edward replied, 'I know.'

A raspy voice behind them. 'You can leave Jack with me. I've been his and Alice's neighbour for thirty years. I'll take care of Jack… and Alice.'

'I'm so sorry,' Edward said in a whisper. He looked up at the decimated building, which included this man's home too.

'Thanks for your help, and you Miss,' the neighbour said, turning to Florence who was still embracing Jack. 'Come on mate.'

Jack peered at Florence, his face cleared of grime with the wash of tears. 'Married fifty-two years.'

Florence touched his arm and didn't know what to say. And so she said nothing.

They carried on making their way to Elizabeth's, the sun had finally broken through and the smell that lay as an invisible blanket across London at last began to disappear. Elizabeth's terraced house remained intact and Florence breathed a sigh of relief. As Florence went to knock (she only used her key at night) Elizabeth opened the door.

'Thank God you're all right, Flo.' She looked over Florence's shoulder at Edward who stood on the small pathway smoking a cigarette. 'Come in.'

Elizabeth took them straight into the parlour and opened the sherry cupboard. 'I think we might be needing this.' She poured three glasses and placed them on the table. 'What's happened, it looks as if something's happened to you both.' She scrutinised them, their clothes, the grime of the Luftwaffe's work covering their faces.

'Two roads away from here, a direct hit. A woman's dead.' She moved closer to Elizabeth and hugged her. 'Edward found her. One of many from last night I'd guess. Did you go to the shelter?'

'I did, love,' Elizabeth replied

'Elizabeth, this is Edward Miller, Edward this is my wonderful landlady, Elizabeth Banwell.'

'Take a seat, Mr Miller, make yourself at home.' Elizabeth turned to Florence. 'I don't think you'll be on that train today up north, my girl. Not after last night.'

Elizabeth had known about her plan to travel to Yorkshire. Florence had even told her some of Anna's story.

Edward said, 'Was your visit important?'

'It was,' Florence replied, deflated.

'I have the use of a car and I'm free for the next few days. I'll take you to wherever you're going.'

Elizabeth handed him a glass. 'I like your style.'

He sipped the sherry. 'And Mrs Banwell, I *love* yours.'

'You look after Florence here.' She drank a mouthful of the thick sweet liquid. 'Not that she needs a protector, but I think, Mr Miller, she could do worse. I can see when two people are meant to be together. It sticks out a mile. My gentleman friend. I knew from the moment I met him in Covent Garden, five years ago now, I just knew. '

Edward nodded politely, but made no comment.

Florence was never quite sure how she felt about the gentleman's adultery, or Elizabeth's part in it, but who was she to make a judgement? When towards the end of the Blitz Florence had found Elizabeth crying in the private back sitting room (she had been brave and poked her nose around the door to enquire) she found out the gentleman's house had been bombed, killing him, and his wife. Luckily their children had been evacuated. Elizabeth was stricken, not only with his death, but that of his wife too. When Elizabeth found out he had made provision in his will for her, and the little boarding house, she'd cried for days, becoming more and more uncharacteristically hysterical at the stark fact of the couple being wiped out by a German bomb.

Florence packed her bag while Edward returned to his hotel. Two hours later he was sitting outside Elizabeth's house waiting patiently for her to emerge. The car was black and sleek, looking out of place on the London street. Florence stood gawping at it, touched the back wheel rim with the pad of her forefinger.

'It's beautiful,' she said. 'So rounded, soft, pleasing to the eye.'

'It's a Lafayette. Shipped over from Wisconsin. A gift for your Prime Minister from our government. It's used for diplomatic errands I'm told. I won't tell you what I had to do to get hold of it for a few days.'

'I just love it.'

He'd hopped out and opened the car door for her. 'Do you want to have a drive a bit later?'

'I couldn't.'

'You can drive a motorcycle. Not that different,' he said with a huge grin.

'And I can drive a car too, but I've never driven one like this.'

'Then today's the day. A bit later you can have a go.' He made sure she was ensconced comfortably in the passenger seat and closed the door.

Sitting next to her he spoke more: 'You can point out your famous English countryside for me on the way. It's a long journey I've been told.'

'I can't ever thank you enough,' she said.

'You have heaps of time.'

She was never quite sure if he meant time on the journey up to Yorkshire, or in the coming years.

Florence felt more comfortable than she'd felt in an age and settled back into the car seat looking forward to travelling up to Yorkshire, hesitant about seeing Anna but determined to help her. As the car rumbled on she thought of Frank on the African continent. She hoped he would return.

34

Frank

North Africa
Autumn 1942

In the ebony ice-cold wasteland Frank manoeuvered the torch so he could see what he was doing. He pulled up his shorts and tightened his belt, wrapped the thick wool army issue coat around him, then tipped the *desert rose's* lid shut with his foot. A converted for purpose petrol barrel, placed hundreds of feet away from the tents, but still too near. He tried not to breathe, wondering how the smell of shit and piss could linger so long in the vast, empty and desolate expanse of sand.

They'd made camp for more than a night and so weren't using the bivvies, the brigade were glad to spend some time out of both their tanks and the slit trenches. In the larger tents they felt a bit of home. England seemed far away.

After leaving Florence in London, Frank had taken the train to Liverpool and boarded a merchant navy ship that took the long route to the African continent. Seven weeks. He'd wanted to throw himself overboard one day into the journey; Frank wasn't a natural seaman, although after three near misses with German U-boats, and a night rescue of men on another Allied ship that hadn't been so lucky as theirs, he'd decided that living with the continual pain in his stomach was better than being dead in the terrifying ocean.

Military life, though, away from the sea, suited him, and when he had time he tried to work out why. Every night he shied away from his conclusion

As he found his bearings he looked upwards, the sky lit by polka dot stars filling the infinite space that if he thought too much about made his head spin and implode at the same time. The moments he did this, which were many, it put a lot into perspective. Frank attempted to hold tight this feeling of owning and admitting to his inconsequential life, although it never lasted long, leaving only minutes after he'd torn his gaze from the limitless wonder that lay somewhere of which he had no comprehension.

He allowed his eyes to fall downward, to the darkness of the evening desert, which gave away nothing, showed no mercy to the uninitiated and punished unconditionally all who toiled within it. And yet the ocean of sand and the domed ink that sat above as a majestic canopy, with its flecks of decorative silver, created an obsessive and powerful draw.

The poetry is in the pull.

So right, so perfect. Frank both loathed and loved the desert and as so many other things in his life he was never able to pinpoint why.

His stomach grumbled. Always hungry, but always unable to keep much inside. His gut was his Achilles heel, and had been since his troubled childhood.

He shone the dimmed torch into the open jaw of the sterile vista. An intrinsically evil place and yet when he'd first arrived in Cairo the country and physical terrain had seduced him; the eroticism, the foreignness, the sheer difference to everything he had ever known. The relief of being absent from his life. His shorts hung from his waist despite the last notch of the belt. He pulled his coat tighter around his midriff.

It was as if he'd been here for years.

After the British Eighth Army had forced the Italians into retreat at the end of January 1941 his division had travelled south to Jebel Akhdar, and another battle. And so, he had killed again. Many times. Frank had an eye for precision aiming, his commanding officer had told him. *A natural.* Frank put it down to years of bricklaying and the symmetry it demanded. It seemed he'd found what he was good at; but this continued natural ability at killing only caused the estimation of himself to crash even lower.

Since joining the army he'd made few friends; the camaraderie other men spoke of was a distant dream to him, an oasis he'd never find. Only with Rab Watkins had he made a proper connection. They were tank gunners who worked together, watched each other's backs, and this brought the two men close, as only the sort of situation they found themselves in during an offensive could do. He'd got on well with Flo's cousin, Harold, too when he'd finally met him.

After a lot of fishing around for information in the main headquarters in Cairo, and even the crossing of hands with a substantial amount of piastres to a handful of knowledgeable locals, he'd managed to locate and contact Harold in Egypt's capital soon after he'd got there, and Harold had spent two precious days of his five-day leave teaching Frank how to properly compass read and navigate the desert night sky.

'More men have died in the desert from bad coordinates than from Nazi bullets and bombs, I swear,' Harold had said as he drank the thick disgusting coffee, which seemed to be the only thing the Egyptians imbibed.

The lack of alcohol bothered many of the newer recruits, but not Frank. He'd found it ironic you couldn't get a drink due to beliefs and customs, but prostitution in the city was rife. Too many of the men had been struck down with illness – and not of the stomach – and long before they were initiated into the horrors of war. Syphilis and gonorrhoea were bastard diseases. The locals thought it hilarious.

Harold continued: *'Learn the art of using the sun as a compass, the art of navigation Frank, the true art of knowing where you are at night by observing the stars, and trust me, you'll have a better chance than many.'*

Frank had learnt quickly. As with killing people, he also had an aptitude for navigation: compass reading, and using the sun and stars to work out where he and his brigade sat on the maps that were forever open inside the tanks. Maybe it was because he was an outdoor man. Frank had very much admired Flo's cousin and was more than a little in awe of what Harold and his compatriots did. Without this lot, the *Libyan taxi service*, as they were known, the British would never have made it this far in attaining some sort of victory in the desert. The taxis, the LRDG (Long Range Desert Group that finally became the modern SAS) had managed to destroy much of the enemy's petrol supplies and airstrips.

He peered towards the camp and turned off his torch – they shouldn't be using them – and all seemed quiet.

The men who weren't on watch duty were in their tents, exhausted, trying to sleep in the glacier temperatures, and undoubtedly dreading the next offensive – *the Big One.* The German enemy, despite the British success at Alam Halfa, had remained glued to the forty-mile stretch of the Alamein front and the Allies needed to remove them, for good.

Frank had been diligent in his eavesdropping, and well-asked questions, and knew Mr Churchill favoured an attack at El Alamein in September, at the next full moon, so as the mine clearers could do their work. Montgomery wanted to wait until October, when the tanks and men would be properly ready, when supplies had reached them.

He and Rab had a bet on who would win the internal battle. Churchill with his September deadline, or Montgomery and his October one. As it turned out, Rab and Montgomery won.

Frank unzipped the tent to the sound of Rab's stertorous breathing. He could sleep through an invasion, and fortunately, also through Frank scribbling letters in the torchlight. He'd somehow managed to acquire a tent where he only shared with one other, and luckily it was Rab. Rab was a short and wiry man, a baker in his other life. Rab was impressed that Frank knew a fair bit about making bread and cakes; stuff he'd learnt from Hilda, in her other life, before her laundry. Rab was a quiet, diligent bloke and easy to share a tent with, despite his tendency for snoring.

Frank sat down and wrapped the blanket around himself, pulled out his notebook and pen from underneath the pillow (some old trousers that he suspected stank nearly as much as the desert roses), and to the rhythm of Rab's snores began writing a letter, first to Hilda, and then to Flo.

He told them both the same thing – at the beginning of the letters: that the war in the desert was far from over, but the British were for once smelling some victory, that the tanks of his brigade (the 7th Armoured) needed a complete overhaul, and Frank and other gunners and artillerymen were being sent to Cairo whilst this was happening. A few months previously Frank had been offered a place on a cargo ship to return to England for two weeks' leave. As his commanding officer had mentioned, Frank hadn't taken proper leave since he'd signed up. Again, as he had whilst in London, Frank declined, saying he wanted to stay where the action was being played out. His commanding officer asked no questions and was probably relieved. Frank didn't tell Hilda about the leave, telling her instead there was no leave for any of his brigade. But he told Flo.

He lay back on the makeshift bed, closed his eyes, sleep drifting towards him. Images of an effervescent Flo on that long ago May Day found their way into his mind, but then he was back in the Wendy house on his allotment, Anna had just left; he held his head in his hands. Then, Anna staring at him from the bed she was sitting on at High Royal. Hilda screaming in their bedroom. Jim dead. He sat up with a jolt and despite the shield of cold hedging him in, sweat exuded from every pore in his body. Bright light filtered through the fabric of the tent, and the noise of a jeep. He looked across at Rab who lay flat on his back, still fast asleep, but oddly now, making not a murmur.

Frank got up and pulled on the trousers that had been working as his pillow, picked up the torch and went outside.

The jeep had swung around and parked up. Two soldiers who he vaguely recognised from Cairo jumped out. As they did so, he heard the far-off noise of machine gun splutter, an Allied camp further into the desert he guessed, testing and clearing their guns. The cluster of night sounds assailed his ears and the familiar feeling encompassed him, of anxiety, of confusion, that he was actually here, and then the feeling of faint exhilaration that soon they would be in battle again.

In the back of the jeep, not moving, were three other men, in uniform but not his own regiment's. He shone the torch into their faces and something in his stomach knitted together. For a moment he thought he needed to make his way back to the latrines. He waited a few seconds and the feeling passed.

'What's going on?' he asked.

It was the driver who answered. 'Three new recruits. They've been sent from the 2nd Armoured. Forty more being transferred over the next few days, in readiness for when the tanks come back home.'

'Couldn't this have waited until the morning?' Frank grunted.

Rab appeared, looking disorientated, his face creased with sleep. His body quivering with the savage night temperature.

'It's a war, Gunner Cullen. Or hadn't you noticed? No night, no day,' the soldier said.

'Where are they supposed to sleep tonight?' Frank mumbled.

'I hear your tent has vacancies?'

Frank didn't answer and walked to the vehicle's rear and again held his torch into the back seat.

Hugh Lambert peered at him. And grinned.

'Hello, Frank, fancy seeing you here.'

Two of the new recruits were already settled with the spare blankets at the periphery of Frank and Rab's tent. They'd made some small talk, drank some of Rab's secret supply of whisky (no one understood why he had it, he was a teetotaler) before falling straight to sleep. Hugh Lambert had drunk several shots and then made his way to the camp's outskirts, saying he needed some time alone. He'd been gone an age and Frank hadn't allowed him to take a torch.

'Think he's all right out there?' Rab asked. 'Might have wandered off into the sand sea, never to be seen again.' Rab yawned and put the flask of whisky that he never drank in the pocket of his coat.

'That'd be a good outcome,' Frank replied. 'He won't have gone far, don't fret. He's a yellow little bastard.'

'Thought you were a bit antagonistic towards him. Do you know him?'

'Unfortunately, yes. Small world, eh?'

Rab nodded and asked not one question about Hugh. That was the beauty of their relationship. The sheer gloriousness of it.

He glanced at Frank. 'I'll wake up old Smelly Tate in the next tent and tell him he's got company. Your best mate Hugh can sleep with Smelly and company tonight.'

'Thanks, Rab.'

'No problem.'

Rab disappeared into the night and Frank put away his notebook. He lay flat on his back. Jesus, the irony. He felt his eyes closing, thinking of Anna, of the mess. Of Hugh Lambert. Frank hadn't said a word to him, leaving the small talk to Rab. His stomach rolling and gurgling, he brought up his knees to ease the discomfort. How was he supposed to fight alongside the bastard? His stomach lurched again. He needed the latrine. Every night it was like this, and every day. Made worse though, with the thought of Lambert breathing in the same air as him.

He stumbled from the tent and couldn't see a thing. Looking up at the sky and despite the contractions overtaking him, he noted two things. The consummate beauty, and the constellation of *Aquila*, *The Eagle*, and its major star, *Altair*, the closest of the stars the naked eye was able to see. Harold had told him that. He knew the latrines were located directly in view-line of the star from his tent, and he began making his way towards his destination. He counted his steps, he knew exactly how many.

He struck a match so he could open the lid.

Trekking back to the camp, he realised how easy it would have been to turn the wrong way and never, ever make it back. Harold's navigation tuition had, and did, save Frank's life many times during the war.

Although it was one of the many things that took his life away afterwards.

35

The Second Battle of El Alamein began on the 22nd of October 1942 and would mark the watershed of the western desert campaign, preventing Rommel from advancing further into Egypt, ensuring the safety of the precious Suez Canal.

The tanks had been repaired, serviced and returned. The men spent the evening digging out the slit trenches as projectile flashes of orange dragged through the night sky, mingling prettily with the silver of the stars; tangerine and silver, a beautiful sight. After a particularly loud explosion Smelly Tate panicked and bolted towards the tank, clambering clumsily into its turret, sat in there and wouldn't move.

'Get out man, it's only Hitler's planes, just a few bombs,' Frank said.

But Smelly didn't budge and it was Frank and Rab who finished digging the trenches, so as they could pitch their bivvies and sleep that night in the midst of the orange and glittering remnants of broken planes that in the distance were shimmering gracefully towards the desert's floor.

The evening before the first offensive they were on an hour's notice to move, but this wasn't anticipated until the early hours of the morning. They were as prepared as they'd ever be. As tank commander, Frank had checked and rechecked the turret, including the six-pounder gun and its metal shield. He checked that the rack of ammo was filled and grenade holders overflowing, that the wireless set and control box were in working order, and binoculars were present. And the important stuff: books, chocolates, boiled sweets, processed cheese, a knife, some biscuits. Frank stood back, admiring his tank. The Crusaders had a habit of developing mechanical problems, unlike Rommel's Panthers, which some said were like the rest of the German army. Invincible.

I wouldn't swap you, Frank mouthed to the inanimate object, whilst patting the cooling metal.

The night prior to battle and the air was laden with anticipation, but permeated too with an underlying fear to which no one admitted. The men busied themselves with jobs and errands – properly cobbled boots, pristine shirts, and clean rifles would ensure victory. Silence in the desert was a strange thing, as it was in the rest of life's long and improvised journey: you fear it, revere it, hate it, all in one go, and for Frank, he craved it, inside his mind, inside his soul.

His fear? That he would never attain the silence of peace again.

Some thought they would see the day after tomorrow, whilst some, like Frank, knew that despite the chirpy rhetoric of their leaders the odds of surviving were abysmally low. Although what had been happening in the previous months – the ongoing massive operation of visual deception in the desert campaign – Frank knew would play a crucial part in a victory, and hopefully lessen the number of casualties.

It had been a master move by Churchill, to create such elaborate decoys in the desert terrain that offered zero opportunity for concealment. In April at Tobruk the ruse they'd used had been spectacular, so much so that Frank had written to both Hilda and Flo in detail about it. How the camouflage team had managed to make a crucial water purification building appear heavily damaged after German attacks, when in fact it was unharmed, and how the limited resources of men and equipment in the Allied army were boosted by dummy tanks, artillery and men. The illusion was completed by 'evidence' of human and mechanical activity – track marks, smoke from 'cooking,' and 'washing' hanging on lines.

It was all very clever and innovative. Churchill would love it all; the artist within the old man would have been easily piqued. The men at the top hoped they'd fooled the Germans sufficiently into making false assessments of Allied strength and intentions regarding this next offensive.

It really was absolute genius and many thought it wouldn't work.

Frank wanted Britain to win the war and was often consumed with the feeling that he cared little if he lived or died whilst he helped his country do so. Only thoughts of his sons, and Anna, brought to him the need to survive, but, this recklessness that surrounded him created a myth of invincibility; so therefore the bricklayer, miner, and tank gunner commander was construed by all as a natural leader. His deftness for aiming well, his compass reading and stargazing talents put him a notch above many. His comrades listened to him, and what he had to say. Most hung off his every word, including Rab. His commanding officer had seen this and it translated into Frank knowing more than the others regarding the logistics of the planned offensive.

Frank peered upwards into a velarium of lustrous flecks, spotting *Aquila* easily. His eyes moved towards the direction of the latrines. Battle the next day, but the desert roses still needed to be sorted, and Frank decided it was Hugh Lambert's turn.

Larry Ramsbottom, their tank driver, a big man and a steelworker from Sheffield, piped up. 'Time you were initiated, Lambert, me boy,' he said to Hugh, who unlike the other men was sitting outside his trench, doing nothing only staring into the blankness of the night.

Frank said quietly, 'Yep, your turn Hugh, you lazy little bastard.'

Rab touched Frank's arm in caution.

Hugh didn't look too good. Military life, and the desert, didn't suit him, but Frank cared less than nothing for this man. A man whose life he had saved, a man who he had then beaten to a pulp.

Hugh finally looked up and peered at Frank. 'Think you're special, don't you? With your books, your walls, your stuck-up wife. Well, you're not. And what about Anna? Abandoned her, you and Hilda. You're a joke. In fact an excuse for a man if you ask me.'

Frank moved forwards, about to pull the little runt from his chair.

But then he calmed himself, and heard the sighs of relief roll through the camp. No one wanted this tonight.

He took a breath and ignored the cramping in his stomach. 'Come on, Hugh. Get up. For once, do something useful in your life. The latrines need clearing. Your turn.'

'It is your turn, Lambert,' Larry Ramsbottom said. 'Here, take a lamp with you, mate.' He handed it to Hugh. 'Keep it dim, though.'

Frank snatched it back. 'Can't have the light.'

Hugh huffed and retrieved a torch from the pocket of the nearest bivvy.

'Time to be a proper desert rat,' Frank said in a whisper. 'Time to learn to get to the latrines in the dark. Everyone else can.'

'You kidding? I can't read the stars like you, you weird bastard.'

'Time to learn then, Hugh.' He smiled at the younger man. 'I'll give you a crash lesson now, as it was given to me. You think you're bloody clever, well show us you are.' He grabbed Hugh's arm and moved him away from the others.

Over a period of half an hour Frank gave Hugh a rushed lesson in reading the constellations of the *Plough* and *Eagle* and the use of their satellite major stars in finding the latrines in the pitch black.

Terror charged Hugh's features. 'I'll get my coat,' he said.

'Yes, I would if were you. You might be out there for a while,' Frank replied.

It was Larry who went to get the coat. Frank sensed Larry felt a bit sorry for Hugh and if he hadn't known him, so would he. Hugh was well out of his depth, and the question of why he'd given up his reserved occupation to come to Africa passed through Frank's mind. He guessed it was probably to get away from a wife he had no wish to marry and a baby that had been a mistake. Another of the little shits Hugh had a tendency to leave in his wake.

He scrubbed away the notion that he was here for not dissimilar reasons.

Larry gave Hugh the coat. Hugh took it and Frank noticed the blue tinge in his fingers, and the same colour creeping into his plump lips. It was colder than normal that night, probably due to the drier air over the last few days. Hugh really did look petrified, and cold. He was showing early signs of hypothermia.

Frank pulled Hugh away from the earshot of the men. 'Easy, Hugh. Just follow my instructions. The stars and a good compass won't let you down.' Without the other men seeing, he took away Hugh's torch and put it in his own pocket.

'What you doing? I need the torch.'

'No light. No lights allowed. Dangerous, might alert the enemy.' Frank jabbed at him. 'Be a man. You seemed to like being a man with Anna.'

'I don't know what you're talking about. I told you years ago—'

'You don't have to pretend with me anymore. I know, I always knew.'

'Look, I lost my head a bit with Anna, just one night in the village. But nothing happened, just a kiss.' Hugh then stood tall as if having a change of mind. 'This isn't about me, is it, Frank?' Hugh looked at him directly in the eyes, didn't flinch, and from somewhere had found a backbone. The little shit. 'It's about you… and Anna, isn't it? You dirty hypocritical sod.'

Frank closed down. 'Like the pit, same here. You know what some of those blokes'll do to you if I tell them what you did to Anna.'

'I didn't do anything to Anna. How many times do I have to tell you? You're looking at the wrong man. I tried to help Anna, guide her. I only wanted to kiss her—'

'Why didn't you ever tell anyone why I gave you a bollocking, eh? Why did you keep it to yourself? Guilt. Pure guilt.'

'I was protecting *your* daughter, and your bloody useless wife. Hilda knew, I'm sure of it. And said nothing, Frank. And yeah, protecting myself too. I didn't want anyone to know I'd tried it on with Anna and she'd refused me, or that Hilda ignored everything I tried to tell her. I'll tell you now what I told you back in 1938, you and Hilda didn't keep an eye on Anna.' He paused and took a breath. 'More to the point though, Frank, why didn't *you* tell anyone? What were you hiding, eh? Anna's quite gorgeous, and you're not her dad, are you? That Wendy house was built for a reason, wasn't it? You filthy bugger.'

'No light, Hugh. I'd do as I say if I were you.' He wouldn't rise to the bait. Wouldn't ask the bastard what Hilda knew.

Finally some arrogance appeared on Hugh's face. 'I'll show you. I can read bloody stars, just like you. Think you're cleverer than me, cleverer than everyone. Think you're a mini Churchill, you sad sod. I'll show you.' Hugh walked into the distance towards the brightest but one star of the *Plough's* constellation.

Completely the opposite direction to the *Eagle* constellation's *Aquila* star.

Frank looked at his watch, turned, and made his way back to the others.

It was Larry who waited for Hugh to return, and Larry who offered to go and look for him. Frank didn't try to stop him but made sure he had a torch. When Larry returned an hour later, with no Hugh, it was Rab who informed their commanding officer, who immediately organised a search party. However, that night a brutal sandstorm erupted and they were unable to search for Hugh Lambert. It wasn't until the first light of morning when a rescue party could go and look for Hugh, but the entire battalion was due to move from the camp at 10.00 hours and so the search was shorter and more hurried than it could have been.

Hugh Lambert was never found; his body never located, undoubtedly due to the oceans of sand that had buried his frozen corpse in the night. It was documented that he had misread his compass and instructions, found himself at night in the desert, and had simply got lost, due to incompetence.

This last conclusion was omitted in the letter that was sent to his new wife.

36

That morning while the search party was looking for Hugh, Rab hardly spoke to him and Frank tried to ignore his mate's frosty stares. He'd given Hugh the tools to read the stars and he hadn't listened. Hugh had the right coordinates and correct star to find the latrines, and his way back from them. He had. Frank told Hugh to use the Altair star to find the desert roses, and then the second brightest star of the Plough's constellation to navigate back to camp. He *had* said this to Hugh, as well as giving him a compass and the correct coordinates to use. Frank pulled at the collar of his newly laundered shirt. The top button flew off, landing in the sand at his feet.

The information he'd given to Hugh was the right way round. Frank never mixed up the stars.

As he and Rab made the final preps in their tank he told Rab, again, and with conviction, that Hugh had the right information to find his way.

'We've all had to do it, clean the latrines in the dark,' Frank rasped. 'It's our job to know this stuff, and it was Hugh's job too.'

'He was green, and you knew it,' Rab said.

'It was his mistake, not mine.'

Rab pulled a little notebook he kept in his pocket, same place as the flask of whisky, and opened up the first page, thrusting it under Frank's nose.

Chief concern – do not endanger your comrade

Do not borrow from your comrade, particularly water and petrol

Do not light fires at sunset

Do not ask for information beyond your job, for idle talk kills men

You do not leave mess behind that will breed flies

<u>You do not give your comrade compass bearings which you have not tested and of which you are not sure.</u>

These above codes are the sum of fellowship in the desert. It knows no rank and no exceptions.

'You remember this, Frank?'

'Course I bloody well remember it.'

'Do you swear on your sons' lives that you gave Hugh Lambert the right coordinates and advice?'

Frank did not waver in his answer because he believed he was telling the truth.

'I swear on my sons' lives.'

'That's it then. We can fight together.'

'I can't believe you wrote all that down, mate, and underlined—' a painful pause, 'some of it.'

'I write everything down. You're not the only literate soldier in this brigade, you know.' Rab looked up to the sun, his hand shading his face. 'Time to kill the fucking Germans.'

That was the first and last time Frank heard Rab swear.

*   *   *

Frank's Crusader Mark III tank was following as close as possible behind the tank in front. Rab sat below. Frank watched Rab's back, and the rest of the team, but when hostilities began Frank and Rab watched everyone else's too.

Frank peered into the hazy distance. This was the tricky bit – getting past the mines. Hopefully most had been cleared by the 44th Division who had prepared the way the day before, so as the 7th Armoured Brigade could pass through the minefields. There was always a slippery little bugger though.

As well as being an excellent marksman, Frank also possessed a sixth sense for danger. He looked through the tank's periscope, the sun blinding him, the wavy air of heat making it impossible to focus. The tank in front had suddenly stopped. There must be unease at what lay ahead in the sand, concern about landmines that hadn't been successfully located. Frank watched as a soldier from the tank in front left his vehicle; Frank guessed to explore. To the naked eye it appeared safe, no giveaway signs the Germans had planted on this stretch.

The man walked leisurely away from his tank; his commander had obviously given him the order to do so, although it hadn't come through on internal communication wireless. But this was an odd scenario.

Frank moved his goggles onto his forehead and spoke to Rab on their own internal. 'Man outside, not sure what he's doing. Communications down with tank in front.'

'The commanding officer in the tank ahead is new to the regiment, less experienced than most, I've heard,' Rab replied.

Hardly experienced at all, Frank guessed. The Eighth Army was desperate for officers with a proven track record, but was unable to find them, as more and more became fatal casualties of the war. Frank scanned the horizon and saw what he knew was the German Korps; he manoeuvered around and looked for enemy satellite vehicles, then spotted a German light artillery tank, but it was at least two miles away, maybe more. They had time. He watched the man outside silently moving on into the distance. Inside the tank you could see, but hear nothing, only the engine's rumbles.

'We need to get him in,' Frank said under his breath.

'Permission to go and help?' Rab said, the sound coming through scratchy. 'Bring him in?'

'No. Wait.' Frank attempted again to contact the tank commander in front via the internal radio. Communications were still down. 'Go ahead. Be careful, Rab. Get the man back inside his tank as quickly as possible and don't wander away. The enemy is, I'd say, no more than three miles away. Let's say two. You have time. But get back in here quick.'

As Rab began to prepare to open the tank's lid, Frank had a change of heart. This shouldn't be happening. Rab shouldn't go outside. He didn't want Rab to leave the tank. But Rab had already clambered out. Frank returned to his periscope. The agile and nimble Rab was making his way towards the errant man, probably shouting but Frank could hear nothing inside the Crusader tin.

The man turned and had begun making his way back to his own tank. Frank sighed with relief and waited for Rab to do the same. He didn't, he was still walking forward. *What you doing, man?* Frank asked inside his head. Panic shot through him, a terrible sense of foreboding. He attempted to speak into the radio again, to the errant man's commander. Still no signal.

Rab walking. Away.

Frank lumbered from the turret to find Larry. 'I'm going outside, I don't have a good feeling.'

'What's happening?' Larry replied. 'Rab must have seen something. German scouts?'

'The stupid bugger. What does he think he can do? On his own, out there? I'll be back, with Rab. Keep trying the radio. Tell Smelly Tate to take position in the turret, keep an eye on the Germans.'

Larry nodded.

Frank lifted the tank's lid and jumped off the metal beast submerging into the sizzling compacted sand. He trudged forward trying to get to Rab. But then as he moved closer, he saw what neither he nor Rab had seen earlier. Only feet away from him the whirl of sand wasn't as uniform as the swathes of sand around it. The Germans had been busy.

Frank shouted Rab's name and wondered then if this was his punishment for Hugh. As the sun thrashed down relentlessly, he sank into the sand, knowing that intentionally he had killed. Again. An image of Hugh as he walked towards the latrine, the scene in the Wendy house. And now Rab, who he'd given permission to leave the tank.

Rab was moving closer to the disparate ripples of toffee-coloured sand. He wished it were he, not Rab. He loved Rab. He loved him as he had loved no other man in his life. He shouted his name. Rab hadn't heard him, the whispering wind of the desert had taken away

313

Frank's voice, taken it far away. Frank upped his sluggish pace and was within feet of his friend. He glanced sideways and it was then he saw a lone soldier, a German sniper, appearing as if from nowhere, and aiming at Rab, and Frank knowing that seconds later the rifle would be turned towards him.

Frank swivelled round, holding up his arms, warning his comrades of the counter attack, and then began trying to run to Rab, expecting at any moment a bullet in the back. Rab rotated and looked at Frank.

Frank was close enough to see Rab's eyes, which looked beyond him and finally seeing the sniper. Rab lifted his arms in a warning.

It was the last thing Rab did.

Frank's world descended into darkness. He didn't feel the searing heat of the gritty sand in his face, he didn't feel the grief of watching his best friend blown to pieces, he didn't feel the flesh of his arm being ripped away from the bone. And he was oblivious to Larry Ramsbottom achieving the best shot of his life and getting the German sniper smack bang in between the eyes.

37

Tripoli, Libya
Three months later
4th February 1943

It was Larry Ramsbottom who woke Frank up that
morning in a warm room in a small house, only a street
away from Tripoli's *Citadel of Raymond Saint Gilles*; a
building Frank had decided was the most beautiful in the
city and built to proportions that pleased his eye. He
couldn't begin to imagine how long it had taken to
construct, and he spent a lot of time in the Libyan
hospital thinking about this. It made it so he didn't think
about anything else.

Frank heard Larry walking towards the bed. He kept
his eyes tightly shut.

'The old man's in town.' Larry's voice grated. 'Rise
and shine, old mate. Your lovely landlady, Mrs Murbati,
has some of that shit coffee waiting for you downstairs.'

Frank turned over, flinging off the thin sheet that
covered him; only February but still hitting seventy
degrees in the daytime, and nights oppressive in the
built-up city, not like the savage beating cold of the
desert. He would never work out what was worse, being
too cold or being too hot. Finally, he opened his eyes
and as he attempted to push himself upward to give
Larry a clever retort, the arm that was still giving him
trouble gave way with the exertion and he fell off the
bed.

Larry laughed, a high-pitched sound and totally out of context with his bulky build. 'Get yourself a wash, mate, and put your uniform on,' he said in a quieter tone. 'Time to celebrate, find some whisky.' Larry perched on the only chair in the room, which was piled high with Frank's clothes. 'And soon we move on to Italy.'

'What time is it?' Frank asked, clambering back onto the bed.

'Just after seven. The parade starts at ten. Our illustrious leader's been in Tripoli since the day before yesterday. He's a man with a hard-on with victory.' Larry shrilled at his own joke, the sound echoing off the plain white walls. Frank's head thumped. 'D'ya think we'll get a pay rise?' Larry added.

'Bloody hell, man, do you never shut up?'

'Hey, mate. I'm just glad you're back with us. You'll be getting a medal, I reckon.'

'What for? Not saving a man?'

'C'mon, mate. You did everything you could.' He hesitated a beat. 'Rab shouldn't have gone forward. It wasn't your fault.'

'I'll meet you downstairs in half an hour.'

They were in the centre of the city by nine; it was much cooler outside than in. The streets were already teeming with locals, many still eating a late breakfast, local sweet delicacies that made Frank's tongue sting. God, how he hated them all.

Men streamed past him, their steps brisk, awaiting the arrival of the British Prime Minister and no doubt wondering what would be happening in their city after an Allied victory. Because for the people who lived there it was only a question of who would be ruling them next.

By nine-thirty the streets heaved and were lined with sentries, whilst armed soldiers covered the rooftops. Frank and Larry had joined their brigade and marched immediately behind the bagpipes. Frank's ears hurt, the bloody noise was worse than the shellfire in the desert. He scanned around; his whole regiment beautifully turned out, anyone would have thought they'd all been inside their barracks for the last six months instead of having marched over a thousand miles and fought numerous battles in that time.

They arrived at the main square, near the sea front, and that was when Frank finally caught sight of Winston Churchill. Smelly Tate was there too, looking, and smelling, very unlike Smelly. Frank swore that at last he'd had a bath. Frank studied his Prime Minister, his old employer; a man who he had spoken to many times about laying bricks, and sometimes about reading, and very occasionally about life in general.

The salty air struck at his nostrils, a 2,900-ton ship had finally made its way into Tripoli's harbour – a moment to be celebrated too – the clearing of the harbour from enemy block ships. The enormous vessel took Frank's thoughts back to his horrendous boat journey to Africa, soon after his meeting in London with Flo. And then his mind moved to the letter he'd sent to Mr Churchill from France. It had been a stupid thing to do. His letter had been a cathartic act and to this day he couldn't explain, even to himself, why he'd done it. He'd never expected Churchill to read the letter, not really.

His gaze settled on the open-topped staff car that carried Churchill, General Brooke and General Alexander. The leaders appeared jubilant, happy, and in control. And so they should be, but the triumph of the moment was bypassing him completely.

As the parade came to its end, Churchill's car made its way to the hotel hosting him and his entourage. The wind was gathering pace in the city's centre, the familiar afternoon bell began ringing out into the sultry but changeable air; the *Asr* time of day, Mrs Murbati had informed him.

He peered at Churchill as he lumbered from the car, cigar in hand, smiling.

Churchill stood on the vivid bright steps of the hotel, hastily whitewashed for his visit only the day before, and viewed the soldiers surrounding him. Frank moved a few steps closer, pushed to the front, eliciting an elbow from a 7th Queen's Own Hussar. Frank smelt alcohol on his breath and gave him a wide berth.

Winston Churchill looked into the crowd and took off his hat, lifted his walking stick and placed his headwear on its end, holding the stick and hat high into the afternoon's gossamer light, and then he turned, making his way inside.

'Time for a drink,' Larry said to him. 'Looks like the old man is just about to have one. He's addressing the troops on the hill later.' He grinned. 'Like Jesus.'

'Thanks, but I might just hang around here.'

'Suit yourself, mate.' And Larry disappeared into the throng of servicemen to find the nearest illicit watering hole.

Two hours later Frank made his way to the outskirts of the city where Churchill was addressing the Eighth Army in full. Hundreds of soldiers surrounded the vast area around the makeshift podium, awaiting the man who many saw as God, not Jesus.

From the corner of his eye Frank glimpsed Larry and other soldiers from his brigade. He took a deep breath and made his way towards them. It had rained earlier, an unusual occurrence at that time of year, cooling the air temperature, drastically for some, a relief for others. Many of the surrounding military wore heavy overcoats, not used to the cold yet, and Frank wondered how they'd all cope once they were back in the grey drizzle of Britain: very well, he supposed. It was only he who felt anxious anticipation at the thought of the end to hostilities.

Larry was sitting on the ground, perched on a stray log; Frank tapped him on the shoulder. 'Been here long?'

'Frank, mate, thought you'd gone back home,' Larry replied.

'Shouldn't be long now,' Frank said. 'Churchill's never late, unless he stayed in the bath too long. I hear they've very nice plumbing at the hotel.'

Larry's face took on an expression of confusion, but said nothing.

As the sun battled its way through beefy clouds a deafening roar filled the air. A black Ford V8 had pulled up next to the podium. Frank squinted around, the small hill full to capacity, the men hungry to see their leader. He turned back, his focus on the car: Montgomery, Brooke and Alexander all accompanying their Prime Minister, who wore the uniform of Air Commodore.

The roar turned into a chorus and every hair on Frank's body lifted.

Churchill walked towards the men standing at the front, shook hands, offered one man a cigar, pushed his hat further on his head, then stood back, palms of his hands resting on his chest.

Looking.

Watching.

Gauging.

That's what the old man did, assessed quickly and moved forward, never looking back, never questioning his decisions once made; good or bad. It was the mark of a leader, a thinker, and a man who was sure of his path and his destiny. A leader, who in all fairness was far removed from common men, but surprisingly in tune with them too. They understood him instinctively and in a way Churchill's own elite tribe did not. He was on their level. Churchill exuded confidence. The working man in the midst of this war admired and felt at ease with Churchill's Americanisms, his brilliance, his pugnacity, and his rhetoric. Yet in the face of a conflict Churchill's own rejected him.

But it is what the common man wanted and needed to hear, and see, and to be a part of. They believed without doubt the old man would lead them to victory, that their country *would* win the war.

Churchill was able to convince the ordinary men in a way he was unable to reassure his own.

The Prime Minister surveyed his troops and the crowd hushed. The rustling wind the loudest of sounds, and in the far distance the call to prayers in the city. He climbed the three steps to the raised podium and pulled out a piece of paper, still terrified of making a mistake, Frank noted, and began.

'I have come to thank all the men of the Eighth Army, and the Allied Air Forces, and other units which participated in the campaign, in the name of the King, the British Government, and the whole of the people. Their deeds will gleam and glow in history's annals.'

More massive acclamation and Churchill waited. Just the right amount of time. Then carried on.

'In days to come when asked by those at home what part you played in this war, it will be with pride in your heart that you can reply: I have marched with the Eighth Army.' He paused, looked up, scanned the crowd. 'You nightly pitched your moving tents, and always a day's march nearer home. Not only in the army's march, but in the war's progress you have brought home nearer. With the forces that are marching from different quarters we may hope to achieve the final destruction or expulsion from Africa of every armed German and Italian. You may later fight in countries presenting serious tactical difficulties, but none… no… none, will have the grim character of desert war, which you have endured and overcome.'

Churchill's soldiers went mad, a clamour of cheering voices punctuated the end of his speech and now the Prime Minister, having soaked in the adulation, stepped down, a mixture of relief and elation covering his stoic features.

Then General Brooke took the helm. Frank listened intently, but it was towards Churchill where he found his eyes settling. Brooke spoke about victory, hardship and the army's patience and fortitude, he made a generous mention of Rommel and in true British fashion the men hooted their agreement. Rommel: the only Nazi the British liked.

The speeches finally came to an end and the Titans of the desert war spoke between themselves. The crowd of men fell into silence. Several NCOs, each holding pieces of paper, mingled amongst the men. Ten minutes later Frank felt a tap on his shoulder.

'Gunner Cullen?' the tall skinny man asked. Frank had no idea who he was.

Frank nodded.

'The Prime Minister would like a word with you.'

Larry elbowed him in the ribs. The others he was standing with stared, then after a few seconds smiled.

Frank mumbled he didn't know what and followed the large twig of a man towards the back of the podium where chairs had been lined up. Five other men followed him, the NCOs asked them to sit down. Frank waited as either Brooke or Alexander spoke with them; semi-private conversations that if he listened intently enough he could hear. It was about bravery, courage in the field. Medals.

Frank's heart pitched. His gut rumbled.

An image of Rab and his notebook hard in his memory.

An image of Hugh in his mind's eye, just about to hit his thirtieth birthday, walking the wrong way into the desert.

He'd murdered him.

And another. Accidentally, but it was a truth. A baby.

Frank tried to block it all out but couldn't.

The other men he'd been brought with dispersed, looking happy, if not surprised. It was something Frank would carry with him for the rest of his life, the humanity of the men he fought alongside, their humility, self-deprecation about what they'd done, and not to defeat an enemy, but to protect and keep safe the men with whom they shared a war.

Frank was not one of those men. He could not accept a medal for Rab, who he had not saved. He did not save people. He killed them.

The NCO who had found him in the crowd took his elbow. 'Mr Churchill would like to talk with you alone, Gunner Cullen.'

He led Frank to the canvas chairs, which were all empty apart from Churchill who sat on the middle one. Without his cigar. The fatigue etched into his face, the jowls hanging as pouches from each side of his lips. Weary but agitated to move, his expression sombre, not the jubilant victor of just an hour before. The war was not over, and word was it wouldn't be any time soon.

Frank looked upward to an overcast sky, undid the buttons of his coat. Felt the moisture under his arms.

'Gunner Frank Cullen,' Churchill said, his voice low, almost inaudible. He took a long breath. 'From Chartwell to Cairo.' He made the familiar sound in the back of his throat, making the statement into a question.

'It's good to see you, sir.'

Churchill moved his body back into the chair. 'War brings strange moments, wouldn't you say? It seems to me the eye you have for a perfectly laid brick is the eye of an excellent gunner.'

'There are many excellent gunners, sir.' Frank allowed himself a small grin. 'Especially in the enemy's army.'

'Rommel has an eye for the best,' Churchill replied, the chewing and incomparable smile finding its way onto his face.

'Indeed, sir.'

'As do I.'

Frank nodded.

'Sit down,' Churchill pointed to the chair next to him. Frank sat. 'My deepest sympathies for Gunner Watkins. Your actions on that day have come to my attention and you have been nominated for the Military Medal. It is with much pride that I'm informing you of this.'

'Sir, with all due respect, I can't accept the medal. I didn't save Rab.'

'It is not only for your actions that day. You are a courageous soldier, an asset to our country, and, Gunner Cullen I will hear no more. You will be awarded the medal.'

'It's not just Rab, sir. Please I don't deserve a medal.'

Churchill leant forward, clutching his cane, balancing himself. 'Are you still reading?'

'Not as much as I'd like, sir. This bloody war keeps getting in the way.'

Grunting with pleasure at the joke, Churchill pulled a Romeo and Julieta from his overcoat pocket. And – as he always had – Frank lit it for him.

'Your friend Florence is a dispatch rider now. Did you know?' Churchill said.

'I do, sir. I saw Florence in London just before coming here.'

'A fine woman, and Mary tells me she is engaged to Edward Miller.' Churchill inhaled deeply, tipped his head upwards to examine the blue smoke that trailed above him in a smooth line. The wind now non-existent. 'I approve of the Anglo-American alliance.'

'Yes, sir. Flo will be good for it, that's for sure.' Silence fell between them for a moment. 'I sent you a letter when I was in France, in 1940, sir. I'm sure you never got to read it—'

'I read no such correspondence.' His tone was impatient but not entirely convincingly so.

Had Mr Churchill read his letter? Frank guessed he would never really know.

'In the letter,' Frank said, 'I told you that my only daughter has been admitted to a mental hospital in Yorkshire.'

'Anna?'

'Yes, sir.'

'I am sorry to hear this. My wife reported that your daughter was very pleasant to have at Chartwell when she visited in the spring of 1938. March I think it was.'

'You have an excellent memory, sir.' The old man's expression though, had suddenly become more sombre. Frank was sure he saw a hint of anxiety settle on the Prime Minister's features.

'Is Anna being well cared for?'

'I think so, sir.' Frank was surprised Mr Churchill had remembered Anna.

'Tell me, Gunner Cullen.' The hint of apprehension was now gone. 'What were you really trying to say in the letter, which I have not seen?'

'The reason I can't accept a medal, sir.' He wanted to tell the man sitting in front of him about Hugh but the words would not come, sticking in his throat.

And he wanted to tell Churchill the real reason he could not accept any medal.

'Continue.' Churchill glanced at his watch and looked towards an NCO who was patiently waiting for him. Churchill inclined his head towards the soldier, who then began walking away from the podium, probably wondering what Mr Churchill was talking to Frank about. The rumours would be flying later.

Frank began to talk, telling his old employer, not about Hugh, but the other thing that strangled him every night in the twilight world of semi-sleep. And even then, on that balmy afternoon on a small hill on the outskirts of Tripoli city amidst the background humming sound of prayer call, Frank was not totally honest. He could not say it all. It would not come out. It would never come out he admitted to himself. Not the real truth.

Churchill shook his head, a judicious movement and then, planting the cigar firmly in his mouth, he slowly pulled himself up, pushing against the thin but robust canvas of his chair; and with deliberation he spoke, relishing the sound of his own words.

'It is my duty to keep our Empire together, to fight and win, as it is your duty too. It is my duty also, to keep my family together, as it is your duty too. And is why you acted as you did.' Churchill turned away, viewing the vast hostile landscape. Frank heard a slight wheeze.

'I have always seen the putting down of foundations,' he carried on. 'Of laying bricks, as a metaphor for life. We do everything we can to make the footings solid, to ensure the quality of the bricks, mix the mortar in just the correct ratio. And indeed, to lay those foundations in just the right place. Why do we build? To keep people out, or to keep people in?' He turned, stumbling. Frank moved quickly to help. Churchill held up his hand. 'I am solid, and you need to be too. You *will* receive your medal, Gunner Cullen.'

Throwing his cigar on to moist African soil, he then placed palms flat on to his chest. 'The wars we fight inside of our minds are of a more turbulent nature than the wars we fight in the open field of human conflict.'

Churchill walked to his waiting car. Frank unsure whether to follow. Then Churchill stopped and looked him directly in the eye. A pause, the profound hypnotic drone of prayer calls drifting through the air.

'Your war will be to ensure your daughter is looked after. Your misjudgement is one that will stay here, in Africa, on the field. There is still much to fight for, causes in other lands that should be dominating your attention now, Gunner Cullen. In building and defending the structures of life, things can wrong-foot us. It is our duty to stay on the path, no matter how difficult it is to do. To stay focussed.'

Frank had no words. He had not told the whole truth, about Anna, or about Hugh, and as the dark clouds intensified he knew he never would.

Later that day, together with the other men, Frank received his medal.

38

Florence

January 3rd 1946

The Times

The Biggest New Year's Honours List In Living

Memory

Order Of Merit Goes To Mr Churchill.

In London on December 30th Mr Churchill was awarded The Order of Merit.

The official announcement from Buckingham Place last July stated that on Churchill's resignation the King had asked him to accept The Order of the Garter, but Mr Churchill begged to be allowed to decline it.

It was then understood that Mr Churchill would be offered The Order of Merit, which, as it comes with no precedence of rank, he would be prepared to accept.

Florence read the newspaper as Edward drove. She knew Frank had probably seen it but she cut it out anyway and placed it inside her diary to send to him, just in case. Mr Churchill so deserved this medal. She, together with Miss Cunningham had thought he should have accepted *The Order of the Garter*; the man was a leader, he'd won the war, for goodness sakes. The old man, though, was bitter about the post-war election defeat, and rumour had it that he'd declined *The Order of the Garter* out of pique, seeing his defeat in the post-victory General Election as the people spurning him. Other opinion – that it was Churchill's ploy to try and repair the reputation, the bad reputation, which still lingered on about him prior to the war years. Florence knew this was not true, it was too out of character. Miss Cunningham pondered that Churchill's reluctance to accept it was powered by his humility. Florence really wasn't sure why he hadn't accepted but she thought he should have done and shared her opinion with Edward.

'He's given everything to this country. Everything. The fight against Hitler nearly killed him, literally,' she said, her feet bare of shoes and her legs tucked under her.

Edward rubbed her stocking-clad thigh. 'The Garter thing?' He smiled. 'No, I don't think he should, I think the reason he gave for not accepting is a valid one. He felt it to be too elitist. The Merit medal is much more in the vein of a proper reward.'

Edward, as was true of many non-British residing in Britain, was better informed about the "system" than the indigenous people of the country often were.

He continued: 'Regarding his election defeat, it was the bee that was stuck and buzzing around in his homburg about Russia, Stalin, and communism that's turned the British people against the man who saved their freedom.' The car veered to a roadway ditch and Florence's legs shot from underneath her.

'Sorry,' he said, grinning. 'They've had enough of war, Florence.' (She still loved the way he said her name and never called her Flo.) 'And Mr Churchill should have known this. But it's not the old man's way – to *not* fight for what he believes in. A black dog with a huge bone.'

She let out a howl of laughter and glanced at her husband and still, only four months after their wedding in a church very near to the Mississippi river that Churchill had used in his famous speech, Florence couldn't believe her luck at finding him. She'd said the very same thing to Mary Churchill when they had met her for tea in London three months before. Mary had been in a fine mood; her romance with Captain Soames was going extremely well. Florence knew what it felt to be in love. Automatically she rested her hand on Edward's knee, forgiving him the near accident.

They were on their way up to Yorkshire to see Anna. It had been on their way there in the autumn of 1940, the day after the Savoy bash and when the old man in London with the leathered face had lost his wife, when Florence had told Edward about Frank's letter that she'd read at Chartwell. She told him about Anna, Frank, Hilda, and her childhood.

Edward had been there for her during that first meeting with Anna, who in all honesty Florence hardly recognised, both physically and mentally. It was Edward who had asked the psychiatrist all the right questions, and Dr Tanner had been writing to Edward regularly about Anna's progress. Edward was probably better informed than Frank. The medical profession stuck together.

Edward had asked her to marry him on the return trip to London. It had been a tornado war romance. She'd fallen in love with him at first sight. He told her he'd fallen in love with her before he'd even met her, through Mary Churchill's description hours before the Savoy bash began. 'I couldn't wait to meet you, Florence,' he'd said. She'd told him she would move to America. 'You're as transparent as gossamer,' he'd said. 'America isn't for you. You're more British than you give yourself credit for. So it's here where we'll bring up our ten children.'

They hadn't managed ten but managed potentially to make at least a thousand. From the first time she slept with Edward on the night of their wedding (they had waited despite the tone of the war and its way of making even the most conservative of girls, which Florence wasn't, do things they wouldn't normally do) she had noted in her diary every single time. From 1940 until Edward's death in 1963.

In one of those wonderful ironies of life she was now a good friend of Miss Cunningham. On the odd afternoon Florence took her mum, who was suffering badly with arthritis and was often housebound, to have a chat with Miss Cunningham. This occurred usually when the Churchill family was away on one of their many holidays. Sometimes on these visits she came across Mary, who'd been helping Clementine Churchill to reopen the house, which was now owned by the National Trust, but with the proviso that the Churchills could live out the rest of their lives there. After the war her relationship with Mary had settled into what it was always meant to be: affable, but as their lives went back to how they should be, the social distance crept back in. Like everything, war changed things at the time of its happening, and perhaps gave a new order in the long run, but the old order remained steadfast. Florence didn't mind. She didn't like the limelight although she loved being the centre of attention in her own circle. The centre of that circle always Edward. She was like the needle of a compass that always swung back to her north. Edward. She had told him early on about Frank, the Marble Arch Hotel, everything. He knew more about her within days than most people who'd known her a lifetime.

It was three o' clock when they arrived in Harrogate. She'd offered to make this visit alone, and by train, but Edward was being clucky with her, as she'd discovered she was pregnant a few days before. They'd decided to make a holiday of it and had booked into a Harrogate hotel that was only a half hour drive from High Royal Mental Hospital.

Edward parked the car in front of the grand-looking building and she let out a giggle of excitement. 'This is just amazing. You spoil me,' she said.

'You deserve to be spoilt.'

'But can we afford it?' Poverty was never far away from Florence's mind; she was aware of Edward's family's wealth, but still, it was hard to crack a nut that's been lying unopened for so long and not worry about money.

'Don't think too much about money,' he said as if he'd read her thoughts. 'I can't believe you do. With everything else, you seem to take in your stride. Anyway, I've been saving up for us for years.'

'I'm not taking going to High Royal in my stride.' She glanced across at him. 'How can you have been saving for me for years when you haven't known me for years?'

'I always knew I'd find you, Florence. I'm glad you're not Frank's.'

'Where on earth did that come from?'

'He has a thing for you.' He said it without malice.

'No, he doesn't. What happened in London, it was a one-off. A war thing. You know that, I've told you.' She touched his cheek. 'You do know that, Edward, please tell me you do? Anyway you've only met Frank once, I don't know where you get that thought from. He loves Hilda, despite everything.'

Edward had met Frank, and Hilda, for the first time, a week before they had taken the ship to America to get married, coming to London to see them. It had been a shock when she'd laid eyes on Frank at the train station. The war had changed him a lot, the way he looked, and the way he acted. The twenty-four hours they had spent with Hilda and Frank had gone as well as could be expected, although by then her and Hilda's friendship was all but non-existent. Yet, the meeting hadn't been as awkward as she'd worried it might have been. She didn't mention Anna, and that helped. Florence's intuition told her it was best to leave all that alone.

Edward jumped into her thoughts. 'You don't see it, but I do. Frank's in love with you.' He'd got out of the car and opened the door for her. 'And I have to say, I don't blame him.'

'He is not.' She looked up at him. 'You don't like him, do you? Because of Anna? I can understand that. But Frank's a good man, a good husband, he's done what he had to do for his sons.' Unsure if she was trying to convince Edward, or herself.

He helped her from the car. 'He's your friend and I accept that, and I will always give him a wide berth because he left you for me to find.'

She leapt into his arms. 'You have no idea how much I love you.'

'I have a very big idea how much.' In the middle of the upmarket street in Harrogate he pulled her against him and she felt his urgency. Florence wondered if the hotel staff would notice that they might be spending the rest of the day in their room. Then she smiled. It didn't matter though did it? They were married. And, she was wonderfully and magnificently pregnant. She was, as her mother had promised her she would be, blooming.

They made their way onto the steps of the hotel and before they'd set foot through the ornate wooden doors the concierge had whipped away their cases and led them efficiently towards the front desk.

Edward spoke. 'Dr and Mrs Miller. We are booked in for five nights.' He peered at the receptionist. 'I asked for a few things and I hope all that's in order?'

'Indeed it is, Dr Miller,' she smiled. 'Would you like help with your cases?'

'No, it's fine.'

They took the elevator to the top floor and made their way to the end of the corridor. Here Edward stopped outside the door that had a small plaque at the side telling everyone that it was The Honeymoon Suite.

'You are a dark horse,' Florence said to him.

He slipped the key in and pushed it open with his foot.

'Oh my God!' she gasped.

The four-poster was huge, with beautiful crimson fabric enclosing it. Clementine Churchill's bedroom and bed were nothing compared to this, and for a moment Florence's mind went back to her life at Chartwell, remembering when she'd rummaged around Clementine's correspondence. To make herself feel better she reminded herself of the time she had gone into Mrs Churchill's bedroom unexpectedly (when she'd known the mistress was in London) and found Mrs Churchill's secretary in there; feet up on Clementine Churchill's chaise longue and unashamedly going through the mistress's entire 'Private' correspondence tray. Florence had thought Mrs Churchill a little stupid in that respect, as by advertising it as private correspondence she was asking for trouble. My Lord, in her home to say something was off limits you might as well say, *come and read this*.

A bottle of champagne perched on a small table, and next to that a bowl of fruit. Winter pansy petals sprinkled on their bed.

'I think,' Edward said, 'it's time for Mrs Miller to take off her cumbersome clothes.'

She giggled and threw off her coat. 'Do you think it's all right?' She patted her stomach. 'Seeing as I'm pregnant?'

'Of course it is. I'm a doctor and I know these things.' He helped her slip off her skirt and blouse. 'But if you're really worried my love, there are other things we can do.'

Florence looked at the man who she adored with more than passion, a man who she not only loved, but also trusted. She knew what he talked of. Things they had not yet done together. It was as if they had been waiting for this trip, for these things. She shivered in anticipation, feeling the hardness of desire through his trousers, which she was urgently beginning to unbutton.

'Will you show me how?'

'Be patient. First you, lovely Florence.' He peeled off her underclothes and she stood, open to him, trusting him. He picked her up and laid her on the bed, her legs draping over its side. He ran his hand over her already expanding stomach, leant forwards and kissed her naval.

The hotness swelled and took her over and she allowed herself to go on the journey. Within only minutes, long and exquisite minutes, the intensity of feeling built like the growing pressure of water within the dam wall. She pushed up her hips and squeezed his hand tight.

And then the world stopped. Every muscle in her body tightened, then finally let go. Edward moved upward, towards her and lay by her side. She kept her eyes closed but felt his breath and a feather touch of fingertips on her cheek.

'Are you all right, my love?' he asked.

'I have never felt as all right as this in my whole life.' She sat up and surveyed him, his body, stocky and lean, tanned and shiny with sweat, and then his face. 'Show me, Edward.'

And he did show her. He taught Florence gently and with patience. And seven months later, what he had taught her to such perfection, was what she was doing when the waters broke with her first child. Their marriage was to be built on passion and humour, and their children.

Over the next two days, Florence and Edward saw nothing of Harrogate and Florence almost forgot to worry about their impending visit to the hospital to see Anna.

It was on the third day that they made their way to High Royal hospital in West Yorkshire.

39

Edward navigated his way along the tortuous road.

'These places,' he said thoughtfully, 'always built so far back from the road and always on a hill, so they have to make the roads really windy to get to them.' He turned and smiled at her. 'It's where the saying comes from, "round the bend."'

'Is that true?' Florence said.

'Very true.'

They stopped at the enormous gravel-covered entrance and suddenly, what had been a startling blue-velvet day turned into a premature early evening January grimness.

She uncrossed her legs in the passenger seat of Edward's beloved beige Standard Eight and pulled out her compact. She fussed with her royal purple hat and then reapplied dark rose lipstick.

'How do I look?'

'You look like I could take you back to the hotel and make love to you all over again.'

He wore a deep brown suit, a chalky white shirt with a crisp collar, and the waistcoat she'd bought him for Christmas. She thanked her lucky stars that she'd worked at Chartwell, because without having worked there she wouldn't know Mary, and so would never have met Edward. The serendipity brought a smile within the gloom of the winter's day.

Her eyes settled on the building and the nervous anticipation struck her again. The hospital, full of damaged people, people who had been long ago

forgotten; people like Anna. She knew Frank hadn't
visited during the war years, and Hilda only very
sporadically. Jem had visited though, Dr Tanner had
informed her. Her feelings for Jem were still splintered.
Florence had made sure she came to see Anna as often
as she could, and had been able to fit in some visits with
her war dispatch work. She had never seen Jem here and
wondered if Jem ensured their visits were always
separate.

Jem. What was it about Frank's sister that made her
feel so uncomfortable? It wasn't what had happened to
Jem with her own father, no, not that, Florence had
come to terms with that tragedy within the Cullen
family, and it was this sorrow that encouraged her to try
and forgive Jem.

A crow settled itself on the lower edge of the
hospital's grand clock tower and at that moment it
struck. 3 p.m. They were bang on time.

Florence got out of the car, stumbling in the gravel.
She looked around. 'This place is so huge. Every time I
come it surprises me.'

'You know it even has its own graveyard.'

'For what?'

'To bury the dead people?' he replied, his face
deadpan.

She thumped his arm. 'I know that, but its *own*
graveyard?'

'For the patients who die here and whose bodies
aren't claimed by the relatives. Over the years there's
been a lot of them. That's what happens, Florence.
Families choose to forget the relatives who are put away
in these places. Some people come in here young and

never get out. Many shouldn't be here, but it's easier to hide people away than deal with the problem. It's the same in the States.'

'You think that's why Frank and Hilda put Anna here?'

'I think it's more complicated than that.'

'How often do you have contact with Dr Tanner?'

'Every month to six weeks he writes to me.'

'It's so good of you to take this interest in Anna.'

'I couldn't let it go, not after coming here that first time with you. I think Anna is one of their more challenging cases.'

'Where did I find you?' she said softly.

'Come on, let's go see Anna.'

The entrance foyer was enormous and the two staircases, which sat each side of the great hall, were both hauntingly beautiful and imposing. As she'd thought during her previous visits, for the visitor this place seemed like a country estate house, but once you moved inwards and into its unfathomable bowels this was not a country house at all. Beyond the double ornate doors situated at the back of the staircases lay an altogether different world: a world of wide clinical corridors, painted in high gloss cream and lime green, tall, lofty ceilings and every twenty feet or so, a sweeping arch, separating the segments of the boundless gallery-like passages that seemed to form a grid within the building's guts. A wired and locked door separated each segment, secure, holding the patients in, holding Anna, and not keeping anyone out because no one would wish to enter willingly.

A strong smell of beeswax, sweet and warm, hit her nostrils and she sneezed.

'Bless you! Dr and Mrs Miller?' A small bespectacled man had appeared as if from nowhere.

'Mr Mowbry,' Florence said. 'Lovely to see you again, and thank you.'

He took her hand, then turned to Edward and shook his. 'It is very good to finally meet you Dr Miller.' He fussed with his jacket, unbuttoning it. 'Dr Tanner is waiting for you both.'

They followed him up the right hand staircase and through a corridor, its floor covered in a rich red Axminster and the walls not decorated in the cream and green gloss, but a rich dark rose matt paint, a muted magnolia on the pretty dados and coving. The heels of Florence's shoes sank into the carpet as she walked towards Dr Tanner's study.

Mr Mowbry knocked and opened the door. 'Dr and Mrs Miller, Dr Tanner.' He then scurried off.

Dr Tanner looked as he had done when she'd last seen him, a few weeks after VE Day, the last time she'd seen Anna. Tall, lean. A greying head of hair, although perhaps a little less of it, but she couldn't be sure.

'Mrs Miller, so good to see you. And Dr Miller,' Dr Tanner said. 'I am so pleased we can finally converse in person again.' He stood up and moved to the front of his desk. 'My belated congratulations on your marriage.'

'Thank you,' Edward replied, hanging an arm over Florence's shoulder.

'And so we've pilfered you from America?' Dr Tanner carried on in an overly jocular manner, his arms gesticulating quite wildly, like a stick insect. 'How are you enjoying working in our country?'

'Early days, but it seems to be going extremely well, thank you. I'm looking forward to helping with the healthcare reforms. Exciting times ahead for the health of this nation.'

Edward, so calm. Organised. Taking everything in his stride. In control, of himself, and others.

Dr Tanner coughed. 'Yes, perhaps it will all be for the good, this idea of free health care for all.' His tone indicating the exact opposite.

'It is for the good. Of course it is. No question,' Edward said.

Dr Tanner coughed again. 'Please sit down.'

'It's been very good of you to keep me informed about Anna's progress, and in such detail,' Edward said. 'I'm only sorry I couldn't have visited in person again before now.'

'The war made many things very difficult,' Dr Tanner said. 'I've been in contact with Mrs Cullen in the hope that she might visit her daughter more regularly, although we did have a long and enlightening chat when she came to see me without her husband in early 1940. January, just after the New Year's ball, as I recall. We—' He looked at Edward, as if about to say something about Hilda but deciding not to.

'Hilda came alone?' Florence asked.

'She did, Mrs Miller.'

'And?'

'And, nothing, Mrs Miller.' He peered at her from underneath heavily drooped eyelids. 'I cannot divulge such things.' He adjusted his chocolate brown bow tie. 'You understand?'

'Not really, Dr Tanner,' Edward answered for her, something he rarely did. 'But I endeavour to try.'

Dr Tanner threw Edward a glance, his expression filled with indicators of his personality, which he'd been managing to hide since the conversation began. Irascibility and impatience. Condescension. Clearly the doctor had no wish to talk about Hilda's visit and hurriedly carried on: 'Mr Cullen, Anna's father, has visited, soon after he returned from overseas. And Mrs Jemima Barnes, Anna's aunt, has been a regular visitor. Very commendable. '

'How did Frank's, I mean, Mr Cullen's visit go?' Florence asked, ignoring for now the mention of Jemima.

'As well as expected. As I've said in my reports, Anna totally refutes that either Frank or Hilda are her parents. Her fixation with the fantasy that she is in fact a "reincarnation" of Mr and Mrs Churchill's deceased daughter, Marigold, is only strengthening. It takes time to filter through these things.' He touched his tie. 'Years.'

'I do understand, Dr Tanner,' Edward interrupted gently. 'And I appreciate the detailed information you've been sending me on Anna's case. But I am no nearer to understanding the root cause of Anna's demise.' He waited a second before carrying on. 'Especially if all the information isn't readily available?'

'Anna is a very difficult study. And, Dr Miller, you more than most, will understand how tricky it can be to dig deep into a mind that refuses to accept reality. It does not help.' He coughed, this time a phlegmy sound. 'It doesn't help that Mrs Cullen has been all but absent in any treatment programme, as has Mr Cullen, but obviously, that has not been his fault.' He peered at Edward. 'I am not at liberty to share every detail with you, Dr Miller. Unfortunately.'

Edward took hold of Florence's hand. 'That is your prerogative, Dr Tanner. But in my view, with proper.' He took a breath. 'Conservative treatment, one day in the not too distant future Anna will be able to leave here.'

'That day, I hope, may come to pass, and if Anna's mother and father are willing to take her back home.' He readjusted his jacket. 'I see no reason why Anna cannot be discharged from our care. In the future.'

'If Mr and Mrs Cullen have no wish to take Anna home, I foresee other possibilities.' Edward's reply was resolute.

Dr Tanner sighed. 'She is nowhere near being well enough for release.'

'I understand that.' Edward peered at the man. 'But I'm confident that with your care and expertise Anna *will* be in the future.'

Florence squeezed Edward's arm.

'With rehabilitation and good care,' Edward continued, 'I know that in the fullness of time Anna'll be able to be eventually discharged from High Royal. You have reported in your correspondence that since being admitted Anna has shown no further acts of violence?'

'That is true, but we must remember what she did to her brother, on two occasions. And we do feel that Anna is a threat to herself.'

'My question is: are you any nearer to finding out a reason to Anna's behaviour?' Edward pressed. He was losing his patience, Florence saw it in the way he pushed both hands into his pockets. Edward was cross that Dr Tanner was withholding information about Hilda, and she suspected, Dr Tanner knew this.

This time, not a cough, but a grunt. 'I feel Anna could be a candidate for surgery,' Dr Tanner said. 'Something I have discussed with Mr Cullen… But he is adamant this should not happen. He is still under the illusion Anna will get better. In my opinion this does not look a likely scenario. Anna would not even speak to him.'

Edward stood. 'Surgery cannot happen. From studies I've read, the data I have, in my opinion—'

'With all due respect Dr Miller, you are not Anna's psychiatrist. I am. It has been interesting for you to follow Anna's case, I am sure, but this is not your speciality.'

'I strongly believe cutting out a part of a patient's brain is not the answer to these complex psychiatric problems, and clearly Anna's father agrees with me. The use of drugs should be adequate. We do not want to see Anna used as an experiment. Anna has been incarcerated within these walls for seven years. You should, by now, have some idea as to what has caused her descent into insanity.'

Dr Tanner settled his eyes on Edward. 'Perhaps it is better if Mrs Miller left the room for a little while?'

Edward peered at the doctor. 'There's no need for that, whatever you have to say, Florence is robust enough to hear it.'

'As you wish,' Dr Tanner said. 'Although Anna says very little, and nothing indicating the reason for being brought here, Mrs Barnes has given me thoughts that might be pertinent, and it would explain much about Anna's case.'

'Please be translucent, Doctor,' Edward pushed. 'What exactly did Jemima say?'

'I really can't divulge.'

'She said that Frank abused his own daughter,' Florence said quietly. 'Didn't she?'

'Stepdaughter, Mrs Miller,' Dr Tanner said.

'This is ridiculous.' Florence said tightly. 'Jemima is in no position to make such wild accusations. She is too biased.'

'Perhaps. And I have not included any of this in my notes. But, back to Anna. She does become very agitated, very easily, and has sunk further into her belief that she is Marigold Churchill reincarnated. That the ex-Prime Minister of our country is her father.' He looked pointedly at Florence. 'Perhaps because her own stepfather is so lacking?' Dr Tanner waited for their response.

'And how does Hilda fit in all this?' Florence said. 'Did Jemima have a theory on that?'

'Mrs Barnes believes that Mrs Cullen loves her daughter and wants the best for her, but is keen that the lives of her other two children are not impacted.'

Edward sighed. 'I feel we are going around in circles, Dr Tanner, with all due respect. I think it's time we see Anna now.'

Dr Tanner smiled in relief. 'Of course. I will take you to the sanatorium block myself.'

Dr Tanner led them through the maze of green and cream corridors, the keys at his hip jangling, the sound ricocheting upward, to high ceilings and wide vacant useless spaces. Finally they arrived at a door with a sign, *The Lounge*, blazoned in black on the background of the shiny green paint. The other times Florence had visited she'd only seen Anna inside her sparse bedroom, or cell, as Florence thought of it inside her head.

The floor was devoid of carpet and the walls were painted in the same high gloss cream that lathered the corridors, whilst the picture rails and skirting boards were all painted in a calm green. The place screamed of sterility. Florence's eyes darted around trying to find Anna.

She saw two women and a man sitting at a table, a board game placed in the middle, all three staring into the space that seemed to hang around them, almost like a physical thing. In the corner a man dressed in white was reading from a book to the several patients gathered around him, although none of them were listening to a word he was narrating. She caught a few of the words and recognised the characters straightaway. It was a chapter from *Peter Rabbit*. Why on earth was he reading children's books to grown adults? It was probably why the patients weren't listening.

A man stood gazing out the window, a patient she guessed. He looked out onto the incredibly well manicured lawn, the green of the inside merging with the colours of the outside. But the man was doing nothing, only staring.

The room was eerily quiet, apart from the hushed tones of the nurse reading the book. There was no music, no nothing, only souls horribly encased within themselves. She knew from her previous visits that the patients who were fit enough were given proper work to do within the institution. She'd found out the place was almost self-sufficient, like a little village in itself. A huge vegetable garden, a laundry, livestock bred within the hospital's vast parameters, and then slaughtered, and butchered for food. A bakery, and even a florist. It was quite unbelievable. She'd never have known.

Then she saw Anna. Anna did not work, only sometimes, Dr Tanner had told her, in the vegetable garden. *Anna enjoys that,* he'd said. *But tires so very easily. One day in the veg garden equates to five days recovering*, he'd finished.

Anna's insanity ran in parallel with her hastening physical decline, and her inherent delicacy didn't help things.

It had only been a matter of months since seeing her last, and if it had not been for the fact Anna wore a red ribbon in her hair, which Florence remembered as the one she'd bought in London, she didn't think she'd have recognised her. The ribbon with black lace, a thin red silk braided through.

Florence walked away from Edward and Dr Tanner, towards Anna. She would now be twenty-three, and so thin that Florence wondered if High Royal fed their patients any of the food they produced. Anna's hair was held in a ponytail, wispy thin and without shine. As Florence got closer she saw the two thick streaks of grey adorning each side of Anna's crown, and faint lines appearing too soon in her life, crossing her cheeks.

'Anna, darling Anna,' Florence whispered.

Anna continued to stare into the space ahead, carried on twirling each thumb around the other. She made no movement and no acknowledgement. Florence felt Edward's hand on her arm.

'Anna?' Florence said again.

Edward gently interrupted. 'Marigold, that's a beautiful ribbon you're wearing.'

Anna turned her head, and the corners of her lips lifted. 'Thank you.'

'And who bought it for you?' he asked.

'A lady from London. One of Papa's friends.'

Edward pulled up two chairs and gently pushed Florence into one of them, then sat down in the other. 'Who is your papa, Anna?'

'Mr Churchill, of course.'

'And who is this, Marigold? This lady sitting in front of me?'

By now Dr Tanner had joined them but stood at a distance.

Anna smiled widely then, and for a moment looked to Florence like the old Anna. 'This is Florence. My parents' friend.'

'Have you said hello to Florence?' Dr Tanner asked.

'Hello, Florence.' Anna studied her, lifting an index finger to her face. 'Yes, I remember you. I took you to see my Wendy house, didn't I? We sat inside and ate Dundee cake and drank squash. You were visiting my parents, I remember that.'

Florence moved closer. 'Do you, Ann… Marigold? You were quite young then, about eight as I remember.' She glanced at Edward and he nodded to carry on. 'Do you see your parents often, Marigold? Do they come here to visit?'

'My papa does. He's been to see me.' She looked up towards Dr Tanner. 'Hasn't he, Dr Tanner?'

Dr Tanner said nothing, only tightened his tie.

Florence said: 'Marigold, was that very recently, that he came?'

'Yes, it was after he'd helped us win the war. I might not be able to go home just yet, will I, Dr Tanner?'

'Not just yet, and your father is very busy.'

'Yes, very busy.' She pulled Florence closer and whispered in her ear. 'It's our secret isn't it, that my mum doesn't really like me that much. That I'm her burden, but you always knew, didn't you?'

Confusion settled within Florence, although Edward was at ease; he seemed to understand so much more about Anna's mind than she did. She really wasn't sure if Anna was being Anna, or Marigold. And in a moment of clarity understood that Anna could be talking about either Hilda or Clementine Churchill.

Sensing her disquiet Edward said, and close to her ear. 'It's best to play along.'

She whispered back. 'Am I missing something?'

He shook his head sadly.

Dr Tanner stepped forward. 'I think it's time for Anna's sleep. We are trying to encourage all of our patients to rest well today, in preparation for the big ball tomorrow night.'

He led them from the room and they made their way back to his office, through the corridors, waiting at each junction for him to unlock each caged door and finally they were back again in the part of the building where there was no cream and green.

'Please take a seat,' Dr Tanner said. 'It is our annual ball tomorrow. You are both welcome to attend.'

'A ball for the patients?' Florence asked incredulously.

'We're famous for it, Mrs Miller. Patients, staff, people from the surrounding villages. It's quite a draw.' He studied her. 'Don't look so taken aback. The patients love it. Anna's been looking forward to it for months.'

'She seems well cared for, but a little thin.' She paused, looked at Edward. 'I do wonder if we should be encouraging Anna's delusion quite this much.'

'Don't worry, Mrs Miller,' Dr Tanner said, his tone brisk. 'It is under control, and the best way to deal with Anna, at the moment.'

Edward said: 'I agree, but I will reiterate again, I do disagree with surgery, Dr Tanner. I believe you have the expertise to do without it. I hope you won't jump on the current bandwagon of invasive surgery. Drugs and therapy are adequate.'

'So tomorrow night?' Doctor Tanner said, skilfully ending the conversation

'We'll be here,' Edward said.

Perhaps with Anna's new openness, tomorrow night Florence might get the chance to ask her more about what had happened in the weeks leading up to Hilda giving birth to Jim, and tell her what Frank would not. Because she knew there was something, and not what

Jem or Dr Tanner alluded to. Frank had survived the war and now she believed whatever he was near to telling her in London in 1940, it was time for her to find out, because whatever had happened seemed to be a secret that had caused Anna's decline; a secret between Anna and Frank, and Hilda, perhaps, and maybe Jem too. Frank had clammed up, and there was no hope with Hilda. Only Anna could tell her the truth and Florence earmarked the ball to finally find out.

* * *

It was quite an event and Florence was glad she'd brought a posh frock. When they arrived, the gothic structure of High Royal was ablaze with light, even the clock tower lit. People scurried around the entrance, and she didn't see one white uniform, even the staff dressed up to the nines. It was Mr Mowbry, and she suspected wearing his finest suit – black pinstripe coupled with a yellow bow tie – who led her and Edward into the foyer. They were then taken to Dr Tanner's office where punch, which took her back to the Savoy, was being served. She slowly fell into the swing of a post New Year Ball held in a mental hospital. Edward did his bit talking to Mr Mowbry on the other side of the room. Hungrily, Florence eyed the hors d'oeuvres sitting on Dr Tanner's grand desk. She picked up a salmon pastry. Pregnancy had sharpened her appetite even more.

'Mrs Miller, you look quite stunning, I'm so glad you and Edward could come,' Dr Tanner said.

She swallowed quickly. 'It's kind of you to invite us, seems that it's a popular event? Do you not worry about… something happening?'

'You mean security? All staff are on duty tonight. It is the one night of the year when we are staffed to over-capacity! Don't worry, Mrs Miller.'

'I'd like to see Anna.'

'We'll be moving to the ballroom in about ten minutes. Anna and the other patients are already there.'

'You really have a ballroom here too?'

'Yes, quite magnificent. Anna's been looking forward to tonight. She does love the post New Year bashes.'

His attention was taken away by Mr Mowbry who shouted, 'Time to start the party properly!'

Florence moved towards the door, taking Edward's elbow as she did so.

'In his element isn't he,' he said quietly.

'Seems to be,' she said, winking.

The opulence of High Royal's ballroom took Florence aback, bigger than the space at the Savoy, and more beautiful in its architecture, colourful frescos on the upper walls, scenes from Shakespeare's Tragedies (Edward informed her later), the ceiling covered in the most ornate gilt, spectacular stained glass windows lit tonight with candles. The room echoed with music from a band on the ballroom's stage, a mini orchestra and a man in a white suit whose voice was strong and distinctive, and familiar. She couldn't place his name but guessed he was well-known. Dr Tanner had pulled out all the stops.

The perimeter of the room was filled with chairs and most of them taken. Florence was unable to see the difference between patients and 'guests' at a distance and it was only as she moved nearer it became apparent. The location of the patients had changed but the vacant stares of most had not. Her eyes skimmed the room trying to find Anna. She finally spotted her, sitting very near to the stage and looking toward the singer who was now in full flow.

Anna wore a red dress that fell just above her ankles, the red and black ribbon in her hair, together with a large silver clasp that glinted in the low lighting. Florence walked towards her; Anna's face alive and animated as she tapped her foot to the music, looking like any other twenty-three-year-old girl dressed up and ready to enjoy herself. A wave of sadness folded over Florence, thinking of Anna's childhood, of Hilda's dismissal of her daughter, of Frank's attempt to make both Hilda and Anna happy, but failing so badly. *What happened, Frank?*

She was now standing next to Anna. She glanced back, Edward was in deep conversation with Dr Tanner.

'Anna,' she said loudly, attempting to be heard over the music. Anna continued tapping her foot to the rhythm, not moving her gaze away from the men on the stage. Florence moved a little closer, noticing again the beautiful silver adornment in Anna's hair that was holding back the strands of grey. 'Marigold?'

Anna turned, her face lit. 'Florence. The singer is good, isn't he?'

She sat next to her. 'Very good. Are you enjoying yourself?'

'I am.'

'That's a very lovely clip in your hair.'

Anna fingered it but didn't reply. Florence glanced at the immense space in front of the stage, people were already dancing. Women with women, whilst the men remained seated at the periphery. Florence wondered if it was Dr Tanner's stipulation there was to be no mixed gender dancing.

'Do you want to dance with me, Florence?' Anna said.

'I'd love to dance with you.'

Anna stood and pressed down the skirt of her dress, pushed back brutally the strands of hair that were coming loose. Her posture erect and sturdy despite her fragility. She smelt of milk and carbolic soap, and sadness.

They began to dance, Florence trying her hardest to accommodate Anna's rigidity, but after a while Anna relaxed and the two women fell into their conservative foxtrot. Anna who was a few inches shorter than Florence laid her head on Florence's shoulder, the sharpness of the silver clasp digging into Florence's cheek.

'Who gave you this beautiful hairclip?' Florence asked.

Anna took her cheek away from Florence's shoulder, looking up at her. 'My father of course, when he came to see me.'

'That wasn't that long ago, was it? So it's very new, your clip. It's nice to wear something new.' Frank had good taste and she was pleased he'd given Anna a gift. Men were sometimes so bad at remembering these things.

'It was a while ago, I think. I can't remember… it was when he came back from the desert. I know that.'

Frank had last visited the previous autumn. 'Ah, so this is the first time you've worn the clip to the special New Year's ball here?'

'No,' she fingered it with love. 'I wore it last year too, and the year before. Papa gave it to me quite a while ago now, the time he came to see me.' She peered into Florence's eyes. 'After he came back from the desert, I told you. He came in a lovely car with some of his friends. No one else here was allowed to see him. Dr Tanner even allowed me to come to his office so I could talk to Papa, and that is when he gave me the clip. That day. He didn't stay long. He's very busy, you know.' She touched Florence's cheek. 'You know that, Florence?'

'I do know that.'

'Dr Tanner doesn't like people to smoke in his office but he allowed Papa to smoke one of his cigars.'

Florence's feet stopped moving as she realised what Anna was saying. And what Dr Tanner had omitted from his conversation with them.

40

Frank

Seven years later
Late July 1953

Miss Betty Cunningham and Hilda had always written to each other on a fairly regular basis, exchanging gossip, recipes and advice. Frank sometimes wondered if Hilda did this only to keep Betty Cunningham sweet, and quiet – because Betty Cunningham knew about Anna being incarcerated at High Royal.

Miss Cunningham wrote to him occasionally too, her last but one letter had been in early 1948, saying she'd like to go and see Anna, that she'd asked Hilda, but Hilda said it was better if she didn't, that it might upset Anna. He told her by all means she should go.

A month later Betty Cunningham wrote back saying she'd been to see Anna: *How sad I found it all, and there must be something that can be done, surely? Can't Anna come back home?* A section perplexed him in the last but one paragraph. *I always think it's better to be as honest as you can, Frank. No matter what's happened. Water that travels under the bridge journeys a long way over these many years. I know Hilda can be difficult, and, Frank, I think I understand.* The last paragraph only saying she hoped to see him, Hilda and the boys in the near future. What had Betty Cunningham meant? She couldn't know. Only one person in the whole world knew.

And he was on the train to see that person now.

In the run up to Mr Churchill's knighthood in April, and again leading up to the Coronation at the beginning of June, Miss Cunningham's letters to Hilda had been prolific. Then a week ago, a letter from Betty Cunningham addressed to him. She was writing, she said, on behalf of Mary Soames.

Her father is not well, Miss Cunningham reported, and Sir Winston has specifically asked for you, Frank. Benjamin is dead, and something about the kitchen wall. I told Mary I would contact you. This is in the strictest confidence. And Frank knew it was; the letter had been delivered to their house by a private courier. The neighbours' curtains had been alive. One of the kids on the street had smudged strawberry jam on the courier's car. Jim had said it was Wayne who lived down the road. Frank was convinced it was Jim, who at fifteen was becoming wilder by the year.

Frank had told Hilda he was going to see Anna; a visit to their daughter was one he knew she'd decline, which she did, saying she had to look after the boys. He loved Jim and Nick but his relationship was not all that it could be, especially with Jim, and he shied away from why this might be so. It was too complicated to think about. Nick, at thirteen, was about to enter manhood and more affectionate than Jim had ever been or was likely to be, but still distant. His sons were close, to each other, and to Hilda. Frank hoped things would change between him and his boys as both grew older but deep inside he knew they wouldn't. Hilda had seen to that, and he'd helped her by agreeing to keep Anna a secret.

It was two in the afternoon when he got off the train at Westerham station. The air was muggy and uncomfortable, a heavy smell of storm in the atmosphere. He perched on the kerb listening to the quietness of the surrounding countryside that even now he still missed.

The man collecting him introduced himself as the gardener. Division and integration of labour. Frank smiled to himself. Communism suited Churchill occasionally, and for expediency.

Frank put his battered suitcase in the back of the ocean-blue Bedford pick-up and made a few pleasantries with the man in an attempt to appear civil. Five minutes into the journey the gardener/driver retrieved a cigar from his coat pocket, ferreted around the pouch that sat in the driver's door and found some matches. He pulled the end off the cigar.

Frank looked at it. 'That's a Romeo and Julieta.'

'It is. Sir Winston gave it to me. Gave me three.' He studied Frank. 'I'm not giving you one.'

Frank shrugged. 'Kind of Sir Winston.'

'He's the best. Just hope he recovers.'

Frank didn't answer. He would find out himself, and soon now. Mr Churchill had asked to see him and Frank wasn't stupid; it wasn't about a wall.

The truck bumped its way up the main road to the house and just before three they arrived at Chartwell. A war, a churning out of office, then back in office, but the house remained as it always had and Frank felt as if he'd come home.

Walking around to the back of the building he knocked on the kitchen door and a young girl answered.

'Hello,' she said, her voice nasal and quiet. 'Are you Mr Frank Cullen, Mr Churchill's bricklayer?'

'I am, yes.'

'A room has been made up for you at Orchard Cottage.'

'That's very kind,' he replied.

He'd noticed numerous expensive cars parked at the front entrance. He glanced around the kitchen, which he'd always thought too small for the scale of entertaining that went on there, and he was sure Sir Winston's entertaining habits hadn't changed. The kitchen was filled with food in various modes of preparation. And then at that precise moment a woman bustled in. Chartwell's full-time cook.

'Tilly,' the cook said, 'we really do need to get on. Twelve for dinner tonight, Lady Churchill is in ice mood. Get a move on.' She began rolling out pastry. 'Take a seat outside if you would like, Mr Cullen.'

'Of course.' He swallowed. 'Is Sir Winston all right?'

She glared at him. 'You'll be "briefed" I'm sure. There's a chair outside.' She capitulated a little. 'I'm sure you know what the master's like. Gets a bee in his bonnet…'

'About the wall?'

'Seems so. And Lady Clementine indulges him, as she always does.' She paused and put the rolling pin down. 'More so at the moment. It's been a busy year.' She looked at the clock. 'With one thing and another.'

Frank wondered what looking at the time now had to do with the year's busyness. 'Seems so, yes. I'll go and sit outside.'

She nodded and carried on making what looked like a game pie.

He sat in the same place that all those years ago he'd eaten the apple pie. The July sun poured onto the small terrace, crashing into his face.

'Mr Cullen. So good of you to come.'

He lifted his head. 'Mrs Soames.'

'Papa is in the studio. He's had a good sleep. It helps with his recovery.' Mary began walking, he got up quickly. 'Your visit today must be kept in absolute confidence, Mr Cullen. Do you understand?'

'I do, Mrs Soames. Is Sir Winston not well?'

'He's getting better.' She took a sideways glance at him. 'Better enough to start thinking of things which do not… tax his brain too much. Of things that have probably been on his mind for years but only now does he have mind-time to address them. He says the kitchen wall needs some loving care.' She stopped walking. 'That's why my father has asked you to come. That is why you are here.'

'Of course,' he replied.

They made their way through the kitchen garden, through Clementine's rose bushes and down the incline that led to Churchill's painting studio.

'I bet Sir Winston's enjoying the time to paint?' Frank said; it was something to say.

'I think he is, Mr Cullen, yes.'

The studio door was open but even before Frank stepped inside he whiffed the familiar aroma, which was only faintly concealed by the smell of oils.

Sir Winston Churchill sat in a mahogany chair, reclining back, his width spread into its wooden pole sides, his back towards them, smoke cresting upwards, a paintbrush in his hand and facing a canvas with an emerging and captivating image of the hills that surrounded them.

Without turning he said: 'Is that you, Mary?' His voice gravelly.

Mary touched Frank's arm and he moved towards the old man.

'Mr Cullen is here, Papa.'

Finally Churchill turned his head and moved the chair back. The paintbrush he was holding dropped to the floor and Mary rushed to pick it up.

'You must not exert yourself too much, Papa. Please?'

Despite filling the chair Sir Winston had lost weight, his face, more creased than the last time he'd seen him. He lifted the arm that had been holding the brush and beckoned Frank to move closer, and then he used the same arm to help his other to move it onto his lap. Mr Churchill wasn't as Frank had last seen him, and he thought about his old gaffer at the pit who'd had to retire just after the war because of the stroke he'd had. He scrutinised Sir Winston who to his eye appeared very frail.

'Frank, come closer and help me stand,' Churchill said.

'Papa!'

'Mary, you go and help your mother with the preparations for this evening.'

She looked at Frank, nodded her head slightly. 'Ensure Sir Winston doesn't do too much?'

Frank glanced at Sir Winston whose face had broken out into a grin, and with the hand that had held the paintbrush, he picked up the cigar smouldering in an ashtray placed next to his palette of oils and took a huge puff.

'I can still hear, Mary, and think. Don't worry, I do not intend on doing very much.'

Mary smiled worriedly and left.

Frank walked nearer to the canvas. 'A beautiful picture in the making, sir.'

'A way to go yet. All these people at the house, all this fuss about me and around me, is not helping it get painted.'

Frank fell silent.

'I'd like to walk to the pond,' Churchill said. 'I have some maggots.' He pointed to a table on the other side of the studio, at a tin box. 'Over there. Let us walk.'

Churchill put the cigar down and shuffled forward in his chair, using only one hand. Frank's immediate reaction was to help him but was hesitant and held back. Finally Churchill was standing, and without his assistance.

'Help me, Frank.'

Frank rushed toward him, the tin of maggots underneath his arm, picking up the cigar, holding it in between his fingers, and together they walked slowly and in silence to the pond.

A table and chairs awaited them. Frank helped the old man sit and gave him the cigar. It took Churchill five minutes to gain his breath.

'There is something I need to talk to you about,' the Prime Minister said.

'The wall, sir? I don't really lay bricks any more. I'm a miner. But I'd love to do any maintenance on your wall.'

'I know you are a miner. A man does what he has to do. I've spent most of my life chained to the deadlines of editors, making a living,' his eyes lifted to his beloved Chartwell, 'to keep all of this, which after the war, I lost anyway, as well as the election. And no, I did not bring you here for the bloody wall.'

'I don't understand, sir?'

'I'm unwell, I had a stroke, as I think you've noticed. I'm recovering well, my physician says, not that I need a physician to tell me how I am doing. No one knows about my illness, only the seemingly hundreds of people passing through here lately. The public must never know. An ill leader is in impotent leader. Leading up to Stalin's stroke in March, he lost all grip on government. A country cannot be governed by an ill man. It's worse than being governed by a stupid man.' He threw the cigar to the ground and pressed into it with his good foot.

He continued. 'Edward Miller has been to Chartwell recently.'

'With Florence, sir?'

'No, Mrs Miller didn't come. It was a business meeting, to talk about the continuation of the health reforms.' Churchill took off his hat and pulled out another cigar from the pocket of his jacket. Put it in his mouth. Frank retrieved matches and lit it for him. Churchill sat back, inhaled several times. 'Tripoli is a long time ago. Where is your medal?'

'In a box somewhere. I didn't want to accept it, sir.'

'We all make mistakes. I, Frank Cullen, should, and will, have made nothing if I had not made them. Swathes of them. If one simply takes up the attitude of defending a mistake there will be no hope of improvement. You did not attempt to defend your mistake and so you are therefore in a position to improve the situation. Which is why you are here. We have to live in the present.'

Frank allowed his eyes to settle on the jewel green of the Wealds.

Churchill continued: 'You are aware of my mistakes. Gallipoli in 1915. Allowing it to be known publicly about the troops that as Home Secretary I sent in reserve to Tonypandy in 1911. I misjudged the situation, although,' he smiled grimly, 'not as much as many newspapers did.' Churchill fumbled open the tin of maggots and threw a handful into the pond. 'Other decisions I had to make that I would rather not have had to make, but someone had to make them. Operation Catapult and the destruction of the French Fleet at Mers-el- Kébir in the summer of 1940, sustained bombing in Germany, knowing about Truman's decision in Japan and agreeing. These decisions were hard but I made them quickly and cleanly.'

'Sir, I believe you did what you thought was best at the time.' Frank had never wholly agreed with the decision to sink the French Fleet and had been horrified with Enola Gay.

'Of course I did. And in the future you must always do what you think is the right thing to do. Follow your instinct, your destiny, and your true convictions; do not be swayed by others. Hold true to what you believe is right.' Lifting his head, Churchill found Frank's eyes. 'You made a mistake, which has had profound effects, and it is now time to attempt to rectify it. Edward and Florence Miller would be happy to remove your daughter from High Royal. I believe your wife is unconcerned about your daughter. But you are, as are your friends.'

The breath caught somewhere in between Frank's lungs and throat. A giant heron swooped down as if from nowhere. The ducks moved quickly, their underwater exertion unnoticeable from above. Frank did not even attempt to defend Hilda.

'My secretary has spoken to Dr Tanner. He is in agreement. I suggest this happens sooner rather than later.'

'I don't know what to say—'

'Give thanks you have friends. I told you many years ago how important they can be, and how listening to advice is paramount. Listen to me now and take my advice. Anna is a lovely woman. She thinks she is Marigold.' Now it was Churchill's turn to gaze towards the hills. He leant forward giving the ducks more supper. The ripples of the lake shimmering diamonds in the lowering sun.

'You've seen Anna recently, sir?' Frank asked, unable to hide the surprise from his voice. How could Sir Winston Churchill recently have seen Anna?

Churchill sucked on his cigar. 'We have to view the bigger canvas of life. Go home and live yours, with your family, Frank Cullen. It is sometimes expedient and necessary for a man to lead a dual if not even a tripartite existence.' He flicked the ash onto the ground. 'Life is not very far away from diplomacy and politics. Always a decision to be made, a compromise and a way around a problem to be found.' He glanced at Frank. 'I think I might need the wheelchair to get me back up to the house for dinner. It's in the studio, could you get it for me?'

Frank nodded and ten minutes later was wheeling the British Prime Minister back to the house. Mary met them at the kitchen terrace and took over. Frank stood watching, Churchill turned his head.

'I hope Orchard Cottage will be comfortable for you. Get in touch with Florence and Edward as soon as you are able.' Churchill held up his good arm, the cigar held tight, and bade farewell.

Frank only continued to stand. He did not move at all, spellbound by Churchill's humanity, self-confidence. Human frailty.

He held the latter in spades and none of the former, at all.

41

December 16th 1953

Westerham Evening Standard
12th December 1953.

Lady Churchill And Mary Soames In Stockholm Giving
An Acceptance Speech On Behalf Of Sir Winston For
The Prestigious Nobel Prize For Literature.

Sir Winston was unable to attend the Nobel Banquet at the City Hall in Stockholm on Thursday due to his meeting with President Eisenhower in the Bermuda Islands, where the two men are discussing Europe's future after Stalin's death.
It is reported that Sir Winston was very regretful that he was unable to be present for this momentous occasion, but made it clear that he is extraordinarily well-represented by his wife, Lady Clementine, and daughter, Mary Soames.

Sitting on the train to Westerham to see Flo and her family, and Anna, Frank read the article Flo had put in the post for him. He'd read similar articles in the nationals, but the old man's local paper wrote a much better piece. He studied the photograph of Sir Winston. An expression recognised by thousands; a fearless lip

thrusting pose, and filled with the old man's inherent
pugnacity. He was pleased he was back on form. Frank
smiled, but then, as he tried to pull his bag from the next
seat, grimaced. His arm would never be right, he
accepted that, but often forgot. The pain that shot
towards his neck when he exerted the muscles in his
injured arm was piercing.

Trying to relax back into the seat, he waited for the
discomfort to cease, which after a few minutes it did. He
put the clipping back in his bag and pulled out a book
with his other hand, looking at his watch. Another hour
or so before he'd reach Westerham. He'd had to wait
two hours in London for the connection, and before
that, three hours on the train from Nottingham. He'd
best get used to the journey because he'd be doing it a
lot.

Opening the cover, he began to read about a man
who was two men. He'd been meaning to read Robert
Louis Stevenson's *The Strange Case of Dr Jekyll and Mr
Hyde* for years. Now was the time. The hours passed
quickly in poor Dr Jekyll's grim London and before he
knew it the train had arrived at Westerham.

This time it wasn't Sir Winston's gardener who
picked him up at the station, and he didn't have to wait
for his lift. Edward honked the horn of his gleaming car
and Frank pushed down a flaring moment of
unexpected jealousy.

Edward and Flo's youngest sat in the passenger seat.
Katie. Around seven now, dark thick unruly hair like her
mum, but she was the image of her dad, narrow face,
and even for a young girl, high and defined cheekbones,
together with Edward's chocolate-coloured eyes. He'd

met her several times since her birth and watched as she'd grown into an uncomplicated, happy and self-assured human being – as were all three of Flo's children. Flo and Edward were doing a fine job of parenting, and as he made his way towards the Millers' car he asked himself again why he hadn't brought Jim and Nick with him. He should have stood up to Hilda on this one but he hadn't, and wouldn't. And now, well now, although the rules had been unsaid of how things would be laid out, laid out they were.

He put the edge of his hand to the side of his forehead in salute to Edward and Edward did the same, his face open and free, and so content. Frank's stomach lurched.

'Frank, so great to see you.' Edward jumped out of the car, opening the passenger door and shuttling out Katie, who faced Frank. 'My mum's put me in her and dad's room. I cleaned my room especially for you, and Anna helped me.'

'Well, I appreciate that, Katie. Come here and give me a cuddle.' His interaction with the little girl had been sporadic but it didn't seem to matter, she rushed over and gave him that cuddle.

'Anna's part of our family now. We rescued her,' Katie continued. 'She's looking forward to Christmas with us.'

'Ah, Christmas my favourite time of year,' Frank lied. 'Well, I can't wait to meet Anna.' He, Flo and Edward had decided Anna's history would be kept secret from their children. More secrets. Florence, though, said she'd tell them when they were old enough to understand. He studied Katie's intelligent expression. It wouldn't be long before their eldest *would* understand.

'She's fun. I like her,' Katie said.

'How's your mum?' Frank asked.

'She's all right but got in a flap this morning after a telephone call.'

Edward said, 'Hop in Frank, let's get home, I'll tell you on the way.' He opened the boot and put in Frank's suitcase. 'Never rains, as the Brits say.'

Katie hung onto her dad. 'I'm a Brit and I don't say that.'

'You're a Brit *and* an American,' Edward said with an indulgent smile.

'I am,' Katie replied with pride.

'So, young lady,' Frank said, 'what are you planning to be when you grow up?' He wondered if he was deflecting from making conversation with Edward.

'I'm going to be a doctor, like my dad.'

'Good idea.' A stab of pain caused his gut to twist, thinking of Anna who at a similar age had said she wanted to work in a hospital and help people.

Katie smiled and got in the back seat, picked up a colouring book and lost herself.

'How's Flo?' Frank asked.

'She's very well.' Edward turned his head. 'We got a telephone call this morning from Jem. She's coming over tomorrow.'

'Oh.'

'You good with that?'

'Of course, she's my sister. Haven't seen this much of her in years. She only left us in Notts last week.'

'She wants to see Anna.'

'Yes,' Frank replied.

'It's nice for Anna,' Edward said.

'I know.'

'Florence's worked up. She's a bit afraid of Jem, I think, between us.'

'Jem can have that effect.'

'Hilda gets on with her, Florence says.'

'She does, Edward. She does.'

Edward let it drop and began talking about all sorts of things, which later Frank was unable to recall.

They pulled up outside a house Frank remembered from his childhood. Good for Flo. A white fence surrounded the property, winter-bare silver birch and rose trees filled the small front expanse of garden. It wasn't massive but double-fronted, and very well-kept. Florence had done all right for herself, living on the edge of the village she'd grown up, and in a house that as kids they'd all coveted.

'Frank, come in, so good to see you,' Florence said wiping her hand on a brightly coloured apron.

After the war, after riding motorcycles and working, Flo had had her children and stayed home. He wondered how long she'd be happy with this but catching sight of Edward touching her lower back, and kissing her on the lips as they entered the substantial sized kitchen he suspected it would be forever; although she had mentioned in one of her letters recently that she was thinking of doing some volunteer work at the local hospital. Flo brimmed with a happiness that he'd never seen in his own wife.

'It's great to see you too, Flo.' He went over and embraced her.

Edward filled the kettle and put it on the stove. 'Tea?'

Frank tried to relax, wanting to see Anna but hesitant. The last time he'd seen her was at the hospital. She'd acknowledged him, treated him as if she knew him, but not as her dad, not as Frank, just a man who had worked for her *father*, Sir Winston Churchill.

Flo turned to Katie. 'Go and get Anna, tell her we have a visitor,' she ruffled her daughter's head, 'and then go and get your brothers in from the garden. It's freezing out there. Tell them there'll be hot chocolate on the table in ten minutes.' She glanced at her husband. 'You do the honours, Edward.'

Flo shuffled Frank out of the kitchen into a sitting room, which was filled with furniture and ornaments that he could see didn't come from England. Gifts from Edward's family in America he guessed. A lamp that dated back to the eighteenth century, Flo told him, a wooden chair from her husband's grandfather, a Pioneer, Edward had told him later. Vases painted in blue and white and all matching, sat in pride of place on the enormous walnut dresser. A Christmas tree, large and beautiful and perfectly decorated sat in the bay window.

Flo gently pushed him onto the colonial-style wooden chair. 'Anna's doing fine here, Frank, and I'm so glad you've come. I've planned the week for us, but I got a call earlier from Jem and she's coming in the morning.'

'It's fine, Flo, honestly. She'll just want to see Anna, and the main thing now is I build a relationship with Anna… a new type of relationship.'

They'd agreed he would visit four or five times a year. They all hoped in the future Hilda would change her mind and come with him, and when that happened ¬– and as all the children grew up – that eventually the truth could be told, and eventually too, that Anna would go back to herself, in time. As far as Flo and Edward's children were concerned Anna was with them forever, she was part of the family. Frank couldn't ever repay the Millers and hoped that soon Hilda would come round. In a way, he'd understood her reticence when the boys were small, but struggled with it now and often conjectured what was really going on in Hilda's mind. He'd probably go to his grave never understanding her. His only solace was that she loved her sons with a passion, giving all of her love to them but to the exclusion of Anna, and him.

'Oh, I know Jem loves Anna,' Florence said. 'But she lives so near and could come over any time.'

'Don't worry about it. It's fine.' He stood. 'Flo, there's something I want to say to you.'

'That sounds ominous.'

'I'm glad you met Edward. He's a good man. Perfect for you.'

'Frank, I know—'

'I'll never mention Marble Arch again, Flo. But I'm glad it happened. I want you to know that.'

'It was good.' She looked at him with no embarrassment. 'Edward had a lot to live up to. And he managed it.' She grinned.

As she spoke, a knock on the sitting room door and Katie came in, followed by Anna. His daughter had been with the Millers for three weeks and already she appeared healthier, although just approaching her thirtieth birthday she looked more like a woman in her fifties. Anna clutched tight a doll in one hand, her other held by a seven-year-old Katie.

'Anna, love. How are you?' he said softly.

'Marigold is fine.'

'It's Frank, lovely,' Flo said.

'I know. My father's friend.' Her eyes swept over the room. 'You're all my father's friends.'

Frank's gaze moved to Katie. How were Flo's children taking all this? As children do, in their stride; their parents taking in a poor woman who needed a home. The guilt skewered through him and momentarily, hatred towards Hilda too for making it like this. But then an image of Jim and his scar dropped into his mind, and finally the realisation that the incident hadn't stopped Flo and Edward taking in Anna. Since the day he and Hilda had brought Jim home from hospital, Anna had never shown any violence again. Hilda though, would not listen.

Things were as things were.

'Hello, Anna, it's lovely to see you again,' Frank said, trying so hard not to gather her into his arms. They were long past that.

Anna held his gaze. Did she know who he was? It was something he would wonder every time he saw her.

'Would you like to hold my baby? She needs a cuddle,' Anna said to him.

Frank's insides curdled as he took the doll and entered Anna's world, because if he did not he would never be part of Anna's life.

'Has she had her milk?' he asked. In his peripheral vision he saw Flo smile.

'Just,' Anna replied.

'Well, I think she needs burping,' he said. 'See, like this.' He put the doll over his shoulder and patted its hard plastic back. As Anna watched him she looked so content; if they allowed her to stay inside her mind she was always all right and happy.

Flo nodded towards him and Anna, leaving them in the American sitting room with the big tree and his grief while she went to get the lunch ready.

*   *   *

The next morning's breakfast, a breakfast of pancakes and maple syrup, bacon and coffee, was served up by Edward and Katie. The boys' job was to pass around the various condiments and cutlery. Already, despite being there with Anna, and wanting to be there, he missed home and his own boys. Watching Edward and Flo together he ached for what he didn't have. But he would make the best of his life, he would see Anna as much as he could, and the two families would not suffer.

His life; a dichotomy, with one existence secreted away from the other.

Flo and Katie left as soon as they'd finished eating. Flo was dropping Katie at school and then going into town to do some shopping. A neighbour had picked up the boys. Anna went upstairs to her room.

It was just Frank and Edward, and suddenly Frank didn't know what to say. A silence swung in the air.

'Frank,' Edward began, studying Frank from the other side of the table. 'Florence's so glad you came. She thinks the world of you.' He coughed, played with the napkin that lay on the table. 'I'm sorry about Hilda—'

Frank knew exactly what he meant and he should have been angry, but he wasn't. He was glad to be able to talk candidly. 'I'll stay with Hilda for my boys.'

'I know.' He waited a few seconds. 'If ever there was anything to happen to me...' He cleared his throat. 'I know that you would take care of Florence.'

Frank smiled. 'You look in fine health to me.'

'I am. But you know what I'm saying?'

'I do know. Flo loves you, Edward.'

'She loves you too.'

Frank slid deeper into his chair. 'I'm glad Flo's happy. I'm glad that one of us is.' His eyes took in the dining room. 'I'm glad that you can give her all of this.'

'You should think about the future, when your boys are older, Frank. We only have one shot at this life.'

'Hilda might change her mind about Anna.' He was just saying that. He knew she wouldn't.

'She might, but until she does, Anna stays with us. And you are welcome here any time you want to visit.' Edward rose from his chair. 'I have to get ready to catch the train into London. Due at my practice later this afternoon.' He touched Frank's shoulder and Frank turned in his chair. The two men shook hands.

Ten years later Frank would wonder if Edward Miller had the gift, or curse, of knowing the future.

Jem arrived at noon. Her husband, William, dropped her off, made his excuses and didn't come inside the house.

And so it was Frank and Anna who greeted Jem, although Anna returned to her room soon after Jem's arrival. At the kitchen table Frank faced his sister, determined to begin a forthright conversation.

'You love Anna, I know that, Jem,' he began.

She didn't reply only stared at him. She was still so thin, even in sitting he saw how her clothes hung from her frame. The grey tinge that coloured in the skin beneath her eyes seemed to have worsened since only a week ago when she'd visited Hilda; not him. His sister didn't visit him.

'I've always loved Anna,' she finally answered.

'And you love Hilda too,' he replied. Jem shuffled forward in her chair and he saw the telltale sign of his sister's rage, and fear; the twitching right eye, the nervous tremor taking over her hands. 'Don't get angry, listen to me.' She receded back into the chair. 'You could change Hilda's mind about Anna.'

'Perhaps I could. Perhaps I could.' She crossed a long skinny leg over the other. 'But, to my mind it's you who should be talking to Hilda... telling the truth.'

His stomach plunged. 'About what, exactly?'

'You know about what.'

'I've no idea what you're talking about.' Had Anna said something to someone? To Jem maybe? No, because if Anna has said something, Hilda would have said something to him, because he knew for sure that Jem *would* have told Hilda.

'Head in sand, as always,' Jem replied, her tone as sharp as a shard of glass. 'Look, Frank, let's just get on.' Her words sliced into him like new cheese wire carving through cheddar. Precise, clean. Ruthless. 'I've come to see Anna, help her settle in. I live nearby, so Anna'll be seeing more of me than she will of you.'

'It's good of you to help.' He really tried to keep the sarcasm from his voice.

'I do try and help.'

'If Hilda had allowed it to happen,' he said, 'Anna could be with us. *You* could have persuaded her.'

'*You* know that's not possible. Can't you understand? Hilda can't be near Anna. She tried and it didn't work. You know Frank, you could never understand what it's like… to be abused. Raped—'

'I was only a boy. What could I do?'

'No matter. Anna's better off here with saint Florence. You know it, and I know it. And Hilda knows it.'

'You really can be a bitch.'

'Can I?' She stood up. 'I'm going to get Anna. Let's go outside. It's oddly mild for the time of year.' She glanced at him. 'Anna can look after her baby in the garden, Frank.'

The cheese wire reached the end of its journey, having sliced straight through.

Frank and Jem were sitting in the garden with Anna, coats wrapped around them and trying to interest Anna in a game of croquet when Flo appeared. Anna was having none of it. She nursed her doll – her baby – spoke to a non-existent Winston and Clementine Churchill, occasionally said something to him, but made more of an effort with his sister.

'Jem, you're already here,' Flo said. 'Has anyone given you a cup of tea?'

'No, not yet.'

'I'll go and make one straightaway,' she said. Flo couldn't wait to get back to the kitchen and out of Jem's way.

'Before you go, Flo,' Jem shouted. 'I brought my Kodak. I want to take some photographs. Come on, a photograph of you, Frank and Anna. Together.'

Jem gathered the three of them in front of the barren flower beds. She stood back and as she was about to take the photo, Katie, who'd just got back from school, ran into the garden and towards Frank, knocking him out of the way as Jem clicked.

The image of Flo and Anna, Frank's trousered leg and foot captured forever. 1953. The year Churchill picked up his Nobel Prize.

The year Frank began phase one of his double life.

42

Richard

2002

Richard was looking at old photos of him and his grandad, most from the late 1960s, but one of him and Frank standing outside the *Churchill War Rooms*, soon after it had opened to the public in the late eighties. He studied the image of Frank. Stern-looking, although Richard saw beyond that expression, and always had.

His grandad had told Richard that apart from going into London for Richard's graduation, and later to see his first court case, that the war rooms visit had been the first time he'd been into London properly since 1965, and Churchill's funeral. Richard laughed, saying he couldn't imagine Frank lining the streets of the capital city waiting for a glimpse of Churchill's coffin with all those masses of people. Frank had hated crowds.

Smiling, his grandad replied, *'I was inside St Paul's. I was a small part of the old man's final chapter.'*

Richard tried to ask more but Frank would give no more away, only telling him the funeral had been the first time he'd cried since the autumn of 1938.

Tearing himself from that part of his grandad's past, Richard thought about a history even further away in time, and picking up his mobile he called Betty Cunningham's niece, Fiona Trott.

'I have a few days off, so it's no problem,' she said. 'I'll make sure I've retrieved everything you're interested in looking at, Mr Cullen.'

'That's so good of you, and please call me Richard.'

'And I'm Fiona. My husband's away for the week, so we'll have time to talk.'

Richard checked his watch. 'I'll be there around five, not too late?'

'Not at all, see you then.'

'Please come in,' Fiona said as soon as she opened the door. She was a tall woman, good posture, thickset, and a sister on ICU his researcher, Nell, had told him.

She waved her arms into the space of the lounge. 'Sorry about the mess, I'm not good at tidying, and hate doing it on my days off from the hospital.'

'I like a bit of mess, Mrs Trott, don't worry.' And he did. Sometimes Gillian's manic quest for order made him want to move into the garden shed.

'Fiona.'

'Fiona.'

'Unfortunately my slovenly ways made it a bit difficult to find what you're looking for.'

Richard tried not to allow his expression to show his disappointment.

'Don't worry, I've found my aunt's things.'

'You've never looked through them?'

'No, one of those things on my "to-do" list.' She gesticulated for him to sit down. 'You've done me a favour. Motivated me to sort out the chaos that is our spare room.'

'Glad to be of help,' he replied with a smile. 'Do you know how the stuff ended up with Miss Cunningham?

'I think it was incredibly busy at Chartwell during the war years. Mrs Churchill couldn't keep up. Some correspondence was lost, not filed, distributed around a bit for secretaries and such like to sort out. My aunt had quite a close relationship with Clementine Churchill, for a member of staff. They knew each other before Chartwell, before Marigold's death, the Churchills' fourth child. My aunt sometimes looked after the poor soul.' She smoothed down the front of her blouse. 'So sad. Betty, my aunt, was given things that she probably never attended to, and these things... well, ended up with her.' She smiled at him. 'I think there was a lot of chaos in those days within the Churchill household, at Chartwell, in London, and at Chequers. Things got misplaced.'

'I can see how that could happen.' He put his hands in his pocket, suddenly feeling uncomfortable. 'Are you sure you're okay with this? You don't know me at all.'

'You're a high-profile barrister. I followed your last case in the papers. Impressive.'

'Ah, I see. Thank you. When did your aunt come to live with you, Fiona?'

She thought for a moment. 'Around 1981. She was mobile, sprightly up until then. She was still going to see Florence and Edward Miller and their family on a regular basis when she came to live with us. She'd take the train to Kent. Lovely couple and family, the Millers. Betty knew Florence from Chartwell, when they both worked for the Churchills, Frank too.'

'How many children do the Millers have?'

'Four. Two boys and two girls. So sad, two died before their mother. Edward passed away in early 1963.

And then,' she scratched her temple. 'The surviving daughter, who was the eldest, I think, had to be hospitalised when Florence couldn't cope anymore.'

'You knew them well?'

'No, not well. I drove my aunt there a few times, but no, I didn't know Florence really well. Betty was always keen to go when Frank was visiting, that's when I tended to take her.'

Richard took in the information he was being fed. All beginning to drop into place. 'When did Miss Cunningham pass away?'

'1986. Would you like a cup of tea or something?'

'No, thank you, I really don't want to take up too much of your time.

She nodded. 'I hope you find what you're looking for. I won't be long.' She went to get Miss Betty Cunningham's things.

Ten minutes later Fiona put a carrier bag in front of him. 'There you go, everything. I'll leave you to it. Sure you wouldn't like a drink?'

'Actually, water would be good.'

She brought him a tumbler and Richard didn't notice her leaving the room as he pulled out a large thick envelope.

After a professional scanning through with his heart beating so hard it felt as if it was going to explode from his chest, he pulled out a letter. And then his heart practically stopped. How had this correspondence never made it into the hungry claws of an historical biographer or a cheap no-holds-barred newspaper?

Because Betty Cunningham had protected both her employers, and his grandad Frank.

Why hadn't Betty burnt them, shredded them? More
salient a question was, why hadn't Clementine Churchill?
The Churchill's daughter, Mary Churchill – Mary
Soames – was still alive – why hadn't these papers found
themselves with her? Mislaid, as Fiona had said, during
the busy war years, and in the big scheme of things,
unimportant. But not to him, and he recognised, not to
the Churchills. Not now.

Richard homed in on several letters from both
Winston Churchill to his wife Clementine, and from
Clementine to her husband.

He read the first one, from Churchill to Clementine,
and then allowed the paper to drop to the floor; he
thought about the allotment, the Wendy house and
Frank's wall.

The wall.

Grandad Frank, you silly bugger.

He picked up the next two letters, both addressed to
Winston Churchill from Clementine.

The first written in March 1938, and sent to a
London address. In it she tells her husband about an
afternoon at Chartwell when she'd invited local young
people from the village.

*It was somewhat of a success, dear Pug, however I do think
that perhaps I should not have allowed so much freedom. The
gardener did find some problematic goings on in the grounds. The
younger generation – what will we do with them?! Unlike our
generation, they seem to have no control. I asked Randolph to
intervene, as fortunately, he was visiting. One of the girls, I think
our old bricklayer's daughter, was keen to return to her
grandmother's home, which did put rather a dampener on things.
The gardener dropped her home, and so all was well in the end.*

But Randolph assured me nothing untoward had happened. I'm not quite sure I believe him…

Richard read the letter a few times. The *bricklayer's daughter*. He foraged through his memory banks, of his conversations with his grandad Frank about his work at Chartwell in the twenties. Benjamin was the name of Frank's immediate employer back then, and from what he could recall, Benjamin hadn't been married, and had no children. *The bricklayer's daughter*. Clementine Churchill must have been referring to Anna. And this tied in too with the letter from Mrs Cunningham to Hilda, which he'd found in the box of correspondence that had been dated late March 1938. And clearly written after Anna's return from her trip to Westerham, when she would have been around fifteen.

Richard scanned the contents of the next letter, which had been written by Clementine Churchill to Winston several years later and in the midst of the war, in between the work she was embroiled with as chairwoman of the *Red Cross Aid to Russia Fund*. Clementine Churchill's letter told him that she'd arranged a visit to a psychiatric hospital in the north of England.

Dearest Pug, I have arranged as you have requested. Dr Tanner is, of course, happy to accommodate on any date that is suitable. You are such a sentimentalist under it all, my dearest.

Richard read on, only momentarily interrupted by a loud noise from the kitchen. Something dropped, a curse from Fiona, and he smiled to himself thinking of Gillian who was prone to the same language with domestic mishaps.

He carried on reading. It hadn't been Clementine Churchill who had visited High Royal Mental Hospital, but her husband.

Richard put the letters back and at the same moment Fiona returned to the lounge.

'Sorry, dropped a glass,' she said with an apologetic smile. She studied him and nodded at the plastic bag. 'Interesting?'

'Quite interesting.' He couldn't make eye contact.

'Glad I didn't get rid of it now. I told Betty I would. But I'm glad I didn't.' She paused. 'Are you all right?'

'I'm fine.'

'Are you going to go and see Florence Miller?'

'Yes, I wanted to visit today, but she's unwell so plan to go tomorrow.' He looked at his watch. 'I need to get on, but I can't thank you enough for all this. Do you mind if I hang on to it?'

'No problem at all. If you find anything in there personal to Betty though, I'd appreciate you sending it back to me.'

'Of course.'

'Sure you don't want a quick cup of tea before you go?'

'Okay, great. Just a quick one.' He felt comfortable with Fiona Trott.

Fiona told him more about her aunt, and her aunt's visits to see the Millers, before and after Edward's death. She told him bits about his grandad, things he'd never known, things his dad had never known, about Frank's *dual existence*, visiting the Miller household on a regular basis. Richard was now beginning to guess why.

A Churchill quote came to mind, probably picked up from Frank: *The opposition is in front of me, but the enemy is behind.*

For Frank, the enemy behind was himself.

Many had protected his grandad. Everyone but Frank.

And Richard would protect him too. He believed what he'd read in Churchill's letter to his wife. Frank had confided something to the wartime leader that his grandad felt he could admit to no one else.

The council wanted to demolish the allotments, the Wendy house, the wall. He would start the demolition himself, he would pull down his grandad's buildings.

And he would, in the process, find out if what he'd read in the letter was true.

43

Richard was certain he broke the law countless times as he drove at speed in near darkness back to his grandparents' old village, and to Frank's allotment. There were still tools left rusty in the old shed that he could use.

He knew where to start – the part of the wall which years ago Frank had been so perturbed he'd been digging around.

Cold sweat smothered his body. Maybe it was all a huge misunderstanding. It wasn't. He knew. He parked the car on the wide street that separated the border of the allotments from the old pit tip and made his way through the back entrance and towards Frank's patch. He could hardly see a thing, but it didn't matter as the layout of the land was ingrained in his memory.

He found the key to the old shed underneath the brick at the back of the dilapidated building, a place it had been kept for years, and retrieved the tools he needed. He began digging into the rigid crusty soil, finding where his grandad had laid the foundations for the wall. Frank had done a good job; pretty solid. He took the weary-looking sledgehammer and began his task, occasionally looking up towards the pit tip; the sun had completely disappeared behind its silhouette and Richard found himself in isolating murkiness. He returned to his dad's car to get the torch he knew lived underneath the back seat and rolled up in a towel. His dad. Jim would find it difficult to accept what his son was finding out, and Uncle Nick too. It would rock and tip over their small world, the stigma would devastate them, their memory of Frank, and Hilda.

Richard stopped for a moment and thought. If what Churchill had written to Clementine turned out to be true, he would have to tell the authorities. Could he keep the secret? Before he did what he was about to do he had to make that decision.

The moon bulged with light. Richard filled up with a portentous foreboding and as he looked upward in question towards the new night sky, he was certain he could see the Plough. He tried to pick out the stars, just as his grandad had taught him.

An hour later Richard located what he had not wanted to be looking for.

He sat down on the cold clammy ground and in obsidian darkness held his head in dirty hands.

After finding what he'd hoped not to find at the allotment, he spent another two hours knocking down Frank's wall and started on the Wendy house too. It was better he did it and not faceless demolition council workers. They might never have found what he'd discovered; they wouldn't be looking for it as he had been – the sadness beneath the bricks – which he had reburied, and deeper than the hole where he'd discovered it.

That night he thrashed around in bed, unable to sleep in the claustrophobic home of his grandparents, feeling the ghosts of the people who had lived there, as well as the one who had never got to live there. He was glad to get up, shower and drink strong coffee, and as soon as the hand on the clock moved to nine he called Celia who told him Florence was feeling much better and looking forward to seeing him.

He went through Betty Cunningham's envelope again, and then sat back in the chair, a strong need to discuss all of this with Gillian washing over him. He tried her mobile, and Beccy's. No answer. He contemplated interfering and calling Carl, to ask if he'd heard from Beccy but thought better of it. Beccy had said she'd dumped him so the conversation could be difficult, although in the depths of his mind he suspected the split wouldn't last long. Beccy could delude herself, and Gillian, but not him. She was young, as was Carl, but it was as clear as crystal that they were in love. Then he thought of the allotment, the wall. What he'd found.

Life. So precious.

He packed a rucksack, locked up the house and drove to Westerham where he hoped he would be able to make sense of the muted kaleidoscope of his family's past.

44

Richard had constructed a picture of Florence Miller in his mind, through the letters, through Celia, and through what Fiona had recounted. Feisty, loyal, a square peg in a round hole sort of woman.

She turned out to be everything he imagined.

As he entered the airy room with Celia by his side, Florence took the blanket which lay across her knees and placed it on the bed. She leant forward in the high backed mustard-coloured upholstered chair that matched the colour scheme of the entire room and pushed herself up, her hand gripping tightly its arms, the purple veins on the back of her hands bulging at the exertion.

'Please Mrs Miller, please don't get up,' he said moving towards her.

'I'm old but I can still stand up… occasionally, Richard,' she said half grimacing, half smiling, her voice filled with the deep burr of a Kent accent but with a hint of American inflection. It was a lovely sound.

Florence Miller was taller than he'd thought she would be. Long hair pushed into a loose bun. Little diamond studs in her ears. She wore a green dress, fitted and with a belt. She was of that limited class of the elderly; not overweight, and not too thin either. Florence's neck, although crinkled, was long and elegant. Because he'd seen a photo of her in her prime, to Richard's eye the old lady had arrived at the age of ninety-three with aplomb.

He liked her straightaway; he'd always known he would.

Florence faced him. Fluid nut-brown eyes, kind, thoughtful, even a bit mischievous. Their luminescence had undoubtedly diminished with the years but beauty and honesty remained.

'Thank you for coming to see me,' she said.

'It's really good to meet you, Mrs Miller.'

She nodded. 'Please call me Florence. Come, sit.' She sat back down, looking exhausted with her show of independence. 'Celia, do you mind getting us some tea?'

'Just about to.' She shuttled from the room.

'You look so very like Frank.' Florence put the blanket back on her lap.

'Yes, everyone always says that.' Richard heard the flatness in his reply.

'You sound disappointed with my observation. Frank adored you. You two were close. I do know that.'

'Not that close that I knew you existed, though.'

'Aw, Richard.'

'I used to love being compared to Frank.'

'Have your feelings changed towards him because of Anna?'

He lifted his shoulders a fraction. 'Can I ask you something?'

'That's why I asked you to come.'

'When did you find out what had happened to Anna?'

'In 1940 I found out she'd been sent to High Royal,' she said softly.

'My grandad told you?'

'Not initially.'

'So, who told you? Gran Hilda?'

'No.' She looked at him. 'I found out through my nosiness. I read a letter addressed to Mr Churchill, from Frank. A letter Frank sent from France in early 1940. He told Mr Churchill,' she shuffled in her chair, 'that he felt guilty he'd allowed Anna to be taken to an institution, but that he had no choice. It was obviously bothering him and he had to tell someone. At the time I was shocked, as you can imagine, but then I felt sorry for Frank. That he'd had to write and tell a man who he knew probably wouldn't read his letter. But that's how I found out, then when I met up with Frank in London, the autumn of 1940, that's when he told me himself about Anna.'

'It is…' He attempted to find the right word. 'Bizarre, that Grandad wrote to Churchill.'

'Yes, it was, but Frank and Churchill did have a sort of "relationship".'

'I found books given by Churchill, to Frank, signed, personal messages in them.'

'As I said, there existed between them some sort of bond. But, these things happen in life, don't you find? Odd alliances and friendships, especially in a time of war.'

'Florence, I have to ask you something, and I need the truth. I've found something out about my grandad.'

'You look so troubled. What? What have you discovered?'

'I wonder if you already know.'

'Tell me, and I'll tell you.'

'I went to see Fiona Trott, who I believe you know?'

'Yes, I do. You went to talk to her about Betty Cunningham?'

'Yes. Fiona allowed me to look at Betty Cunningham's things, letters, and correspondence. I found a letter written by Winston Churchill from Tripoli in 1943, to his wife, Clementine.' He stopped. Should he be this honest? He glanced at Florence and felt guilty that he might be causing so much upset to an old lady.

'Go on, Richard.'

'In Tripoli Frank told Churchill that Anna had had a baby—'

'A baby?'

Florence didn't know. No one knew, only Frank, Anna, Winston Churchill and his wife, Clementine. And probably, Betty Cunningham.

'Anna gave birth in the allotment, in the Wendy house, to a stillborn baby. No one knew Anna was pregnant, until the day she found Frank in the allotment, about to give birth. Frank buried the stillborn, probably I suspect, to protect Hilda, and her pregnancy, and to protect Anna.' He peered at Florence. 'He didn't do a very good job of protecting Anna, did he?'

'Oh, Frank,' she said. Her statement directed towards a man who had died the February just gone. 'No, I didn't know. I can't believe I don't know. But perhaps this is a misunderstanding. Frank was badly injured at El Alamein, and probably not himself when he spoke to Mr Churchill?' She stopped talking and thought a moment. 'It might not be true?'

'It's true.' The air in his lungs seemed to stagnate. 'I know it's true. And it's the reason Frank initially refused the medal, I suspect.' Florence sat upright in her chair, looking as if she was about to say something, but didn't.

'I've been to the allotment, Florence, where my grandad buried the baby. I found the remains.'

'Dear God.'

'The allotments have been earmarked for redevelopment. Frank's memory, Hilda's. It will upset my dad, my uncle.' He swallowed. 'My whole family. It happened over sixty years ago. Frank and Hilda are dead. The baby was stillborn. There's nothing to be gained from me saying anything. What will happen in the future, will happen.' He moved closer to Florence. 'Do you want me to say something? Do *you* think I should?' It was rare for him to ask advice.

'It won't help Anna,' she said quietly.

'No, I don't think it would, not now.'

'You're a barrister, how do you feel about this?'

'Some things are better left.'

'But if the land is redeveloped?'

'I'll cross that bridge when I approach it. Churchill's letter is potentially explosive. It's better that it remains a secret. I do though plan to get in touch with the family. Mary Soames.'

She nodded. 'Yes, it needs to be destroyed.'

'It seems,' Richard said, 'that Churchill was as flawed as Frank. Keeping secrets. Not telling the truth. Condoning what my grandad did.'

'I am shocked, very, by this news, but it explains so much.' She glanced towards the window, as if she were talking to herself. 'Poor poor Anna. Frank never told me. All those years and he never told me, and neither did Anna. But come now, Richard.' Her tone reminded him of his favourite primary school teacher. 'There was a war on. Frank was fighting for his country. Churchill was fighting for the world's freedom. Perhaps values were skewed at the time of their exchange. Frank made a terrible mistake in keeping the birth of Anna's stillborn baby a secret.' Her eyes were moist. 'It seems, retrospectively, it ruined his life, in many ways, and explains much. He made a mistake in burying the dead baby and keeping it to himself. And.' She stopped talking, took in a gulp of air. 'The worst thing he did was make Anna keep that secret. That was Frank's biggest error, because it is clearly this that caused an already fragile Anna to tip over the edge. But I think for Churchill, at that moment in Tripoli, it's something Churchill would have done, I feel. What Frank did, how can I put this, wouldn't have been the end of the world to Churchill. But, to Frank it was. Churchill was in the position of having to make the most difficult decisions during the war. Hard choices, and someone had to make them. For him, forgiving Frank and helping him was an easier decision. And, Richard, it explains Churchill's great insistence in advising on Anna's future care.'

Richard didn't answer. He had no answer. The conflict inside was a conundrum he was unsure he'd ever be able to unravel.

Florence continued: 'Churchill went to see Anna, at High Royal, during the war.'

'Yes, I gathered as much.' He turned to her. 'It's a strange story.'

'It certainly is. Mr Churchill kept up a correspondence with Edward, right up until Edward's death in 1963.'

'Unbelievable, but as you say, somehow not. You've been a widow for a long time. It must have been lonely for you.'

She rested her eyes on his face. 'I have.' Twisted her fingers together. 'I haven't been lonely, Richard… I had…'

He waited but she said no more.

'I went to see Jemima, after Hilda's funeral,' he said finally.

'I thought Jemima would go to say a final goodbye to Hilda. They liked each other. They were close. Jemima and Frank didn't get on.'

'No.'

'What did Jem have to say?' she asked.

'She told me what happened, why Anna was admitted. And… and that my own great-grandfather was a…' He was unable to carry on.

'That is true. I'm sorry, but you know many families have dark hidden secrets.' She pulled the blanket upwards, tucked a wayward strand of hair behind her ear. 'Did Frank keep his medal?' she asked, wanting to change the subject. 'Have you found it?'

'Yes, and yes. I found it with the other stuff.'

She nodded and Richard saw her contemplating what to say next. He recognised the familiar expression and pause, which he'd seen so many times on the faces of defendants after a particularly probing question: *should I be truthful, or not? What will be the consequences?*

Finally she said: 'Frank didn't want anyone to know. First you should understand why he was awarded it. He tried to save a man's life whilst serving in the desert. The man died, but not from a lack of Frank's efforts. Frank risked his own life to save another's. Many years before, Frank rescued a fellow miner at the colliery where he worked.' She took a sip of tea. 'The man was called Hugh Lambert. And in that rescue, Frank *was* successful.'

'I feel there's a reason you're telling me this?'

'I'm telling you that he saved Hugh Lambert's life at the colliery because of what I'm going to tell you next.'

'Hugh Lambert. Jeff Lambert's dad,' he said, almost to himself.

'Yes, I believe Jeff was the name of Hugh's son. Frank didn't want to accept the medal because although Frank saved Hugh's life in the colliery incident.' She fiddled with the edges of the blanket. 'Frank was probably responsible for Hugh Lambert's death whilst they were both serving in the desert campaign.'

'*How* was he responsible?'

'Because Frank believed Hugh had raped Anna, or at the very least coerced her into a relationship, and that might be what caused Anna's decline. I never could understand his complete vitriol towards Hugh. Of course, now, after what you've told me, I do understand. Clearly. Frank believed the baby belonged to Hugh, and Frank could never properly confront Hugh, because of what Frank had done.' She picked up her tea again and sipped for what seemed like minutes. 'Buried Anna's stillborn. A pregnancy which Anna didn't realise she was experiencing, just as Hilda hadn't realised she was pregnant sixteen years before. History repeating itself, mocking. Frank did it to protect Hilda, and he thought, at the time, to protect Anna too. That's what I'm guessing.'

'That does seem to be a likely scenario.'

'Frank thought if Hilda found out in the last few weeks of her pregnancy, and carrying a baby that both she and Frank had been longing for, the shock might have caused Hilda another miscarriage. So in a moment of sheer madness, Frank decided to bury the dead baby underneath the wall in his allotment?'

He nodded. 'I think you're right, yes.'

'Churchill was aware of Anna's fixation with his daughter, Marigold. And now from what you've just told me, Anna's obsession with Marigold and babies is more understandable. Frank had always admired Churchill, spoke about his family, his children, as did Betty Cunningham. As a young child Anna picked up on this and as she dipped further into her own world, she convinced herself she *was* Marigold. Edward and I decided it was easier to allow her to stay in that world, and inside she stayed all the years she was with us. I think that Dr Tanner, Anna's psychiatrist at High Royal when she was first admitted, didn't altogether agree. But what could he do when one of the most powerful of men intervened, agreeing Anna would be much better off with us, and being Marigold? It soothed Anna, this delusion. Who were we to attempt to change it when it was unchangeable? And Mr Churchill was aware by then that there was nothing that could be done… only to help Anna in the best way possible, to give her as normal a life as possible, with us.'

'You took Anna in didn't you? She was the fourth child Fiona spoke about? It was you who gave Anna a life, not Frank. You and your husband? It must have been hard after he died, three children, and Anna?"

'With guidance from Mr Churchill, Frank, Edward and I decided Anna should live with us, and our children.'

'It's a wonderful thing you did.' Richard raked his hand through tangled hair. 'Did Hilda know about the arrangement?'

'She did, Richard. She knew about… both arrangements. Hilda didn't want to tell your dad and Uncle Nick about Anna. Too difficult, she said, and Frank went along with her. He knew Anna was safe with us, and happy. Hilda just couldn't cope with the thought of Anna.' She glanced at him. 'And Jem agreed with Hilda. Frank went along with them both. By that time, Frank's misplaced guilt about Jem and their dad was deep. I'm sorry, Richard. I had to go along with it. I was in no position to have an opinion, really. Although, I don't know why Frank didn't tell me about Anna's baby. Everything could have been different. I could have helped him.' She caught his eye. 'I had plenty of time to help him.'

'You said "both arrangements?"' Richard was beginning to see. His grandad and those lengthy quarter yearly trips.

'I'm sorry, Richard. No one knew, only Hilda. It didn't begin until a good few years after Edward's death. Edward knew he was dying. He had bowel cancer. He asked Frank to take care of us, all of us. It seemed so natural. Hilda didn't want him, but Frank didn't want to leave your dad and Nick. He didn't want to break up a family.'

'You and my grandad?'

She met his gaze. Unflinching. 'Yes, me and your grandad.'

'I see it all now.'

'Are you angry?'

'No, I'm not. But I wish I'd known before he died.' He jerked his shoulders in conflict. 'Although I'm struggling to understand why, as time went on, Grandad didn't tell the truth about Anna's baby.' His mind untangling the information as he spoke. 'There had to be something more, something we don't know about. Something Churchill didn't know about.'

'I have no explanation, I'm afraid. But, what caused Anna to turn the corner into madness was, I think, holding the secret which Frank encouraged her to keep.' She slumped, frailty overcoming her.

'Florence, would you like me to leave. I can come back later?'

'No, I'm fine. We need to talk.'

'Tell me more about Hugh,' he asked, and yet hesitant for the explanation.

She sighed deeply. 'You won't like this either, but it's time to be honest, for all the secrets to be uncovered. My cousin, Harold, was out in Africa the same time as Frank during the war. Hugh Lambert was posted to the desert in the autumn of 1942, just before El Alamein. To the same brigade as Frank. The irony, eh?' She moved in her chair and pushed a small fist into her back, wincing.

'Harold, my cousin, was a member of what would come to be known as the SAS. He taught Frank the intricacies of compass reading, reading the stars, the sun, how to move about the desert without getting lost. Frank was much more accomplished than many in the army with this skill.' She took a breath. 'One night, Frank gave the coordinates to Hugh. Hugh was on latrine-cleaning duty – the latrines were always placed a long way from the tents. Hugh never made it back to camp.'

'And?'

'And perhaps Frank gave him the wrong coordinates.'

'Purposefully?'

Florence slumped in her chair. 'Frank always said that he hadn't been as diligent as he should have been in teaching Hugh the coordinates. But there was a terrible sandstorm that night and Hugh got lost, caught in it. Frank blamed himself, and could never say for sure, to me, if he'd given the correct coordinates.'

Richard's gut retracted. 'Do you think he did it on purpose?'

'I think he did...'

'And did Churchill know about this?'

'About Hugh and the coordinates? No. Frank only ever told me, and Edward. But it was because of Hugh why Frank at first refused the medal... I'd thought.' She held up a thin arm. 'Come closer, sit by me on the bed.'

'I can't forgive him this.'

'Frank is dead. He punished himself enough. Trust me. You must remember all the good and precious moments you had with your grandad. You must. He adored you.'

She leant sideways and with an agility that surprised him, pulled an album from her bedside table, opened it, and indicated for him to flick through. 'Photos of Edward Miller, the father of my three children, the man whose suggestion it was, along with Mr Churchill's, that

Anna come live with us. I loved Edward, and I loved your grandad.' She gazed at the photos herself, of her children, of Anna, and many photos of his grandad.

'My grandparents put away a young woman and left her to rot.'

'Frank never left Anna to rot. He visited all the time, even before Edward's death. He came to our home in Westerham four or five times a year, and it wasn't easy for him. And there was your dad and Nick. How could Frank tell them without Hilda agreeing? In the end it was easier to do it the way we did it. And better. For everyone.' She found his hand, held it. 'It really was.'

'I can't thank you enough, on my behalf, and my dad, and uncle, what you've done for Anna.'

'Anna gave my family, and me, another meaning to our lives. She gave as much as she took, probably more. Edward adored her, as did my children. I'm only sorry Anna had to go back to High Royal, but you know in the end, it really is the best place for her now. Frank and I never thought she'd live this long. Please don't judge Frank too harshly. I don't. And Hilda too. Forgive her. Hilda was more tortured than any of us... except perhaps Jem.'

'Grandad Frank should have told someone about the baby. He should have told you. All the years he came to see you. He should have told you.'

'As time went on it must have become more and more difficult for Frank, and you know Richard, by the time he could say something, it was far too late for Anna. And she was really happy here with us. Me, Edward, our children Katie, Tom and David, and then later with just me... and Frank when he came.'

'I'm so sorry about your children, Florence. Tell me about them, if you'd like to.'

'I love talking about my children. Katie, my eldest, died in 1969. She was twenty-three. She died of glandular fever. She was training to be a doctor. Bright girl, gifted, like her dad. Anna was distraught. They were close. Anna had been living with us for sixteen years when Katie died.'

Talking about her children seemed to soothe her. 'Tom, our middle child, died of a heart attack in the early eighties. Sudden, and unusual, and devastating. He was thirty-five, he left a wife and two children. David, my youngest, went to live in Australia in the early nineties with his family. He has two girls, and one grandchild. They come over every two years.' She took a sip of water and then let out a quiet sigh. 'No parent should outlast her offspring.'

'No, that shouldn't be the way, Florence.' The thought of losing Beccy sent a sharp current of discomfort through his body. 'When did Anna go back to High Royal?'

'When I moved in here, eight years ago.'

'Did Frank want Anna to go to him, and Hilda?

'It was never an option. Hilda would not have Anna. I'm sorry to be brutal, but she wouldn't have Anna in the early years, why would she have her back in the latter? Your grandad went up to Yorkshire to see Anna every month.'

'And you?'

She smiled, 'Every two months.'

'I can't believe it.' He scrutinised her features. 'I can't tell my dad and uncle, I just can't. They loved their mum.'

'I know they did. I know. Don't tell them.' As if attempting to lighten the atmosphere she said, 'I know you've a daughter, and a lovely wife. Celia said. But Frank told me a lot about you all too. He loved all of you.'

Richard nodded. He knew Frank had loved them all. He knew that. 'Yes, we have Beccy. Seventeen.'

It must have been something floating around in the warm air of the nursing home but he ended up telling Florence all about Beccy, and her being pregnant. Celia had been in with at least three cups of tea. He began to feel guilty that Florence was ready to sleep, but he recognised the adrenaline rush in the old woman. The bolt of sharing, getting things off your chest, of smoothing the crumples of life out and the satisfaction it gave. Obviously, it still happened in your nineties. Christ, he hoped he'd be like Florence at ninety-three.

'It would seem, Richard, that there is some circular movement within the Cullen family as far as pregnancies are concerned?'

'It would seem so.' Her humour was priceless and he saw completely why his grandad had loved Florence.

'Will your daughter keep the baby?'

'I think she will.' He looked at his watch. 'But Gillian isn't as easy with the upset as I am.'

'Seventeen is very young. I started late, especially for my generation.' She caught his eye. 'There's a lot to be said for starting a family younger?'

'Maybe, yes.'

'What about the father of Beccy's child?'

He flattened down the fabric of his jeans. 'Nice guy. An impoverished musician. I suspect he'd stand by Beccy, if she gave him a chance to.'

'See what the future holds, eh?' she said.

He checked at his watch again.

'Please, don't feel you have to stay.'

'No, it's not that. I have to contact Gillian and Beccy. They've gone off for a few days to the Peaks. I wanted to call them to see if they'd got there okay.' Suddenly it became important that he spoke to his wife and daughter. He felt his phone inside his jacket pocket. 'I'll leave you in peace now. One last thing. I want to go and meet Anna, and I know that my dad and uncle will want to too. Are you well enough to perhaps come with us?'

Florence's face brimmed with contentment. 'I'd love to come with you and see Anna. I haven't managed to visit her since this bloody chest problem. More than two months ago. Celia takes me.'

'Great. I'll arrange it as soon as I can. It would be nice if my wife and daughter came with us. I'd love you to meet them.'

'It will be a pleasure to meet your family, Richard I very much look forward to it.'

He pulled his phone from his pocket, switched it on and peered at the screen. Some missed calls but not from Gillian or Beccy.

'Excuse me, Florence,' he said. 'I need to check this.' He nodded to his mobile sitting in his hand.

She smiled. 'Of course. Modern technology. We're always too available.'

As he nodded in agreement he listened to the voicemail. It was Nell.

She'd had a call from the Derbyshire Police. They needed to contact him. Urgently.

The gaily painted mustard room became white. He tried to gather himself, and using all the acting skills he'd acquired in his twenty-five years as a barrister he bent forward and kissed Florence on the cheek. 'I'll be in touch soon.'

As he walked from the room a text came through from Nell, giving him the number he needed to call and the books residing on his internal bookshelf fell with force from its end. Thoughts of Frank, Anna, Hugh Lambert, and a buried baby were demolished. He stumbled towards the nursing home's entrance and to his dad's car.

Richard got in and held his head in his hands.

45

On automatic, Richard checked the petrol gauge. He could make it up to the Peaks without having to fill up and his stuff was already in the back of the car. He looked at his hands that gripped the steering wheel, knuckles as white as new snow. He picked up his phone from the car seat where he'd thrown it and called the number Nell had sent to him.

'DS Malone speaking.'

'Hello, my name is Richard Cullen. My colleague's just called me… regarding my wife and daughter?'

'Ah, Mr Cullen, I'm so sorry. Where in the country are you?'

'I'm in Kent. I can be in Derbyshire in a few hours, three, maximum. Have you located Beccy yet? My daughter, Rebecca.'

'Not yet, but we're certain we will. The mountain rescue team's searching.'

'Which hospital has my wife been taken to?'

'Chesterfield Royal Hospital, Calow. She's okay, Mr Cullen.' The line went quiet. 'Mrs Cullen has a fractured ankle, but has also a shattered her pelvis. The surgeons are trying to stabilise her condition so that she can be taken to theatre.'

'Do you know what happened?'

'We don't know exactly, as I'm loathe to talk to your wife just yet in detail, as she's still very shook up. But the proprietor of the B&B, a Jack Sivers, says that your wife and daughter had an argument this morning, before they left for hiking. We really don't know any details yet.' She stopped talking again. Richard thought she'd hung up.

'DS Malone?' he said into the phone, barely recognising his own voice.

'The weather is closing in up here on the Peaks. I don't want to cause you more concern, but we'd like to find Beccy before the night sets in.' She stopped again. 'Early reports on your wife's car show there was a problem with the brakes. We think this is what caused the accident. Mr Cullen was there anything, any conflict, going on within your family recently?'

He nodded but didn't reply.

'Mr Cullen?'

'My daughter recently found out she was pregnant. But no real conflict—' He swallowed. 'Tell my wife I'm on my way and please call me if you hear news about Beccy.'

'Of course, and please drive carefully.'

Richard disconnected and as his chin dropped to his chest, he saw the tears that had fallen from his cheeks, turning dots on the salmon pink shirt he wore into shades of red. He started the engine and began to drive. He wanted to call his mum and dad but stopped himself, deciding to wait until he knew more. He'd only had the car serviced weeks before and his mind was moving quicker than the needle on the dash.

The rain, which had been forecast, started. Richard flicked on the windscreen wipers and found some comfort in their rhythm.

His phone vibrated on the passenger seat, and glancing at it, saw it was his dad. He pulled into a layby and against his better judgement answered.

'Richard, you're not driving are you?'

'No, Dad. Are you okay?' He wouldn't say anything yet, not until he'd got to the hospital. He tried to compose himself hoping it would translate into his voice.

'Fine, son. Just wanted to let you know. There's been a reprieve from the council about the allotments. Seems the petition actually worked.'

'That's great news.'

'You all right?'

'I'll call you later. Just about to start driving.'

'Okay, speak later.'

A reprieve on the allotments. Reporting what he knew was buried in his grandad's allotment was pointless, for both Anna and his family. Some things were better left untouched, no matter how much it went against the grain of who he was, and the truth he believed in.

He started the engine, moving the gear stick straight into second. Never knowing how he actually drove to the hospital in Chesterfield, he arrived at just after eleven in the evening. He called DS Malone, who told him to call her Jess. That was when he knew the ominous feeling he'd been having for days, which he'd convinced himself was connected with Frank, Anna, Hugh's death, and a baby that was buried on his grandad's reprieved allotment, had in fact been a warning about his own immediate family.

Getting lost in the Peaks was not good, but he was logical enough to know that the percentage probability of finding Beccy was high, unless of course she'd fallen somewhere unseen: he stopped himself from going there. Then, an image of Gillian played in his mind, the last time he'd seen her at Hilda's. Looking beautiful.

He texted Jess Malone as he made his way towards the hospital's entrance.

I'm at the ICU. Richard Cullen

An immediate reply.

Give me twenty minutes. Jess

He stood outside the double doors of the unit and pressed the buzzer. He gave his name and the door clicked open. A nurse greeted him as he took a step into the sterile environment.

'Mr Cullen. So glad you're here. Please follow me through. Your wife is in the side room,' the nurse said. She was close to him and he smelt the faint aroma of chocolate on her breath.

'How is she?'

'I've paged the consultant to come and talk to you. He'll be here soon.' She was very short and peered up at him. 'The consultant feels though, that we've got your wife stable enough for surgery on her pelvis within the next twenty-four hours.'

They were standing in the small anteroom, Gillian lying in the bed that sat in the middle of the space.

'I'll leave you alone for a few moments.' The nurse delved into her uniform pocket and pulling out a half-eaten bar of chocolate, in readiness he thought, to finish it off in the staffroom.

Richard moved closer to the bed. Gillian's eyes were bruised black and deep lacerations covered her face. He took in the tubes and lines that reminded him of Beccy's tangle of leads in her bedroom, of every hair appliance known to man, and looked at his wife. Underneath all the cylindrical wires and the impossibly starched sheet that was placed neatly over her, Gillian appeared like a spindly bird.

He saw flashes of their life together, unarranged images of random events over the last twenty-five years. He'd met her when she was doing her A levels: a seventeen-year-old schoolgirl. Same age as Beccy was now. She was an Ealing girl and he'd met her at a Dire Straits gig at the Marquee on Oxford Street. He was living in digs in Shepherds Bush, on his Pupillage, six years older than her. The only difference between him and Carl, really, was that he was seen to be a good catch by Gillian's mother because of his chosen profession. Gillian had known about his dream to be a pianist. She saved up enough money to buy him a piano in those early days. For a long time he didn't have the heart to tell her that he would never play again. Only when Beccy was born did he find an excuse to sell it. Their house wasn't big enough, he'd explained. He thought of Beccy and pulled out his phone, which he'd had to switch off. But still expected a text or something from Jess Malone saying they'd found his daughter.

It was then that Gillian opened her eyes.

'Hello, Richard.'

'Hello, darling.' He squeezed her hand. 'Can't leave you for a few days, it seems.'

'It would seem,' she replied. 'Richard—'

'Don't talk, Gillian,' he said, his voice a whisper.

'Mr Cullen?'

He turned. A small woman, dressed in a sensible black trouser suit, red cropped hair. Pale skin. Kind-looking, was standing a few metres away. Looking back at Gillian he said, 'I won't be long. Get some rest.'

Gillian closed her eyes.

'Richard Cullen? Jess Malone.'

He took her hand. 'Thank you for coming… Any news on Rebecca?'

'Not yet, but we *will* find your daughter. We'll go into the visitor room and talk? There's no one in there.'

Richard followed her through a short corridor.

'We've spoken to Jack Sivers,' she said, closing the door. 'And another guest from the B&B. The guest saw Gillian and Rebecca having an argument around about 4.30 p.m. A Domenica Rossi, the B&B's cook, saw Mrs Cullen limping towards her car at 5.00 p.m. Upset. Mrs Cullen told Domenica that she'd sprained her ankle on the way back to the B&B. Domenica, who had spoken quite a bit to Rebecca during their stay, asked Mrs Cullen where Rebecca was. Mrs Cullen didn't answer and got in the car, driving away at quite high speed. Initial reports are telling us there is something wrong with the brakes on the car, but also that Mrs Cullen had sustained a nasty right ankle injury, which Mr Stone, her consultant, has verified. Her ankle is broken. I think Gillian probably thought she'd only sprained it. The ankle fracture could have happened in the car accident, or prior, in the stumble Gillian reported to Domenica Rossi…'

Jess Malone moved her weight from one leg to the other, pulled a can of coke from her rucksack and took a large gulp, then continued, 'Domenica has told us that Rebecca told her that she'd left her mobile phone at home in London. And because Rebecca didn't want to ask her mother to use her phone, Rebecca asked Domenica if she could use the B&B landline located in the B&B's kitchen. Domenica overheard Rebecca speaking to a "Carl" saying, *yes, I will marry you and I want our baby*. Rebecca told Domenica that she wanted to call her dad, but couldn't remember his mobile number. Your mobile. I've checked the phone records and Rebecca called a number in a town in Nottinghamshire?'

'My late grandma. I was staying there. Beccy would remember that number, it's been the same since she was a child.' He found her eyes, soft and gentle in the visitor room's laser-like lighting. 'Beccy's a seasoned hiker. She knows what to do.'

He saw what had happened between mother and daughter. Gillian and Beccy had argued about the baby and Beccy had tried to contact him to talk about the disagreement. That had always been the way. Between the three of them they'd always managed to sort things out, his sanguine temperament balancing his wife's more phlegmatic stance regarding their daughter.

'Please try not to worry, Mr Cullen,' Jess Malone said, 'We will find Rebecca.'

Richard returned to Gillian's bedside but she was asleep. He spoke with the consultant who told him they planned to take her into surgery as soon as possible. The nurse on duty persuaded him to go and get some rest in a proper bed.

He turned up at Jack Siver's B&B at 2am. Jack didn't bat an eyelid, asked no questions, and just showed him his room. Richard couldn't sleep, but must have dozed off around the time he was woken by gentle tapping on his bedroom door. At the same time his mobile rang out.

He ignored the door and answered the call. The rescue team had found Beccy. Alive. Thank God.

He pulled on his trousers and opened the door. It was Domenica; he'd briefly said hello to her not that many hours before.

'They've found Beccy,' he said to her. He took hold of the Italian woman he did not know and hugged her.

Beccy had been taken straight to hospital but Jess Malone had said she was absolutely fine, just a precaution. Richard went first to see Gillian. The room was quiet but for the rhythmical sounds of various monitors. He went over and kissed her on a warm dry cheek. 'I love you, Gillian.' Then he made his way to the general medical ward where Beccy had been given the only available bed in the hospital.

She saw him as soon as he entered.

'Dad,' she cried.

Richard rushed over, enveloping her.

She looked up at him. Pale, drawn and devastated. She'd obviously been told about Gillian. 'It's all my fault. Dad…'

'It was an accident.'

'It was my fault. What's happened to Mum.'

He took in his daughter, his eyes moving towards her stomach. 'Your mum's going to be fine.'

'She's not going to be fine. Nothing is going to be fine ever again.'

'Don't talk silly, Becs.' He sat down in the chair next to the bed. 'I called Carl, do you mind?'

'No. I don't. I'm glad you have.'

'His dad's bringing him up, to be with you.'

'I love you, Dad. I love Mum too.'

'Shush, don't talk. It's all going to be fine.' As his life slipped further away, he was losing his vocabulary too.

He moved, sat on the edge of the bed and held his daughter as he had held her as a baby.

Carl and his dad arrived that evening at seven, two hours after Gillian was taken down to theatre.

At seven thirty-four Gillian suffered a minor heart attack whilst undergoing crucial surgery to her pelvis.

Life is linear, we travel only one way, but the way you choose to go is often not of your own accord, not really, no matter how much you attempt to pull the reins and guide. It is impossible to stay on the path you wish to remain. When he'd met Gillian, a wild and beautiful seventeen-year-old girl at the Marquee in London he thought he would spend the rest of his existence with her, he'd never questioned it. What had happened though, made him question how with one swipe of fate's hand, his entire existence could so easily be compromised.

He had no idea how he was going to steer Beccy through this because it would be the most difficult task of his life if her mother died.

46

Florence

One month later
November 2002

Florence was not a superstitious person at all, but when she got a call from Richard a few days after he'd visited telling her about his wife, she told Celia there was something going on in the universe. But Gillian had pulled through, thank goodness. *A miracle, if I believed in them*, Richard told her later.

She did not know Frank's grandson properly, she did not know his daughter, she did not know his wife, but she had been married and she had grieved and had had more than her fair share of anguish. She had been both blessed and cursed in her life. To have so much to love was a huge gamble but one you do not have a choice in taking. To love is to open yourself up to pain. To *not* love is to live in an abyss. Love is wonderful but possesses its dark fringes. It had made Frank's life something he could not understand. But she had known Frank, and loved him. Many years before she had loved Hilda too. And she'd always loved Anna; from the first day she'd set eyes on her in Hilda's parents' home; the first time she had picked up the bonny and healthy ten-pound baby. It was Florence who had changed Anna's nappies, for weeks, when Hilda would not go near her daughter.

And so Florence's heart had been as lead inside her chest when Richard called to tell her what had happened to Gillian, and had become light, like a feather, when he told her his wife had survived. She liked Richard, perhaps because of his connection to Frank; but no, it wasn't only that. She *really* liked him.

Frank had often told her that his grandson Richard was special. What was it he'd said? She unpicked the fogginess that sometimes fell inside her brain, which was happening more and more these days. She sat very still and gathered her thoughts. *Not like me, Richard isn't, everything I wanted to be and everything I'm not. Jim and Nick are good boys too, but with Richard there's no hidden meanings, no conflict between us. I love my sons, but they love Hilda more than me, as if they knew, somehow, I wasn't who I made myself out to be. Richard on the other hand, takes me for who I am. Richard is the generation to let go of everything I brought to my own.*

And that was why Frank had never shared the secret of Anna with his sons. She had once asked him on one of his visits to Westerham, after Edward's death – in the late seventies and when Richard was deep in his studies to become a barrister – why he hadn't told Richard about Anna. *I will, one day*, Frank had said. But he never did. And the secret did indeed pass to the next generation. By the time Florence realised she could keep Anna with her no longer and when telling Richard would have been the sensible thing for Frank to do, Beccy was a toddler. Florence (who knew more about Richard's life than she had let on to him) was aware Gillian was having problems conceiving another baby, something connected to Beccy's birth and so she'd not pressed Frank to discuss Anna with his grandson,

Richard – simply because the pain of Hilda and Frank's barren years was still imprinted inside Florence's mind.

And so, as it is prone to do, time went on, and Frank had died, and Florence said nothing to Richard at Frank's funeral; she hadn't even introduced herself to him.

It had taken her too long to do something, and for that, she disliked herself.

A knock on her door and Celia poked her head in. Her hair was a different colour, a bit darker.

'You had your hair done?'

'I have, you like it?'

'I do. Suits you.'

'I've just spoken with Richard.'

'Is he all right? And Gillian?'

Celia began tidying around as she spoke. 'Yes, both are okay, Florence.'

Florence's enormous heart opened for Richard. Finding out about Anna's baby, and then the worry of Beccy going missing, Gillian's accident. He'd shared with her his angst and soul-searching regarding how he'd handle the situation of the baby's remains. She'd tried to guide him. He had changed his mind and wanted to inform the coroner. She told him, *there is no point. Anna's life is nearly over, it would be cruel to get her involved in questions. The allotment isn't being redeveloped, the little body might be found one day, or it might not. See what the future brings, Richard.*

Not telling the truth was difficult for Richard. *Not saying anything isn't lying*, she'd carried on. He didn't believe her, Florence knew that, but he chose to take her advice and she wondered if he'd discussed it with

Gillian. She was certain he had. She'd ended gently, *there's no need to assuage your conscience on this, Richard.*

He had listened to her, probably thinking of his dad and Uncle Nick, as well as Hilda's memory. And of Frank. He'd gone on to tell her that he'd told Jim and Nick the truth about the wall, and the secret buried there. As she'd foreseen, the two brothers stuck with Richard, agreed with everything he had planned. The tragic news increased their love for Frank rather than diminishing it. This, she knew, was a relief to Richard.

Celia gently interrupted her thoughts. 'Richard said he plans to go and see Anna, and are you still up for going with him? Gillian won't be going, she's still recuperating.'

'I certainly am,' Florence said.

'He asked if next week would be good?'

'Yes, definitely.'

'Richard'll pick you up. He said that he'll book a hotel so you don't have to travel there and back in one day. Beccy, Jim and Nick will be with him.'

'It'll be lovely to meet Beccy.'

She hadn't asked Richard about his daughter's pregnancy. It had crossed her mind that the trauma of what had happened might have caused the decision to be made for her. She closed her eyes, tiredness swallowing her.

'You have a little sleep, Flo. I'll save you some lunch,' Celia said, closing the mustard-coloured curtains.

47

Ten months later
August 2003

Since her visit to High Royal the previous November
with Richard, Beccy, Jim and Nick, Florence had
managed to fit only one more in to see Anna. It had
been a month later, and in December when Celia had
driven her up to Yorkshire – the same time she'd visited
all those years before with Edward. The visit had
coincided with the toned down High Royal New Year
celebrations. On that visit she'd attempted to draw Anna
in about that fateful day at the allotment, but Anna
hadn't responded to her gentle questioning at all. If
anything, she'd seemed more fey than ever; although
Anna surprised Florence in remembering Richard and
Beccy, and had asked about them. This was a unique
thing, as Anna had never, in all the years, connected with
the present, or the people who inhabited it. Richard,
Beccy, Jim and Nick, had all introduced themselves, but
it was Richard and Beccy who Anna had kept within a
part of a mind that everyone had thought was long gone.

The newly refurbished NHS hospital hadn't hosted
the annual New Year's ball on her visit, and instead of
the once grand affair of the past it had been Indian-style
snacks, dips and Doritos. Dr Tanner was long dead, the
place run by a "director" who was not medically trained.
The ballroom locked up and never used. Florence had
got the distinct impression the director would have
loved the High Royal New Year's ball's fare more than

he'd liked the buffet, which had been laid out on Dr Tanner's old desk.

Today, it was Beccy and Carl who were picking her up to take her to High Royal. They were driving from Nottingham. She glanced at her watch; she was looking forward to seeing them. She loved being with young people. Richard was meeting them at the hospital. He and Gillian had moved to Nottingham a few months before, sold their Ealing house and Richard had taken a job at a Chambers in the city. Their daughter, her boyfriend, and his granddaughter were living with them. Richard had told her that the incident in the Peaks and Gillian's accident had somehow changed his wife's views on quite a few things, and that it was her idea to move away from London. Florence spoke with Richard regularly on the phone, and often with Gillian too. These days, Richard felt like a son, and as with a son she felt his pain as if it were her own. She never said it to him but he was more like Frank than he realised.

The revelations about Frank had profoundly affected Richard and caused him much internal conflict. She wished Frank had told Richard; about Anna's existence, about Hugh, about the baby, but it was in the past. They must all live in the now. Not look back and not look too far forward. It had taken her over ninety years to truly appreciate this advice.

Leaning sideways she opened the door of her bedside cabinet and pulled out a bright yellow tiny dress with little black polka dots. Celia had picked it up from Gap for her. She touched the fabric lovingly.

Richard met them on the familiar gravel driveway, his

granddaughter in his arms. These days High Royal had a big board outside announcing the NHS trust to which it belonged. Every time Florence had been there in the years since Edward had died, she made a point of visiting the institution's graveyard. Long ago now the hospital had stopped burying deceased patients in its cemetery. The dead now were put to rest in the local church's graveyard. There was talk of making it into a memorial garden, something Edward had suggested once to Dr Tanner many years ago, to remember all the poor souls who had died over the past hundred years, without family or friends. Forgotten. Within the elderly population at High Royal – the few oldies still alive had been inside the institution's walls for a good part of their lives – Anna was one of the only long-term patients who still received visitors.

Richard gave the baby to Beccy and helped Florence from the car. He'd lost a lot of weight, his once sturdy frame now too lean. He'd greyed significantly too, his full head of hair shone like polished silver in the high and hot noon sun.

'You look well, Richard.' It was good to see him again.

'No, I don't, but you do, Florence. You're amazing.'

They embraced.

Florence took a step to Beccy and the baby, touched its face, the little girl gurgled happily.

'There's a bag in the back of the car,' she said to Carl. He'd been subdued on the journey but then again he'd been driving. It was apparent he was a quiet youth. She liked him, a lot. He and Beccy made a wonderful couple.

Carl gave her the bag, which she gave to Beccy. 'A little something for your little girl.'

Beccy pulled out the dress. 'Oh, Florence, I love it! Yellow's my favourite colour.'

'Maybe leave the baby with Carl outside for a bit?' Richard said to Beccy. 'We'll see Anna, how the land lies with her.' He glanced at Florence. 'What do you think?'

'I think Anna would love to meet the baby, but yes, let's see. Anna loves babies,' Florence said to Beccy. 'A bit obsessed with them. Babies and being Marigold. Her years living with us, we bought her so many dolls, and all were her children.'

She took a sideways glance at Richard. Anna's obsession with babies was undoubtedly linked with her own. In all the years with them, Anna had never ever mentioned the incident at the allotment, burying deep what had happened. Florence though, guessed Dr Tanner had his theories, and even now, this many years later, she remembered Dr Tanner's hesitance at telling her and Edward that New Year in 1946 about the meeting he'd had with Hilda early on in the war. Hilda had told Dr Tanner something, and they had never found out what it was. His case notes on Anna had been passed on to the new psych, who had taken over after his death, a few years before Anna had come to live with them in 1953 – the autumn after Mr Churchill's stroke. The new psych hadn't pursued Dr Tanner's thought patterns. 1938 was a long time ago and he had other more pressing cases to deal with. Academic interest in Anna's case had long ago subsided, the early notes on her, lost.

She, Richard and Beccy made their way into the grand building. A reception desk had been installed when the hospital had been given Trust status, and they signed in. No need anymore to talk with Anna's psychiatrist first before visiting her.

They were informed Anna was in the Day Room.

The three of them made their way down the familiar corridors, still painted cream, but matt as opposed to gloss, and no green; the tiled floor now carpeted in a calming aqua blue. Instead of wired doors, fireproofed wooden ones with frosted glass had been fitted, but still locked and controlled digitally. At each doorway they pressed metal buttons on the panel to let them through.

The Day Room was new; it had been constructed as an annexe to the old part of the building. It held a television, a snooker table, and a vending machine in the corner that didn't need money to be fed into it to get what you wanted.

Anna sat at the far end of the room, staring out from the open patio doors onto the still wonderfully kept garden that housed a swing, which hadn't been there on Florence's last visit. Anna was now eighty. An old lady, like her. In the last years an always sylph-like Anna had become much rounder, and was now verging on the obese. Florence noted the bandages covering ulcerated legs and Anna's once wonderful hair so thin that the glassiness of the skin on her skull glinted in the August glow. She also noticed the doll sitting on the chair next to Anna.

'Hello,' said Florence.

Anna turned her head but found it difficult so rotated her body. Arthritis spared no one.

426

'Hello, lovely,' Florence continued. 'It's me, Florence. Are you looking after your baby?'

She nodded and touched the doll's cheek. 'I know it's you. Are my parents coming today, do you think?'

'I don't think they are, lovely girl. Just me, and—'

'Some others?' She peered up at Richard and Beccy. 'Do you remember them? Richard and Beccy?'

Anna scratched her head, pushing back a tendril of thin pewter grey hair behind her ear. 'I still have the ribbon you gave me. I forgot to put it in today.'

Florence smiled at her. 'Do you mind if we all join you?'

Anna scrutinised Richard and Beccy. 'I remember these others. No, I don't mind. There are some extra chairs and coca cola in the machine. I like coca cola, but I don't think my parents like me to drink too much of it. And my baby can't drink it, of course.'

'No, I don't think that would be a good idea,' Florence said.

Beccy pulled three chairs to where Anna was sitting.

'It's nice to see you again, Anna,' Richard said.

Anna looked at him directly in the eyes. 'It's nice to see you again… Richard.'

Florence's breath trapped in her throat. Anna never recognised anyone, always in her own world. She caught Richard's eye. He was thinking the same thing.

It was Beccy who spoke. 'What is your baby's name, Anna?' She touched the doll.

'I'm Marigold not Anna. My baby doesn't have a name.'

'Yes, it's difficult to think of one sometimes,' Beccy said calmly. 'Marigold.'

'Do you have a baby?' Anna said, her voice staccato.

Beccy turned quickly towards her dad, looking for guidance. He nodded gently.

'I do,' Beccy replied.

'How old is your baby?' Anna asked.

'Just two months.'

Florence shuffled her chair closer to Anna's, and Richard got up to help her.

Anna stayed silent. Everyone stayed silent. Beccy fussed with the doll.

Finally Anna spoke. 'Is your baby a boy or a girl?'

'A girl,' Beccy said.

'What's your baby's name?'

Beccy looked at her dad again, then at Florence. 'My baby's name is Anna.'

Anna's face lit up and her wrinkles seemed to disappear. Her dark and phlegmy eyes sparkled. 'I once knew someone called Anna.'

Florence watched Richard gently poke his daughter in the side.

Beccy said: 'Did you like her?'

'I did like Anna. But she went away. She had to go away. She was sad, but sometimes she comes to visit me. She says, *Marigold, you are so lucky, I'm glad I'm now you.*'

'Would you like to meet my baby?' Beccy asked, her tone light.

'I would,' Anna replied. 'I like babies. And I know I will like Anna. And my baby,' she touched the doll's arm, 'will have someone to play with.'

Beccy smiled. 'She will.'

Anna scuffled in her chair and turned towards Richard. 'Anna told me you are Frank's grandson.'

Confusion filled Richard's face.

Florence interrupted. 'I think Marigold means her friend, Anna, not Beccy's baby, Richard?'

'Ah,' Richard said. He carried on, talking to Anna. 'I am. Do you remember me telling you that? When I came to see you?'

Florence remembered him saying it, and had worried it would upset Anna at the time, but it had seemed to brush over her. But clearly, it hadn't.

'I do remember,' Anna said. 'And I remember that you said you had loved Frank. Anna loved Frank too. Very much.' She stopped speaking, and again stared into the garden. She glanced at Beccy. 'You could go on the swing?'

'I will later – maybe while you take care of little Anna for me?' Beccy replied.

'Yes,' Anna said. 'And I think Richard should go outside too. Leave us all together with baby Anna. No men for a bit?'

'That's fine. I'll go and get some sunshine,' Richard said.

'Come on then, Dad,' Beccy said.

Beccy returned fifteen minutes later with her baby and without Richard. She gave a contented baby Anna, to Anna.

'She's beautiful,' Anna said.

'She is, isn't she… Anna?' Beccy said, her voice hardly audible.

Anna lifted her head. 'Yes.'

Beccy stole a glance at Florence.

'You go and play on the swing, Beccy,' Anna said.

Florence moved closer to Anna ensuring little baby Anna was safe. 'Yes, why don't you, Beccy? Just for a while.'

'I'm not sure,' Beccy mouthed to Florence.

'It's fine,' Florence whispered.

Reluctantly, Beccy made her way outside.

'What is it, Anna?' Florence asked gently. 'Because you *are* Anna today, aren't you?'

Anna stroked little Anna's cheek. 'Frank thought Hugh was my baby's father.'

Florence swallowed, her throat felt as if it were coated in grit. 'I think he did believe that was so. But it's all in the past. It doesn't matter now.' Florence touched little Anna's arm, and then Anna's. 'You can care for this little one when we come to see you.'

'It wasn't Hugh. It was a man at Chartwell. It happened when I went to visit Grandma Cullen and Jemima, and I was invited to the big house for the afternoon. It happened after the lunch that Mrs Churchill had put on, just a cold buffet in the garden. We were in the grounds, all of us, mucking around. Mr Randolph and his London friends were there too, egging on the boys from the village, egging on the boy who liked me. The boy and I made our way a long way from the house. I told him to stop, but he wouldn't stop, and I didn't want to make a fuss, didn't want to upset Mrs Churchill, or anyone. It was the gardener who found us. I was so embarrassed, although later that night I tried to tell Jemima, but I don't think she wanted to know. I was so upset, and the next day I told my gran I wanted to go back home to Nottinghamshire. And it was after that, when I got home, that Hugh started following me, pestering me. It was as if he knew something had happened to me in Westerham, at Chartwell… He said he'd tell my mum, but Hilda didn't care about me.' She peered at Florence. 'I thought the boy at Chartwell liked me. I thought he was being kind. I wanted someone to be kind to me apart from my dad. I didn't know I could get pregnant. Hilda never explained anything. I never liked Hugh, but I think he was the only one who guessed anything. He cared about me in a funny way. I did let Hugh kiss me, and only a few weeks after I got back from Westerham. But Hugh only kissed me. He didn't do what the Westerham boy did. Then Hugh walked me home and said I should never go with a boy again. Said he'd know if I did, because he followed me, you see?'

Florence's stomach buckled. She thought of Richard. He would never know. Never. Frank had truly believed Hugh had raped Anna, and had thought the stillborn baby was Hugh's. She wanted to ask why now, why was Anna talking now?

'The man who's just left, Richard – I didn't want him to know,' Anna said.

'Know what, lovely?'

'Richard told me he loved Frank. I remember him telling me that when I saw him last.' Anna hugged herself. 'Frank didn't mean to do what he did. I didn't want Richard to know what really happened to my baby.'

Anna had seen Richard soon after Gillian's accident and Beccy being lost in the Peaks. He'd been so open with Anna in that meeting; talking about his grandad Frank, how much he'd loved him, as if he were opening his heart to his great-aunt, a woman he didn't know, and perhaps thinking Anna wouldn't understand, although

431

hoping she would understand. Florence mused, it seemed that Anna had indeed understood.

'Anna wants to tell you something else,' Anna continued.

Florence was now feeling a little dizzy. She needed a glass of water. 'What does Anna want to tell me, Marigold?'

'My baby girl wasn't dead.'

Anna held little Anna to her chest and the baby grizzled and a panic gripped her. Florence wished Beccy wasn't outside. She moved closer to Anna, thinking to take the baby from her.

'She was born alive,' Anna said. 'My baby was very small, but alive. She was early, I think. Frank cut the cord and took my baby from me. He was holding her so tight. I know it was an accident. He was holding her too tight. He was crying. I'd never seen him like that. My baby died in his arms. Then he said he was going to tell Hilda, and the police, and I couldn't stand it all. I made him promise never to say anything. To anyone. I made him swear. But I knew my baby would come back.'

'Why didn't you want to say anything? To Hilda… your mother?

'Hilda was never a proper mother to me. When my baby came out, when I saw her, I wanted to be a proper mother.' Anna's eyes brimming with lucidity. 'I didn't want Hilda to know, she would ruin everything. And then… the next day, afterwards… I pushed Hilda, because she was going to have *her* baby. And mine had gone. But, my baby came back… Marigold came back, and we became like one. The three of us, Marigold, my baby, and me. Together.'

'Carry on,' Florence said gently.

'When Hilda brought her baby home, Jim, it was snowing. She came into my bedroom. She told me she knew what had happened. She told me I was disgusting.'

Florence tried to suppress a gasp. Hilda had been so much more tortured and mixed up than she'd ever known, than Frank had ever known. But Jem knew.

'And that's when I hurt Jim. I'm so sorry.' She looked at little Anna. 'I won't hurt this baby.'

'Aw, Anna.'

'So I stopped talking and thinking and never said anything and I don't want Richard, or Beccy to know. Because I don't want them to be like Anna. Marigold doesn't want them to be like Anna.' She gave little Anna to Florence and the relief that flooded through her, drowned her. Anna continued, 'When Richard came here to visit me, he reminded me of my dad,' She surveyed the room. 'He didn't visit me in this room, but another one. This one is new. Richard is nice and good, like my dad. But Richard doesn't smell of cigars.'

'Anna…' Florence whispered.

'Anna's gone now. And I have to go too. I'm tired. It's time for my nap.' She got up and touched Florence on her shoulder. 'I hope you come again soon.'

The nurse at the door led Anna back to her room. Florence, with little Anna in her arms, rose and steadily walked towards the vending machine. Holding the baby, she was unable to retrieve a can of coke from it.

Beccy returned. 'Is everything all right, Florence?'

'Everything is fine, Beccy. I don't suppose you could get me a can of coke?'

The young mum smiled. 'Course I can.' She pushed a few buttons and the can dropped into the tray beneath. Beccy put it on the table and took little Anna from her.

Florence picked up the can, managed to open it with her arthritic fingers. Took a sip, then said, 'I think it's time to leave.'

Florence would go to her grave holding Frank's remaining secret.

No one must ever know, especially Richard.

And somehow Anna had sensed this.

48

Richard

A week later

Leaning back on the new sofa that he and Gillian had chosen together, Richard cast his mind back over the last eighteen months: what he'd discovered about his grandparents, about Anna, and Frank's forty year affair with Florence, as well as what had happened to Gillian. She was only just recovering properly, and very unlike Gillian, she'd made no complaints about having to find a new teaching job in Nottingham, because she had no intention of looking for one. She was happy to stay at home. Happy to be the doting grandma, and was happy to have Carl around. The reality was – it could have been Gillian and Beccy… and an unborn little Anna in the car together. The car's brakes had been faulty, but it had been inconclusive if the cause of the accident was the brakes, or due to Gillian's fractured ankle. All of this had added to Beccy's early angst, because she'd blamed herself for the accident – because she and Gillian had argued – and during that argument Gillian had slipped into a pothole. The doctors had ascertained that Gillian's ankle had probably been fractured prior to the car accident, and then due to the rush of adrenaline Gillian had overcome the pain, rushed off in the car to find her daughter, who in a huff and angry had disappeared into the darkening Peaks.

Richard hauled himself up and went into the kitchen where he brewed tea, which he took upstairs. He checked in on his sleeping baby granddaughter, and then on his slumbering wife. All quiet.

As he made his way to his study he thought about the immediate future. Beccy was starting college in September, continuing her A levels; she hadn't had a problem moving institutions and had enrolled at a local college in Nottingham. Carl had applied and secured a place at the London College of Music. He was starting in September too but intended to spend his holidays in Nottingham.

In his study he picked up the pile of papers pertaining to Frank and Hilda, the stuff he'd brought from Hilda's house; letters, the correspondence, as well as the bag Fiona Trott had given him, which included the letter from Churchill to his wife – about Frank burying a stillborn baby and never registering the birth – a legal requirement in 1938.

A Churchill quote came to mind, his grandad had been full of them, as well as Churchill's platitudes too. But this was a quote he'd read and remembered from all those years ago at the war rooms.

It is a mistake to look too far ahead. Only one link of the chain of destiny can be handled at a time.

He could not stop loving his grandad. Florence had forgiven Frank utterly. And so would he.

Putting the file on his knee he fished out the letter from Churchill to Clementine and studied it again. He should shred it, but this was a slice of history, an insight into a man who, despite his place in history, so little was known. This letter did not belong to him; it belonged to the Churchill family.

He'd asked Nell months ago to contact Lady Soames' secretary to establish where he should send important and confidential correspondence. In the past, the Soames' family had had some dealings with his Chambers in London and so the dialogue had been easy to set up. The secretary had emailed Richard directly, asking what the query was about. As soon as Richard mentioned correspondence from Winston Churchill there followed a steady stream of polite emails, and even one phone call. Richard had been putting it off, but it was now time. The secretary suggested a courier to take the correspondence to Lady Soames' residence.

He clicked on his computer to write a letter to Mary Soames, which he planned to print off. He closed the document and opened a drawer, taking out his headed notepaper from the new Chambers. He'd write longhand, somehow it seemed more suitable. It took him over an hour to compose.

He laid out the entire truth about Hugh Lambert's death/manslaughter and the veracity of what Frank had admitted to Churchill concerning Anna's baby, about Mary Soames' father visiting Anna all those years ago at High Royal. He read what he'd written and put a line through the mention of Hugh Lambert. He redrafted.

Finally, Richard put the letter in the package that held the evidence and sealed it all up. As he finished, he heard little Anna beginning to stir. He checked on Gillian, she was still asleep. He made his way to the baby's room, fed little Anna, changed her nappy, and then arranged for a courier to pick up the package.

An hour later he received a call from Celia.

Anna had been taken very ill and wasn't expected to last more than a few days. She had diabetes and her heart was weak. The nurse told Celia, and Florence, that it might be better to go and see Anna sooner rather than later. He looked at the clock and then texted Beccy. Did she mind him taking little Anna to see Anna? He explained why. Beccy and Carl were away for the night. A little break, courtesy of his mum and dad.

She texted back immediately. *Cool.*

Then he called Florence.

'I can't go, Richard, I'm not feeling that well myself. I've seen Anna, I've made my peace. You go. She likes you, very much.'

'I want to tell Anna that we will bury her baby properly,' he said.

'Richard, it's better to leave it. Better for Anna. Don't unburden yourself on her. It's not fair. She's dying.'

'Perhaps you're right, Florence.'

'I am right.'

Next, he called his dad and told him, and then wrote a note to leave for Gillian. He placed it on the bedside table.

Within an hour Richard was in the car with baby Anna strapped in the baby seat – on his way to pick up his dad and Uncle Nick to take them to see their sister.

Anna was in the infirmary part of the hospital, lying in bed, her eyes closed, but her lids fluttering. A nurse pulled up chairs and all three men sat down, his dad holding little Anna.

'Anna's in and out, so don't be surprised if the poor lamb doesn't wake up,' the nurse said stroking Anna's whispery hair away from her cheek. She then leant closer to her patient. 'Three men to see you, and a lovely baby, love.'

Richard glanced at his dad, and then his uncle. The discovery of Anna had hit them both hard. Both had been to see her as much as they could over the past year. The staff had told him that Anna had never had so many visitors and Richard's heart continued to break.

His uncle touched his sister's arm but said nothing. His dad moved closer to her. 'Hello, Anna. We've brought the baby to see you,' he said.

No answer. Anna's eyes remained closed, but her eyelids flickered rapidly.

'Hello, Anna,' Richard said. Her lids finally opened. 'Would you like a sip of water?'

She shook her head and then lifted it from the pillow. 'Can I hold her?' She looked at the baby.

Richard helped her to sit up in the bed. When he thought she seemed comfortable he took the baby from his dad and placed little Anna in her arms. The baby was perfectly content.

Anna held her, smiling. 'My great-great-niece.'

She had an understanding. He should tell her.

'That's right, Anna. She is,' Richard said.

'And my dad's great-great granddaughter.'

'That's right too. You've been thinking about this,' Richard said gently. 'I always get really confused with all this – relatives and the way we're connected, the right titles,' he rambled.

She moved her gaze to his dad and uncle. 'And you are my brothers. I know that.' Her eyes settled on his dad. 'I'm sorry about what I did to you.' Leaning forward, she touched the scar on his cheek.

'Makes me more handsome.' Jim smiled awkwardly.

'My dad wanted to protect me. He loved me,' she said.

'Mr Churchill wanted to protect you?' Richard asked with tentativeness.

'No. Frank.' She kissed the baby's forehead and held her out to Richard. 'Thank you for bringing her to see me.' She sank back into the pillow and closed her eyes. 'I'm tired. It's time for Marigold and me to go now.'

It was Richard and Anna's two brothers who were still sitting by her bed when an hour later Anna Cullen passed peacefully away.

* * *

The day after Richard returned from Yorkshire a courier delivered a letter from London. He'd just lowered himself onto the sofa and with more than a little hesitation he opened the envelope.

Dear Mr Cullen,

Thank you for your package. I cannot begin to explain how much my family and I appreciate your understanding on this issue. I also would like to express my sincere gratitude for your detailed explanation of events.

I remember my childhood at Chartwell very well, and sometimes, as if it were only yesterday. I do of course remember

Florence and her husband Edward, to whom my father, during and immediately after the war years, was close.

I do remember vividly, too, your grandfather from Chartwell, when both he and Florence worked for my mother and father in Kent. I also remember Anna, and playing with her in my Marycot. We got along famously!

My father sent the letter, which you have kindly given back to my family, to my mother from Tripoli in 1943. After reading its contents my heart goes out to you and your family.

I have been through my mother's diaries and correspondence and it would indeed seem, as you have suggested in your letter, that my father made a visit to High Royal Mental Hospital in 1943, which would have been a very busy time in his life. It is clear that he (and my mother) were moved enough by Frank and Anna's plight to involve themselves in such a tragic set of circumstances.

This was my father all over. Despite his many faults, he was a man who thought deeply and acted (some would say) too spontaneously. He possessed an innate understanding of people's plights and battles, and this was always very apparent in his relationships with the people who worked for him, and with him.

I hope that his visit to Anna, and his advice regarding Anna's future care were of help to your family.

On a final note, I was with my father at Chartwell in the summer of 1953 when he was so terribly ill. Frank Cullen's visit cheered my father up immensely. I believe they spent the whole afternoon talking about bricklaying and books. My father found it such a tonic.

The letter you have returned I will shred. I believe this is the best course of action considering the contents.

With the most kindest wishes,
Mary Soames

Richard took the letter to his study and put it in the shredder.

49

Florence

The Waterside Nursing Home, Westerham
Eight months later
April 18th 2004

'You have a visitor, Florence.'

Florence opened her eyes and squinted. Celia's face was close to her own, her expression troubled. 'Who?'

'Jemima Barnes.'

'She's here? Now?'

'She is. You can say no. She can get back in her taxi and return to the station.'

'No, send her in.'

Celia disappeared and came back with Frank's sister. Despite never having liked Jem, her appearance shocked Florence. Jem couldn't have weighed more than six stone and Florence saw something more than old age etched into her face. She recognised it these days. The claws of cancer.

We all, though, have to die of something.

'Thanks for agreeing to see me.'

'Take a seat,' Florence replied.

'Nice décor. I like the mustard.'

'Why are you here, Jem?'

'I've come to talk. I'm going to die soon. I have pancreatic cancer…' She collapsed into the chair next to Florence's bed.

'I'm sorry to hear that. I really am.'

'I've come to give you something.'

'And you had to wait until you were dying before you did?'

Jem lifted her stooped shoulders. 'I'm sorry I didn't encourage Hilda to tell Jim and Nick about Anna.'

'Why didn't you? Hilda would have listened to you.'

'I was wrong not to. I see that now. Why? You know how I felt about Frank. The resentment I've held for him was deeper than even I acknowledged. Making my brother's life difficult was my aim. I tried to make things right by telling Jim though, and the family. But... too late.'

'It was a bit,' Florence said. She really couldn't be bothered with Jem, coming here to off-load her guilt. Why had she agreed to allow her in?

'But I did love Anna.'

'No. You didn't love Anna. You didn't even go to her funeral.'

Jem ignored her, carried on regardless. 'I'm unsure how much you know, Florence, and if this will come as a surprise, but Anna got pregnant in 1938. She gave birth to a stillborn baby. Frank buried it in his allotment.' Jem waited.

'I know all this.' She would never tell Jem what had really happened. That would stay between her and Anna.

Jem's features twisted into confusion but she gathered herself quickly. 'Richard found out?'

'It doesn't matter how I know, I just do, and to be honest I'm disgusted you kept this to yourself. I'm guessing Hilda knew too?'

'Hilda had suspected Anna's condition for weeks. That day, Hilda made her way to the allotment after

Anna returned home upset and confused. Hilda watched Frank, with the bundle. He didn't know Hilda was there as he placed it in the hole and filled it in, and then laid the concrete.'

'*If?*' Florence had no words for Jem's coldness.

'The baby. Hilda didn't tell me this for years, Florence. And by the time she did, there was no reason for me to intervene. Too late. But trust me, Hilda suffered too. Every day. Hilda wrote to me only weeks before she died, asking me to tell Jim and Nick the truth when she passed, about Anna's existence, about Anna's baby. Despite what you might think, Hilda felt enormous guilt about Anna, which she took to her grave.' Jem wriggled uncomfortably in her chair and Florence wasn't sure if it was with mental discomfort or from real physical pain.

'Would you like some water?' Florence asked.

Jem shook her head. 'One afternoon at a cattle market, and then the malicious gossiping of villagers, ruined Hilda's life. Have you any idea how hard it is to love and be with a man after what Hilda and I went through? How difficult it was for Hilda to love Anna… and the man who she'd adored most her life – Frank. No, you don't, and you never did.' She looked at Florence. 'The man who you'd have taken away from Hilda, if you'd had your way. To be honest, I often wish you two had ended up together, properly. You both deserved each other.'

It had taken twenty minutes for Jem to revert to form and Florence didn't smart at Jem's words; she was long past that. She tried to regain her inner composure. It needn't ever have been like this, and Jem was talking as if they were all still clenched within their pasts. If Hilda had been honest, even years later, life would have been very different, for Hilda, Anna, and Frank. Frank had wanted to take care of both Hilda and Anna. Florence couldn't forgive Hilda, as she could not forgive Jem.

'You and Hilda ruined Frank's life, you know that don't you? *Don't you*?' The last two words Florence shouted and it hurt her throat.

'Frank ruined his own life.'

'And Anna?' Florence rasped.

'Anna was fine with you and Edward. It suited everyone, including Frank.'

'Why did Hilda keep what she knew to herself? If she'd supported both Anna and Frank the world would have been a different place for everyone. Anna would never have been institutionalised.' She tried to hold back her tears. 'You, and Hilda… are monsters.'

Jem picked up a large handbag and pulled out a batch of letters. 'Hilda posted these to me the same time she asked me to tell Richard, Jim and Nick about Anna. They're unopened.' She put them on Florence's bed. 'I'll leave them with you.'

'What are they?'

'Letters Hilda wrote to Anna in the years she was at High Royal, and the years she was with you and Edward. Letters she never posted. Hilda wanted me to have them so no one else found them. I never opened them. I told her to get rid of the stuff in the loft years ago, but she wouldn't. Probably wanted it "all out" once she was gone. I was going to give them to Richard, but I know he's had a rough time. And I know you two are close. So I'm giving them to you.' She put the bag on her shoulder. Jem seemed to have lost height and even more weight during the time she'd been inside Florence's room.

'Stay and have a cup of tea before you leave?' Florence said.

'I don't think so. The nurse asked the taxi to wait for me.'

'All those years ago, Jem, I did tell Frank to go home to be with you.'

'Maybe you did. But he didn't, did he? That was the evening my father went all the way.' She turned, shuffled to the door and didn't say another word.

A few minutes later Celia poked her head into the room. 'You okay? Your friend got the taxi.'

'I'm fine.' She really didn't feel fine at all. 'Celia, what time is it?'

'Just after four.'

'Too early for a sherry?'

'Never too early for a sherry. I'll bring you one. Then I'll be indisposed as I'm full-on organising your birthday party,' She said attempting a smile. 'Try not to worry.'

As Celia bustled from the room, Florence's thoughts moved to the long dead Dr Tanner. For a reason that would never be known, Dr Tanner had obviously done as Hilda had wished and remained silent about Anna's pregnancy, because he had known, she realised that now.

The only written record of Anna's baby's birth had been in the correspondence Dr Tanner sent to Hilda, she guessed, and correspondence Hilda had probably shared with Jem; but eventually evidence of which Hilda disposed. Erasing everything about Anna.

Hilda and Jem's friendship had been based upon their mutual anger towards the men who they perceived had ruined their lives. The man who'd raped Hilda, and Jem's own father, and to some extent Frank. It was as if all these years Hilda and Jem had fed off each other. Florence could only guess at her childhood friend's damaged state of mind. And by ignoring the existence of her only daughter, Anna, as well as the birth of her baby – Hilda's own grandchild – proved this.

To Florence's shame she'd not truly understood the depths of Hilda's torment, or the magnitude of Jem's. As Jem had never exonerated her young brother for his non-intervention in their father's abuse, Hilda had never forgiven herself for Anna's conception. Never forgiven Anna. But Florence could not forgive Hilda for abandoning Anna, for not being honest with Frank. She would never tell Richard about Hilda knowing.

Florence put her glasses back on, and pulled out a photo of her, Hilda, Frank and Jem. 1928. Just before Frank, Hilda and Anna left for Nottingham. She'd gazed at the photograph so many times over the years, and only now did she see the true animosity in Jem's expression as she looked at her brother.

One by one, she opened the envelopes that had been sealed for too long. A letter for each year Anna had been in High Royal, pre and post Anna's time with her, Edward and the children. The letters all said very much the same thing but in the last one, dated 2001 and the year before Hilda died, Hilda said it with eloquence and clarity. Finally, at last, after seventy years, Florence understood Hilda properly. She could not absolve her inside her mind, but she understood.

As much as she wanted to show the Cullen boys these letters, she could not because then they would know the extent of Hilda's culpability. And she had to protect them, especially Richard. Even Jem had known that.

Dear Anna,

I am sorry for what I said to you. You are not disgusting. You were a girl looking for love, and I was remiss in not explaining the facts of life, remiss in not being a proper mother to you, remiss in allowing you and your dad's secret to remain a secret. I have no explanation why.

I had loved Frank, had loved him for most of my life. When a man raped me and made me pregnant, it was me who felt disgusting, and so revolting, and so I couldn't marry Frank. He waited for me, but I didn't want to marry him, I wanted to marry no man. My love for Frank disappeared the day at the cattle market, the day I was raped. It disappeared forever. When I thought he didn't want me anymore, that was when I agreed to marry Frank. When I thought Flo was taking him away from me.

Anna, you were not raped, you told me that. I was angry with you for choosing, voluntarily, to follow the same path as me. I was angry with you for being born. I was angry with myself. I was pregnant with Jim, and that day at the allotment when I guessed what had happened, I could see everything being taken away from me again. I'd guessed you were pregnant, Anna. I am so sorry for not being there for you.

I guessed too that Frank would not tell me, and I guessed you had sworn him not to. I knew you would not tell him that I knew. You are my daughter and I knew you would make Frank promise to keep quiet, and I saw what it had done to you. I am truly sorry for High Royal.

I'm sorry, Anna, for not loving you as you deserve to be loved. I'm sorry for ruining your life, Frank's life, and my own. Sorry that you never knew your brothers. Sorry that you lost a baby. You wanted your baby because you are a finer woman than me. I didn't want mine, not you, not then, not with him.

I'm sorry, Anna.

Every day I try to love you, but God doesn't allow me to. Inside my head I've given up with God because he did not give me the fortitude to be your mother.

I will die and go to purgatory, I know that, and it is where I deserve to be.

Your mum, Hilda

50

May Day 2004

Florence opened her diary. Saturday May 1st. Exactly seventy-six years since the May Day dance in Westerham and her first kiss with Frank – years that had passed with both the quickness of a heartbeat and the slow ebb of an ancient stream.

She had celebrated her ninety-fifth birthday the week before. Celia had organised, with great gusto, a tea in the Waterside's enormous lounge, as Florence hadn't been up to going anywhere else.

She was tired.

Her remaining child, David, his wife, her four grandchildren, three great-grandchildren, Richard, Gillian, Beccy, Carl and little Anna, Jim and Nick and their wives had all been there. As was Celia of course, who had brought her husband. Not any others.

She had outlived them all. All of them gone. Jem had died a week after coming to visit her. It was Richard and Gillian who had gone to the funeral in Ireland.

Florence snapped her diary closed and laid it in her lap, and leaning sideways, she opened her photo album that Celia had left within easy reach on her bed. She flicked through her life. So much love.

She found the photos of Edward, her children, including Anna, and gently touched them with the pad of her finger. Anna had given them so much. She plucked out a photo of Frank standing next to Churchill on a hillside in Tripoli. She'd been lucky to love two men, because she had loved Frank, since childhood, from that first day in the woods when she saw him crying. She and Hilda had both loved him. And back then she and Hilda had loved each other. The best of friends. *Thick as thieves* everyone said about the three of them.

Her gaze moved towards Edward's image. He'd understood and accepted her love for Frank, always knowing there were two men who'd held her heart. Edward was the gatekeeper to her soul and had carried out his job, always, with the prerequisite of her freedom in his mind. He'd guarded both her soul, and heart, with profound sublimity until his illness, when he'd asked Frank to take over.

She took off her glasses and laid them on the bed. Closed her eyes. So lucky.

A beautiful whiteness came, enveloping her, and then an impossibly young Frank and Edward took hold of Florence's hands, Frank the right, Edward the left; her two children and Anna were there too, so very close.

The five of them leading her away.

The Mississippi keeps on rolling.
Let it roll, let it roll, to broader lands and better days.

ABOUT THE AUTHOR

Jules Hayes lives in Berkshire with her husband, daughter and a dog. She has a degree in modern history and holds a particular interest in events and characters from the early 20th century. As a former physiotherapist and trainer – old habits die hard – when not writing Jules likes to run. She also loves to watch films, read good novels and is a voracious consumer of non-fiction too, particularly biographies.

Jules Hayes' second historical novel, which is due for publication in late 2020 is another dual timeline story.

Jules also writes contemporary thrillers as JA Corrigan.

A NOTE FROM THE AUTHOR

Dear Reader,

I do hope that you liked reading my story as much as I loved writing it.

If you enjoyed *The Walls We Build* do mention the book to your friends, or tweet and share that you have finished the novel. Alternatively, please leave a review on Amazon and/or Goodreads – reviews mean *so* much to an author.

Thank you.

You can contact me in these places:
Website: http://www.jules-hayes.com
Twitter @JulesHayes6
http://www.twitter.com/JulesHayes6
Facebook Author Page: JulesHayesAuthor
http://www.facebook.com/JulesHayesAuthor
Instagram: JulesHayes6
http://www.instagram.com/juleshayes6

Writing thrillers as JA Corrigan, I can be found at:
Website: http://www.jacorrigan.com
Twitter: @juliannwriter
http://www.twitter.com/juliannwriter
Facebook Author Page: JACorrigan
http://www.facebook.com/jacorrigan
Instagram: corriganjulieann
http://www.instagram.com/corriganjulieann

ACKNOWLEDGEMENTS

The nuts and bolts of a novel are put in place by the author, although as with most endeavors in life it is often a team effort, and the creation of my book is no different.

I would like to offer my heartfelt gratitude and thanks to my initial early readers and friends, David Evans, Jan Beresford and Claudia Cruttwell. Also to Emma Haughton, Richard Gillis, and Glynis Peters.

Thank you to Essie Fox, my friend and mentor, who gives me wise advice ranging from syntax to the care of a cockapoo, and makes me giggle a lot too. My huge thanks to Laura Wilkinson who despite her busy schedule reads anything I send to her. My thanks to Anne Williams and Michelle Ryles, two wonderful book bloggers/reviewers within the writing community. My gratitude and thanks to both Nicola May for her practical advice and unswerving positivity, and Sarah Ward who, at the eleventh hour, gave me the confidence I so desperately needed.

I'd also like to thank Debz Hobbs-Wyatt, Debi Alper, Carolyn Gillis, Kim Nash, Sally Spedding, Emma Mitchell, Rachel Gilby, the awesome members of *Think Tank*, and my fabulous cover designer, Stuart Bache. Thanks to my tutor and fellow students at the Faber Academy, including Ana Garcia, Jo Hoare and Tory Kingdom. And to my small but perfectly formed writing group, Daniel Culver and Stela Brinzeanu.

A huge thank you to my brilliant and erudite editor, Arzu Tahsin, whose encouragement was instrumental in me pursuing this novel's journey to the very end.

I spent a fair amount of time at Chartwell in the early days of writing this book and it was there where I found the conviction to tweak, a little, Mr Churchill's off-the-page historical role. On that note too, a thank you to Sir Winston Churchill himself, whose life and times were such a rich source of material. As with many stories, mine began with a kernel of an idea, powered by an image of Churchill addressing his troops in Libya, 1943; I imagined Frank being amongst those soldiers.

My thanks to Steve and Nicola Corrigan, for their love and ear during the darker moments of a writer's life. Gratitude to my parents too. *Love you Mum and Dad.* I want to mention the late, generous and gorgeous Susan Roebuck who was always, and unfailingly, so supportive to me as a writer.

Thank you to my lovely friends, the enormously helpful Michelle Flood and hugely talented Andrew Johnson. My gratitude to Paul Bacon and Kam Chahal who manage to say the right and very wise thing during my frequent bouts of insecurity.

Lastly, to my *White Knight,* Steve, and Rhiannon, for their support, patience, strength and love.

Without them I'd be unable to write a word.

Printed in Great Britain
by Amazon